AN AMERICAN ANTHOLOGY

MECHANIZED MASTERPIECES 2

EDITED BY PENNY FREEMAN

Other Anthologies by
Xchyler Publishing:

Forged in Flame: A Dragon Anthology

Moments in Millennia: A Fantasy Anthology

Shades and Shadows: A Paranormal Anthology

Mechanized Masterpieces: A Steampunk Anthology

A Dash of Madness: A Thriller Anthology

Terra Mechanica: A Steampunk Anthology

Legends and Lore: An Anthology of Mythic Proportions

The Toll of Another Bell: A Fantasy Anthology

AN AMERICAN ANTHOLOGY

MECHANIZED MASTERPIECES 2

EDITED BY PENNY FREEMAN

M. K. WISEMAN, M. IRISH GARDNER
SCOTT W. TAYLOR, D. LEE JORTNER
J. AUREL GUAY, J.R. POTTER
JAY BARNSON, MEGAN OLIPHANT
NEVE TALBOT, SCOTT E. TARBET

Xchyler Publishing
an imprint of Hamilton Springs Press, LLC
Penny Freeman, Editor-in-chief
www.xchylerpublishing.com

1st Edition: February 2015

Cover and Interior Design by D. Robert Pease, walkingstickbooks.com
Edited by Penny Freeman and MeriLyn Oblad

Published in the United States of America
Xchyler Publishing

TABLE OF CONTENTS

Foreword

Combine airships and locomotives, submersibles and mechanoids, alternative histories and anachronistic technologies; mix well. Season to taste with Nineteenth Century sensibilities and culture (hefty dosage recommended). Garnish as desired with the supernatural, paranormal, and/or macabre. Spread generously over a wide swath of the globe. Steam well.

The challenge to our seasoned Xchyler authors: reprise our most successful anthology, Mechanized Masterpieces, Steampunk expansions of classic literature, this time with a distinctive American flavor. Herein find the *pièce de résistance*, ten engaging tales compiled to create a sumptuous repast. *Bon appetit.*

A Princess of Jasoom

J. AUREL GUAY

With a steady hand, Elizabeth carefully held the dropper over the flask of green liquid. Her brilliant blue eyes peered intensely at the droplet that formed as she applied gentle pressure to the rubber bulb. One drop was all she needed. One drop and no more.

‘. ._.. .. __.. ._ _... . _ .... _ ___ _.. ._. _. . . _. _. .. ... ___ _. ... ___ .._. .._. .. _._. . ._ ... ._ .__. ._._._’

The sound of the telegraph startled the young researcher, and a whole cascade of drops slipped into the flask. A flash of brilliant light and a plume of dark smoke immediately clouded her petite round spectacles. The container slipped from her grasp and broke on the laboratory bench-top, releasing its contents to ooze toward the floor. The wood started to dissolve with a slight vapor and an unsettling hiss.

Elizabeth pulled off a glove and gripped the crystal that hung from her neck. “Fergusson, will you please help me clean this up? Fergusson?”

With her free hand, Elizabeth smoothed a frizzled bit of coppery hair behind her ear as she turned. The telegraph continued to tic.

"Fergusson?"

She found the shell of the mechanical automaton hunched in the glassware room where it had been restocking shelves. Elizabeth's thin lips pursed as she grimaced and approached the silent machine. Turning a latch on its back, she opened a door and inspected the contents within. Everything seemed to be in working order. The fittings of the crystal shard held it secure. The couplings were connected. Oh. His little furnace had burned out.

Elizabeth retrieved a handful of coal, and with the strike of a match, Fergusson's fire was burning again. With the hiss of steam and the internal clinking of cogs and chains, the humanoid machine came to life. It turned to look at her with large eyes that reflected the soft, white glow of the internal crystal from each side of its smooth, featureless face.

Elizabeth reached for a pail and a mop and thrust them at the automaton.

"Fill this with water and soap. Then clean the bench and floor." She was careful to touch the crystal again and to think clearly of each element and action in the commands. Automatons were marvels of technology that could carry out many orders but required very simple and clear instruction. Otherwise, any manner of confusion and disaster could result.

As Fergusson clomped away, Elizabeth pulled her timepiece from her pocket and started at the sight of the hands on the dial.

No wonder her mechanical aid had run down; she had worked through the night and half a day. She had already missed at least one meeting that she could think of, and all she had to show for it was the steaming pile of goo on her bench-top.

With a sigh, she stomped over to the telegraph to collect what she was sure would be a reprimand for her absence at the monthly progress meeting. Elizabeth enjoyed her new career as a researcher but could do without the constant meetings, discussions, and lectures. Since the accident in Arizona, the one that sent her dearest friend to the grave, she had been reassigned with the near impossible task of understanding the uncanny crystalline shards that Automaton Incorporated mined from a desert mountain beyond the Great Plains. She felt close to her greatest ambition, the creation of the first synthetic shard.

The shards, first discovered in the American West by Automaton Inc., or A. I.'s founder, Henry Powell, were an aberration of nature. They had the ability to transmute and redistribute energy in such a way that could animate any manner of mechanical device. What's more, a paired "control shard" tuned the animated machines to human thought and allowed them to carry out any simple command. With training, they could even learn more complex tasks.

The means of this process were a complete mystery. However, extensive study had unveiled the substance of the shards, and Elizabeth felt sure she could create more like them. If she could discern a means of synthetically producing them in the laboratory, the current revolution of technology would no longer be limited strictly to the wealthy and powerful.

Alas, Fergusson diligently mopped up her latest progress to the tune of his rattling cogs. She was fortunate to be working directly for A. I., otherwise, she would not likely have such an aid to clear away her frequent mishaps. This good fortune was due to the even better fortune of her late uncle, John Carter, known to her as Uncle Jack. The riches he found in those Arizona gold mines and the dictates of his will paid for her privileged education and secured her a position in what would become A. I. The company owed its existence to those gold-exhausted tunnels and the crystals that remained, bequeathed to Henry Powell, the grandson of the man with whom Carter discovered the mines.

Picking up the tape spooled out by the telegraph, her hand moved to her cheek and her heart skipped as she read the transcript:

'Elizabeth to Dr Dennisons office ASAP STOP Regards second Arizona site STOP'

"My apologies for missing the progress meeting this morning, Dr. Dennison," blurted Elizabeth as she burst into the research administrator's oak-paneled office. "It won't happen again, I promise. Your telegraph said something about Arizona—did they find evidence of Mr. Brooks?"

Dr. Dennison, who would normally have interrupted her excessive prattle before it started, seemed at a loss for words.

In the end, he mustered little more than to gesture toward the leather chair beside Elizabeth. She jumped in surprise as a tall man rose and turned to her.

Her world stopped at the sight of his face. She beheld the very visage of the late James Brooks. How could it be? She had been there. She had narrowly escaped the cavern collapse that claimed his life. Yet, before her stood the man declared dead more than a year before, with all of his dashing good looks and strong brown eyes.

Elizabeth did not know whether to faint or to rush to embrace him. Instead of doing either, she found herself choking out muddled questions. "James, but—how? What happened? Where have you been? I—"

"Miss Carter, I presume?" he returned with nervous politeness.

"But of course! James, don't you—"

"It seems Mr. Brooks suffers from amnesia," interrupted Dennison. She turned her attention to the man behind the desk, perplexed. "He was found wandering the desert in Arizona. Some settlers took him in for a time, but when he came to the mines looking for work, the foreman recognized him immediately and sent him on to Boston right away. That was not long after my visit to the excavation site last month."

Elizabeth again looked at Brooks.

"But how did you escape?"

"I wish I could tell you, Miss." Mr. Brooks fiddled with the bowler in his hands as he spoke and seemed hardly able to meet her eyes.

"Mr. Brooks' late mother passed during his absence, and his family's wealth was appropriated by the state. It will take some time to sort out, I'm afraid." Dr. Dennison could not take his eyes off his reappeared employee any more than could Elizabeth. "In the meantime, Mr. Powell has kindly offered to employ him and provide for his lodging. Since you knew him best, Miss Carter, I have decided to assign him to you."

She started. "To me?"

"Yes. It is rather a reversal, I admit. Instead of aiding Mr. Brooks in finding new crystal deposits in the field, Mr. Brooks will now assist your research into manufacturing them here in Boston."

Elizabeth's heart fluttered. Her mind skipped to and fro, unable to settle between attempting to understand how the past could be rewritten so easily, and wondering what her future with her secret love interest may now hold. She stood blinking for a good minute, first at Brooks, then at Dennison, before realizing that she ought to say something.

"Yes, of course, Dr. Dennison. I would be delighted. Perhaps it will help Mr. Brooks' memory."

Elizabeth turned abruptly to Brooks. "Shall we?" She motioned toward the door.

Brooks had little time to respond as the small woman herded him from the office.

"Thank you!" she called a little more happily than she intended as she closed the door behind her. Dr. Dennison had not yet lifted his pen when the door reopened and Elizabeth again peeked her head inside his office.

"Oh, and the report will be on your desk in the morning."

"See that it is, Miss Carter," replied Dr. Dennison with a smirk.

As the weeks passed, Elizabeth had absolutely no success in reviving Mr. Brooks' memory. He recalled none of their journeys together across the western frontier in search of crystals or his love for geology, travel, and adventure. Of course, James would not remember her feelings for him, as she had never spoken of them. Neither did she mention them now. It seemed unfair to prey on a man whose history was a blank slate. However, she took no small delight in his constant presence during the long days and nights in her little laboratory.

Thanks in part to James, she did make commendable progress in her research. In his prior life, James Brooks had been a prospector and frontiersman. At that time, the shards held no interest in themselves beyond paying for the next shot of whisky and the supplies to get him back out into the wild. However, in his new role as assistant to Elizabeth, he proved to have an uncanny familiarity with the shards and was of significant help.

"It just doesn't make sense," muttered Elizabeth looking at a small gray crystal through her magnifier. "It has the same chemical makeup as an indigenous shard, but does nothing when placed in a machine."

"Perhaps the elements are not in the right order," commented Brooks as he entered from a back room. In his hands he carried a complicated contraption. “The indigenous shards must have some kind of organization at a fundamental level that makes them unique. Something beyond the simple lumping of chemicals together.”

Elizabeth suddenly thrust out her palm to stop him from going any further. She placed her hand to her temple. She could not afford to have the fragile shadow of revelation escape her. “Of course! The process of synthesizing the crystals is entropic! The sum order is less than that of the parts . . . But if we can reverse the entropy . . .”

“But how?” James interrupted her whirling internal calculations.

“We feed more energy into the crystals as they form, of course. But it has to be the right kind of energy.” She put her finger to her lip as she continued thinking aloud, unaware of the amused smile on James’ lips. “Heat won’t do; the crystals would never solidify. In fact, we will have to chill the entire process to prevent the excess energy from disrupting the crystallization.”

She slapped the table as the conclusion came, startling even herself as the contraption James had lain there rattled from the jolt.

“Electricity!” she proclaimed, then looked down at the thing on the countertop. “What’s this you’ve found?”

“It was lying in the back and seemed interesting,” James replied. He grinned again, and this time Elizabeth noticed. He seemed perpetually amused by the ease with which she was distracted.

"Oh, this is one of my early creations," Elizabeth cooed at the thing, recalling the hand-machined parts she once labored over. "I wanted to test the limits of complexity that a shard could manage. I never quite got around to testing it."

"You were saying about electricity?" James prodded, still smiling.

"Oh, yes! Go and ask Mr. Otto if we can make use of his generator."

After a few weeks of hard work and trial and error, James and Elizabeth stood over a steaming vat that glowed with energy. James watched as, using long forceps, she pulled from the effervescent liquid a gleaming green crystal the size of a walnut. James' heart leapt at the sight of it. Yes, they had done it this time. He was sure of it.

With a sweep of his arm, he cleared a space on the nearest workbench. Elizabeth's expression gleamed nearly as much as the crystal as she laid it down. Setting a small horn to her ear, she tapped the crystal gently with a tuning fork. James found himself holding his breath as he waited. Elizabeth's eyes fluttered and her smile widened.

"It's asynchronous," she whispered, still listening intently. "Just like a natural shard."

"You've done it, Miss Carter!" James exclaimed.

"Not just yet. We still have to test it." Elizabeth put her instruments down and stared at the emerald shard. "It's strange how its hue is green instead of white like all the natural shards. . . . What shall we test it in?"

Both she and James looked around the lab. The space had become rather disorganized in their hurry to test the latest hypothesis. Various tools, instruments, and dirty flasks lay scattered about the place. James wondered if he had been so ambivalent to disorder before he lost his memory. Regardless, it only slightly bothered him now. He soon spotted the many-jointed contraption that he found in the supply room on the day their flurry of investigation began.

"Here," he said, picking up the device.

"Oh, but James," replied Elizabeth doubtfully, "I'm not certain that even works. I only just finished it before switching projects."

"Well, the coupling is intact, and it certainly should give us some kind of feedback if it works." Not waiting for a response, he filled the little spherical boiler and set it on the bench-top in front of her. She opened the device and began preparing the fittings to receive the shard.

"Fergusson, come lend me one of your coals," James called.

Elizabeth sighed and brought her hand to her crystal pendant. "Fergusson, come here and let us have a coal, please. You forget the control shard, James."

Elizabeth removed the crystal pendant from about her neck and gave it to James. As his skin made contact with the smooth surface of the shard, he felt a sudden sharp shock to his hand that made him exclaim. Both Elizabeth and Fergusson paused.

"Must have been static somehow," he responded to Elizabeth's questioning look. He shook his hand to rid it of the sting and proceeded on. However, Fergusson remained motionless.

"Miss Carter, look at this," James called, looking at the automaton. Elizabeth approached and took in the change that had overcome her mechanoid's eyes.

"How curious," she remarked. "I've never seen a crystal turn blue like that! Does he still respond to commands?"

James held the crystal pendant out in front of him. It also showed the strange blue color. "Fergusson, bring one of your hot coals to the table."

Without hesitation, the machine resumed its steady march toward the table and opened the hatch of its hotbox. Elizabeth shrugged and returned to the preparations on her old mechanical creation.

"It is very curious," she said. "We will have to look into it later. Let's not worry about it so long as the control shard works. Which brings up the point, how shall we test our new shard if we have no control shard to match it?"

James thought for a moment. He had learned from Elizabeth that control shards and their larger counterparts within the working machines were essentially identical. Pairs were made between them by matching their resonance energies such that the smaller could communicate commands to the larger. His brow furrowed as Elizabeth retrieved a coal from the larger automaton's hotbox and placed it into the furnace of the smaller device. He set it down to let the boiler pressurize.

"I suppose making a new shard is out of the question. There is no guarantee that they will match."

"Most likely they won't," commented his partner. "There is only one thing to do: we will have to cut the shard we have."

She reached for the control shard about her neck, then remembered that James still held it. "Have Fergusson get his cutter fitted and let's set him to the task."

"But supposing he breaks it?" James questioned nervously.

"If we don't take the risk, we will never know."

Nearly thirty minutes later, they breathed a collective sigh of relief as a pea-sized sliver of the green shard fell to the work-bench beneath Fergusson's powerful cutter.

"Well done, Fergusson. Now, go refuel yourself," James ordered the machine.

Using her ear horn and tuning fork, Elizabeth tapped the smaller green shard and listened, then repeated the process on the larger shard.

"They're close," she said, straightening. "It's the best we can do. Let's hope we can get at least some sort of movement out of this little contraption."

Using a small set of forceps, she carefully placed the larger of the green shards into the device on the counter. James handed her the smaller control shard with a smile.

"Would you like the honors?"

"But what shall we call it?"

“Hmmm, what about Spot?” James suggested. He had recently met a black and white dog with this name and thought it very clever.

“No, no, what about Jack? It was my favorite uncle’s name,” Elizabeth countered.

“Oh, I know: let’s call it Edgar.”

“Fine, then. Edgar,” conceded Elizabeth. “That happens to be my favorite cousin’s name. Let’s just get on with this.” Her chest heaved as she took a deep breath and closed her eyes for a moment, clutching the small control shard like a rosary bead.

“Edgar, raise one arm.”

For a moment the contraption of steel and brass did nothing. Then all of its many jointed arms began to twitch and slither about on the counter top. Very slowly, one slender metal tentacle rose into the air.

“Ha ha! We’ve done it, Elizabeth! We’ve done it!” James could hardly contain his excitement. He gripped his partner’s shoulders in a collegial and gentlemanly embrace. He ran a hand through his dark hair and stared at the machine as Elizabeth gleefully leaned closer to inspect the animated creation.

A sudden motion and a sharp cry from Elizabeth snapped James from his reverie. Elizabeth shook her hand, trying to rid herself of the sting of a slapping tentacle. The mechanical creature snatched up the green control shard from where it fell and tucked it under its shard hatch.

Both researchers stood back as the automaton raised itself to its full eight-inch height on ten stubby metal tentacles. A pair of more slender and longer tentacles curled beneath its body under two large round optics that gleamed with the green light of the shard. Its tiny pistons hissed at Elizabeth.

"Now you listen here, you little devil." She shook her finger at the creature. Its vents whistled in retort and it lunged toward her reprimanding hand. However, being only moments alive, the metal menace tripped over its own limbs and toppled over.

James acted quickly. He slammed a large glass beaker over the autonomous machine. Once it was contained, he joined Elizabeth in staring at it as it pushed and poked at the sides of its transparent prison.

"It—it's acting on its own. I've never seen any shard do that before," Elizabeth whispered.

"It's a miracle," added James.

A smile emerged at the corner of his partner's mouth. "It's kind of cute, like a little metal octopus."

"A very naughty one," commented James as he watched the thing ram the side of the beaker in an attempt to break the glass, an attempt thwarted by a firm hand on the top of the container.

"Yes, and that's what we shall call it, Nautilus—'Nauty' for short."

"But you already gave it a name, and it doesn't much look like a Nautilus."

"Oh, hush. It didn't like its other name, and I don't rightly care what it doesn't look like. I shall call it Nauty."

"Very well, then." James knew there was no reasoning with her when she spoke in that tone. "What shall we do now?"

“We wait.”

“Wait for what?”

“For its boiler to run down. It has to lose steam eventually. If it won’t respond to a control shard and wants to act like a little beast, we shall simply treat it like one.”

As it turned out, Nauty learned very quickly that it required a steady supply of coal to keep its boiler hot and responded very well to being trained with coal ‘treats’ by Miss Carter. Within a span of two days, it became quite friendly and even affectionate, particularly to Elizabeth. It developed a habit of perching on her shoulder where it could watch her at her work.

The unveiling of their synthetic shard resulted in surprising disinterest—even apprehension—from Dr. Dennison. His nervous hedging hinted at an impending development with the natural shards that would make their discovery of “little significance.” When Elizabeth persisted in her argument with no small amount of red-faced blustering and monologue, he recommended they show their creation to Mr. Powell himself. Powell would return from inspecting the mine in a few weeks, at which point he could decide if their discovery fit with A. I.’s business agenda.

After Miss Carter’s fiery exit from the meeting, James found himself alone and so returned to the laboratory. It was not long before she barged in, still flushed and with several slips of paper in her hands.

He attempted to dampen her discouragement of the day’s meeting with Dennison with lighthearted banter. “Ah, Miss Carter, you’re back! What have you there?”

"Tickets, of course," she nearly spat. "Dennison said we should see Mr. Powell, and so we shall."

"Oh, I see." James clearly did not. Though he lacked a proper memory, he was very observant, and in the few months spent with Miss Carter he learned very early to tread lightly whenever she raised her slender eyebrows that high on her forehead. Secretly, he wondered how he ever survived her temper during the explorations the two of them had reportedly shared.

"Of course, Dennison expects us to wait for Powell's return, but that won't stop us, will it?"

"No, I suppose not."

"I have booked our tickets. Now, pack your things. We'll be leaving for Arizona on the train in the morning." Miss Carter shoved a set of tickets into James' hands and turned to stomp out the door, Nauty still perched precariously on her shoulder.

James looked around the lab. He picked up his coat and bowler from the nearby hat rack. "Well, I'm packed," he smiled. "Are we taking a train all the way?" It was true that he had little to his name, though this did not bother him in the least. In his attempt at humor, he hoped he would subdue Miss Carter's wild temper.

Elizabeth turned to face him again and her countenance suddenly softened.

"Oh, I'm sorry, James," she said. "And no, we are not taking a train all the way to the mines. The railroad can get us as far as Denver. We will have to ride in a coach from there."

"What about the experiment?" James motioned to the large contraption from which they had formed Nauty's shard. For the past week, the processor had maintained its quiet humming and churning as a new synthetic shard formed within its cauldron.

"I'll ask Mr. Otto to keep an eye on it. I'm sure he won't mind, and the longer it goes, the larger the crystal it should yield."

"Heaven forbid there ever be a larger version of that little hellion on your shoulder!"

Nauty gave a sharp hissing whistle at this and waved several curled limbs in a threatening motion, but Elizabeth took no notice.

Several days later, James and Elizabeth stepped from a stagecoach into the glaring Arizona sun. Behind them spread an expanse of hot, dry desert and rolling hills. Before them rose the mountain ridge where, years before, Elizabeth's uncle discovered gold and Powell, later, discovered the crystals. Thus, A. I. became the exclusive source of the remarkable shards that became the center of a new booming robotics industry.

The bulk of these mechanical marvels were in service on the East Coast. However, a small army of mechanized wonders slaved tirelessly under the blazing Arizona sun. Marching in their slow, deliberate steps, they moved in and out of the myriad of gaping tunnel entrances dotting the mountainside. For every dozen or so automatons, a human worker wandered among them, giving directions and carrying out such tasks that might require some judgment.

Noticing their arrival, one such human worker approached them, riding a most remarkable machine that rumbled along on four sets of treads. A plume of steam escaped from its sides as it pulled up in front of them.

"What are you doing back?" barked the foreman, recognizing James.

"We have come from the research office to meet with Mr. Powell," responded Elizabeth confidently.

The man's mustache wrinkled under his dusty Stetson. Placing his hand to a bracer on his left forearm, he touched two out of several crystals and gave the order, "Escort these two to Mr. Powell's tent. But do *not* let them inside."

Two top-heavy automatons approached and flanked the visitors. "I'll go and inform Powell that you are here," the man grumbled.

"Do be sure to tell him we have a breakthrough to—" The man moved away, and the hissing and clanking of the travelling device that bore him drowned out her voice. "Oh, drat."

Something about her expression made James smile. The automatons beside them began to move. Whether their escorts were guiding or herding them James could not be sure, but they saw very little of the mining operation as they were hurried off.

They stood in the merciless sun for quite some time before Mr. Powell made his appearance. He was a barrel-chested man, thick through his middle but surprisingly nimble on his feet. Accompanying him was the man that intercepted them earlier, now divested of his mechanical transport. Neither gave the visiting pair so much as a passing glance as they entered the spacious tent. Elizabeth and James attempted to follow, but the solid metal bodies of their escorts moved to block them.

Elizabeth stamped her foot, and James saw that familiar fire in her eyes. He was debating the risk of intercepting her next move, which was sure to be of an impulsive and regrettable nature, when Powell's voice called from within the tent.

"Come in, Miss Carter."

This time, the guards did not prevent them. The inside of the tent was stuffy, with only yellowed light penetrating the canvas roof. Despite this dingy pall, the interior of the space was furnished with lavish and masculine accoutrements and innumerable mechanical contraptions. Powell sat at a side-facing desk with an expression of impatience glowering through his "friendly" mutton chops. Behind him stood the solemn and suspicious foreman.

Elizabeth seemed suddenly unsure. An awkward silence spread until Powell gestured with his broad hand.

"Well?"

"Yes," replied Elizabeth automatically. She smoothed her traveling skirt. "As you know, Mr. Powell, I have been in the process of researching means of synthesizing shards that will match those that you mine here."

Powell's fingers drummed impatiently on the table.

"I have come to show you in person the remarkable break-through that I have made, with the assistance of Mr. Brooks, of course."

"Get on with it, Miss Carter. I have a schedule to maintain."

Elizabeth hastily poured out the contents of her bag onto the desk, and out came Nauty in a tumble of waving tentacles. Righting itself, the little creature spurted a small puff of indignant steam and took in its surroundings with its luminous green eyes. Powell seemed little impressed until he saw the green hue of its gaze.

"And you made this shard?" he questioned.

"Yes, sir." Elizabeth flashed a proud smile at James.

"Show me what it can do. Make it lift that tea kettle." He gestured to the iron kettle that sat on the desk.

"Nauty," Elizabeth called in her kindest voice. "Please fetch me that kettle."

The creature looked at Elizabeth, then at the kettle, then at Powell. Everyone seemed to hold their breath. The mechanical device crawled slowly toward the kettle.

Reaching the heavy teapot, it surveyed each of its spectators again. Finally, it pressed its small face to the black iron side. With a mighty shove, it knocked the kettle clear off the desktop.

Everyone started at the crash, and Elizabeth gasped in horror as the little device chuffed merry bursts of steam at its clever ruse.

Nauty scurried about the desk, cheerfully scattering papers and pens to the floor. "Miss Carter, get control of your beast," bellowed Powell.

"I am so sorry, sir," Elizabeth blurted. "I'm afraid I have yet to perfect a means of controlling the shard."

She scooped up her little creation and set it upon her shoulder, whispering words of condemnation, which seemed only to further amuse the creature.

"You mean it has no controlling shard?" Powell raised an eyebrow high.

"Not yet, sir."

Powell glanced at his companion. Whatever their silent exchange meant, James could not discern, but Powell's manner was once more dismissive when his gaze again turned toward Elizabeth.

"It is an interesting curiosity, Miss Carter. Yet, without a means of control, I fear it is of little use to us."

James saw her countenance drop, and his heart followed for her sake.

"Still, I will ask that you leave the shard and its device here for my further inspection. You may return to your duties in Boston but will create no more of these aberrations without prior knowledge that they can be safely controlled."

"But sir, I already have a second and larger synthetic shard in production. Mr. Otto is governing the incubation. How could I possibly know how to control them without first experimenting?"

"An excellent question and one I am sure your scientific expertise will overcome. In the meantime, I will see to it that Dr. Dennison enforces my order explicitly. We cannot have vagrant devices of this sort running amok in Boston. It would dissipate all public trust in our automatons."

Powell rose and moved toward Elizabeth with outstretched hand, demanding the disobedient creature. Elizabeth stepped back, nearly bumping into James.

"But Mr. Powell, this is my first and only creation."

"And, as you are in the employ of A. I., it is my property. Do not forget that your joining this corporation was only due to the stipulations of John Carter's will. But there is no such requirement for your retention in the face of disobedience. I have wanted to be rid of your foolish endeavors for some time."

James saw the color in Elizabeth's pink cheeks drain to match the canvas that shaded them, then flush red again as, with a tremor, she forced her posture as straight and stiff as an arrow. Nauty, meanwhile, wrapped several of its long arms around her shoulder and hid itself from Powell's outstretched hand behind the loose chignon resting at the base of her neck.

"Mr. Powell," she retorted with only the slightest quaver in her voice, "I am in much gratitude for your obedience to my dear uncle's last wishes. However, I have proven myself worthy of this company on countless occasions. That said, you will no longer have to endure any of my 'foolishness.' I resign forthwith and request only the time permitted to return to Boston and set my private laboratory in order."

Powell grinned wickedly, further enraging the petite woman.

"And you shall have my synthetic shard no sooner than my affairs in Boston are concluded."

With that, she turned abruptly and whisked out of the tent with all the air of a reproached royal princess. James, once again left in the vacuum of one of her volatile exits, saw Powell move to follow her with rage in his eyes. He was prevented, however, by his foreman who, muttering certain advice under his breath, dissuaded his master from escalating the conflict.

James later found Elizabeth at the edge of the camp. She gazed out across the flat Arizona plain with reddened eyes. Nauty reposed nervously in her cradling embrace. James could find no words of comfort, for indeed there was nothing to say. He merely chose to stand beside her in hopes that, through the silence, his presence would support the heaviness of her heart.

Presently, one of their large steel escorts arrived bearing a note. In professional but none-too-cordial terms, it instructed them to take lodging in the tents shown to them while they awaited the arrival of the morning coach.

It was already dusk, and as the cold Arizona night overtook the land with uncommon swiftness, it was quite dark when they reached their lodgings. Elizabeth entered her tent without a word. James saw there was nothing to do otherwise, so he, too, settled himself into the meager accommodations made for them.

It had been a long day's travel and so, despite the turbidity of his emotions, James fell into a dreamless sleep. He did not know how many hours later he awoke to the sounds of a struggle.

From next door, he heard feminine shouts and the clang of metal knocking against metal. Rushing out, James found Elizabeth's tent half collapsed and undulating like a turbulent sea in the clear Arizona moonlight. Rushing in, he found

Elizabeth and two mechanicals engaged in a competitive but vain attempt to capture the scurrying Nauty.

James leapt to action. One automaton, preoccupied with capturing the elusive mechanical octopus, fairly trampled Elizabeth under the narrow wheels on which it rolled. Leaping onto the back of the nearest machine, James quickly found the trap door that hid its crystalline shard.

He tore open the hatch and reached for the glowing crystal within. However, on contact, he received a terrible jolt that sent him reeling off the back of the motorized beast. Curious and unnatural visions flashed through his mind. Though it seemed far longer to him, the jolt only removed him for a moment from the conflict. Jumping to his feet again, he saw his initial adversary slumped and the other hot on the heels of the scurrying Nauty.

The frantic little creature rushed to him and clambered up his back. The automaton came fast in pursuit, and poor Elizabeth lay watching from where a downed tent pole had tripped her. The mechanical monster reached for Nauty with its steel pincers, which both James and the little beast did their best to dodge and duck. The creature grew tired of that game, and simply gripped James by his shirt collar, lifting him into the air.

His feet dangled and thrashed and his hands instinctively rose to his throat.

"Help!" he managed a strangled scream.

Before he had time to make a second cry, a heavy object hurled itself into the automaton that suspended him above the ground. Tumbling to the earth, James stared in awe as the form of the first automaton dealt such damage upon the second as to appear in a deadly rage.

James scuttled toward Elizabeth, thinking to protect her. Finished with its work, the metal golem rolled toward them. The glow of its eyes shone a gleaming blue instead of the common pale white, and with them, it fixed its gaze on the two humans and their tiny pet machine. Closer it rolled until, not three feet from them, it stopped.

James stared up into the unblinking eyes. The machine stared back, motionless. He rose to face it, and soon felt Elizabeth's small hand on his shoulder.

"It looks like it's waiting," she whispered.

Shouts rose in the camp as the slumbering supervisors of the mechanical giants awoke and hurried toward the disturbance. Elizabeth's hand gripped James' shoulder more tightly.

"We've got to move," he whispered.

The pair backed carefully away from the machine and began to scuttle stealthily through the camp. James was not sure where he was leading them. Perhaps they could find some horses on which they could escape or one of the treaded vehicles they had seen that day. He knew they must leave the camp at all costs. James felt certain Powell was behind the botched attack, and from such a man they could assume no assurance of safety.

Groups of men and machines streamed about the camp searching for them, forcing their path toward the mountain as they struggled to remain hidden. The manhunt compelled them closer to the mines and higher upon the ridge. Rounding the shoulder of a rocky outcropping, their eyes beheld a startling view.

Below them lay a work site quite separate from the rest of the mine. Electric lamps illuminated it from all sides. Several guards stood about, armed with repeater rifles. In the very center lay a massive crystal. Elizabeth gasped when she saw it. She shielded Nauty's luminescent eyes under her waistcoat.

Nearly five yards long and a quarter as much in width, it was faceted all over with sharp angles that reflected the light of the electric lamps. It added to those lights its own soft glow, which was of a pale, almost sorrowful blue. Attached at regular intervals were blocks of what looked like a foreign metal.

The spying pair ducked down on seeing someone enter the protected space. Powell. Still buttoning his jacket, he approached the crystal confidently. He paused before it briefly, as if to gather his thoughts, then placed his palm firmly against the smooth, glowing surface.

A splitting pain erupted in James' head, such that he nearly collapsed over the embankment. The whispers of Powell rang with deafening clarity in his mind.

CAPTURE THE MAN AND THE WOMAN. BURY THEM IN THE MINES, BUT BRING ME THE GREEN SHARD!

All at once, the pain slackened and James opened his eyes to see Powell leaving the guarded crystal by the way he had come.

"They're going to kill us. Did you hear it?"

"Hear what, James?" Elizabeth's face was stricken with concern and confusion.

“We’ve got to get out of here.”

Standing to make his way back down the ridge, James suddenly reeled with dizziness and lost his footing. A fist-sized rock tumbled down the embankment and into the sanctuary of the immense crystal.

Powell turned at the sound. “There they are! They’ve seen the Master Shard! *Shoot them now*!”

The guards did not hesitate a moment. A volley of lead hurtled towards James and Elizabeth. The girl fairly threw herself down the opposite side of the embankment with James close behind her. Just as he thought they were out of range, a force like the kick of ten mules struck his shoulder and knocked him headlong down the ridge.

Elizabeth was beside him in a moment.

“James, are you alright?” Her hand touched his throbbing shoulder and came away wet with blood. “You’ve been shot!”

“We have got to get out of here!”

“But how? We have no way to travel but our own feet, and you are wounded!”

Through the pain James could see only one solution. “We need one of their machines!”

No sooner had he spoken than up to them raced the blue-eyed automaton that first attacked, then defended them back in the camp. It waited for no assistance nor order but carefully collected the bleeding James Brooks in its steel arms.

“No, Elizabeth must come too,” James groaned as he struggled to maintain consciousness. The machine turned and looked over its shoulder as if waiting. Cautiously, Elizabeth set her foot on the ridge of its torso swivel, and then set her hands as high upon its shoulders as she could reach.

The machine did not wait a minute more. Down along the ridge they swept on rolling wheels. Out into the moonlit night they raced at a terrific speed. With every bounce and bump, a sharp pain reminded James of his wound. A glance behind them revealed a pursuing party from the mining operation. Whether they were men, machines, or both he could not tell.

They had a good head start since it took some time for their pursuers to realize that they had procured a means of travel. However, their mechanical transport soon began to slow. It was running low on fuel and steam.

When they reached a water hole, James found the pain in his shoulder had slackened. They quickly replenished the water supply of both Nauty and their unusual friend. Dead branches would have to suffice for fuel to charge the boilers.

As James pondered their next move, two shots rang out in the night. Powell's patrol had found them. Both humans mounted the back of their ride and fled.

A narrow ravine spilled them onto a wide plateau. It afforded no cover and few choices but forward. Far too quickly, the lights and whoops of their adversaries rose up at their rear and spurred them to hurtle headlong through the rocky wastes.

The two human and two mechanical fugitives eventually found themselves traversing a rocky mountain trail. With a high cliff rising sharply to their right and an equally steep precipice dropping off to their left, they wound their way up a mountain-side until they reached a cave. A distant commotion confirmed that their pursuers had taken an easier pass out of the hills.

They dismounted at the small mouth of the cavern. James moved to search out a safe place to rest, but his partner stopped him.

"James, don't you remember this place?" Elizabeth asked.

James paused. He looked behind her at the Arizona landscape emerging in the premonitions of dawn. Its stark, rolling hills and tall cacti looked strange in the death throes of night—almost like another world. Something stirred in him, but he could not place it. Shaking his head, he looked back at his companion.

Her welling tears glistened as she looked into his eyes. "This is the very cave in which you were lost nearly two years ago."

In the long silence that followed, James scanned the dusty trail at his feet, searching desperately for any clue that would unlock his memory. Vague images tried to break the surface, but they seemed to have nothing to do with prospecting or a cave-in. What strange circumstance led them to this place at this time?

He knew the story well enough. He had talked it out with Elizabeth during their late nights at the laboratory. Two years prior, they had scouted for new crystal deposits, Elizabeth the expert in the mineral, and James her intrepid guide. According to her, the entrance opened into a large chamber. A myriad of tunnels and smaller caverns fanned out beyond. In one of those occurred the collapse that separated him from his memory for so much time.

Dawn came on in earnest, and the bitter cold of the night began giving way to the sun's golden rays. Elizabeth refused to enter the cave, and he agreed to sit at its mouth and rest. Their strangely benevolent ride stood motionless before them, while Nauty amused himself by dropping pebbles over the cliff opposite the cavern entrance. Exhausted and distressed, James leaned his head against the rock wall and turned over the recent events and his own mysterious past over and over again in his mind.

Finally, Elizabeth roused herself.

"James, you were shot. Let me see the wound." She pulled back his shirt to expose his shoulder. The tenderness of her delicate fingers alone seemed to bring strength and healing to him. He watched as her brow furrowed.

"What is this?" she murmured. James could just see from the corner of his eye. The sizable but shallow tear in his flesh had already begun to heal. Yet it did so by the strangest of means. Specks and shards of brilliant blue crystal mingled in the dried blood and inflamed tissues.

Elizabeth lowered her hand from the wound and startled at the touch of something on his chest. Before he thought to stop her, she pulled back the cotton fabric of his half buttoned shirt and gaped. A brilliant blue gem, larger than a tea saucer, interrupted the surface of the skin. The look in her eyes told

James that something must be gravely wrong, but he did not understand.

"What is this?"

He looked at his chest, seeing only what he had seen since finding himself alone in the Arizona plain several months gone. "How do you mean?"

"The stone, the crystal in your chest!"

"Is there something wrong with it?"

"Wrong with it? It should not be there at all!"

James did not know what to say. "I—I didn't know. I never thought about it, really."

"Never thought about it!" Elizabeth's eyes flashed as she looked away. A curious fear and bewilderment that he could have been so ignorant overcame him. Elizabeth moved stiffly. He could not begin to guess the feelings she struggled to control.

"I'm sorry, Elizabeth," James tried to console her. However, she backed away.

"James, order that machine to jump in its place," she demanded suddenly.

"What?"

"Just do it!"

James consented without hesitation, although he did not understand her intent. The heavy rollers of the automaton rose from the ground, rather unimpressively, and returned with a solid thud.

"Machine," Elizabeth called to the automaton immediately, "jump!"

The machine stared at James in silence. Not so much as a puff of steam escaped it.

"I saw you in the camp, James." She glared back at him, almost venomously. "You touched its shard. Just as you touched Fergusson's control shard. Do you see its color now? Changed, just like his. And now it obeys you without a control shard. I wonder, would Fergusson have obeyed me even if I had held the control shard after that day?"

She paused. The tears again welled in her eyes.

The expression on her face as she looked at him sent a pain through him greater than he had ever known. He was not a heartless machine and he knew it. He could think of only one way to prove it to her. He opened his shirt, gripped the crystal, and pulled.

"No, James, stop!"

He felt the shard give a little. He could do this. The cold transparent stone began to glow as it slowly pulled away from its resting place. Elizabeth was saying something again. Her voice seemed so far away. He kept pulling. His vision began to blur. His body felt far away. His legs no longer listened to him. Was he falling or floating . . .?

James woke with a start and a feeling of pressure against his chest. A feminine face hovering close to his quickly retreated. He sat up, trying to recall what happened. The early morning sun still labored to warm the Arizona landscape. Elizabeth stood sobbing nearby. He felt for the shard in his chest. It was still there, pushed back into place by hands not his own.

James approached, trying to console her. “Elizabeth—”

She stepped back. “How do I know that shard does not control you,” she whispered through her tears, “just as you control this metal brute? Who are you really? What are you?”

James paused at the words. He struggled with the thoughts and new memories that flashed through his mind at the touch of the automaton’s shard. They were all fragmented and jumbled. He saw a large crowd bidding him well on some voyage, then a sense of something gone terribly wrong. There was also a brief image of a tall man, first standing, then slumping in the mouth of the very cave by which he sat, but he could make sense of none of it. Now that he stopped to consider them, he could not place them in the history of James Brooks as he knew it.

“I—I don’t know.”

The next few hours passed in miserable silence. Elizabeth continued in her isolation, fear, and grief.

Presently, she rose. “I cannot stay here.”

She moved past him and down the trail. Nauty left the tower of rocks it had been building, and scurried up to her shoulder.

“And you will not follow me, James Brooks, or whatever you are,” she asserted, forcing her belligerent tenacity over her anxiety.

James could not possibly let her go alone, but she looked ready to pounce on him if he ventured after her. An alternative struck his mind, however. He spoke quietly to the machine that stood ever vigilant and ever silent nearby.

“Stay close to her, Machine. Keep her safe, obey her, but do not leave her.”

The coming of dark found Elizabeth still stamping across the Arizona desert. Nauty, perched on her shoulder, drooped lethargically nearly as much as she did. Ten paces behind her followed the tall automaton. Across its steel chest were several dusty scuffmarks where it had been assaulted by its charge. She had taken to throwing rocks as a means of dissuading it from following her. However, nothing she could do would make the metal minion deviate from the directive given by James.

The twilight came on with that unnatural swiftness to which the Arizona plain is prone, and for the first time Elizabeth truly considered the gravity of her situation. She was alone in the desert with no food and no water. Initially she thought she would march to the nearest outpost, which lay "only" fifteen miles from the mines from which they fled. Now, as she faced dehydration and exhaustion in all their stark reality, she felt afraid.

She was confident she was going in the right direction to reach the outpost. She had only to follow the dry riverbed which flowed down to the tiny settlement. However, as to how long it would take her to reach it, she could only guess. Elizabeth was aware of her propensity for rashness. Perhaps this had been a poor and hasty choice.

The clunking of the automaton behind her brought her thoughts back to James. She no longer believed him to be the same man she knew before the cave-in. No, that James had been a haughty and brash frontiersman, flirtatious but detached.

She wondered what she had ever seen in him. This man, this thing that animated James' body, never displayed the same self-important attitudes. In contrast to the aloof and reckless James she once secretly adored, this man was kindhearted and courteous, even noble. All her life Elizabeth had put her dreams of success ahead of everything else, and as such, she had few genuine friends. Now she realized that James—this new James—had been such a friend to her as she had never known. And she had left him behind.

She turned and faced the machine that followed her. Her mind was made up. "Machine, take me back to the cave at once . . . please."

The machine acknowledged her only by turning its back and allowing her to climb its hulking frame. Making much better time by wheel than on foot as she had so stubbornly chosen at the outset of her journey, they rapidly made the return trip. Elizabeth soon found herself approaching the cave. However, James was not there.

Although she was no frontiersman, she thought she could distinguish his tracks leading away from the cave and back west, in the direction of the mines. Had he gone mad and returned to Powell's camp? Elizabeth called her iron companion.

"Machine, can you take me to James?"

The automaton looked at her with its expressionless eyes, and then looked into the west, in the direction she was certain James had gone. Without waiting for consent, she and Nauty climbed the machine's back once more and they sped off through the moonlit night.

As they reached the camp, Elizabeth could see that the men were not asleep as they ought to have been, but were making a great commotion. Men were crowding around something on which they focused so exclusively that they did not see Elizabeth speeding up on the back of the mechanical man. Just outside the crowd, she spotted a severely damaged automaton with a shard that glowed the unusual blue that marked James' touch.

Elizabeth realized what James had been doing. He returned to the camp to test his curious talent on another shard. It seemed that the experiment worked, but that Powell's men overpowered both James and the newly turned machine. That meant that, in all likelihood, she would find James himself at the center of the jeering crowd.

"Fetch James, and get us all to safety!" she shouted to the machine over the clatter of its pistons and the rumble of its wheels across the cold dry ground.

The automaton plowed through the crowd as a cue through billiard balls. Startled men scattered in every direction. She soon saw James, bound hand and foot on the ground before her. The marvelous machine did not slow in the slightest, but caught James by his tattered collar and continued up the mountain. It raced toward a small dark patch in the mountainside, and just when Elizabeth was about to scream for fear of colliding with some unknown black thing, she found herself suddenly enshrouded by the darkness of a mining tunnel.

The machine stopped. It was pitch black in the tunnel, save for the soft blue light that emanated from the eyes of the machine, and the weaker green light that likewise shone from Nauty's. Nauty was excited to see James again and skillfully applied its slender arms in assisting Elizabeth in untying his bonds.

"Elizabeth, what are you doing here?" he asked as soon as she pulled the gag from his mouth.

"I should ask you the same thing!" she retorted, fussing over the ropes tied tightly around his wrists. An awkward silence followed.

"I did it again," whispered James eventually out of the black. "I changed one of their machines."

"You are a fool, James. Those ruffians could have killed you."

"But I remember! With each new shard I touch, I remember more of who I am!" The excitement in his voice suggested a smile that the darkness of the tunnel veiled.

"Yes, but James, how are we to—"

A startling sound in the darkness interrupted the woman. It was the clanking of metal. Following it came the sound of hissing steam, and a soft white light cast shadows on the tunnel walls ahead of them.

"They have set the machines after us," cried Elizabeth.

"Then they have sent our salvation into our hands," smirked James. He rose confidently. As he did so, a curious thing happened: along the walls of the tunnel several crystals hidden in the darkness began to glow with the same powerful blue hue of the shard belonging to the changed automaton. She could see James' smile now as he marveled at what was surely his own unconscious ability. He beckoned the larger automaton to follow him as he crept stealthily toward the oncoming lights. Elizabeth, so bold in the face of duty to an endangered friend, now crouched against the tunnel wall, clutching Nauty tightly.

James and his metal servant slipped out of sight around the corner, and the crystals in the walls dimmed again. There followed a terrific crashing and clamor that brought Elizabeth's heart full into her throat. She waited for what seemed like an eternity.

Her fears were unfounded, however. Soon James returned with no less than four metal golems, each with glowing blue eyes.

"The men are leaving," he told her. "They have loaded up almost every automaton and started hauling them across the desert."

"But why?"

"I am not certain. I heard them say something before you rescued me. Something about Powell moving up his plans because of us."

"Whatever could they mean?"

"I don't know, but we should be safe here for a short time. This is an old, unused mine, and the men are quite frightened now that they realize I can claim their machines as my own."

Elizabeth was not quite sure how to feel about this confirmation of James' inhuman nature. "What are we to do then? Wait 'til they leave?"

"I doubt they will all leave," replied James thoughtfully. He seemed to her suddenly bold and confident. "The mining operation will go on eventually, I am sure. They certainly do not want to lose their claim. They don't know quite where we are and are avoiding the mines at the moment. It is almost dawn out there. I suggest we wait until it is dark again and then take our flight."

"It seems that we must. Yet how shall we make our way? It will not be safe for us to travel the rails again—not if Powell's men are looking for us."

James scratched his chin, and in the dim light cast by his new minions, she thought she saw a strange twinkle in his eyes. She marveled at what manner of man he was becoming. She thought she should fear him for his unnatural abilities, yet, when he gazed upon her, she felt a warmth and peace in her heart that she had never before felt.

"I think I have an idea," he grinned.

James and the automatons separated themselves a short distance from Elizabeth and Nauty. The little cephalopod wanted to follow and investigate, but Elizabeth pulled him back when she heard the sounds of hammering and grinding of metal against metal.

The desert sun that rose was perceptible only as a slight decrease of the dimness in their deep tunnel, even when it reached its brightest, and that soon faded away. James continued with the deafening noises of construction. She wondered how he could go on working without having eaten or slept in nearly two days.

She woke sometime later, when James' strong arms gently picked her up and placed her onto some sort of seat.

"Hold on," he said, as if sorry to disturb her sleep with such a trivial thing as escaping their mountain prison.

They were soon moving through the tunnel under the power of steadily pumping steam pistons. The dim light of the cave gave no indication as to what kind of contraption carried her. It clattered and clanked but moved smoothly over the floor of the tunnel. Reaching the cave mouth, they peered out. James had been correct. The majority of the camp had moved out. Plenty of men stayed behind to defend the mines, and a few automatons remained to continue the work. However, most of the machines had been taken for some other purpose.

A tent stood at the foot of the mountain and lights shone from it. Those must have been the men placed to watch for their appearance from the tunnels. What could have been so important that Powell took leave with so many of his crew and supplies?

Stealthily, James directed their vehicle out of the mine and along the side of the mountain. However, it did not take long until a sharp cry and the sound of gunshots told them they had been spotted. James gave a shout of command and pushed a lever on their machine. It leapt forward with a sudden burst of speed. Elizabeth realized now that the device had no wheels or tracks, but ran across the ground on five pairs of stout legs of steel. She caught her breath and gripped Nauty all the more tightly.

A bullet glanced off the side of their peculiar carriage, but soon they were well out of range. Away they sped out over the rolling Arizona hills, faster even than their first automaton ride that took them across the plain the day before. It was not until the coming of the dawn that blinded them with its vermillion rays that Elizabeth breathed a sigh of relief. They made their way east, toward Boston, not knowing what they would do when they got there, but sure that they would find safety within the bounds of the civilized city.

The journey took many days, and many stops were made to rest, refuel, and escape detection. They spoke few words between them.

At some point, crossing the Taconic Mountains of New York, Elizabeth leaned forward from the rear seat to place her hand on James' shoulder. She could see Nauty perched on the head of the machine, watching the trees speed by with unending fascination.

"James," she said tenderly, "I'm sorry I doubted you. You are a good man and rather a better one than the James I knew. I am glad to be with you."

"Are you sure of that?" he replied with a guarded tone.

"Of course I am. Look at all you've done these last days, risking your life to—"

"No, are you sure that I am a man?"

Elizabeth did not know how to respond.

"Elizabeth, you said your uncle discovered the mines, right?" he asked after an awkward pause.

"Yes, it was my Uncle Jack—John Carter."

"He was a tall man with dark hair, wasn't he?"

"Yes, he was that way from the time I first remember him 'til he died. But how did you know?"

"Was he with us when the cave-in happened?"

"James, what is with all these absurd questions? Of course he was not there. He has been dead and laid to rest in Virginia more than ten years."

James did not respond. Then, as though struggling against the words, he spoke again.

"I think you were right. With every crystal shard I touch, my memories return. However, they are not the memories of James Brooks. They are memories of far-off places, strange people, of a man who was there in the beginning. He was there at the mines, before they were mines, and he was there at the cave."

Elizabeth remained silent. She could find nothing to say. Instead, she leaned forward and placed her chin delicately on his shoulder.

"There's more," continued James. "I can still hear Powell when he touches that shard." His words were strained, as though he did not want to admit his abilities even to himself.

"He is back in Boston preparing for something. He controls all the automatons with that shard, and he has some evil plan for them. There is only one thing he fears can stop his designs, one thing he has ordered his minions to stop at all costs."

He paused and Elizabeth raised her head attentively.

"They will be waiting for us."

"All the more reason we must alert the authorities," she affirmed. It was a bad situation indeed, but she felt strangely secure with this mysterious man . . . or whatever he was.

James fell into silence again. Elizabeth stretched her arm around him and placed her right hand on his left shoulder. Her forearm rested against the stone lodged in his chest, and when he felt it, he gently moved her arm upward, away from the evidence of the unnatural trait. However, he did not push her away completely. She rested against him in the silence as their mount charged on. When she next opened her eyes, it was dark and James was saying, “We’re here.”

They were indeed. The sprawling streets of Boston lay all around them. Most of the tightly packed houses were dark, and only the streetlights shone under the moonless sky. Their mechanical steed moved along quietly, keeping to the shadows as much as its bulk could manage.

“Should we go back to the lab?” asked Elizabeth.

“I fear there is no time,” replied James in a whisper. “Powell seems to have moved up his plans again on hearing that we escaped, and took control of some of his automatons. I have heard him directing groups of machines near the harbor all night.”

“Then we must go there. He is a madman, and you are the only one who can stop him. He’ll never suspect—”

“Shh—” James drew their ride to a stop. “They’ve seen us.”

Ahead of them, six pairs of pale glowing eyes stepped from the doorways of their masters’ homes. The automatons came toward them with the clinking and clattering of their steady, rapid footsteps and the sharp hiss of their boilers. James wasted no time. A combination of his thoughts and a movement of levers on their many-legged mount sent them charging towards their foes. The three rows of upturned spikes at the head of their steed made short work of the sentinels. However, the next corner they turned presented them with several more of the silent adversaries.

At the sight of them, James dismounted. He spoke a word of direction to their beast to protect Elizabeth. She was shocked to see him turn and advance unarmed toward the oncoming automatons. She wanted to scream and call him back, but her fear prevented her.

Reaching the first, a clunking domestic serving machine, he thrust his hand against its chest before it could act. A blue flash resulted and the machine burst backwards, separating into its myriad components. The same happened with the second and the third. In the midst of the chaos, Elizabeth noticed that the pieces were not all falling lifelessly to the ground. They flew away, only to roll or slide back to James' feet where they began to assemble themselves about him.

His growing abilities terrified her and left her in awe. The street was soon cleared and James stood garbed in what could most closely be described as a suit of brass and steel. Enshrouded in cogs, pistons, and the blue glow of crystal shards, James stood nearly ten feet tall on mechanical stilts. Metal contraptions likewise artificially extended his arms, and a second set of independent arms worked for him by means Elizabeth could only imagine. As he turned to face her, she saw a pair of large reflective spikes that looked like tusks extend upward from his collar plating and past his face. He motioned for them to follow him, which they did at a safe distance.

From the next group of automated attackers, James fashioned weapons in keeping with his alien armor. His right arm gripped a jagged length of steel that he swung like a scimitar, and the left hand of his second set of arms thrust with a pointed scrap that he used as a short sword. In this manner, they progressed through the city.

Any onlookers that woke from the disturbance doubtless ran back to the safety of their bedclothes. Elizabeth once spied a mounted police officer speeding away and presumed that he was either a hopeless coward or sensible enough to summon reinforcements before engaging in the sortie. They were thus unimpeded by men in their advance through the winding streets.

Upon reaching the A. I. compound, they found it silent and vacant. James' mechanical arms tore open the gates, and they advanced quietly. Elizabeth could feel her heart in her throat. For half a moment, she considered going back and allowing James to finish the work alone. However, the memory of that dastard Powell and his responsibility for James' gunshot wound breathed new fire into her. Beyond that, she knew she could not leave James. Something in her forbade it.

The interior of the complex was gloomy and dark. James inched with stealth through the scattered buildings within the gates with singular purpose. Elizabeth did not understand how he knew which direction to head, but they drew ever nearer the large tin-clad warehouse on the wharf. Upon reaching it, they found the building completely dark and the broad sliding doors partially open.

James motioned for her to stay back and the mechanical beast on which she rode stopped obediently. However, as James slipped into the darkness within, Elizabeth slid to the forward seat.

"Shall we try it, Nauty?" she asked, taking the controls. The imp of a machine puffed in the affirmative and leaned forward on her shoulder in anticipation. She was pleased when the walking machine responded to her working of the several levers and controls.

Engulfed in the darkness within the warehouse, she could not help but whisper into the shadows. "James . . ."

The sudden hiss of steam all around her and the pale lights of a hundred pairs of crystal-powered eyes sparked to life. Electric lights crackled on and illuminated the rows of armed automaton soldiers standing at silent attention before her. She quickly spied James' towering suit on the opposite side of the mechanical regiment.

"Welcome!" shouted an unpleasant voice. On the catwalk above strode Powell, followed by Dr. Dennison. Dennison looked pale and thin, much more so than usual.

"Whatever technology you have developed to bring you here so quickly, Miss Carter, I am afraid will belong to me, just as your synthetic shard technology." He pointed to the east side of the room where a massive green shard hung over the water near the indoor loading dock. They had taken it from its incubation at her laboratory.

"Leave her out of this, Powell," barked James, taking the man quite by surprise.

"Ah, Mr. Brooks! You have finally found your voice. I've received telegraphs on your mysterious doings and was quite hoping you would come." Powell eyed the cogs and gears of James' mechanical suit.

"I am here for the Master Shard," returned James, undaunted by Powell's hubris. "It is not what you think it is; none of the shards are."

Elizabeth wondered what new memories he gained through the many shards claimed in the streets of Boston. She spied a stair to the upper catwalk and directed her steed closer to it.

"You know James, I believe you are right," laughed Powell. "But unlike our dear Miss Carter, you will find me most unscientifically pragmatic about such things."

Pulling a tarp from beside him, Powell revealed the large, pale blue crystal. Attached to the anterior wall by clamps and heavy cables, it towered over the motionless automaton army below.

"With the Master Shard, I control every device on earth powered by crystal shards. The army that stands before you is only the reserve force. They will support the myriad of devices already positioned throughout the city, in the homes and factories of what will soon be my subjects. The days of fruitless unguided struggling of the individual will soon be over and replaced by the clean efficiency of progress for the common good!

"And now, Miss Carter, Mr. Brooks, I must ask that you hand over the brilliant technology on which you ride and surrender yourselves."

Elizabeth stood poised next to the stair. Neither she nor James moved an inch but stared intently at Powell.

The broad man sighed with exaggerated dismay before grinning wickedly. "As you wish." He took two steps toward the control shard and placing his hand on it, bellowed, "Destroy them!"

The silent army sprang to life and advanced on James and Elizabeth. James swung furiously, cutting down machines on all sides, but there were so many of them! Moving toward her, the metal soldiers found themselves faced with the raking tusks and trampling feet of her mechanical steed. Elizabeth slipped from her seat and hurried up the stair. If only she could get to the control shard, she could stop these monsters! But, how to get past Powell?

Powell stood clutching the rail with white knuckles as he stared at the scene below. On the floor lay scattered bits of more than a score of his mechanical soldiers. James battled furiously against them with an uncanny skill. He was pinned by the near wall, unable to advance. Yet, every swipe of his weapons incapacitated another of his foes.

Some of the automatons, on contact with James, suddenly ceased in their attack, and then, with a new brilliant blue hue in their eyes rejoined the battle, this time against their brethren. Unless the hero exhausted himself soon, Powell would run out of soldiers.

"Dennison! Drop the green shard!" Powell bellowed to the researcher.

The scientist squirmed. "But Mr. Powell! I've been telling you that it won't—"

"That is exactly the point! Now go! Release my Kraken!"

The man complied with his master. Moving across to the catwalk opposite Elizabeth, Dennison pulled a great lever and the green crystal plunged into the black water below. Elizabeth saw her chance.

Slipping as quickly and quietly as she could, she moved closer to Powell and the Master Shard. Powell was entranced with the strange green glow that emanated from the now churning water at the far end of the warehouse. She was not even a stone's throw away now. She had only to touch it.

She sprinted toward the large glowing shard and stretched out her hand. 'Stop! Stop! Stop!' she screamed in her mind. Her outstretched finger was an inch away from its target when a strong hand gripped her wrist and jerked her violently away.

"It's no use now, my dear. Behold!" Powell forced Elizabeth to the rail where she saw something coming up out of the waters. Long metal tentacles reached upwards and coiled around the steel pillars that held the roof. To the surface rose a pair of menacing green orbs atop wildly swinging tentacles.

"You see, Miss Carter, even 'foolishness' such as yours can be put to good use in the right hands!"

A steam spouting blur flew up Powell's arm as Nauty threw itself at the man. Powell released Elizabeth as he struggled to extricate the tentacles of the vicious little device from his face and neck. She immediately turned to reach for the control shard once more. She only paused when, from the corner of her eye, she spotted Powell hurl Nauty to the ground below where the aimless foot of an automaton crushed him into twisted metal and rolling gears.

A massive tentacle wrapped around the catwalk near Dennison, and pulled it down to the water's edge, taking the scientist with it. The jolt shook the entire suspended walkway and Elizabeth soon found herself on a slanted floor, sliding towards the battle-engulfed James.

"James!" she cried as she left the walk for open air. Her scream caught in her throat as the hard floor rushed toward her.

Already out of his armor, James stood on its shoulders facing Elizabeth when the platform shifted. Summoning all his strength, he leapt toward the catwalk. His outstretched hand found her flailing arm. He caught the edge of the crooked walk in his free arm, stopping their descent with a jolt that tore at his shoulders.

Towering over the crowd of automatons, the four-armed suit continued its battle in spite of James' egress, though with less efficiency. The terrible metal Kraken continued its advance, crushing and tearing at everything within its great reach. Suddenly, all the blue-eyed automatons, save for the unmanned suit, left the battle and engaged the hideous machine rising from the water.

With help and great effort, Elizabeth scrambled up James' body and onto the remaining horizontal segment of the catwalk, then aided in pulling him up as well. Illuminated in the soft blue of the control shard, he had never been more pleased to see her. Before James properly got his footing, a dark figure loomed up behind Elizabeth and dragged her to the opposite side of the shard.

"Not another move, Brooks!" screamed Powell, holding a revolver to the young lady's head. James froze in his tracks.

"Powell, this is madness! You have to turn your soldiers against the beast!"

"Never!" bellowed Powell. James had to get Elizabeth away. Powell's monster would bring the building down on them if he did not act quickly.

"Then let me purchase her freedom. Let me save her." James moved his hands to his shirt collar.

"You have nothing I could want, fool!"

"I will give you this," James tore open his shirt to reveal the gleaming blue gem buried in his chest.

"James, no!" cried Elizabeth. He felt a rush of tenderness as he saw the understanding and new fear wash over her face. They both knew the depth of what he offered. The shard was bound to the automatons he claimed and controlled, as it was to the body in which he walked. Where did his newfound humanity reside? There was no time to consider such dreadful possibilities.

A sudden screech of twisting metal disrupted the moment. The Kraken was upon them. It gripped the catwalk near the stair

Elizabeth had ascended and tore it down. With the scraps, it swept aside the remaining soldiers that were single-mindedly engaged in attacking James' fighting suit.

Again, the catwalk lurched as its supports gave way. James saw his chance. Gripping the shard in his chest, he pulled with all his might. The sensation of disjointed floating came over him, and he could barely feel the limb that held the shard. By sheer force of will, he hurled the crystal at the Master Shard.

The crystal from James' chest bounced off the surface of the Master Shard with a sharp ping. At first, the sound was drowned out in the clamor of the battle around them. But instead of dying away, the reverberation steadily grew until the rafters shook with the deafening ring.

"James!" Elizabeth screamed. She tore herself from the bewildered Powell and rushed toward James' limp form. A blast of energy from the control shard interrupted her. Its pale blue glow deepened to a brilliant cerulean radiance of palpable intensity. Bolts of energy shot out from it in all directions.

Powell attempted to flee from the Master Shard, but a steel tentacle tore that section of the walk from beneath him, and he fell nearly two stories to the ground below.

The electrical charges struck the cog-riddled floor again and again, changing every shard to the familiar blue. The Kraken paused only a moment in its thrashing of the little automatons that came against it. It then charged all the more fiercely, bellowing mingled clouds of smoke, steam, and unbridled rage.

On the floor of the factory, the strewn mechanical parts began to move. Swept up in some uncanny magnetic force, they flowed around the fighting suit. They shielded it from view behind a swirling array of electrically charged sheets of metal, cogs, and hulking bolts.

Just as the Kraken reached out to strike the cyclonic mass around the four-armed suit, there leapt from the center a colossal machine like Elizabeth had never before seen. It still bore the additional limbs of its predecessor, but rather than a long slender form, this machine was broad and powerful, enhanced by a myriad of pumping pistons and hissing steam. It stomped toward the other beast on two short legs and the massive knuckles of its middle set of limbs, like an ape. The Master Shard, still fastened to the anterior wall, continued to gleam its brilliant blue energy as the beast beat the metal boilers of its mighty chest and taunted the Kraken.

The Kraken wasted no time, and the cries of its rage shook the rafters of the large building. Elizabeth watched in awe and horror as she knelt beside the body of James on the catwalk. She felt unable to do anything else. The brutal battle of coiling, constricting tentacles against the pummeling, crushing strength of the four mighty fists raged all over the factory. One by one, the ape-machine tore the tentacles from the Kraken's body. It was not long before a wild blow hit the catwalk for a third time and the structure fell, carrying with it Elizabeth and James' lifeless body to the floor below.

⁂

When Elizabeth next opened her eyes, the ring and clash of metal continued, but at a different tempo somehow. A steady pounding and hammering replaced the random clashes and collisions of the battling mechanoids. Raising her sore body, she took stock of her surroundings. As her thoughts came into focus, she searched for James' body, but to no avail. A single, massive construct stood in place of the destroyed automatons that had littered the factory floor.

Dozens of reconstructed mechanoids with blue glowing eyes moved about it. They hammered, bolted, and welded across the length of the craft. Indeed, now that she saw it clearly, it could be described as nothing else. Far longer than it was wide, and pointed at its forward end, it looked like a ship pulled from the water. The vessel, with its clean lines and gleaming hull, made a sharp contrast with the mostly destroyed factory interior.

A ray of pure golden sunlight suddenly glared in her eyes and Elizabeth realized that the machines were carefully disassembling the roof of the building and applying parts to finish the vessel. As she watched, dumbfounded, a side door opened on the craft. A ramp extended like an accordion and out came the familiar form of her faithful Fergusson.

The mechanical man approached her slowly, with gleaming blue eyes. In its arms it carried a squirming thing that leapt into Elizabeth's arms. The reconstructed Nauty embraced her with all the affection that its metal form could give. Fergusson handed her a parchment that was rolled and fastened with a silver chain from which hung a blue crystal.

My Dearest Elizabeth,

Please accept these parting gifts. You were right all along, I was never James Brooks. In gratitude, his body has finally been laid to rest. I was born among the stars and am made for traveling thence. I am the vessel, or rather, the heart of the vessel, that first carried the man you know as John Carter to this world. An accident caused us to crash on this planet, known to us as Jasoom. John Carter is not dead, I assure you. But, he has yet to recover full memory of his past, or of me. I must return to him. He has made his own way home and there I must join him.

I know not whether my capacity for the sorrow I feel in leaving you has always been within me or if it is some vestige of my interaction with the brain of your late friend. Yet, I know that I will never forget you. Thank you for everything. You will always be my princess, my dearest Princess of Jasoom.

Love,

James

Elizabeth's eyes misted. She looked up to see Fergusson walking back toward the mysterious craft. The automatons had ceased their work and moved to board the ship. Her face flushed. James was leaving her. After everything they had gone through, he was simply going to leave. Hot tears welled in her eyes and she chased after Fergusson.

"You will not abandon me like this!" The machine strode on, indifferent to her tears.

"I spent my entire life in the study of these foolish shards to the loss of all other loves. And now, I find the one person on this earth who I care for and who actually cares for me in return and you are just going to leave?"

She barely thought about what she was saying, nor did she care. Her heart burst open in a torrent of emotion that she did not even know she held. The automaton finally paused. They were near the ramp now. Fergusson looked at her with his voluminous blank eyes.

"I've dedicated my life to these shards—to you! You simply cannot deprive me of all that I know and all that I love!"

"I am sorry," came a familiar voice. She knew that voice: James', and yet somehow different. It emanated softly from both the ship above her and from the automaton before her, and mingled with a pure, high, bell-like ringing that added an undefinable musical quality to the words.

"Elizabeth, you need to be with your own kind on your world, and I must return to my own," it continued. Fergusson stepped onto the ramp and it retracted with him to the waiting doors of the vessel.

Still weeping, Elizabeth slumped in her dirty, ragged clothes before the solid door of the shuttle. No one would trust shard technology again. A. I. would crumble without Powell. She would be destitute and without a career. But these were not the thoughts that most consumed her as she wept.

"Don't you see? You and the shards are one and the same—everything I have ever cared about. There is nothing left here for me. If I am to be alone, I would rather be alone with the wonders of the shards and the heart of the man I love, than with a world full of men that would never understand me. The James I knew was not a man like you. Your courage, your kindness, could not have come from him, and what would I care if they did? You have become so much more than a friend to me, James. I cannot bear to lose you."

The craft began to vibrate, luminous sails of pure energy formed along its top and sides. She wept for her loss all the more, until a loud click resonated from within the craft. With a hiss and the clattering of gears, the doors slowly opened and the ramp descended once more. The light of a thousand pulsing, luminous crystal shards bathed the interior.

Elizabeth Carter rose slowly and stepped onto the ramp. She did not know where James was going, nor did she care. She but knew that she would be with him and that he would protect her, no matter the cost. The ramp drew her into the heart of the great machine with the mind of the man she loved.

A brilliant craft with sails made of sunlight rose from the wharf and floated higher and higher into the sky. Into the heavens it carried its peculiar cargo on to a future of uncertainty, but a future together.

Styled after *A Princess of Mars* by Edgar Rice Burroughs

Winged Hope

MEGAN OLIPHANT

"Hope" is the thing with feathers
That perches in the soul
And sings the tune without the words
And never stops at all
And sweetest in the Gale is heard
And sore must be the storm
That could abash the little Bird
That kept so many warm.
I've heard it in the chillest land
And on the strangest Sea
Yet never in Extremity,
It asked a crumb of me.
—Emily Dickinson 1861

San Francisco, 1889

The soft clank of metallic feathers whistled overhead and Beatrice Cosgrove glanced up again, tracking the flight path of her bird. The little creature stayed between the rooftops of the tight alleyway, always within sight of her. Bea took a sharp right, another right, then a left where she slid to a stop, barely avoiding a fruit cart and its irate owner, her soft leather soles no match for the constantly damp cobblestones of San Francisco's misty streets.

The sound of her bird disappeared in the cacophony of the Chinatown market, but she knew where to look. Scanning the rooftops, she finally spotted it. The brass sparrow, its wings no longer shiny with youth, hopped on a faded red awning across the street, the Chinese symbols in stark black contrast across the front.

Bea wove her way across the market, careful to step out of the path of the ubiquitous street sweepers that added their sound and stink to the chaos of the crowded square. She shook her head at the folly of town fathers that decided clean streets were worth the complaints about the sweepers. They caused more congestion than the refuse would have with their constant breaking down and mindless insistence on running through every intersection regardless of right of way. Michael had even taken a new design to the mayor when he was only fifteen and they both still lived at St. Sebastian Orphanage. The groundbreaking innovations of an enclosed, self-renewing combustion system and intelligence to react appropriately made them much more functional than the ones in service.

That had been his first brush with government bureaucracy and the O'Reilly family who held the contract with the city to supply and repair the sweepers. That particular interaction had taught him a very valuable lesson: innovation for innovation's sake was failure waiting to happen and could get you threatened by one or more powerful groups. But it was his boldness at that young age which had brought the Chamberlins into his life, rescuing him from the orphanage where he and Bea had met, and fostering him in their home on Nob Hill. It also brought his best friend, Alexander Chamberlin, into Michael's life. It was Alex who had been her greatest strength since the accident that had robbed her too soon of her beloved husband.

The memory of Michael sent a pang through her chest, as it always did. But now it combined with the greater worry over Delia, and the weight of them both threatened to crush her.

She entered the shop and almost wished she'd stayed outside, her nose assaulted by the combination of bizarre herbs and other unrecognizable ingredients. She scrambled for a handkerchief to block some of the scent, but instead its delicate lavender smell just added to the mix, sending her into a sneezing fit.

The noise brought an ancient woman through the curtain who examined Bea's watery eyes with a knowing look.

"Ah. You need cure for cold, yes?" Without waiting for Bea's reply, she moved to her shelves, muttering to herself.

"No!" The old woman stopped and looked over her shoulder. "No," Bea repeated in a softer tone. "It's not for me. This"—she lifted the handkerchief—"was just a momentary thing. I'm here for my daughter. Alexander Chamberlin said that you would have what I need. She is very sick."

The older woman put a hand to her chest and her face softened. "She has the Blue-face?" She put both hands to her chest and made a vague motion of congestion, then faked a cough. At the glimmer of understanding on Bea's face, she said, "I so sorry."

At the unexpected sympathy, Bea felt her control crumple and she covered her face with her hands. The worry that she should never have had to bear alone released as suddenly as a burst pressure valve.

Soft hands pulled her gently towards a nearby chair and Bea sank into it, grateful for the small kindness. Things had been so hard since Michael's death just two months ago, and now Delia struggled with the terrible illness that plagued the city, killing so many, mostly children and the elderly. Bea had done what she could to protect her daughter, barely letting her out of the house, but still she had contracted the disease that left people wheezing and turning blue with every coughing fit, unable to eat or drink, until they withered away.

She took a deep, shuddering breath, trying to get hold of her emotions. Finally, she dabbed at the tears with her handkerchief and looked up at the woman who stood next to her, her gentle hand on Bea's shoulder giving her strength.

"Thank you." She nodded at the woman who smiled and gave her a final pat on the back before moving to the shelves full of glass jars holding her wares. The woman moved with practiced ease, her old hands quick and light as butterflies as they flitted from jar to jar, gathering ingredients. In moments a small pouch sat on the counter, and a wave from the woman brought Bea near.

The shopkeeper pointed to the small purple bag in front of her. "This for the Blueface. You must . . ." She started to pound a fist into her other hand. At Bea's blank stare, she huffed and walked over to a sideboard, bringing back a small mortar and pestle. "Crush, see?" Bea nodded her understanding. "Mix tiny bit"—she pinched her thumb and index finger together—"in honey."

Her bent finger poked at Bea with a quick jab. "She sick many days, yes?" Without allowing Bea to respond, the Chinese apothecary continued, "She very sick. White people no come shop unless much fear."

She held up eight fingers. "Must give same medicine this many first day. Next day this many,"—she lowered a finger—"next day this many," as she held up only six fingers. "Every day one less. Then one time many days, until medicine gone, yes? Do or she no live. Dead."

Bea's throat closed up and she clutched at it, desperate for air. The old woman grabbed Bea's hand from her throat and held it gently in both of hers. "Still hope. My son of son live with this."

The old woman placed the small bag in Bea's hand. She paused and looked Bea over again, her eyes narrowed. With a quick jerk of her chin, she said, "Yes. She live."

Bea took the medicine and tucked it into her reticule. "Thank you. I don't know what to say." She pulled out her coin purse. "What do I owe you?"

"No money."

Bea shook her head. "No. Certainly not. This will save my daughter's life. Surely you expect some recompense for that?"

Her smile was cheeky. "No money, but you do this: when child better, tell others about shop."

Bea returned her smile, feeling for the first time that there was some hope for Delia. "Thank you." She reached out a hand to touch the other woman's in gratitude. "I will do exactly as you instructed."

The hand turned under hers and gripped it hard, startling Bea into meeting the other woman's suddenly intense stare. "Avoid Chamberlin. He is the eel that waits in hole—strike like lightning. He eat you before you know he attack." She disappeared behind the separation curtain before Bea could more than blink her surprise.

Bea followed Sparrow back from Chinatown, paying only enough attention to the bird so as not to get lost. Her mind tumbled over itself, thoughts chasing through consciousness in random spurts. Hope and worry over little Delia combined with the constant sorrow of Michael's loss. And this new and disturbing information about Alexander Chamberlin.

Alexander had always been their friend, since he and Michael first met. That Alex had come from money and Michael had not never seemed to matter. In fact, Alex had been Michael's biggest supporter, acting as a patron as Michael had made discovery after discovery. He had never been anything but kind, helpful, and generous when Michael and Bea had married and Michael tried to find a market for his innovations.

After Michael's untimely death, Alex started coming by two or three times a week. He or Victor, his disturbingly lifelike automaton and manservant, would stop by the house. After each visit there would be a basket full of foodstuffs on the kitchen table or several dollar bills tucked into the cookie jar. She couldn't reconcile the kind man she knew with what the strange woman had said.

The familiar streets of her neighborhood came into sight, and Bea released a breath she hadn't realized she'd been holding. She was almost home, just a few minutes from giving her child the medicine she so desperately needed. The front door was nothing to look at, its weathered gray color blending in with the rest of the rundown row-houses on the street. As she always did while she waited for the mechanism to engage, she traced the loopy "M" Michael had carved in the center panel, looking like a bird in flight. She could feel the familiar hum of the house, a constant embrace from her husband. Sparrow landed on his perch above the door and it swung open without a squeak.

She peeked into the little parlor where she had left Delia asleep on the settee. The small lump under a pile of blankets remained in the same position as when she left fifteen minutes before. The coat rack followed her into the kitchen, beeping a quiet reminder to hang up her pelisse. After obliging it, she slipped on her apron and fetched the medicine from her reticule.

She pushed the appropriate button on the food preparation panel to request warm milk to help wash down the medicine Bea was sure would taste disgusting. All the best medicines did.

Ten minutes later the medicine and milk were arranged on the tea table, with a few of her daughter's favorite cookies. "Delia, Mama has brought you a special medicine, sweetheart." Bea followed the rolling table into the parlor and approached the makeshift bed, stopping to lift the spoonful of medicine-laden honey from the table. Her daughter didn't stir. "Delia? Sweetheart?"

Suddenly nerveless fingers dropped the full spoon onto the floor. Bea scrabbled at the still warm blankets that no longer held her sick daughter. No golden curls dimmed with sweat and illness, no deep blue eyes so like her father's. Gone. Her baby was gone.

The scream tore from her chest in a rising crescendo that she couldn't seem to stop. She raced through the house, hoping to find Delia. Playing in her room. Asleep in a corner. Anywhere. But every room she entered bore silent witness: someone had stolen her dying daughter.

"Thank you for coming so quickly, Alex. I didn't know what else to do."

Alex draped his overcoat over the waiting rack that hummed contentedly as it slipped into its corner.

"Of course I would come." He grasped her elbow and led her

back into the parlor. "Tell me what happened." He steered her to the settee.

"No!" She jerked her elbow out of his hand. "I can't sit where . . ."

"What was I thinking?" Alex brushed a hand across his forehead. "Of course not. Here." He gestured at one of the other chairs. "Come. Sit."

With a nod, she followed him over to the two chairs near the window. She picked Delia's blanket off the table, hugging it tight while she shared with him the morning's events.

"And you haven't contacted the police? Surely they can help you," Alex said when she finished.

Bea looked out the window. While a bit run-down, it was still a perfectly safe part of town, with mothers out walking children, elderly couples strolling arm in arm, and the occasional courting couple. Respectable. Not someplace where children were kidnapped.

She shook her head. "I'm not sure. You were the first person I thought of." Her eyes widened. "Oh. I should have called them. What will they think?" She jumped to her feet, ready to rush out the door.

He grabbed her hand. "No. It's all right. We will need their manpower to search for her. A moment longer to collect yourself is understandable." He tugged at her hand until she sat again.

The sound of fluttering paper caught her attention, as did the opening of the sweeper door. She glanced down to see the small machine next to her foot, chirping at a piece of paper. The scrap didn't seem familiar. "Yes, you can dispose of it."

Alex glanced at her. "But it could be a clue, a hint of some kind. What if . . ."

"Oh!" She dropped the blanket on the sweeper as she snatched the note out of its reach. The little machine slid out from under its shroud with another chirp that sounded like a mix of hurt and confusion, then sped back behind its door, closing it with a snap.

A small smile tilted Bea's lips as she looked from the offended machine to the paper in her hand. It seemed normal enough, but when she saw the scrawled words, it slipped from her fingers into her lap.

Wordlessly, Alex picked it up and cleared his throat. She stood with a jerk, one arm wrapped around her waist, the other clamped over her mouth. She wanted to rush from the room, to wake from this nightmare her life had become. Instead she got only as far as the door, unable to go further.

"We know that you are in possession of your husband's research," Alex read. *"You will leave it wrapped in brown paper under the bench in the park across from your house by midnight or you will never see your daughter again."*

The pair remained silent for what seemed like forever but must have only been a minute before Alex spoke. "What would you like me to do? You know I would do anything for you and Delia." He stood and put his arms around her.

She looked up at his hope-filled face. "I-I can't, Alex." She stepped out of his grasp and picked up the blanket off the floor. "I can't think about anything—anyone—but Delia right now. She needs me. She needs me to find her. To save her.

"I have something these mysterious people want, apparently." She nodded at the paper Alex still clutched. "And they have something I want. I have to do what I can to see if, by some miracle, Michael wrote down his plans somewhere else besides his work journals. But as far as I know, they were destroyed in the explosion."

Alex shifted away, his bearing stiff. "But surely he worked here as well. The Michael I knew was always working, always scribbling something."

"Yes, he did," she said. "But when he did work from home it was always in his most current journal, which he took back and forth with him to the warehouse. He rarely left anything here, and if he did, he would come back and fetch it." She smiled. "I miss that, you know. The way he would tear in here, hair mussed like Finch or Sparrow had nested in it, calling out for me to help him find that journal." Her smile faded. "Delia will never really know her father. She will only have everyone else's memory of him. If she lives long enough to realize it." Her voice caught as her throat tightened around the words.

Out of the corner of her eye, she could see Alex's arm coming to encircle her again and she moved out of reach, straightening her skirt. "How long do I have to produce this miracle?"

"Until midnight."

"I should start looking."

Alex began to remove his suit coat. "Let me help you. I'll start in the basement."

She put a restraining hand on his arm. "No. I need you to go to the police. And search the warehouse."

He feigned confusion. "Warehouse?"

"He knew, you know."

He gazed down at her hand, his face a mix of pain and something she couldn't define. "He knew what?" he asked finally, meeting her eyes.

"He knew that you did what you could without his permission, like buying the warehouse to make sure his work wasn't disturbed by a landlord who wouldn't understand. He could let you do things like that. I'm sorry if his . . . secrecy hurt you."

She patted his arm and stepped back. She saw the disappointment on his face but ignored it. "Will you go search the warehouse? I know it has been a long time—maybe too long—and too damp for anything to have survived, but I know where to look in my house, where I wouldn't even know where to start there. Please? That is the biggest help you could give me."

With a sigh, Alex retrieved his overcoat from the rack and stepped into the midday sun. "I'll go over it with a fine-tooth comb. If there is anything to find, I will find it." He leaned down and kissed Bea on the forehead. "I love Delia, too. I would be devastated if anything happened to her."

He disappeared into his waiting carriage, a silent Victor at the reins.

"They wouldn't even come inside, Alex. They wouldn't even look at where I had left her sleeping with all the alarms on. They just brought me here." Bea threw her hands up and gestured at the walls, the shackle on her wrist rattling the chain against the floor.

Alex grasped her flying hands, holding them still. Bea closed her eyes and slowed her breathing, hoping that would help calm her thoughts, but all it did was bring back the Chinese woman's warning about Alex. She opened her eyes again, studying her friend. His warm brown eyes gazed at her, full of concern. She could see nothing in him to be afraid of.

He gave her hands a squeeze before he stood and moved to the door. "Let me speak with someone. My father's connections should be good for something."

Bea nodded and watched him walk out of the room. His soothing presence gone, her anxiety and desire to be out searching for her daughter washed over her again. Who would have taken her? She had nothing. The explosion of Michael's warehouse on the docks had robbed her of a husband, Delia of a father, and the world of his brilliant mind. She wished she did have his research, if only to turn it over to Alex and have those marvelous things come to fruition.

Alex had counseled him to find a better, safer place, but Michael had refused. That was the only time she'd seen the two almost come to blows, they were both so furious.

"I won't take it, Alex," Michael had yelled, throwing the wad of money back on the table.

"You are an idiot." Each word came bitten off as Alex had stood nose to nose with his friend. Bea had been in the doorway, soothing the baby after their raised voices had awoken her, watching both men clench and unclench their fists as they resisted the urge to clock each other.

Finally Alex stomped away and threw himself into a chair that creaked ominously at the abuse. He turned a basilisk stare on Michael. "I'm trying to invest in you, damn it! It's like Michelangelo and the Medici family. They made sure he was fed and clothed and sheltered so he could create his art. Why wouldn't I do the same with you? Why do you refuse me all the time?"

"You do take care of me." Michael folded his arms. "Too much. I don't need some fancy new workshop in a better neighborhood. I'm happy where I am."

Alex just shook his head. "That makes no sense. I'm prepared to build you a state-of-the-art facility. Won't that help you develop things faster? Better? Why do you insist on that run-down place on the docks?"

"Look around you," Michael replied, waving his hands at the room they were in. It seemed normal with its wood paneling and slightly shabby furniture and a little too-threadbare carpets. But they all knew that behind the walls lived the heart of the house, which cared for all the furnishings and people inside. At first it had taken time for Bea to get used to its quiet hum. But now she could not dream of being in the house without it. All the machines, great and small, worked autonomously, caring for everything from dusting to garbage removal. Bea was able to care for her family and spend time with them without the physical tasks that one either did for oneself or paid help for.

It had taken him most of their first two years of marriage, but when he was done, the things even the meanest home took for granted had transformed into something almost magical, something the richest maharaja would pay millions of dollars for. "The automation of this house is a gift to my wife and mother of my child. But it was entirely built with things that others discard and think of no value. I scrounged it all. Because I saw their worth where no one else could."

Alex shook his head. "What does that have to do with having a better place to build your inventions? I will have the contents of every scrapyard along the coast brought in if you want."

Michael was already shaking his head before Alex finished talking. "You forget. I grew up there. The docks were my home long before Nob Hill was. I understand want. Need. Lack of proper shelter or food or clothing. And that was before my parents died. It only grew greater afterwards."

He walked over to the window and gazed out. "Even our neighborhood now is so far from my early days." He turned and met Alex's confused stare with eyes bright with excitement. "What if the things I've done could be adapted for others? From the grandest home here to the rudest hut in darkest Africa? Can you imagine how life for the whole human family might change? Improve? Become something we've only imagined?"

Alex's stare grew intent. "What is it? What are you talking about, Michael? What have you dreamed up?"

Michael shook his head and said, "I'm not ready to speak of it. But it will take time. Probably most of my life. It's a sacrifice I'm willing to make, as is Beatrice, I think." He walked over to Bea where she stood and slid an arm around her waist, giving her a squeeze at her acquiescing nod.

"I am," she affirmed. "I knew who you were when I married you."

Alex took a sudden step forward, and Michael's hand tightened at her waist, pulling her closer to him. "Let me help you, Michael," Alex insisted. "If it is so important to you, why won't you let me help? For heaven's sake, you won't even let me come to your workshop." He threw his arms out. "I can do more if I know more."

Michael shook his head again. "It's not ready, Alex. *I'm* not ready. And frankly, I don't think you are, either. Please wait. Have faith in me, and I promise to tell you everything in time."

Alex sighed, a rueful smile on his face. "I can't out-argue your stubbornness with my own, can I?" He gathered his hat and coat from the rack that had quietly delivered it from the corner. "But I can be patient, too. I will not stop asking. Perhaps one day you will realize that it is not charity when I am benefiting as well."

He shrugged on his coat before walking to the front door. Pausing, he had turned back to his friend. "I hope you know that I want you away from that rough place for your own safety and the protection of your inventions."

It had been Michael's turn to look rueful. "I will think about it, Alex. I remember how 'autonomous' you let me be during school. I want—and need—to be able to come and go as I please."

A grin had broken across Alex's face as he stepped back in to give his friend a big hug. "It wasn't you who needed a friend, old man."

Bea wiped tears from her face in the detention room as the memory faded. Surely that woman had mistaken Alex for someone else. He had been nothing but kindness personified.

The door rattled and Alex came back into the room, followed by an abashed young officer holding a ring of keys. "Here we go. Lift up your arm, Bea."

She obeyed so the young man could unlock the manacles. As she rose to her feet she rubbed her released wrist, surprised at its tenderness. "So I may leave?"

"Yes, ma'am, but the chief would like a few words, if you'd be so kind."

"I would like to have some words with him as well. Like why was I hauled in here as a common criminal when my daughter has been kidnapped?"

The young policeman's face blushed bright red. "I'm . . . I'm . . ." He cleared his throat. "I'm sure the chief will be able to answer any questions."

They followed the officer out of the room and into a hallway flanked with jail cells, some more full than others. For the first time Bea was fully aware of her surroundings. She'd been near hysterical when they'd brought her in. And while she'd been shackled, she had also been blessedly separate in the interrogation room. When several men hooted at her, Alex slid a protective arm around her shoulder. While she normally wouldn't have allowed it, she welcomed his protectiveness in this unfamiliar place.

"Hey! Quiet down, you bunch!" The young officer slammed his stick against the bars, which only brought further catcalls from the inhabitants.

"Sorry about that, ma'am." The young man blushed again as they left the cells behind and made their way to the other side of the police station. When they arrived at the chief's office, he rose and greeted them pleasantly, as if she had not been hauled out of her house like one of the riffraff back down the hall.

Confusion and anxiety roiled in her stomach and she only gave him a brief nod before blurting, "Why did you arrest me? Why is no one searching for my daughter?"

"Please sit, Mrs. Cosgrove." He nodded at a nearby chair. She sat but perched on the edge, as if prepared to take flight at any time. "I realize that you are greatly upset by what you perceive to be a kidnapping—"

"Perceive? *Perceive*? I am not imagining the disappearance of my daughter, sir. My very *ill* daughter."

"Yes. About that." The man stroked his mustache with one hand. "If she was so ill, why would you leave her alone? Not even a neighbor to stay with her for half an hour? What if something were to have happened?"

"For the same reason your officers refused to come into my home. My daughter is ill with the China Cough."

Both the chief and the young policeman leaned away from her. Just a little, but enough. She lifted an eyebrow. "How brave you all are." Both the policemen bristled. "That was exactly the reaction my neighbors had when they refused to come in the house," she continued. "I had no choice but to leave her, but I could look after her anyway."

"Not well enough, apparently," the police chief said.

Bea felt her frustration building but swallowed it back and said, "May I open your window for a moment?"

He raised his eyebrows in confused acceptance, and she stepped to the sash. She lifted it and held her hand outside. In a flash, Sparrow perched upon it and she carefully brought the creature inside.

"A mechanical bird?" the chief snorted. "I've seen those. A plaything for children."

Alex shook his head. "It's not a toy."

"Look." Bea touched just behind the right eye of the bird. With a quiet whirring, the bird spread its wings and exposed a small screen on its back. Holding it so the chief could see it as well, she said, "Kitchen."

The screen flickered several times, but a picture did come into focus. It was her kitchen, complete with the herb bag and the still dirty mortar and pestle on the table. "Parlor," she said, and obligingly the picture changed, showing the room that had held her daughter just a few hours ago. Her heart lurched, but she quelled it. She had to convince the man. "Front door."

The picture appeared more distant, as the camera was mounted on a lamp post instead of inside a room, but it was clearly her house, the familiar 375 above the door, with an unfamiliar policeman standing in front of it, ignoring the stares and questions of the passersby.

"How . . ." The chief's fingers no longer stroked at his mustache but yanked in what could only be a painful way at the ends that drooped around his mouth.

"That was the genius of Michael Cosgrove," Alex said.

His comment produced her wistful smile as Bea touched the same spot on the bird and the wings closed over the screen. It preened a feather before she took it back to the window where it swooped up to the roof to continue its sentry duty.

"That's not all it is, Chief"—she paused to glance at the placard on his desk—"Chief Murphy. It is also the key to the house. You cannot get in without Sparrow sitting on its perch." She continued even as he blinked and gaped at her like a fish. "There is an alarm that sounds when someone attempts entrance without Sparrow in his spot. You can ask our neighbors. It roused them more than once while Michael was working on the system. They were not best pleased. And if someone does try to gain entrance, Sparrow lets me know with a distinct, piercing whistle."

"So this bird is the only way in? No staff? Not even a maid that comes in once a week?"

"There is no staff. The house is self-maintaining and –cleaning. Another of Michael's little inventions." Her smile dimmed as she continued. "There was another bird, one for Michael, though being his prototype, its long-distance viewing system rarely worked. It was a finch that we presumed destroyed in the explosion."

"I've never heard of anything like what that bird can do. It's amazing. Can you imagine what could be done to dissuade or solve crimes throughout the city?"

The chief suddenly stopped, his eyebrows coming together. "Explosion? Do you mean the one on the wharf?" At Alex's nod, understanding filled his eyes and he turned to Bea. "I'm so sorry at the loss of your husband. If that bird was just a trifling thing, it truly is a tragedy to have lost him so soon."

"Do you see now, sir?" Alex stood and moved towards the door. "There is a great mystery here. Someone broke into this house without triggering the many protections built into it by her now-deceased husband. We need to find the child, and fast. She will not last much longer without the medicine her mother went to fetch."

Bea blinked several times to keep the sudden tears from falling. This delay had cost her precious hours. Taking a deep breath, she focused on Chief Murphy, begging him with her eyes to release her.

The chief cleared his throat. "I can see there is more going on here than we initially supposed. You're free to go, ma'am. We will do all we can to aid you in your search."

"Thank you, sir. I so appreciate it."

Alex shepherded Bea out of the office and onto the street. A jerk of his head summoned Victor and the carriage. Bea stepped up into the cabin, grateful for the seat's softness as she sank into it. Guilt swelled within her and her eyes flooded again.

"I have enough tears to fill San Francisco Bay." She attempted a watery smile at Alex to alleviate his concern. "It's just that I felt so comfortable as I sat down, but my poor Delia is suffering, alone, afraid, with strangers. Or . . . worse." She took a swift intake of breath, sucking down any darker reflections.

They drove the rest of the way in silence, both of them lost in thought. The carriage pulled to a stop and Alex helped her down while Sparrow whistled a greeting as he landed on his perch and the door swung open.

She tried to withdraw her hand from Alex's grasp, but his fingers tightened over hers. "Are you certain you won't let me help search the house? The note seemed to imply that they knew you had this research. Even if all Michael did was tuck it away somewhere, two people searching is better than leaving you alone to do it yourself."

"No. I can do this. Besides, no matter how many men you have searching the warehouse, it is really only you that understands Michael enough to know where to look and what to look for. Please."

He sighed. "Very well. Of course you are right. Michael was always about the details." Alex smiled. "It would irritate me to no end that he excelled at Latin while I was failing. 'Alex,' he would say, 'you have to pay attention to the little things, or you will make a mistake.'" He shook his head. "I hated it when he said that. I hated it more that he was right."

"Me, too!" A giggle burst out of Bea. She immediately covered her mouth, shame washing over her.

"I never did master Latin as he did." His hand tightened over hers. "That's the first time I've heard you laugh in weeks."

She shook her head. "It is the hysteria. I have nothing to laugh about."

"It's still a good sign."

"A sign? A sign of what?"

His smile was soft. "That you still have hope. And hope is what you need to hold tight to right now. I don't know how, but I know Delia will be returned to you and all will be well."

She gripped his fingers, seeking to draw some of his confidence into herself. "Do you really believe that Delia is fine? But what of her medicine? She is so ill. She has been sleeping more and more, asleep more than she has been awake." Her voice came out as a whisper. "She is all I have left."

Alex put his arm around her, pulling her close. "Cling to the hope that she will be returned to you soon," he said softly into her hair. "All will be well."

She pushed him gently away. "Thank you, Alex," she said through her tears. "Thank you for everything."

He returned her watery smile with a tip of his hat. "I will let you know as soon as I find anything." He climbed back into his carriage while Victor held the reins. With a snap, they moved down the street.

She walked through the door and leaned against it, listening to the clatter of wheels as Alex rolled away. Suddenly her knees buckled and she slid to the floor. Wrapping her arms around her belly in a futile attempt to keep herself from shattering to pieces, all the grief and terror she had held in came pouring out in great, hulking sobs.

She wasn't sure how long she cried, but when she finally looked up, she found herself surrounded by a myriad of household helpers, all chirping concern in their own way. It sounded like an orchestra of crickets all out of synchronicity, and she gave a soggy hiccup of a laugh.

She sat up. "Thank you for your concern. I only wish you could help me find this mysterious information. Do any of you know where to find Michael's secret store of inventions?"

She gasped when as one they chirped and spun on their tiny wheels and sped down the hallway toward the kitchen. When she didn't immediately follow, they stopped and turned, waiting.

After a moment, it registered in her sorrow-fogged mind what they wanted and she stumbled to her feet to follow them. They veered as one to the right, where glass-fronted cupboards lined the interior wall of their home shared with the neighbors. The individual chirping started to take on a rhythm, like they were talking to each other, the pitch gradually rising to a high whine. She wanted to cover her ears against it, but when the glass fronts started to flicker, she forgot all about the noise.

The picture jumped and stuttered, but Michael's beloved face appeared on the glass, broken up by wooden slats and cupboard knobs. His hair was askew, as always. She put her hand to her mouth as he smiled and seemed to look straight at her.

When his voice came from the various machines that vibrated on the floor, a choral echo of his voice, she held her breath. She didn't want to miss a single word.

"Beloved Bea, if you are receiving this message, then something awful has happened to me. And you have suffered things I'd hoped you'd never have to. But things have changed, and I wanted to leave you something so when you were ready, you could know what I suspect. And who could possibly be my murderer.

"Several months ago someone broke into my warehouse. I was not here and nothing was taken, but I couldn't see who it was because they wore a cape and hood. The cameras showed little but that someone was here."

He shook his head, lines of sorrow deepening the dimples of his cheeks. "I know you never quite understood why I wouldn't let Alex come to the workshop." He looked away from her, his gaze distant and full of pain. Finally he returned. "He didn't know that he's the only one that understands how important this place is."

He sighed and rubbed his hand over his face. "You and I grew up at St. Sebastian's. We know how to hide things in plain sight—how to make something desirable seem not worth stealing. Alex never understood that. It's why I never let him come here. It looks like a junkyard, but his very presence would have made it obvious there was something here to steal. I had the security in place, but I'd never needed it. Not once. No one who lived and worked around here would have known what to look for, anyway.

"That break-in put me on my guard. I started digging into his business dealings. Then he started asking me more questions about my work. He hinted around at first, but eventually he got more obvious. Really angry. Finally, I told him a few things—wrong things. Once I told him that I would need quite a bit of copper to make stuff work. Within a month, one of his father's companies bought two of the most lucrative copper mines on the continent. I knew then that Alex wanted my brain, not my friendship. A golden goose. All he cared about was the money and the power it would bring him.

"I thought I had been subtle, but just a week ago he came to me, demanding to know everything. He sounded like an O'Reilly, with not so subtle hints about using muscle to get his way." Michael sighed, and Bea's own throat thickened when she heard the tears in his voice. "I loved him, Bea. Like a brother. I trusted him with so many other secrets. Why couldn't he leave it alone?"

At this, he walked away from the instrument he spoke into and put his face in his hands for a few moments. When he came back, while the evidence of tears was still on his cheeks, his eyes held a new resolve.

"Bea, if you are watching this, I am dead. I know it. Alex has become crazed with his obsession to own our vision. We want to help the entire world become a place without hunger, but he thinks this is something that one person can own, can control. No one can control another human being. Not really. No matter what one man does to another to control the body, the mind will always seek freedom. And Alex will never own that. He will never own me.

"He will be searching for that one 'machine.' If he hasn't asked you about it as you watch this, then you must find a way to develop it on your own. Make sure it gets into the hands of the people who need it most.

"If Alex threatens you, Bea, or there is some other reason that you need to give these plans over to him, then for your own safety, please do so. Please. Give it to him. And then run. Run far away. My secrets are not worth the cost of your lives." His face grew wistful. "I hear Paris is beautiful any time of year." He stepped to the side and picked up something before coming back into view. He held up a thick folder with a string wrapped around it. Michael had scrawled "SECRET" across the front.

"I have put this folder behind the china cupboard. Where we keep our nicest plates, the ones we haven't used since Delia was born. If you look in the bottom right corner you will see a small tab of ribbon. Pull that and the false back should come right out."

He swallowed hard. "I love you, my darling Bea. You have always been my rock, my muse, and my heart. I will be by your side in this life, and wait for you in the next. Goodbye, my love."

The vision faltered and disappeared, the whine from the machines lowering to a normal pitch. They moved slowly out of the kitchen, each heading to their assigned spot.

In a daze she walked over to the cupboard and opened it. There sat the ribbon, completely unnoticed all that time. With slow, deliberate movements, she took the plates and put them on the table. Then she pulled the ribbon. The false back fell forward with a soft whump and she stared at Michael's life's work.

Bea's preparations took all of the afternoon and most of the evening, longer than she wanted. The sky had deepened to an inky purple by the time Sparrow swept down to his perch and opened the door as she returned to the house. The papers tucked into the crook of her elbow gave her a bit of courage.

She left them on the kitchen table and headed to the basement. She went to the far wall where she touched a sliding panel that blended in with the rest of the brick foundation. She gasped. An automaton stood in stasis mode, eyes closed. It was the exact copy of Victor, Alex's manservant. She shook her head as more pieces of the puzzle fell into place. Michael had clearly planned for this eventuality long in advance.

Climbing up on a stool, she reached behind its left ear and felt carefully for the spring latch. With a soft click, the top of its head loosened and Bea lifted it off. She held it in one hand while she reached inside the head cavity.

She had not worked on things with Michael since Delia's birth, but the knowledge came back swiftly as she started up the system she'd helped build, though she never realized what he'd had in mind. She had never had Michael's vision, but her mechanical abilities had been one of the things that had brought them together in the orphanage. First as friends, then later when he sought her out just shy of her eighteenth birthday.

A soft hiss began to come from the automaton as it came to life. She re-secured the head panel, careful to smooth the hair into place before gesturing for it to exit the wall alcove. It took a step forward and stood, awaiting instruction . . . The hiss was barely audible now, sounding like human breath in a metal chest.

It was just like Michael to have built it and hidden it from her, another surprise gift like so many others. She gave it the specific directions it needed before she sent it on its way.

With a sigh, she followed it back upstairs to the kitchen, where all of the various household tools hummed, waiting for her. One last task and then she would have to wait. It killed her not to rush out the door to where she now knew Delia was, but Michael's plan from beyond the grave was solid—an ironclad cage to snare Alex and free them from his grasp forever.

Carefully popping the control panels of the household helpers one by one, she rearranged the wiring of each. Soon they were all finished. Now it was time to wait.

When the clock struck eleven, she picked up the short note she'd prepared and headed into the park. The street lights didn't reach far into the shadows of the trees, but she had travelled the paths often enough with Delia in healthier days. The paper tucked where the ransom note had demanded, she returned to the house.

She tried not to stare at the mantle clock as time crawled by. Bea jumped from her chair when Alex burst through the door at 11:45. The ever silent Victor followed him in and shut the door behind him. She could hear the whistle of Finch as the other mechanical bird greeted Sparrow as if they had never been separated.

Alex stalked into the parlor where she stood, waiting. "What do you think you are playing at?"

Bea's hands tightened into fists hidden in the depths of her skirts.

"I am not playing at anything, Alex. It is you that is playing games, pretending to be my friend, to love me, love Delia. I knew you must have had Finch, since that was the only way you could have gained entry into the house to take Delia in the first place. You went through this elaborate and desperate ruse to steal Michael's legacy. You threaten Delia's life by exposing her to the elements while she is so ill."

He leaned back against the doorjamb, all semblance of politeness and caring gone from his face. His handsome features made ugly with disdain, she wondered that she had not seen it before. All the softness, the kind words, had been a ploy to deceive her.

"If I did, I hold all the winning cards. I know you have it. His research. I want it. Now." He stepped forward, clearly trying to use his size to intimidate her.

She held up a hand. "I would not do that if I were you."

He raised a single eyebrow. "And who would stop me from just taking what I want? You?" He laughed, a harsh, brittle sound. "You have only one thing that I want. I have Delia. This can be a . . . mutually beneficial arrangement. There doesn't have to be any ugliness between us."

She just shook her head. "I think you are mistaken. You do not hold any of the cards you think you do. I hold them all."

"Really? Pray tell, what cards do you hold that trump Delia?"

She stepped forward and looked him in the eye. "I have Delia."

His face froze for a moment then relaxed. "No. You cannot. You did not even know I had her, let alone where she was. That was a clever trick, by the way," he added. "How did you figure out I had her to begin with?"

"I didn't. Michael did."

He straightened, confusion clear on his face. "Michael? But—"

"He's dead? Yes. I know. Another thing you have robbed me of. Why did you have to blow up his workshop?"

He blinked at her. "How did—" He broke off, his voice full of unease.

"How did I know? Michael knew you had purchased property and built a state-of-the-art facility with your father's money. He knew that the time would come when you would try to force him to work there instead of in the workshop he designed." Bea's small smile held no mirth. "Michael understood, much better than I, who you had become. I thought of you always as our friend. But he knew that your greed had corrupted the idealistic young boy who had befriended him all those years ago."

Alex shook his head, eyes distant. "He wasn't supposed to be there, you know. No one was supposed to get hurt." When she didn't immediately respond, he focused on her again. "If only he had cooperated. I tried to figure out what he wanted, what he needed in a laboratory, to support him in his goals. But he wouldn't even let me come near the place!" He pounded a fist into his other hand. "I was forced to sneak in there like a common burglar to see what he was doing. But there was nothing there. Nothing but piles of scrap. I couldn't even find any of those journals." He sighed. "I just wanted to help."

"You just wanted to help yourself, you mean." She glanced at the clock. Just a few more minutes.

He lifted a single shoulder. "If there was financial gain to be had, why not me? Why did he keep it from me? Didn't he trust me?" He shook his head again. "If he had just let me in, explained to me what he was doing, I wouldn't have had to stoop to such subterfuge. I wouldn't have had to blow up that dilapidated warehouse to force him to my facility."

"And that's the crux of it, isn't it? You wanted to own him. To own who and what he was. He wasn't a tool, Alex." She could feel the heat rising in her cheeks. "Just because your family 'rescued' him from the orphanage, that never meant you owned him like a puppy. Or a golden goose. His goals were much loftier than that, something that would benefit all of mankind, not just to line your pockets."

The clock chimed midnight, and Sparrow and Finch began a whistling duet. It was time.

Alex paid them no heed. "It doesn't matter now. What matters is that you will hand over the research. I will give you Delia. We never need cross paths again."

"You would leave us penniless? You really care for no one but yourself, do you?"

His face grew cold. "'Survival of the fittest,' as Mr. Spencer said." He stepped away from the door and towards her. "The time for polite conversation is over. I want the information now."

"No."

His eyes went from cold to furious. "No?" He grabbed her arm. "Where is it, Beatrice?"

The coat rack spun out of its corner and slammed into Alex. It knocked him back, loosening his grip on her arm. She jerked away and he fell into the wall. He spun to stare at the coat rack, which slid a few inches closer.

"What is going on?" He looked at her. The coat rack lunged forward again, this time ramming the tall center pole into the middle of his back. He flew across the room and crashed hard to the ground. The noise echoed in the small space.

"I would advise you not to touch me again." Bea straightened up from the chair where she had fallen when the coat rack first attacked. "You will be stopped."

Alex stood, careful to stay out of reach. With a fast movement that she felt more than saw, he whipped off his coat and wrapped it around the top of the rack, pulling it forward with a jerk. It fell over with a thud, its small wheels spinning uselessly in the air.

He brushed back the hair that had fallen across his forehead, smoothing it as best he could into his normal neatness. He advanced on Beatrice. “Now what will protect you? The floor sweeper? The revolving bookshelf?” He threw one hand in the direction of the shelf in the corner. “What will they do, throw books at me? Sweep me into submission?” He chuckled. “With all of his inventions, Michael can’t protect you from his grave. Besides,” he gestured for Victor to come into the room, “state of the art automatons like Victor are still better than cleaning toys made from scrap and garbage.”

Alex jerked at his cuffs. “Victor, search the house. Leave nothing untouched. Tear holes in the walls and floors if you need to.” He smiled at Bea. “It will be a pity to lose this little love nest he built for you. Unless . . .” His voice faded, the intimation left hanging in the air.

“*Audite vocem meam.*” Bea said the Latin phrase for ‘obey me’ and Victor stopped in his tracks. “Victor,” she continued in English, “please restrain Alex.”

The automaton’s arms surrounded Alex across the chest from behind, pinning his arms to his sides.

“What? Victor! Release me at once!” He struggled, but Victor remained as immovable as a mountain.

Bea’s gaze stayed as firm and unwavering as Victor’s arms. “You will be still and listen to me. Victor is my creature now. He will obey only me.” She walked to the doorway. “I have a proposition for you that, if you will behave, will benefit us both.”

The sudden trill of the birds preceded the opening of the door. "Delia!" Bea rushed over to the other automaton that held a small shape, bundled by several blankets.

"Mama?" Delia's sleepy voice came from within. "I dreamed I was flying through the air like Sparrow. It was very cold."

"It was just a silly dream, sweetie." Bea carried her daughter upstairs and tucked her into bed. Upon returning to the parlor, she found Victor still holding Alex, though Alex no longer struggled. Instead he looked back and forth between Victor and the other automaton who stood at the front door. They were identical, down to the last detail.

He frowned in confusion. "Victor was supposed to be one of a kind. I outbid a prince, two Rockefellers and a sheik for him. How—" He stopped, realization washing over his face. "Michael."

"Yes, Michael. Even I didn't know that Victor was his creation until tonight. But now that we both have an understanding of what our positions really are, will you negotiate? If Victor releases you, will you discuss terms?" She gestured at a chair.

His narrowed eyes shot daggers at her. After a long moment as he visibly ground his teeth, he gave a begrudging nod.

"Release him, Victor. But please stay near his chair." She turned to speak to the other machine in the hall. "And Thomas, please stand at the ready if Mr. Chamberlin should show any aggression."

They sat in the same chairs as they had earlier that day but as adversaries instead of friends. Though she supposed he had never been her friend. At least not for a very long time. With a sigh, she began.

"You still have something I want. Peace." At his raised eyebrows, she continued. "I know with the resources at your command there is nowhere we could go that would fully escape your search, should you so choose." A single nod from Alex encouraged her to continue. "I am willing to give you what you went to such great lengths to get from me. But on my terms. And only on my terms. If you do not agree, I will sell it to the highest bidder."

Greed ignited in his eyes. "I'm sure whatever your demands are, they will be easily met."

Bea refrained from shaking her head at his hubris. He would learn soon enough. "First, after we come to terms, you will agree never to contact me or Delia ever again. You will not search for us. It will be to you as if we never existed."

"Done." His smile was small but still full of pride.

"My second demand is that as payment for this information that will make you one of the most powerful and wealthy men in the world, you will agree that I and my descendants in perpetuity will receive thirty-three percent of all gross profits of your financial enterprises due to your acquisition of Michael's research. In addition you will give us one hundred thousand dollars up front."

During this stipulation, his face had grown gradually redder, until at the mention of the cash, he jumped out of his chair. "I won't! That's extortion!"

Victor dropped a heavy hand on Alex's shoulder, pressing down until the man collapsed, almost against his will, back into the chair. Alex frowned, looking like a scolded school boy.

"You will," Bea said, leaning back into her own chair. "You will because we both know that with the amount of money that this will bring into your coffers, this paltry initial investment will be as a single grain of sand on a beach. You will be as rich as Croesus."

He glared at her, only increasing the impression she had of a naughty child, but she merely said, "We both know I'm right. And without your acquiescence, this will go to some other competitor who will eventually crush you."

She turned to the automaton in the hall. "Thomas, please fetch the documents from the kitchen table." It nodded and in moments returned carrying a slim stack of papers.

Alex sat forward on his chair. "Is this it? Michael's research?"

She shook her head. "No. This is the contract you must sign or all that you want will go to another."

"Fine. Give me a pen, Victor." Alex held one hand out, the other looking through the paperwork. The automaton did not move.

After a moment, Alex looked up and realized what had happened. His eyes met hers. "Please tell him to give me a pen."

"Of course." She did her best to hide her smile as he took the now available pen and began to sign on the marked pages. After a couple of minutes he handed over the endorsements.

"Now, Michael's research," he demanded.

She shook her head. "You will not see even one scrap of this information for two months. Enough time for Delia to recover and the two of us to go far away from you and San Francisco."

"You—" He cut off an epithet. Instead, he picked up his suit coat where it lay across the tipped rack. He put it on with care, taking time to adjust his cuffs before speaking to her again, his glacier cold eyes boring into hers. "This is not over. It will never be over. If I ever suspect you are holding out on me, I will annihilate you."

Outside Paris, 1912

Bea took the newspaper Victor proffered with a nod. Katriona, her maid, continued to style her hair even as the door burst open and her young grandchildren, Philippa and Michael, ran into the room, their mother close behind. They both ran to the window where Sparrow and Finch hopped, the children whistling and trying to capture the birds who would fly just out of reach and then land on the sill, only to take off again as little hands grabbed for them.

"I'm sorry, *Maman*. They escaped me again." Delia leaned against the doorframe, her seven month pregnancy very evident. Her daughter again amazed Bea at how much she looked like her father. Her hair had darkened to Michael's chestnut, setting off the deep blue eyes they shared.

Bea smiled. "It does not bother me, you know that. I love to hear the squeal of my grandchildren in the house."

"So you say, but I have seen you cover your ears before." Delia sat down heavily on the corner of the bed as the children raced back out of the room. All three women sighed with relief. Bea and Delia's gazes met in the mirror, and they burst out laughing.

"I do love them, but perhaps the nurse can take them outside for a nice long walk around the pond? The trout pond?" Bea suggested. "And have Thomas accompany them. You know how much they adore him."

"The trout pond? That's at least a kilometer away. Oh," Delia laughed. "I will definitely recommend that to Nurse." She struggled to her feet. "Perhaps I will take a nap. Charles is due back this evening, and I would like to be able to talk to him about his trip to America without falling asleep halfway through."

"An excellent idea, my darling. Come give me a kiss and then take that nap. You need it."

Delia exited the room and Katriona left soon after, taking the tea tray with her. Finally alone, Bea looked at the newspaper headline.

"Billionaire inventor Alexander Chamberlin killed in factory explosion."

She put the newspaper aside and looked up at Victor who stood near the window. "Sparrow and Finch, to Victor." The birds flew into the now outstretched hands of the automaton. As one, they turned their backs to her, heads down to connect to the power couplings Victor had exposed in his wrists.

"Show me Michael." The birds spread open their wings until they touched, the panels on their backs receding until the tiny screens were fully exposed. A flickering image started to glow above them, flashing faster and faster until Michael's beloved face appeared. She had watched this countless times over the years and could recite his words by heart, but she sat quietly to listen to him speak.

"Bea, my love. I know if you are seeing this that you have found the file I have hidden in the kitchen. And that somehow I am no longer there to build our dream of using the refuse from the developed world to benefit all of mankind. I am sorry that I will leave you to carry this burden on alone.

"I must assume that Alex has the rest of my research. Alex was many things, but he knew how to make the most of an opportunity. With what we allowed him, he will most likely have expanded his businesses exponentially. I also know that the information I had you remove from the file will have kept him from commercializing our dream.

"I do not know when you may be able to move forward with our plans. But if the time ever comes that Alex will no longer be a threat, I hope that you will take what I have left you and make it happen. Bless the world with the lack of want for the poorest among us.

"I love you, my dear heart. I pray you never see this, but if you do, know that I will be with you. Always."

The image disappeared and the birds closed their screens. They flitted back to the windowsill with a soft metal clank.

She stood and patted the silent automaton on the arm. "Thank you, Victor. It is always bittersweet to see his beloved face. May I have the file?"

With a nod, the automaton reached into his coat and extracted the small sheaf of papers. She traced the loopy M with a finger, missing the feel of wood under her fingers. Then giving herself a mental shake, she said, “It’s time to begin. I hope the world will be a better place when we’re through.”

Inspired by Emily Dickinson

Brayden,
Enjoy the adventure!
Jay B

The Van Tassel Legacy

JAY BARNSON

Samuel Chase persevered through six years of the top technology institutes in Vienna and Munich with ambitions loftier than becoming a common pharmacist. His fellow graduates who remained in Europe found immediate and comfortable employment as researchers for governments, wealthy patrons, and prestigious universities. But along the eastern bank of the Hudson River, in the aptly named village of Sleepy Hollow, such an education meant little.

In 1842, the Old World obsessed over recreating Viktor Casimir's legendary experiments of the 1700s. The promise of armies with new weapons and rich men with extended life fueled a frenzy of scientific activity. They joked that a man with expertise in physiochemistry ranked higher than many noblemen, for it took no exceptional skill to produce more noblemen.

An entrepreneurial man like Samuel created his own opportunities, even while acting as a village pharmacist. Like his grandfather's own inauspicious beginnings in Sleepy Hollow, he planned to turn his humble start into a successful career. To the old judge, the land had been an investment, let to tenants for years. Unlike the absentee landlord who had never had intentions of setting foot in this quiet hamlet again, Samuel meant to make it his home.

He couldn't believe his luck when he learned that his inheritance was so near Van Brunt Industries of neighboring Tarrytown. The company was unique in all of New York—if not all the United States—in that it produced medicines and devices of physiochemical origin. Thus, Samuel spent his last penny repairing the house and constructing a modest laboratory within, rather than return to Europe.

His only regular client, Katrina van Brunt, paid him quite well for her curiously specific orders. As he ambled along the road to her home—a mansion the locals still referred to as the "Van Tassel house," after Mrs. van Brunt's father—he wondered briefly if his grandfather would approve. Probably. The man never allowed old grievances to interfere with profit.

As he approached the enormous pre-Revolutionary mansion, Samuel's good mood soured. Peter van Brunt stood near the front door, adjusting the saddle of his horse. Tall, blond, and two decades Samuel's elder, Peter had seemed charming when they first met. That impression hadn't survived their second encounter. Peter scowled as he mounted his horse.

Politeness demanded a greeting. "Good afternoon, Mr. van Brunt," Samuel said with a small wave.

"What business do you have here, Mr. Chase?"

None of yours, Samuel almost snapped. Instead, he motioned to the cotton satchel over his shoulder and answered, "I've brought medicines for your uncle."

Darkness flashed over Peter's expression, replaced by an automatic smile that projected no warmth. "Ah. That's right. You said you were a chemist, didn't you?"

"A physiochemist."

As in their previous conversation, Peter showed no sign that he grasped the distinction. Though sibling sciences, the broader field of physiochemistry bore more in common with the alchemy of Isaac Newton and Tycho Brahe than Robert Boyle's offshoot. Physiochemists noted with considerable pride how much their field had elevated medicine beyond the state of quackery practiced at the beginning of the century. The technology was the foundation of Peter's company, but his ignorance of it baffled Samuel.

Peter shrugged. "Right. You should see about coming to work for me."

"I did, two weeks ago. Your man said I could help unloading and loading at the dock on Tuesdays and Thursdays."

"Oh? Good. Did you accept?"

Samuel stared at Peter, unsure if the man was joking, deliberately insulting him, or serious. He didn't answer.

Peter glanced back at the mansion. "If my uncle is too sick to see me, he may not be your customer much longer. If you find that land too expensive to maintain, my offer on it is still open."

Samuel couldn't bring himself to feign gratitude out of politeness. He simply waved to Peter, who did the same before kicking his horse into a canter and riding off.

Samuel fumed. Certainly they could use another physio-chemist on the staff! But no, they hadn't acknowledged his credentials. Then, to add further insult, Peter had offered to buy Samuel's property for one-fourth the assessed value.

Samuel's good mood returned when Miriam Janssen answered his knock at the mansion door. Her blonde hair was tightly braided behind her head, and over her simple work dress she wore a leather apron. It was the kind that men who worked with sharp objects or dangerous substances might wear—like a blacksmith, or one in his own profession. He'd never seen a woman wear one before, and this one showed signs of use. While it surprised and intrigued him, he found it did nothing to mar her attractiveness.

"Hello, Mr. Chase. Please come in. My aunt is with her husband right now, but she'll be up shortly. Did you bring the medicine?"

Samuel nodded as he crossed the threshold. The palatial entry hall always amazed him, after a lifetime of living in tiny Connecticut and New York apartments and even smaller European dormitories. It combined Old World architecture and American materials and sensibilities. It also carried the gravity of maturity, a feature taken for granted in Europe, but something of a novelty in a nation younger than the oldest men in the village. Sadly, although he could detect no hint of dust, the stately mahogany furniture bore subtle cues of having fallen into disuse over the years.

He withdrew the sealed jar from his satchel and handed it to Miriam. “This should be stored in a cool location, and it will start breaking down and losing potency in three or four months. I’d advise you to use it all before then.”

Miriam placed the jar on a table. “Our previous supplier shipped it from upstate, so it lost as much as two weeks in the transport. I’ve not been very successful making it myself.”

Samuel raised an eyebrow. “It’s not a trivial manufacturing process.”

“No, it’s not. The catalytic process is unforgiving. And allowing it to cool too quickly can damage equipment, I discovered.”

Samuel grinned. “I learned the hard way, too, my third year at university. I haven’t met another physiochemist since I returned to New York. I didn’t know any of the higher schools admitted women.”

“None that I know of.”

“Where did you study?”

“At my father’s knee.” Behind her faint smile, her eyes flashed, as if she waited to pounce should he say something stupid. Samuel had little social contact with women during his years of study. He knew he was going to say something stupid.

“Oh,” he answered. It was awkward and definitely stupid, but hopefully harmless.

Katrina van Brunt's arrival from another room saved him from further dialogue. In her late sixties, Katrina wore her age as comfortably as her simple cotton blouse and wool skirt. A moderate, healthy plumpness smoothed out her wrinkles. She remained a handsome woman, but her face now bore an angry frown. Samuel inclined his head to greet her. "Good evening, Mrs. van Brunt. I hope you and your husband are feeling well."

Katrina shook her head, but her frown faded. "Perhaps with fresh medicine, Brom may improve, but unless you can brew me a cure for an affliction named Peter van Brunt, I hold little hope for my own well-being."

Samuel said, "I saw him depart. He didn't look happy."

Katrina's frown faded. "He gets that way when he doesn't get his way. Enough about him. Now, Miriam tells me that you are trained in physiochemistry, and that you studied in Germany. Are you familiar with the works of Viktor Casimir?"

Samuel felt his head swim. What a strange village Sleepy Hollow had proven to be, where the head of a major technology company was ignorant of physiochemistry, while a farmer's wife inquired of the world's greatest physiochemist in casual conversation!

"That was my specialty at the university, ma'am," he said. "But that's hardly unusual. Everyone wants to recreate the *Dauerrüstung*."

"What's that?"

"It was the cavalry armor he tested during the Revolution. He intended it to keep injured soldiers alive long enough to receive medical attention after a battle, but in practice, it made them keep fighting for hours through fatal wounds. Our soldiers thought they were monsters. Casimir thought the same, I think. He destroyed all the prototypes and all of his notes to prevent the armor from ever being used again. He died in prison over that."

"Oh, that thing," Katrina said, waving her hand dismissively. "Anything else? Did you study any of his other machines?"

Both women stared at him intently. Samuel realized he was being interviewed, but for what purpose he couldn't fathom. He had endured examinations from professors who seemed less interested in his answers than these two women. "Of course. But not much else had such practical value."

The women exchanged glances. Was the examination concluded? Katrina looked back to Samuel and asked, "I assume you have sought employment with Van Brunt Industries."

"I have, but they didn't seem interested. I understand your husband is a partner. Perhaps he could put in a good word for me?"

Katrina shook her head. "Brom's recommendation would be worth nothing. Or less. He and Peter haven't gotten along in many years. I would advise against working for Peter, anyway."

"Why?"

Her frown returned. "He's a ruthless snake who fancies himself the next Van Buren. He's not known to be kind to his employees, either. That's all I'd like to talk about that subject tonight. It is near suppertime. Mr. Chase, if you have no other plans, we'd be pleased if you'd join us for dinner."

“I wouldn’t want to trouble you.”

“It would be no trouble. Brom . . . rarely joins us for dinner these days, and it would be nice to have a male voice at the table.” The right corner of her mouth flicked upwards. “And you look like you could use a few more good meals.”

Samuel caught himself glancing sideways at Miriam, who studiously looked another way. Katrina, catching the glance, added with a half-smile, “Miriam will be joining us, as usual.”

Samuel offered a polite bow of the head, hoping it might conceal any blush. “Thank you. I’d be delighted.”

As he took his leave after dinner, Miriam followed Samuel out onto the spacious veranda formed by the jutting eaves in the front of the house. He lingered, enjoying the crisp evening air of the early autumn but more particularly Miriam’s company. Miriam likewise seemed reluctant to return inside.

Miriam had changed into an evening dress with puffy upper sleeves. He’d seen the style in Germany two years earlier. Undeniably attractive, she wore it as comfortably as she had the stained leather apron, but somehow Samuel felt that it didn’t suit her as well.

They spoke of trivialities as the sun set. Miriam spoke of growing up in Sleepy Hollow, the quiet times so far removed from Samuel’s own childhood and adolescence in bustling New York City, where his father shared a legal practice with his grandfather. While Samuel considered little of his schooling in

Vienna and Munich to be noteworthy, the notion fired Miriam's imagination.

"I have read so much about Vienna," she said. "Did you ever visit the zoo?"

Samuel nodded. "I didn't have much time to explore the city, but I did visit the zoo once. They had giraffes—strange spotted creatures with alarmingly long necks. I thought the whole design, legs, neck, and all, seemed exceptionally spindly, and wondered if they weren't some bizarre man-made creation of clockwork to fool the public."

Miriam grinned. "I've seen sketches of giraffes, but I have never seen a real one. I went to a circus once, as a young girl. They had a striped horse—a zebra. I asked Papa why they'd painted stripes on the horse. He just laughed, and I didn't understand why. Then he asked me if I thought it was a black horse that they'd painted with white stripes, or a white horse with black stripes. I grew upset, because I didn't know how he expected me to know such things, and he wouldn't tell me the answer.

"I obsessed over the question through the rest of the circus. On the way home in our wagon, I announced to my whole family that zebras must be naturally white with black stripes, because the black stripes seemed to taper and the white did not. Everyone but Papa laughed. He just nodded and told me that I'd made perfect sense. I was very pleased with myself."

Samuel chortled. "I had a professor like that in my second year. My classmates hated him. I did, too, at first. He'd never tell us if we were right or wrong . . . we'd always have to prove our hypothesis."

"You hated him at first?"

"He told us that out in the field, there'd be no one to tell us if our conclusions were sound. We'd have to think for ourselves, and live by our own mistakes. Like everyone else, it frustrated me at first, but I came to think he was right."

"That does sound a little like Papa."

"Does your family still live here?"

"No, they moved to Germany when I was seventeen. I stayed with Aunt Katrina and Uncle Brom."

"Is your father Katrina's brother?"

Miriam laughed. "No. Katrina was an only child. I think we're actually first cousins twice removed or something like that. I just grew up calling them my uncle and aunt."

"Why didn't you go with the rest of your family to Germany?"

Her expression turned somber. "That's a story for another night, Mr. Chase."

Darkness set in, and the air grew chill. Samuel could make no more excuses to linger. "I have been delighted by your company, Miss Miriam. With your permission, I would like to call upon you again."

"I think I would like that as well. Goodbye, Mr. Chase."

The following week, Samuel visited Tarrytown to pick up an order of potash salts from Van Brunt Industries. The substance could be volatile and possessed no medicinal properties, so Samuel didn't keep a large stock available. He could easily have asked his neighbor to deliver it, but after Katrina's warning, he didn't want to involve Peter in his dealings any more than absolutely necessary.

When Samuel arrived in the plain wooden office, Peter dismissed the clerk and greeted Samuel personally. "I'm so sorry, Mr. Chase, but your order isn't ready yet. However, I have been guaranteed that it will be filled by this evening. It wasn't medicine for Brom, was it?"

"No, just potash salts."

Peter's blank expression suggested that he never sullied his hands with the details of his company's products. He shrugged and asked, "So, just how is my partner, anyway? Have you seen him?"

"No, sir. I've only delivered medicines to the house."

Peter's face showed exaggerated solicitude. "Does that strike you as odd?"

Samuel shrugged. "I don't know. I'm a scientist, not a doctor. I'm not even a pharmacist, really. I am just glad to render assistance to your partner's family."

"I'm sure." It almost sounded like an accusation. "I'd bring your order with me, but I won't be returning home tonight. I have business keeping me in Tarrytown until late, and I do not like to travel home after dark. You understand why, of course."

Samuel shook his head. Peter continued. "Our most famous story is of the Headless Horseman. It is the phantom of the

Hessian cavalryman from the Revolution that seeks a head of the living to replace its own."

"Of course. I imagine everyone in New York has heard the story." It had certainly impacted Samuel's family, although his grandfather never spoke of it. If the story had been less well-known, Samuel may have been born with a different name. He had other reasons for being intrigued. "Personally, I think I'd like to meet this Headless Horseman, assuming he would leave my head where it is. A few of the cavalrymen from the Hesse-Darmstadt landgraviate wore special armor during the Revolution. Do the stories ever mention his armor?"

Peter's face darkened. "Do not make light of the horseman. He has been the end of several men of the region, including Katrina's old tutor, Ichabod Crane. Crane ran a school on the Van der Boors' property near the brook. They say that if you walk by the clearing where the schoolhouse once stood, shortly before dawn, you can hear the ghost of Ichabod Crane whistling to himself."

Samuel tried to hide his amusement. "That would be something to hear."

"Not from what I have been told. Those who have heard it say it leaves a chill up your spine. But I suppose a man of learning such as yourself has little time for tales of spooks and specters."

"Apparently, this afternoon I have plenty." More impatience came through his voice than he'd intended.

"I'm sure your order will turn up. Come back this evening, at closing time—six o'clock—and we'll either have your delivery, or a replacement. You have my word."

Resigned, Samuel spent his afternoon buying a lantern and oil for his return trip, and then strolling along the bank of the Hudson. His thoughts frequently wandered to Miriam. She was a young woman of great beauty, intelligence, strong will, and independent thought—not to mention at least a passing knowledge of practical science gained from her doubtlessly brilliant father. Certainly dozens of men must be courting a woman like that, Samuel reasoned. He had no idea how to compete, but he vowed to try.

He returned to the offices of Van Brunt Industries promptly at six o'clock. A clerk handed Samuel the two-pound ceramic jar, which he placed gingerly inside his satchel. There was little chance of the potash salts igniting from mere jolts or jostles, but he'd once witnessed a fellow student burn his face and blind himself from too-casual handling of acids. Ever since, Samuel treated volatile substances with additional care.

With his order in hand, the evening's chill pierced his clothing as he made his way up the road to Sleepy Hollow. His lantern gave off scant heat, but the light comforted him. By the time he crossed the bridge near the "old" Dutch church—rebuilt after a fire in 1837, he'd been told—the night was fully upon him. The sliver of moonlight revealed indistinct gray outlines of the road, trees, and hills around him. He found it easy to let his imagination run wild and envision such haunts as Peter had suggested lurking amidst the dark silhouettes.

On the hill near the road, he thought he saw a figure on horseback standing amidst the trees. He silently cursed his imagination, but then the figure moved out from the shadow and into the scant moonlight. While it was impossible to make out clear details, it was definitely a horse and rider.

A headless rider.

Samuel's mind raced. While the impossibility of what he perceived warred with his subconscious dread, the rider turned on the saddle, facing him. Some tiny, conscious part of Samuel's brain wondered if it was possible to look without eyes. If so, his lantern was a beacon in the night.

The figure on the hill turned the horse, and descended on a path parallel to the road, accelerating before Samuel lost sight of it through the trees. No matter how his conscious mind sought to rationalize it, no matter whether the horseman was man or fiend, Samuel recognized on an instinctive level that he had become prey. He must fight or flee.

A quick scan of the road in the lamplight revealed no fallen branch or rock to use as a weapon. But that didn't mean the student of physiochemistry was defenseless. On the chance that his approaching enemy was mortal, Samuel set down his lamp and opened the jar of potash salts. He dumped half the contents on the road. Before him, the hoof-beat rhythm turned to a gallop. Samuel fought his own shaking fingers to open the base of his lamp, and poured most of the oil into the pile, forming a noxious, flammable mash. Only then did he dare look up.

The rider was a shadow against the darkened road. It spun a bundle overhead like a medieval war-flail as it charged.

Samuel leaped backwards. He hesitated the span of a heartbeat to time his attack, then hurled his lamp at the mound.

He had a moment to shield his eyes before the night exploded with the brightness of noonday and a sound like a rifle shot, hurling white-hot sparks several feet into the air.

The horse screamed. Samuel reeled to the side of the road. Over the ringing in his ears, he thought he heard a muffled voice crying, "What in blazes?" The horse fled.

It took half a minute for his vision to clear after the instant of light. Any remnants of burning oil from the lantern had been completely extinguished. A formless lump lay near the shattered remains of the lantern. Samuel moved slowly to investigate.

The lump proved to be an old flour-sack that the horseman had dropped, with the split remains of a pumpkin within. While he had no doubt the impact at such a speed could have caused grave injury, fatality would have been unlikely. Knowing his attacker hadn't intended to murder him didn't help. Samuel didn't stop shaking until he was safely within his home with the door bolted and barred.

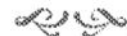

Samuel didn't leave his home the following day. While the terror of the encounter with the horseman dissipated with the morning light, the suspicion that his assailant had been a mortal from the village left him feeling angry and betrayed.

After lunch, much of his anger had subsided. He still had a commission from Katrina to complete, which he'd intended to start after his excursion to Tarrytown. It was a two-day process, most of which involved waiting. He focused his efforts into the job, trying to push his memories of the attack to the side.

He completely forgot about making himself dinner. At some point in the night, he fell asleep at his table, a book acting as a pillow.

He was awakened several hours later by a determined knocking. He brushed his hair back with his hands and straightened his shirt as he made his way to the door, but it did little good in making him look any more presentable. Resigned, he unbarred and unbolted the door.

He squinted and shielded his eyes from the noonday sun. Miriam Janssen stood on his porch, in a simple light-brown summer dress with wide, short sleeves and lace along the collar, and a small white bonnet with silk flowers. In her hands, she held a wide, closed basket. Samuel's self-consciousness turned to pure embarrassment, which doubled when he opened his mouth but couldn't think of anything to say.

Miriam looked him over from head to foot, and said, "I suppose that settles part of the mystery."

"Mystery?" Samuel repeated, finding a portion of his voice.

"The one going around town about whether you still live, or were taken by the Headless Horseman of the Hollow. Or my private fear that you somehow managed to blow yourself up with your experiments Thursday night."

"Oh, that. Yes. I mean, no." He stepped onto his porch to join her. "May I take your basket?"

"Thank you. Now, when did you eat last?"

"Lunch," Samuel answered, placing the basket on the railing.

"You have already had lunch?"

"Lunch yesterday."

"Then open the basket. I took the liberty of preparing some food." After a beat, she added, "at Aunt Katrina's insistence." She opened the basket, standing close enough that her clothing brushed Samuel, and he felt lightheaded. He told himself it was a symptom of hunger.

Pulling fruit and cheese from the basket, Miriam said, "The town is currently a-roar with rumors, you know."

"What rumors?"

"Some people say they saw lightning strike out of a clear night sky. Others claim they saw the Galloping Hessian himself. Some even say he was fleeing. And somehow people know that it was you who returned home late from Tarrytown two nights ago. What really happened?"

Samuel shook his head. "I had an encounter, though I doubt it was with the supernatural." As they ate together, he shared his story with her. She laughed and applauded when he spoke of the explosion, and what he thought was an exclamation of surprise from the supposedly mouthless rider.

"Do you think it was Peter?"

"Probably. Or someone he'd convinced to do it in his stead. He delayed me until dusk, and insisted on bringing up the stories of the Headless Horseman. I just don't understand why."

"He wants you to stop helping Brom. Maybe he wants your land, too."

“Why? He doesn’t need it.”

“He moves in circles that represent very old money, and medieval impressions of economics. They haven’t come to grasp the wonders of industry yet, and still measure wealth in terms of acres.” Miriam’s eyes glinted. “I think you should make your reappearance tomorrow, at church. It will cause quite a stir. From what I have heard, many believe that you share the fate of Ichabod Crane and have become the horseman’s newest victim.”

Samuel rubbed at his chin, and found it raspy with stubble. “Does everyone believe the horseman killed Crane and took his head?”

Miriam shrugged. “No, not everyone. Some do not believe the horseman ever existed.”

“How about you?”

“Can you keep a secret, Mr. Chase?”

“I would love to,” he said, grinning again.

“It would be a shame to spoil a wonderful legend. I do know the horseman—the dead Hessian, that is—was real. But I have reason to suspect it was no ghost that attacked Ichabod Crane that night.”

Samuel smiled. “I have my reasons, too. But how do you know the horseman was real?”

“A Van Tassel family story, from Katrina’s father, Baltus. He saw the decapitated mercenary. But as to any appearance of the ghost afterwards, I can’t say.”

“I would like to know more about the mercenary. Do you know if he was wearing any armor?”

"You mean the armor you spoke of the other day—what did you call it?"

"*Dauerrüstung.*"

Miriam nodded gravely. "For any more information, you'll have to talk to Katrina. That is not my story to tell. Now, will you sit with us in church tomorrow?"

"I'll be there. Hopefully of better appearance than you found me today."

"Good," she said. With another impish smile, she added, "Because right now, you smell of burnt potash salt."

Samuel was nearly late for the Sunday service, and his entrance caused a stir. The talk grew even louder on his seemingly bold decision to seat himself next to Miriam and Katrina. As the preacher began the service, Samuel thought he detected the hint of smugness in Miriam's tight, thin smile as people stared in her direction.

Peter van Brunt and his wife were the only ones who seemed to make it a point to ignore him.

After the service, villagers surrounded Samuel, begging for his account of the Headless Horseman. Samuel repeated the story twice, but out of concern for the curious boys listening, he omitted the ingredients of his makeshift explosive. He also omitted his suspicions that the horseman was a fake, as he didn't want to be seen as accusing anyone. Still, he noticed some of the men smirk, no doubt imagining a wonderful prank that Samuel had turned against the prankster.

The crowd finally thinned, allowing him to escape. He found Katrina and Miriam in a pointedly polite conversation with Peter.

"So sorry my good uncle could not make it to church today," Peter said. "I've not seen him in months. I do hope he gets better soon."

"As do I, Peter," Katrina agreed. "He is an old man, and some days he is stronger than others. But I assure you, he is as lucid as ever, and grows quite animated when I mention you to him. Should you catch him on a good day, I'm sure he would be pleased to discuss matters with you."

Something she'd said brought Peter up short. He tipped his hat to the two women before walking away, scowling and ignoring Samuel as he did so.

When Peter was out of earshot, Miriam muttered to Katrina, "He will act soon, I'm sure of it."

Katrina nodded. "At least he still fears Brom. For now." She looked at Samuel. "Do you have the medicine ready?"

Samuel said, "It should be finished this afternoon."

Katrina said, "I think I need to rest this afternoon. Miriam, would you mind going to Samuel's house and picking it up for me?"

"Of course not."

Katrina flashed a knowing smile. "I didn't think you would."

A week later, a boy from the village summoned Samuel from his house with a message that Mrs. van Brunt needed him immediately. Samuel grabbed supplies and stuffed them into his satchel, then raced to the Van Tassel home. Two carriages sat in front of the manor. The double door stood open, raised voices carrying through. Samuel knocked twice on the doorpost, and then entered.

Peter van Brunt stood in the front room, flanked by Constable Franklin and two strangers in dark clothes. Katrina stood facing them with crossed arms, Miriam behind her. Miriam let her blank mask slip a bit as she saw Samuel, hinting at her desperation.

"I don't care how sick he is, Katrina. Nobody has seen my uncle in weeks, and we must speak with him. Some in this town suspect that he may no longer be among the living, and that for some unknowable reason you have concealed this fact. I understand that losing a loved one can be very distressing to the gentler sex, and that in your state of mind—"

"There is nothing wrong with my state of mind, Peter van Brunt, and there is nothing unknowable about why you'd prefer my husband dead." Glancing past the party before her, Katrina said, "Samuel, please accompany Miriam and help roust my husband from his sorely needed rest and help him get ready to receive these inquisitive visitors."

Samuel opened his mouth to ask a question, but the elderly woman's expression allowed no disobedience. He silently followed Miriam down a hall, but not up the stairs, as he would have expected. Instead, Miriam produced a brass key and unlocked a small door next to the staircase, motioning him inside. Behind him, Samuel heard Katrina offering the men some tea while they waited. For the present, Katrina had control of the argument, as they waited on the long-missing master of the Van Tassel house.

The room behind the door was small and dark. Familiar chemical odors penetrated the masking scent of dried herbs, bringing with them memories of the university. "What are you working with in here?" he asked.

"Shh. Not now," Miriam said. "And mind your step." She struck a friction-match and lit a lantern on a shelf by the door. As she carefully closed the door and relocked it, Samuel took stock of the room. While it served as a storage room for food and herbs, a stairway down into what appeared to be a cellar dominated the far end of the room. Miriam silently descended the stairs, and Samuel followed.

The chamber at the bottom might once have served as a wine cellar but now was dominated by laboratory equipment more impressive than Samuel's own. Two chairs, a cot, and two trunks made up the furnishings of the chamber. A machine took up an entire wall, its intricate clockwork mechanisms powered by three swinging pendulum weights, connected with tubing to fluid-filled glass containers and an object that resembled nothing so much as an oversized glass coffin.

A coffin, Samuel realized, which held a body.

Miriam moved to the machine and began adjusting the dials with obvious familiarity, while Samuel marveled. "This looks like the designs of Casimir's Rejuvenator," he said. "But how is this possible? He never completed his research."

"He did. He even built it," Miriam said, not taking her eyes off a gauge as she made tiny adjustments. "But we think he was disappointed with it, and he and his patrons were more interested in his next project. That was the armor, I believe. His assistant, Heinrich Ritter, took the machine for his own use when Casimir died. He intended to sleep inside it for years to escape Casimir's fate. Unfortunately, he didn't adequately train his brother in its maintenance. Ritter died inside."

"I can't believe this. How did it get here?"

"When Brom first showed symptoms of the palsy thirty years ago, Katrina enlisted my father's aid. He had informally studied physiochemistry, among other things. Katrina and Brom paid him to travel to Germany to learn more about Casimir's armor."

Samuel nodded. "He, and everyone else in Europe."

Miriam finished her adjustments and moved on to another control. "Instead, he tracked down Ritter's nephew, who had this machine, and several of Ritter's notes. The nephew had no idea how much it was really worth."

"And your father put it all together? From Ritter's notes?"

"As best as he could, yes. Now I need help to get Brom safely out of the machine."

Deactivating the machine safely required two people, Samuel discovered, as well as precise timing and coordination. Samuel followed Miriam's instructions carefully, and just as carefully observed her actions and movements. He waited until she paused before asking questions, and savored each word of instruction or response.

This machine was a discovery of a lifetime, and it sat in a cellar in Sleepy Hollow, quietly fulfilling its intended purpose.

"We can't just cut off the flow of chemicals into his body all at once," she explained as she gingerly closed a valve. "The shock would kill him. We must do it slowly, in stages, and introduce the counteractive agents. Including one that you created for us just a few days ago."

"How well does the machine rejuvenate him?" Samuel asked.

"It doesn't. It lets him sleep for weeks instead of hours. He's usually stronger for a few hours, sometimes even days. He doesn't even shake. But while the machine slows age and infirmity in his body, it doesn't halt it." She paused her narrative to give Samuel instructions. "Please pull that brass handle to your right, and turn the dial next to it to halfway between five and six."

"What does this do?" he asked, locating the knob and carefully judging the midpoint between values. When creating medicines, he was always aware that his precision might mean the difference between life and death. This was no different.

Miriam checked a gauge, and pulled out a pocket watch and noted the time. "Twelve minutes," she said. "The machine is now passing his blood through a filter, warming it, and then returning it to his body a bit at a time. It is supposed to take ten minutes, though we've found it works best for Brom at twelve. He may be a bigger man than Casimir's test subjects."

Samuel watched the tubing fill with red fluid, and looked at the pale figure in the glass container. "So your father taught you how to use the machine?"

"Yes. He took what he'd learned and went into business with Brom and Peter. Brom provided the funding, my father the inventions, and Peter handled the business. For a while, they did extremely well. My father could afford the finest tutors and books for my brother and me."

"For a while?"

Miriam hesitated for several seconds before answering. "Papa met my mother in Germany. They went back six years ago for a visit, with hopes that he could obtain access to more of Ritter's or Casimir's notes through the universities. While they were gone, the murder of a company manager came to light. Peter claimed to have evidence that it was Papa's doing. His leaving the country seemed proof of his guilt to some. Brom was already in the machine more often than out, and by the time he found out what had happened, it was too late. All we could do was warn Papa not to return."

"And you were left here?"

"Someone had to help Katrina run the machine." She checked her watch. "Get ready to turn off the blood filter. Turn the dial back to zero, and then return the brass lever to the off position." She stood ready for the next procedure, watching the hands move on her pocket watch.

While he waited, Samuel tried to memorize every control and pipe-fitting. At twelve minutes, he deactivated the filter. Miriam opened the glass case, and delicately removed equipment from Brom's naked body with the mechanical familiarity of years of practice. For two tubes, Brom had permanent connectors inserted into his left arm and right thigh. She gently stoppered the implants, and then asked for Samuel's help to move Brom to the bed.

Once Brom was out of the case, Miriam covered him with the blanket, retrieved some clothing for him from one of the trunks, and excused herself from the room. In spite of his slow, regular breathing, Brom appeared more like a cadaver than a man. When his eyes fluttered open five minutes later, it startled Samuel.

A similar shock registered on Brom's face, as well. "Crane?" he croaked. "Ichabod Crane? Have you come to take me to hell?"

"No, sir, I am not he. My name is Samuel Chase."

Brom raised himself to a seated position. "You look like him. I did him wrong once, but for the right reasons. I fear I may have done him grave injury."

"You were the Headless Horseman."

Brom experimented by taking a deep breath, and seemed satisfied with the results. "That night, I was. I took him for a coward and a weakling, and thought Katrina deserved better. But then, neither of us knew I would become this . . . this cripple." He sighed and shook his head. "And now, Mr. Chase, you know one of my secrets."

Samuel answered, "Then I shall tell you one of mine. Ichabod Crane changed his name to Abraham Chase, and became a successful lawyer and judge. He found a woman who loved him, and they had a son and three grandsons, of whom I am the youngest. Whatever injury you may have done to him, I do not think he died with regret."

"Abraham Chase? The man who bought the land north of Peter's property?"

"The same, yes. I inherited the property when he died earlier this year."

Brom scratched at the stubble of his beard. It seemed to be only two days' worth of growth, but he'd been within the machine much longer. Like his hair, it was snowy white rather than gray. "I only met his agent, and then briefly. Peter and I both had our eye on it, but we were waiting on Van Dijk to drop his price. Chase came in and snatched it from beneath our noses." A faraway look appeared in his eyes, and his lips curled into a wry smile. Then he shook his head and asked, "But, why would Ichabod Crane buy land in Sleepy Hollow?"

Samuel shook his head. "I can't tell you that. Even my father didn't know about the property until after my grandfather died. But knowing him, he probably intended to resell it for a tidy profit."

Brom grunted. "In better times, he'd have been correct. I'd have paid him half again what he paid Van Dijk. Now, what are you doing here in my cellar, Mr. Chase?"

"Assisting Miriam, as I am somewhat familiar with the creations of Viktor Casimir. Your nephew, the constable, and two other men are upstairs demanding your audience. They believe you are dead."

Brom offered a raspy chortle. "They are very nearly right, I'm afraid. Please assist me in getting dressed, Mr. Chase. I will enjoy disappointing Peter one more time."

Peter's voice boomed. "He's not been seen in weeks, Katrina. If you do not take us to him immediately, we shall be forced to declare him dead, and the stigma of hiding . . ."

Peter seemed to be struck mute the instant Brom entered the room. Brom's presence commanded attention even as he leaned on a cane for support. He was accustomed to respect and obedience. In a quiet voice that allowed no argument, he said, "Kindly refrain from using that tone of voice with my wife."

Peter and the two strangers wore expressions of confusion, but Constable Franklin smirked. Brom banged his cane against the floor as he stepped up to Peter, drawing himself to his full height so he could look down on his nephew. "Now, what business is so urgent that you cannot allow an old man to get his rest? Unless, of course, you've come to bring me my share of the profit from last quarter?"

Peter stammered before answering, "No, we made no profit last quarter. It is being swallowed up by interest. We need to clear the liens on your property."

Peter looked away from Brom's withering stare. "I see," Brom answered at length. "It is really too bad we lost Luther. His talent at invention could be handy right now."

Peter hesitated before replying, "Truly unfortunate."

"In the meantime, is there a reason you brought the constable and two strangers—lawyers, I assume—into my home? Do you wish to charge me with a crime, perhaps? I'm sure that would prove very interesting to everyone."

Brom's voice was not at all playful with this accusation. Peter visibly blanched but quickly recovered his composure. "Of course not, Brom. I was simply seeing to your continued well-being."

"My well-being demands peace. Now, if you have no further business to discuss, would you kindly see yourselves out? Thank you. And Mick, it's good to see you again."

Constable Franklin gave a courteous nod. "I'm very sorry for the disturbance, Brom. I'll make certain it doesn't happen again."

Once the four men were safely out of the house, Brom collapsed onto a chair. He brought his hand up to rub his temple, and it quivered. "Damned palsy," he muttered. "It didn't even leave me alone for an hour this time."

Katrina turned away from her husband. "You must be starving," she said. "I'll help Mrs. Harper with dinner."

Miriam rose to assist her, but Katrina shook her head and said, "No, see to Brom." With a hint of undirected seething, she added, "Make certain he is well." She turned to go to the kitchen, but not before Samuel and Miriam both noted the tears in her eyes.

Miriam came to Brom's side, but he waved her off with a twitching hand. "I'm fine. At least, as fine as age and this degeneration will allow." Turning to Samuel, he asked. "And what's your interest in all this, Mr. Chase?"

"He's a real physiochemist, Uncle," Miriam offered. "He studied Casimir's experiments."

Brom offered a ghost of a smile. "Did you ever study his armor?"

Samuel shrugged. "Of course. Everyone studies his armor. But we only have a few notes from his assistant, as he destroyed all of the prototypes after the Revolution. No complete model still exists."

"One does," Brom said.

Miriam looked curiously at Brom. She didn't seem surprised by this revelation, only that Brom had admitted to it.

Samuel looked between the two. "What are you talking about?"

"Follow me," Brom said. Waving off Miriam's assistance, he rose to his feet, leaning firmly upon his cane. They descended the stairs and returned to the chamber holding Casimir's machine. Brom tried to open one of the trunks, but his shaking, weak hand betrayed him. Samuel assisted him. And then audibly gasped.

A suit of leather, brass, and steel lay within. Bits of tubing, not unlike the tubes found in the machine beside them, wound under the protective metal plates, connected to metal capsules and cylinders strategically placed between layers. The capsules had thin glass windows along one side, marked with measurements and Casimir's own unique chemical notation.

Samuel felt as if he were a Knight of the Round Table laying his eyes upon the Holy Grail. As with the night of the horseman's attack, the impossibility that a surviving *Dauerrüstung* should exist here, in his neighbor's home, warred in his brain with his acceptance of what his own eyes were seeing.

"This was taken from the Headless Horseman?" Samuel asked in a whisper.

Brom nodded. "Katrina's father found the rider's body. The rider had been beheaded by a cannonball, but the armor held him fast astride his horse, which was grazing on the property. Baltus buried the body and took the horse. He also, wisely, preserved the armor. All his life, he told no one but his wife and daughter about it. Katrina was better educated than any of us, and guessed what the armor was. When I became sick, she enlisted Luther, Miriam's father, to restore the armor, thinking it would help me. Luther went to Germany to learn how to repair it, but instead came back with the Rejuvenator."

Brom eased himself into one of the chairs. "Can you fix it for me, Mr. Chase? When I am done with it, it shall be yours, to do with as you will."

Miriam shook her head. "Brom, no. It will kill you." Brom just shrugged in response.

Samuel answered, "You offer me the opportunity of a lifetime, Mr. van Brunt. But Miriam is correct. It will not extend your life by any worthwhile length. In the war, it merely allowed the dead and dying to continue exerting themselves for several hours before expiring. Just wearing it would put stresses on your body that would kill you."

"I'm dying already, Mr. Chase. I don't know that I will survive another sleep in that machine, or another week outside of it. I should be long dead already."

"But why accelerate it?" Miriam pleaded.

"Because I'm done surviving. I need to live again, if only for a few hours. I need to be strong, bold, and brash. I need to become Brom Bones again. Can't you see what I am asking? Do you understand what a gift it would be for a man to choose not only when but in what manner he finishes his mortal life?"

Samuel said nothing. Miriam sighed, and said, "Katrina will never agree to it."

"Maybe not. I'll speak with her. But this is my decision, not hers. Mr. Chase, will I have your assistance?"

Samuel considered, and said, "I will try. But I don't know if it can be fixed."

Brom nodded. "I don't know if I will survive until it is fixed. But I, too, will try."

Katrina spoke with Samuel the following day, when he arrived with a rented cart and horses to retrieve the trunk and its unique contents.

"Can you fix it?" she asked.

"I don't know. There is far more to it than medicines and chemicals, as my professors long suspected. But I promised your husband I would try. He and Miriam said you would object."

"I did. For several hours. But when we put him back into the machine this morning, he was not in a good state. I've worried for years, each time we placed him inside that horrible glass case, that it might be the last time. But today, I knew it. If he awakens again, it will be the last time."

"I'm sorry, Mrs. van Brunt."

The sunlight glistened in her eyes. She nodded. "I've been living with this for a long time. I am used to not having him around. Brom was never a perfect man, but he was a dutiful husband. I owe him his final wish. If you can give him a few hours of his youth and health back, you'll have my gratitude. I wish I could offer you more, but once he is gone, I may not be in a position to offer much."

"What do you mean?"

"It doesn't matter. Just do what you can, Mr. Chase. I'll send Miriam by to see if you need anything."

Returning to his home with the armor, Samuel was immediately consumed with the realization of a dream. He forgot to eat or sleep for a full day, pouring his attention over the tiniest details of the suit by lamplight until morning. He learned more in those hours than all the greatest minds in his field had pieced together in fifty years.

Samuel could spend years studying the suit, but he had only days to repair it. Fortunately, the suit was undamaged mechanically beyond the entropy of time. The chemicals were another story, but the containers were helpfully labeled with Casimir's own shorthand, as familiar to Samuel as the German language on which it was based. Some of the markings had faded with age, requiring educated guesswork. He considered making another trip to the Rejuvenator for comparison, when fatigue finally overtook him, clouding his thoughts and memories.

He woke up from his desk to the distant sound of knocking. Thinking it might be Miriam, he hastened to the front door, running his fingers through his hair in a last-moment attempt to make himself presentable before opening the door.

Peter van Brunt stood at the threshold, immaculately dressed in a black suit with a pointed, dark burgundy cravat and a tall hat. He smiled as he saw the look of surprise on Samuel's face. "May I come in, Mr. Chase? I have some business to discuss with you."

Tact overcoming suspicion, Samuel let him inside. "Can I get you anything?" he asked his unexpected guest.

Peter removed his hat, but held onto it rather than offer it to Samuel. "No," he said, "but thank you." Scanning the hall, he inclined his head towards the laboratory and asked, "Is that your workshop?"

"What is this about, Mr. van Brunt?"

"I will be brief. I do not know your business with my uncle and aunt, but I do know you've been there frequently. I have also come to learn that you studied abroad, specializing in Casimir's life-extending devices. I don't know if you realize this, but my company was founded on some of Casimir's technologies. We've expanded a good deal since then, but a man of your credentials could command a very high salary at a place that has need of such an unusual specialization. Enough, perhaps, that you could secure a very nice future for yourself and a particular young lady."

Fatigue overcoming tact, Samuel snapped, "Two weeks ago, you didn't even seem to know your own company's business or physiochemistry. I don't know why you suddenly took an interest in such things, but I'm not interested in working for you."

Peter's eyes narrowed, and his jaw hardened. "Let's be direct, then. You are a nobody, Mr. Chase, but you've attracted my attention. Brom is not long for this world, and when he finally expires, I have enough claim on his property and friends in high places to ensure I inherit everything."

"Nonsense. Katrina will—"

"Katrina will get nothing. Her father's property legally belongs to her husband, now, and it will soon pass to me. Widows have no right or need of inheritance in this state, and even their dower can be contested. Stop doing business immediately with Katrina and that uppity niece of hers, or I'll see to it she gets nothing. I don't want her wasting one more penny of her husband's money. Unless you want to see them cast out on the street in the middle of winter, you'll make the sensible choice."

"You wouldn't dare."

"I would, and I have. In the end, Mr. Chase, it is your choice, not mine. Think about it, but don't take too long. Once things are set in motion, they cannot be recalled."

Peter flashed a fake smile at Samuel. Then he put on his hat and left Samuel's home without another word.

Samuel seethed, temporarily forgetting his fatigue and hunger. Peter might be used to dealing with local farmers easily cowed by a rich, politically-connected would-be magnates, but this provincial bully could do little to Samuel. Once Samuel had uncovered the secrets of the *Dauerrüstung*—and, having kept his promise to Brom, had possession of the only working model—his own future would be assured. He'd have more wealth than Brom and Peter combined, and more than enough to make up for whatever losses Peter might try to inflict on Katrina and Miriam.

Samuel convinced himself that rage and hunger fueled the shaking he experienced after the short interview, rather than fear, as he returned to the lab and continued his work. Once again, he fell asleep at the workbench.

Five days later, Samuel had nearly completed repairs on the armor and manufactured all of the compounds he knew how to make for the suit. It wasn't perfect, and he'd had to make some guesses. He estimated two more days of final adjustments and testing. Then, if all went well, he would deliver it to Brom.

During his work, his sense of guilt overshadowed his ambition, robbing him of the joy he knew he should feel. The *Dauerrüstung*'s completion meant not only Brom's death, but hardship for Katrina and Miriam. He promised himself that he would care for them, but if Peter made good on his threat, it might be months before Samuel would be able to afford to provide for himself, let alone the two women. He had to make a decision in the next forty-eight hours that would haunt him forever, regardless of its outcome.

The thought nagged him as he tried to sleep, turning over and over in his mind with no resolution. Samuel finally threw back the covers in his bed, determined to salvage the night and turn his restlessness to productive action. He dressed in the chilly darkness of his room. He'd barely entered the hallway when he heard glass shatter behind the laboratory door.

Was it a thief, come to steal the priceless *Dauerrüstung*? Samuel flew to the laboratory, and in horror spied the flickering glow against the wall before he saw the flames. A pool of oil burned on the floor, sparkling on pieces of broken glass from the bottle hurled through the window.

In that moment, for the briefest instant, a temptation whispered to him to flee, leave the house and the *Dauerrüstung* to be destroyed by the fire, and allow fate to remove the awful decision he faced. Temptation and fear caused him to hesitate for a fraction of a second, but then training overcame instinct.

He threw treated blankets over the flames to extinguish them. However, the blankets became soaked in oil. The smaller fires spread to one of the cabinets. Samuel charged forward. As he heaved it out the broken window, its contents shattered around him.

An oil-soaked blanket had caught fire. The flame snaked toward him and the scattered chemicals. A broken jar of potash salts lay in its path.

Samuel leaped away from the mess moments before it ignited. The potash salts exploded in a sputtering belch of smoke and sparks. The flying, white-hot cinders touched off more blazes. A canvas on a workbench caught fire, as did the other oil-smeared blankets.

The renewed conflagration spread quickly. The air filled with noxious smoke and chemical vapors. The battle was lost.

Samuel swept the *Dauerrüstung* into its trunk, along with all the materials and notes that he could grab in the seconds that remained to him. Behind him, glass shattered. The room glowed a hellish red as flames spread. Ignoring the pain from his burns, he dragged the trunk to the front door. He half-crawled along the porch and into the yard, finally collapsing onto the trunk in a coughing fit.

At first, he welcomed the crisp night air against his hot skin, but within a minute he started to shiver. Through the windows and the open door, he watched helplessly as the flames destroyed his home and all his worldly possessions.

He was only distantly aware of the fervent clanging of the church bell. He never learned who covered his shoulders with a blanket. The village formed a bucket brigade, but they could only prevent the fire from spreading to the rest of the town. By dawn, little remained of his home but two stone chimneys jutting out like bones from a smoldering heap.

The following day, Samuel stood alone at the Tarrytown dock in the fading sunlight, resisting the temptation to look upriver towards Sleepy Hollow. A selfish part of him wanted nothing more than to return, to bask in Katrina's hospitality one or two more days, and to pretend the events that would unfold were beyond his control.

Instead, he'd returned the *Dauerrüstung*—repaired but nonfunctional without some of the concoctions that had been destroyed in the fire. Then he'd made a deal with the devil himself, in the form of Peter van Brunt.

"I am leaving, Mr. van Brunt," he'd told Peter. "I will leave all to fate, if you promise to do the same. Leave Katrina van Brunt and Miriam Janssen alone; allow Katrina to keep her dower without contest. If you will promise me this, I will leave. You will only hear from me once more, in one year's time, and that will be to deed you every acre of property I inherited from my grandfather, if Mrs. van Brunt vouches that you've kept your promise."

Hours later, the words still tasted like the ash from the fire. Peter had enthusiastically agreed, after swearing that he'd had nothing to do with the inferno that had consumed his home. Samuel tried not to think about why he'd believe a liar's promises.

The air grew chill. Samuel welcomed the discomfort, as it matched his mood. Eventually, he'd have to find a place to stay the night, as the boat wouldn't arrive until after dawn.

He would try and make his way back to Europe. It would be difficult, as he would be near-penniless without his grandfather's land. But even without the *Dauerrüstung*, without admitting that he'd seen Casimir's devices firsthand, he should be able to excel at some laboratory in France or Austria. While he'd regret never being able to see Miriam again, and doubted she'd ever forgive him, he would sleep easier knowing that he'd spared her some degree of misery.

He stared out over the river, now scattering the last purple hues of sunset in its ripples, and tried to convince himself that he was making the right decision. The sound of hoof beats rose behind him. He didn't turn to look, almost hoping it was the ghost of the original wearer of the *Dauerrüstung*, come to take his head. He heard the horse approach him, then stop, and the rider dismount. He turned slowly to face Miriam.

"Mr. Chase, I have come to enquire as to why you are late for supper. And lunch." Miriam's voice was chillier than the evening air.

Samuel couldn't bring himself to look into her face. "I don't think I shall be there for supper, Miss Janssen."

"You'll pardon me if I say that sounds ridiculous, as your own kitchen has burned down. And pardon me further if I say it sounds foolish to be standing so near the water in the cold. And again if I say that it would be even more foolish if you sought passage to New York City, as I've heard report."

Rumors flew faster than hawks in small communities, it seemed. There was no way to flee her wrath now. "I'm sorry, Miriam. I have made a deal with Peter van Brunt. He guarantees your security in exchange for my land and my . . . absence. You and Katrina will be safe from his legal attacks on her property when Brom dies. It is for the best."

Miriam stood in mute silence for several seconds. Samuel didn't dare say anything further, or look directly at her. At length, Miriam turned towards the river and muttered, "I am such a fool."

Samuel once again knew he was saying something stupid, but he didn't know what else to do. "No, of course not. You are the smartest woman I have ever met."

She shook her head. "It's flattering that you say that, but it's a lie. I turned down four offers of marriage. Do you know why?" At Samuel's silence, she continued. "Because they were thoroughly uninspired dullards who saw only my appearance, and assumed that they were my intellectual superiors. They believed that they were more capable of knowing what was good for me than I. I hoped that I would meet someone who actually had a thimbleful of real brains, and would respect me enough to seek my counsel in matters involving our mutual futures. And for these last few weeks, I had stupidly believed that I had found him." She glared at him. "At least those four men were merely uneducated and didn't know better. Even they wouldn't be so stupid as to enter a deal with Peter van Brunt."

Samuel felt as though he were drowning. His noble rationale crumbled before her disappointment. "Please try to understand," he said, mentally grasping at what had seemed clear two hours earlier. "Peter doesn't get the property for a year. He has to prove . . ."

"You try to understand! Peter doesn't need your property. That's secondary to him, and he has enough friends in high places to wrest it from you a piece at a time if he so chooses. He really needs you gone, just like he needed my father gone, and just like he needs Brom gone! Brom knows things that keep Peter in check, and Peter blames you for Brom's continued survival.

"If you leave now, you are making the same mistake as Brom. He thought he could deal with a scorpion to protect us, all those many years ago. It has haunted Brom for half of his life. A scorpion doesn't change its nature for all the promises made to it."

The truth of her words hit him like a physical blow. He turned away from Miriam's harsh gaze. "I think I may have compounded my mistake," he admitted. "I am an idiot."

"At last, we agree upon something!"

"But I gave my word."

"To the man who destroyed your home, and for whom promises mean nothing! You gave us your word first, so who is more worthy of betrayal?"

His thoughts reeling, he finally looked into her eyes and said, "Miriam, come away with me. Let's just flee this place. With Katrina. Perhaps we can all go to visit your family in Germany. Peter's arm is not that long."

Miriam's voice softened. "Katrina will not agree, even after Brom passes. This is her home. Her family turned these forests into farmland when New York City was little more than a distant trading post. She'd rather die than surrender it."

Samuel didn't answer for several moments, and Miriam did not prompt him. He thought he was doing the right and noble thing, but Miriam's words only ignited the sparks of doubt that had smoldered within him for hours.

"I'll stay, if you still want me," he announced. "But I have nothing left. Nothing to offer you. No means to fight Peter."

"Maybe you have a thimbleful of brains after all, and that's something. We need your trust, Samuel. Your trust, and your aid in restoring the armor. I believe Brom has a plan, and I trust him. Can you give us that much?"

"I will give you all that I have, Miriam. It's what I thought I was giving you all along. As grand gestures go, I suppose it was a stupid one."

She reached up and touched his face. "You saw how ruthless Peter can be. You wanted to protect us. Yes, it was a stupid gesture, but I know what it meant."

"I am about to do something else very stupid," Samuel said. And he kissed her. She returned it with equal measure.

Three days later, Samuel and Miriam completed work on the armor.

Samuel had been able to replace some of the materials destroyed in the fire with supplies cannibalized from the Rejuvenator, but there would be no way to refuel either machine afterward.

It didn't matter. Brom could not survive many more hours, inside or outside of the Rejuvenator.

Miriam and Samuel didn't speak as they removed Brom from the machine. They waited in awkward silence, uncertain if he would regain consciousness.

Katrina looked at the young couple and pursed her lips. "I'm not the fragile flower Brom married fifty years ago, you know," she said. "I knew this day was coming and that I would lose him. You can quit trying to protect my feelings. I've seen how you two look at each other, and I can see how you are so careful not to look at each other in my presence. You are allowed to be in love. Now, you two go on upstairs. Brom and I will be along presently."

It was an hour before Katrina and Brom came up to the main hall. Brom clearly looked worse than he had before. His body twitched as he sat himself on one of the great claw-foot chairs.

"Are you ready, sir?" Samuel asked.

"Not just yet," Brom said, his voice weak but determined. "I have a lot to do, and perhaps not much time. But first of all, I want to know your intentions regarding Miriam."

Miriam turned away, feigning disinterest in their conversation. Samuel said, "In her father's absence, I would like to ask your permission to ask for her hand."

Brom nodded. "She's of her own mind on such things. You aren't the first. I'll give you my blessing on one condition. You must tell Miriam and Katrina your secret. But no one else."

"My secret? You mean my grandfather? That's not much of a secret. He's always been Abraham Chase to me. The other name is meaningless."

"To you, yes. But not to them. They are the ones that matter. For everyone else, let the legend endure. They don't need to know that their favorite ghost was just Brom Bones being a hooligan."

"Yes, sir. You have a deal."

"Very well. Miriam?"

She turned and approached Brom, cheeks flushed, eyes glistening. "Yes?"

"I apologize, but I do not have time for a long courtship between you two. This young man wishes to become your husband. Do you accept?"

Miriam suppressed a smile at this indirect proposal, but answered, "Yes. Yes, of course."

"Good. You can handle things more properly in my absence. But this gives me one more task for today, and that is to get you your wedding present."

Miriam shook her head. "Brom, you know you have more important things to do."

"No. It is the most important thing I can do on my last day. Or rather, the second most important. And by far, the most enjoyable. Now, will you help get me inside that contraption?"

They struggled to outfit Brom in the *Dauerrüstung*. He could offer very little assistance on his own. As the last needle entry point was tied down and the final buckle fastened, Brom reached for his cane, then thought better of it. "Please saddle my horse. I have many places to go today."

Samuel and Miriam walked together to the stable to prepare Brom's horse, while Brom tarried with Katrina. Finally, with all ready, he gave his wife of fifty years one last, lingering kiss. Then, with the confidence and strength of a man half his age, he mounted his horse in a single motion.

To Miriam and Samuel, he said, "I commend your handiwork." His voice boomed with confidence and vigor.

"We don't have much time, Brom," said Miriam. "What can we do to help?"

Brom shook his head. "It's messy business. I don't want you to be involved."

"With all due respect, sir," Samuel said, "let us help you make the most of what time you have left."

Brom frowned. After a few moments, he reconsidered. "Very well. For your wedding present, I am giving you my share of our company. If I am successful today, you will not have to worry about Peter being your partner any longer. I just need time to convince some men that it's in their best interest to testify against him."

"Convince?" asked Miriam.

"Convince. Threaten. Promise. Blackmail. There are a few of us here who know where the bodies are buried, but are afraid to speak against Peter individually for fear of repercussions."

"You are speaking figuratively of bodies, of course," Samuel said.

Brom said nothing.

Miriam broke the awkward silence. "Once word of what you are doing reaches Peter, he's going to try to stop you. By any means he can find."

Brom nodded. "My testimony won't be of much value alone, especially not when I am dead."

Samuel said, "I think I know how we can help. We'll meet you in Tarrytown."

Samuel and Miriam loitered in the center of Tarrytown. To all eyes, they appeared a couple courting, enjoying a cool autumn afternoon. Miriam was the first to spy four riders emerge from the road to Sleepy Hollow, led by Brom clad in the black armor, headed toward the constables' office. Time to create a distraction. The two hastened to Van Brunt Industries.

A clerk in the front office asked with a disinterested monotone if Samuel wished to place an order. "Yes, I do," Samuel said, trying to keep his own voice almost as flat as the clerk's to hide his anxiety. "I order you to come with us to the manufacturing floor to show us your processes."

"Uh, what do you mean, Mr. Chase?" the clerk asked.

"I mean come with us and show us around." He stepped to a large door. "We'll start with this room."

"You can't go back there," the clerk said.

Miriam could hold her peace no longer. "No, I'm quite certain we can."

Samuel opened the door, and Miriam walked inside. He looked back at the clerk. "Come along."

The clerk obeyed.

The workshop behind the door genuinely disappointed Samuel. His own humble laboratory had been better equipped, and far better maintained. He expressed his dismay without pretense to the handful of workers operating the equipment.

"What are you doing here?" As Peter stormed into the workroom, red-faced, his carefully maintained composure vanished. "You have gone too far, Samuel Chase. I warned you, and you are going to regret ever setting foot in my town."

Samuel hesitated. "We're conducting an inspection," Miriam prompted.

Samuel nodded. "For a workshop of this size, you should have at least eight fire blankets." At the word, "fire," a rising fury restored his courage. "You are clearly aware of the danger of a fire in a physiochemical workshop."

Peter's face turned purple. After a breath, the older man's mouth curled to a vicious smile. "You can contemplate the ramifications of that fire in your jail cell, Mr. Chase," Peter seethed. "Your trespassing here will not go unpunished!"

"We're not trespassing," Samuel replied. "We represent your partners."

Peter's smile collapsed. "No. No, that's not right. You cannot do this."

"You weren't expecting this?" Miriam demanded. "Did you think that simply because they were personally unavailable that they would never have a delegate protect their interests?"

Peter shook his head furiously. “No. This won’t stand. You’ll be removed, and when the lawyers are done with you, you’ll have nothing left but regrets. I’ll own it all.”

Samuel glared at Peter, turning his own lips into a thin smile. “I’m delighted to get the lawyers involved. I grew up in a family of them—the best in New York. I’m sure it will prove a most enlightening process. In the meantime, why don’t you show us around?”

Peter shouted, “I’m going to get the constable to have you thrown into jail!”

“Yes, please leave,” Miriam agreed. “Take your noisy self off. I need peace and quiet to look over the financials. Brom is concerned about irregularities.”

“Somebody get the constable for me!” Peter bellowed. “Now!”

A workman fled the room. Fuming, Peter monitored Samuel and Miriam while they stared back at him, waiting. Samuel didn’t mind. Their objective had been to distract and delay the man. He hoped it had been enough.

It was almost an hour before the workman returned. “Constable says he’s not coming,” he said.

“Why not?” demanded Peter. “You told him what was happening here?”

“Yes. He was busy meeting with your uncle.”

“He was meeting with Brom? Here?”

“Yes, sir. And some other men.”

“What other men?”

“I don’t know. Men from Sleepy Hollow, I think.”

All color drained from Peter's face. Without casting another look at Miriam and Samuel, he fled the building. By the time they'd followed him outside, Peter had mounted his horse and rode north towards Sleepy Hollow.

"I don't know if he's fleeing or up to something," said Samuel. "We should let Brom and the constable know."

"You go. I mean to secure the financials. They might disappear if we leave them unattended. They need to get used to seeing Luther's daughter in the office, anyway."

"Will you be safe?" asked Samuel.

She nodded. "These men knew my father. And they know Brom. I'll be fine. I'll send them home and lock up behind them. Go."

There was a crowd outside the town offices when Samuel arrived. He pushed his way through curious villagers just as Brom exited the building. Samuel quickly informed Brom of Peter's flight.

"He's too late to stop this, even if he got one of his judge friends to delay and complicate matters," Brom denied. "They have my testimony, and they'll soon have all the rest." He strode towards his waiting horse, and chuckled grimly. "If I don't leave now, I may spend the rest of my life in jail."

"Do you think Peter has time to destroy evidence?" asked Samuel.

Brom shrugged. "I'm more concerned about him following through on his threats. I need to stop him."

"Alone?"

For an answer, Brom mounted his horse. He winced as he did so.

“Something is wrong,” said Samuel.

“It’s just been a long time since I’ve been in the saddle. Aches and pains of an old body.”

“You shouldn’t be able to feel that through the armor. Come down, and I’ll check it.”

“If any of these little bottles are empty, can you refill them?”

“No,” Samuel admitted.

“Then there’s no point in wasting the time. I’ll go as far as I can.” He patted his horse’s neck, and glanced to the west at the fiery ripples of the low sun’s reflection on the Hudson. Then, he leveled his gaze at Samuel and said softly, “We have cleared Miriam’s father of the murder. Her family would love to be here for the wedding.”

Samuel nodded solemnly. Without another word, Brom rode towards Sleepy Hollow.

A new lantern in hand, Samuel set off on foot behind him. Dusk settled around him as he made his way up the road. Before he’d reached the bridge by the old Dutch church, darkness had fully obscured his path, and he resorted to the light. Instead of comforting him, its glow made him feel exposed. The darkness fueled his imagination, transforming every sound into distant, approaching hoof beats of the Galloping Hessian, or Peter in the guise of the same, or Brom Bones in the horseman’s armor returning in triumph. But each time, he was alone on the road.

A gunshot split the silence from the other side of the river, amplified by the featureless night. Samuel hastened across the bridge, slowing only when he heard the sound of hooves on the road before him.

"Brom, is that you? Is all well?" Samuel asked the darkness.

The horse and rider entered the nimbus of his lantern light. Instead of Brom, Peter raised a long pistol and aimed it at Samuel's chest.

"No, I do not think anything will be well for Brom ever again, no matter what sort of concoctions you give him," said Peter. "You planned this all along, didn't you?"

"I don't know what you are talking about."

"You knew Brom's intention. Did he tell you what I promised would happen to his family if he ever went to the authorities with what he knew?"

Samuel said nothing. Peter's smile was feral. "Welcome to the family," he said, cocking back the hammer of his pistol.

"You haven't finished with me, yet," Brom shouted from the darkness outside the lantern's glow.

Peter turned in his saddle, away from Samuel, waving the gun in the direction of Brom's voice.

Samuel threw himself at Peter's arm, pulling the older man off his mount. They hit the cold ground separately. The horse bolted away.

A huge, dark shape lunged out of the shadows. Peter, lying on his back, jerked his gun towards the figure and fired. Flame roared out of the muzzle in a deafening blast. In the next second,

Brom dove on top of the man, and pounded Peter's head with his fists.

"You will never hurt or threaten my family," Brom roared between punches, his wrinkled face twisted in rage. "Never, ever again."

Peter's resistance ceased, but Brom didn't let up. Samuel stepped forward and tried to pull the older man away, but his hands slipped on slick blood coating the armor. Brom halted in mid-blow, and looked towards Samuel. He then ran his fingers across the armor. With a great sigh, he slowly stood, and staggered backwards. Samuel caught and supported him.

Samuel helped Brom sit down next to a tree by the side of the road.

"I'm afraid I've put a hole in your armor, Samuel," Brom said. "I'd hoped to return it undamaged."

Samuel shook his head, and kneeled beside him. "It's nothing. I'm sure I can repair it."

"You weren't supposed to try and protect me. It's not like another ball would have made a difference."

"I couldn't help it."

Brom nodded. "I believe that. You are a good man. Miriam chose well." He looked down at his blood. "I've not always been a good man. I've done some things I've not been proud of."

"Like scaring my grandfather?"

Brom's somber expression broke into the hint of a smile. "No. I admit, I was always a little proud of that one." He made a weak coughing sound. "You and Miriam will do great things, and have a good life together. As for me, I'm beyond mortal justice now." He glanced at Peter's motionless body. "But he's not." He winced, and his breathing became labored. "My chest . . . it hurts."

"Is there anything I can do?"

Brom winced. "You did. You gave me one last, good day. That's over. I think my heart is trying to die, and your suit is trying to fight it."

"It's not my suit."

"It is now." He winced again, trying to speak through the pain. "Take care of them."

"I will. I promise."

Brom nodded. "You figure the rest out. You're smart. So is Miriam." He hissed through gritted teeth. "Done talking. 'Bye."

"Goodbye." Samuel never knew if Brom heard him.

He'd only known Brom a few days and couldn't understand why the night felt darker and colder at the moment of the old man's passing, nor why he had to blink away its chill sting. He hardly noticed when Constable Franklin and several men from the village crossed the bridge behind him. They'd come to arrest both of the Van Brunt men, but Brom Bones had departed Sleepy Hollow forever.

Styled after *The Legend of Sleepy Hollow* by Washington Irving

Invested Charm

M. IRISH GARDNER

A Charm invests a face
Imperfectly beheld—
The Lady dare not lift her Veil
For fear it be dispelled.
But peers beyond her mesh,
And wishes, and denies—
Lest interview annul a want
That Image satisfies.
—Emily Dickinson, 1891

I never thought my girlhood days on the Amherst apple farm would lead to parties among the Boston elite. The Brahmins, they called themselves. The influential. The blue-bloods with their own way of speaking the same words with the same meanings, but not the same worth.

Their clothing, the finest from France. Their furniture, all from Italy or Spain. Their households operated with the most up-to-date inventions designed and manufactured by my uncle,

Waldo Rigby. He wasn't Brahmin. But he wasn't not one, either. The wealthy took his mechanical creations under their wings and he often followed in a consequential wake.

My uncle had fashioned new ideas since before I was born. When he and my father were boys, a homemade brass cricket held their interest for hours on end. Its magnifying-glass thorax would burn from the sun's rays and trigger a tiny spark and explosion into its legs. A hop every three minutes.

That was the only product I ever understood. Uncle Wally explained it to me once and displayed the bug's shiny, intricate guts, still cared for after so many years. After that, I could only witness the results of creations without knowing how they accomplished their purpose.

But I didn't need to know. More often than not, I didn't want to know. My face held enough unnatural handiwork to satisfy my curiosity for too many lifetimes.

They called me lucky when I survived that cursed night. The night when the center of Hades broke loose and swallowed up my mother, my father, and my little sister, Ruth. I was only fourteen, and though I think I remember it well, I have come to understand the impossibilities within those memories.

For now, I'll only speak of the outcome.

Starting at my hairline, just above my temple, and jaggedly edging below my right eye, over to my nose, and comprising half my mouth . . . is an internal mask of machinery. It parades uncovered down to my chin, along the right half of my neck, and stops just below my collar bone. It whirs a little, but otherwise emits no sound. With all the gadgets and joints, I would have thought some cranking and clacking would be a constant part of my existence, but my uncle has spent years recalibrating his personal Mona Lisa.

Without it, I would die. My face would return to its collapsed state and I would either suffocate or starve.

With it, my ability to manipulate future events is enhanced.

In Amherst, when I was just a small child, my forecasts were simple. Obvious. Events are subject to laws—just as objects are, according to Mr. Newton. An action in a state of uniform motion tends to remain in that state, unless acted upon by an external force. The same can be said for a sequence of actions. All have a natural order about them. My rapid calculations allowed for a measure of prediction. But that was only when I was little.

As I matured, my ability advanced. I learned to discern a person's aura, especially a man's—not of his personality, but of his soul—and with that knowledge, I could bend the natural order. I could will it in a new direction as long as I aimed the individual the right way first.

My mother warned me about abuse of the power. She, an itinerant French Romani—a Tsiganes—understood it all too well. The blood of all her female ancestors ran thick in my veins. I took her seriously and showed great discipline.

After the accident, however, my mental dexterity reached its potential, and a new opportunity presented itself within Boston's upper crust. I moved in with my uncle, and my constant veiling caused secret whispers in gentlemen's clubs. Uncle Wally knew of my talents and helped generate the gossip where it would be most effective.

For, during that time, a growing problem plagued the city. A single man, Duilio Falco, with his mastery of beguiling minds, controlled more than half the police force and vulnerable businesses. A cloak of wealth and influence portrayed many sinners as saints, and that was where my uncle and I would find many of Falco's minions.

It wasn't long before we gained access to their circles and worked against the crumbling system. Only a select few ever saw my face. I found that it came with its own curse—if seen during one of my readings, it would seal a negative fate, even if I had just prescribed a redeeming one.

Thus, my uncle and I agreed to keep me hidden from society. Brahmins knew to contact him to arrange a meeting. I was kept relatively safe, despite the heavy blows I delivered regularly. Those doomed by my divination did not survive long and never had a chance to expose me. Those blessed by the same curse within me would know victory and never felt the need. Both paid a hefty coin for what they initially considered a fine amusement.

"I do believe I am next, Charlie. But if you care to go first, be my guest."

I could hear the exchange between two gentlemen outside the darkened study.

"Please, Robert. I am certain you are correct. After you."

The door cracked open, allowing a pillar of light to enter the room. The shadow of a man slipped across the threshold and the door gently closed behind him.

His eyes would adjust in a moment or so. My table in the corner was blocked from immediate view by a tall burgundy curtain, but a single gas lamp sat on my table emitted a soft glow.

I heard his boots clack against the hardwood floor as he approached. My stomach grew taut and my fingernails pressed into my palms with anticipation.

"Madame Mauve, I presume?" He poked his face around the drapery and raised his eyebrows.

"Come," I said gently and extended my gloved hand. "Sit with me, Robert Bartlad, and I shall show you wonders."

His eyes already searched my figure, analyzing what *wonders* resided beneath my black silk and lace gown. He would never know. No one would, I was certain.

He sat in the chair across the small table from me and took my proffered hand.

"Hmm. You are not the man you say you are."

He stiffened but said nothing.

Tracing my fingers across his palm, I stared into his eyes. "You portray a falsehood. On the outside, you are generous and mild, but on the inside, your heart is greedy and vicious. Deception is your game. Manipulation, scheming. All merriment to one so distorted as you." I leaned closer and whispered my words. "Especially when men's lives are playthings for your pleasure. You thrill in exacting an innocent's reckoning by spilling their blood, don't you?"

His head cocked back in surprise. Those deep azure eyes shadowed. "Of what do you speak? You have no proof of this slander!" He glanced around in the darkness. "Who is there? What sort of game is this?" He tried to let go of my hand, but I held tight.

"You, demon who calls yourself Robert Bartlad, reek of deceit and betrayal. You frolic amid the powerful, but you reside with the weak and desperate. I can feel how your merciless thumb is pressed down upon those lower than you."

He pulled his hand again, but the effort was that of an aged man. His eyes welled with tears of anger. It always happened that way. And that quickly.

"You want to know your fortune? Your future? You thought this only a sport when you first came to this evening's festivities, but know this and know I jest not: death will come swiftly and soon. That angel who regulates the passing of souls will administer the same fate to which you damn others. Yet . . ." I paused. Narrowing my eyes at him through my veil, I caught an important shift in his aura. The soul-fire which had fed his deeds over the greater part of his life had left his eyes. But that did not alter his sentence.

"You will do the act yourself, won't you? No shame enters your heart; nonetheless, you know your days of afflicting horror are complete. No more fun to be had, is there? And *you* will end it, not to rehabilitate honor, but because you cannot live without your sickness."

I released his hand.

"Do you wish to die, Mr. Bartlad?"

He only blinked in response.

"I didn't think so. You may lose the resolve. The courage. Let me help you stay the course." I brought my hands to my veil and slowly lifted it, tucking it into place upon my miniature feathered top hat.

His focus grew abnormally sharp and his eyes painfully wide. His chest no longer brought air into his lungs. His chin quivered.

I grinned, knowing I was lipless on the right side of my face, my teeth and gums fully exposed.

I lurched forward and put my hands on the edge of the table. "You will be haunted by this image until the end of your days! Abandon your existence and your ill-gotten gains, and escape what surely awaits you if you don't!" I jabbed a finger at my face and huffed a breath which made steam burst out of the spinning gears in my cheek.

He scrambled backward and tipped over his chair. Rolling out of the burgundy enclosure, he tore out of the room and didn't slow down through the crowd of gentlemen waiting. I could hear the host calling after him, but a few moments later, the slam of the front door confirmed my feelings. The wicked had gone.

My plastered-on smile left my face and I returned the veil to its rightful position.

I heard the gentlemen whispering outside the door. What had happened to their friend? Why had he left in such a state? I felt their nerves heighten and agitate. That was never good for business, but there wasn't much I could do. What must be done, must be done.

After another two minutes, a braver man entered the arena, though with caution.

"Madame Mauve? Are you here?" Charles Vanderhook whispered after he had closed the door behind him.

"Indeed, sir. Follow the light and you shall find your way."

He bumped into a side table as he walked in the darkness, but finally rounded the corner and smiled timidly at me. "Hello, Madame."

"Hello, Charlie. Please, sit, and I shall show you wonders."

He nodded, righted Mr. Bartlad's chair, and sat down on the edge of his seat.

"Take my hand, Charlie Vanderhook."

He obeyed, and at his touch, I inhaled earthy, cool, autumn air—the scent of tired blossoms, salty sea, and soil—and could envision the changing leaves that lived right outside the covered window.

I released a slow exhale, careful not to create steam, and smiled. Even though the innocent men could not see my smile beneath the veil, they would hear it in my voice.

"It has not always been easy, has it, Charlie?"

"I beg pardon, Madame?"

"The choices. The pressure to sink while simultaneously soaring. Yet the difficulty of denying yourself the temptation never caused you to succumb. Such men as you are few and far between."

"I-I'm not sure I—"

"The strength of your resolution comes from deep within and cannot be tainted. You focus not on religion or law to guide your way, but the ethical moralities which logic demonstrates every day. You know what guarantees sorrow, and what feeds happiness, don't you?"

He shook his head. "You speak so strangely, and still I feel I understand"—he touched his chest—"in here."

I nodded. "Yes. Your soul speaks to you and you listen. That is what has made you the man you are today . . . and what saves you for your future." I leaned forward. "Charlie Vanderhook, tomorrow is your day. You will find the key to the happiness you seek. It will shine brighter than all else around and it will whisper your name. Embrace it. Live it. And share it with others. That is your fortune. That is your destiny."

He stared at me intensely. I knew what would come next.

"I believe you, Madame Mauve. I don't know why, but I do. And . . ." He trailed off. They also had a tendency to do that.

He reached his other hand up slowly. "Your voice is so strong yet delicate. Your words have rent me in two. May I gaze upon the face which has granted me freedom this night and caused such a stirring in my breast?" His fingers touched the bottom of my veil.

"If you see me, Charlie," I whispered, "the charm will be annulled."

He paused.

"Wager for now or live for tomorrow?"

His breaths came in short puffs. He bit his lip in consideration, but finally dropped his hand.

I relaxed my tensed shoulders. "Go to your men. Enjoy your evening, for tomorrow, you will see."

He frowned, nodded, and stood up. "Goodnight, Madame."

I waved him away. After only two readings, I was finished. Exhausted. "Uncle Wally, I'm done for tonight."

"They're always harder when so opposite, aren't they? You must feel completely bounced around inside." He emerged from the shadows and leaned on his cane. I wondered if his bad leg was bothering him.

I eased out of my chair despite my wobbly legs and walked to the door. "How many will we miss tonight?" Peering through the tiny crack, I saw a disorganized line of at least half a dozen more gentlemen ready to hear their destiny. They seemed to all be enjoying a good lark and had little idea of the seriousness of their chosen entertainment.

"None that we can't secure another evening, my dear." My uncle wrapped a shawl around my shoulders. "We can only do what we are able."

I nodded but was distracted. A man stood separate from the small groups of gentlemen. He was dressed less extravagantly than the Brahmin boys, but he still caught my eye. In his hands, he held an intricate apparatus which he inspected thoroughly—a metallic puzzle of sorts, perhaps with origins from Lemarchand's design.

Suddenly, the box popped open. The man smiled. Growing obviously conscious of his surroundings, he quickly put the contraption back together and placed it on the mantle behind him.

"Who is that man, Uncle?"

I gave him room to peer through the crack. "Ah, Inspector Warrick. He's new in town. Or relatively so. He's climbing the ranks quickly, I understand."

The name sounded only vaguely familiar, though I sensed my uncle's worry. "You wonder why a man like him is at a function such as this?"

Uncle Wally huffed out a laugh. "None of that with me, my dear. Come, let us tidy up and be on our way." He propped his cane against his hip as he began undoing the enclosure.

I sighed. "These young ones always need to get a few diversions out of their system before they become their staunch, discreet parents. If I were another lady, I would wonder if perchance the wicked could eventually change their ways. But I am who I am, and I know they will not."

"Undoubtedly, Mauve. Were these men mercilessly checked in their ways by the good ol' boys of law enforcement, perhaps an opportunity could arise to stimulate change. Yet, you know as well as I that Duilio Falco has nearly every officer in his pocket. And these stagnant stones would gather all the moss of the forest without your intervention.

I nodded my head at my uncle's words. What I would give to pour a little accelerant on Mr. Falco's fate. Such an act as that, however, would possibly destroy me. After even the smaller fish of that evening, I was drained. There was a reason we limited my readings to the naughty young bucks of society rather than the hardened devils from hell.

I peeked again at Inspector Warrick. So young for his position on the force. His ebony hair and eyebrows seemed to pull light from the room in their depths. Yet, his eyes were the warm grey of approaching clouds. Elusive memories tugged at my mind.

He glanced up and I pulled back from the door. It was time to depart.

After packing away our belongings, we found our way through the house to the servant's entrance, never once encountering a single guest. The contract guaranteed it. I would not associate with any person outside of my readings.

My uncle settled me into the awaiting AirRidge, his latest twist on an antiquated transportation method, and went back into the Federal-style home to collect his fee. I peered out the window at the moonlit city.

Who was I fooling? The moon may have been somewhere in the sky, but the light permeated from artificial sources—flames and gasses and steam out of this orifice or that. The city never retired for the night and I had not seen a star since I was fourteen.

A fleeting memory haunted me from my days on the apple farm. As a bit of a wild child, I would sneak out on summer nights to lounge in the center of the orchard, where a large clearing lay. No tree would grow there, for some reason, despite all the efforts of my father's ancestors. I would snuggle into the tall grass and study the expanse of the sky. Even the neighbor boy would join me on occasion.

Abel Bronson.

I say 'neighbor,' but he lived two miles down the old dirt road. Of course, that didn't stop him from waiting until his mother was asleep to dash away and see the stars with me. He seemed to always show up just when I wanted him to.

When we were little, we only ever talked and laughed and played games in the dark. As we grew up, we fell into a comfortable silence under those twinkling stars and let our fingers gently tangle together.

Sure, we would play during the day, jumping in the swimming hole, or hunting rabbits in the orchard, but it was nights with him that etched themselves upon my mind.

I hadn't experienced anything like that since then.

But those days were far away and it is useless to relive what cannot be. My family was gone and stars fade into the background when in competition with synthetic brilliance.

My uncle returned and we headed home, he likely already half-asleep, and I prepared for another fitful night's rest.

"You better get shakin', Mauve Rigby, if you're to eat your breakfast before lunchtime."

Rebecca pulled the window coverings back to reveal a sunless, disconsolate day. I moaned. For only having twenty-two years on my bones, I could not believe how ancient I felt.

I stretched and received a toe cramp for my efforts. "Lud, that hurts!" Sitting up, I quickly massaged it. Then I noticed pieces of my hair had escaped my plait and gotten stuck in my gears. Thankfully, not the ones protecting my mouth.

I eased the strays out and asked Rebecca to bring me my veil.

"But it's just me, child. You're so beautiful without it."

I cocked my head at her and glared. "I'd trade you in a heartbeat."

She just shook her head and made me perform my morning rituals before providing my security blanket. Once again, it was black.

Three firm knocks sounded on my uncle's front door, heard from three floors up. Ours was a tall and slender building squished between two quaint businesses—a laundry facility which used pleasantly scented soaps, and a bookstore to which I had an unhealthy attraction.

Before our butler could open the copper door, the three knocks sounded again, more furtively than before.

Something was wrong. I could feel it. I stilled Rebecca's fussing hands and went to open my bedroom door to listen down the spiral staircase.

"Inspector Warrick for Mr. Rigby, please."

Our butler closed the door after the man entered. He walked into the study, and a moment later, Uncle Wally's voice and uneven gait echoed in the entryway. "Ah, Warrick! Nice to see you again, sir! Please, come in."

"Thank you, Mr. Rigby, I—"

"Oh, call me Wally. How have you been? I haven't seen you since worship services last week! On any interesting cases?" They entered the study, but the door remained open.

"That's actually why I'm here . . . Wally. Have you seen the papers this morning?"

I eased around the banister and descended the stairs to the second level to eavesdrop.

"I have," he responded. "Nasty bit of business, that."

"The pictures hardly do it justice. Mr. Bartlad was found at four a.m. when the baker went to start up his Bake-O-Matic. One of your designs, I believe."

"Indeed! Yes, crafty little thing! You simply put in your ingredients and out comes whatever you pre-select!"

"Well, it seems Mr. Bartlad decided to season this morning's pastries."

There was a brief pause. "Right," said Uncle Wally. "Inspector, what can I do to help?"

"Mr. Bartlad was last seen at the Cabots' last night. I believe you were there, correct?"

"Yes! I provided some diversions for the gentlemen."

"If you say so," Warrick said. "I personally do not understand the draw. Seems a tad crooked. She is your relative, is she not? Is this exploitation what she wishes?"

I grew uncomfortable. Warrick's contempt wafted through the air.

My uncle took his time to respond. "She is a grown woman with her own choices to make. Is there something specific you need, or can I show you the door?"

"I am interviewing everyone that was there last night. If she is truly free to decide, please let her know I'll expect her at my house on Square Street at seven this evening . . . unless you think she'd oblige me by meeting at the station."

Silence ensued. I inched down the second set of stairs to the ground floor and hid around the bend in the hallway.

"No? Then if she refuses to show, I'll know to investigate the both of you further. Good day, Mr. Rigby. I'll see myself out."

I peeked around the corner as he strode determinedly out of the study and toward the front door. The shift of my position caused a squeak in the floorboards, and Inspector Warrick paused.

For a frozen moment, he glanced over his shoulder toward me. His silhouetted profile contrasted against the overcast light from the door's window. My pulse raced with apprehension. If he discovered me and confronted me then and there, I would surely buckle under those persuasive eyes and confess all my dark deeds. Why did his emanation feel so familiar, so powerful, to me? I would need to fortify my defenses to face him that evening.

He finally turned and exited, closing the door behind him.

I exhaled and stepped out.

"Not to worry, my dear Mauve," my uncle said as he joined me in the hall. "You won't need to see him."

"Are you sure that's the best course of action, Uncle? His suspicions will only heighten at such behavior. Besides, what harm can there be? I was not the one to push Bartlad into your machine. No one was. He did it himself."

He narrowed his eyes at my reckless attitude. “Likely safe to assume. But what will you say to the inspector? What if he interrogates you on your craft? Or demands you expose your face? What then?”

“Then disaster would befall him, as with the others, and our worries would again be over.”

He bit his cheek, mulling over his thoughts. “I believe Inspector Warrick has done a great deal of investigating already. You feel confident there is nothing to worry about?”

I hesitated for a fraction of a second, and I’m sure he noticed, but I replied, “I don’t know that we have any other choice.”

I needed fresh air, and a chance to think before my meeting with the inspector. Toward the afternoon, I grabbed my old parasol, headed down to the cellar, and dashed into the tunnel leading downtown. I always left a lantern and matches at the entrance so my way would be lit. It was only a quarter mile to the Old South Meeting House, and the rumbling of machinery and locomotives overhead allowed my mind to cover all sorts of possibilities regarding that night’s clandestine meeting. What returned over and over: might Inspector Warrick ask of me something that may cause his demise?

The rain continued to fall as I exited a railway station a block away from the red brick building with a world of history—a place I went often to collect my thoughts. I opened my parasol but soon discovered a few leaks. It must have been years since I’d ventured out during a downpour. The curls in my hair slowly lowered with the weight of water. It was better than nothing, I supposed.

Hurrying down Washington Street, I noticed a woman on the opposite sidewalk. She stood out as a beam of light from a gap in the clouds dropped down upon her. Her angelic appearance stopped me in my tracks. I stared as she tried to avoid the rain by ducking underneath the baker's canopy—the same store which had received an unexpected fatality during the night. She tried the door handle, but with Bartlad's death, the shop would have been closed up until after the investigation.

A man barreled down the sidewalk in her direction with a newspaper over his head. Not looking much past the front of his nose, he almost ran straight into her. At the last second, the woman called his name just as the beam of light grew brightest.

He skidded to a stop only inches in front of her. From my distance and the pound of rain, I could not make out any sounds, but I didn't think they spoke anyway.

They stared into each other's eyes and I suddenly felt like an intruder. The beam of light vanished, and the man shivered. Regardless, he took off his hat and placed it on her head with a smile.

It was Charlie Vanderhook, and I then recognized the woman. A young widow with a sizeable fortune left behind by her late husband. She smiled up at Charlie who deftly removed his overcoat and held it over her as protection from the rain.

They slowly walked away from the bakery, he with a bit of life in his step, and she leaning into his warmth.

By then, I was drenched. I cared not, for I rarely witnessed the fulfilment of my charms, but there was no way I could enter Old South in such condition. Starting to feel a chill, I returned the way I came until I reached the underground railway entrance.

My intuition alerted. Something inky black called within the hollow void. Its poison sank in my core. I adjusted my hat, veil, and dress, and grabbed the lantern. I never avoided such encounters. They were an integral part of my life.

After thirty yards or so, a man stepped out of the shadows along the side of the tunnel and into the light of my lantern.

"You'll not get away with what you said to me, Madame Mauve. Remember me? Lucas Duran?" He removed his top hat, which I could see had deteriorated after a week exposed to the elements. I wondered if he had been home since my reading four days before.

"I can't say you made a strong enough impression upon me to be remembered, sir, but I do know whatever I said to you is true and your condemnation shall find you."

He sneered. "You think you can just deal whatever hands tickle your fancy without consequence? I've been driven mad over the past few days simply because of some witch's words spoken to me in a dark room! And I'm certain the face I saw was concocted of my own imagination! It's not possible! I will not live my life in fear at the hand of a deranged woman!"

I sighed. "Then why do you cower beneath the city?"

"Because I've been lookin' for you. I heard tell that you make your way 'round this city underground. Not surprising for the rat that you are. You told me the first man to see my face would grant me an exit out of this world! What a ridiculous notion! I'm done hiding, mark my words, but not without punishing you first!"

He came toward me at a run. I braced myself but did not shrink away from his charge. Before he crashed into me, I heard a noise to my right, and Lucas suddenly disappeared from in front of me, taking out my lantern in the process.

Two bodies landed hard against the rounded brick walls. Muffled words were grunted back and forth. One of them gained the upper hand.

I heard a knife unsheathed and heavy breathing. "I don't know who the hell you think you are, Mister, but now you're gonna die, too." Lucas lunged forward. The two collided and I widened my eyes to detect their movements in the dark, to no avail. The struggle continued, one man rolling into a superior position atop the other. Finally, after grunts and growls, a yowl escaped from one of the men as the knife plunged into the wetness of his body.

Then nothing.

There was no sound except the heavy breathing of the survivor. My own was stopped within my breast. The winner struggled out of the dead man's embrace and stood up.

"Mau—" he started but then cleared his throat. "Madame Mauve?"

"Is that you, Inspector?"

He grunted and I heard him come closer, enough that should I extend my hand, I might touch him. His chest still heaved from his struggle.

"Did you even *try* to tell him you were the police? Maybe he would have surrendered."

Warrick chuckled darkly. "I told him several times, but his arm was around my throat."

"Well, I thank you, I suppose—for stopping Mr. Duran. I think he intended my demise."

"And why would a man be driven to such extremes because of your words, Madame? Is that all you do in those dimly lit rooms with them?"

I touched my hand to my veil. "I'm not certain what you imply by your question, but I provide a very straightforward service, Inspector. Forgive me, but were you following me?"

"It is my duty to inspect and investigate. Should that come as a surprise? And please, call me Abel."

I stiffened. The fine hairs on my neck prickled. There must be thousands of Abels in Massachusetts. I shook my head. Purely coincidence. Either way, I couldn't think what to say. And it suddenly became painfully apparent that I was standing in the dark, soaking wet, surrounded by dash-fire, and a dead body *sur le côté*.

"Forgive me, Inspector. I believe shock is setting in. I need to return home."

"I would be honored to escort you," he said, knowing his chances were slim. "You never know what type of fellow you might meet in an underground tunnel."

I sensed it then. He was neither innocent nor malicious. He had committed wrongs in his life, most definitely, but their necessity was born from the greater good. And though few, his heroic choices redeemed the guilt and frustration retained by living on the border of good and evil.

My insides buzzed and I failed to squelch them. Reaching my gloved hand up, I found his face and touched his scruffy cheek. "You will leave the way you came, and I shall keep my appointment this evening. Ask me what you will then." I dropped my hand and walked past him further into the tunnel.

I heard his boots crunch the gravel as he strode away from me. He couldn't be *the* Abel. Different last names, and yet . . .

It had seemed impertinent that he ask me to call him by his given name. Especially since I appeared worthy enough a suspect to be followed. He wanted me to know it. He knew the significance. But that was impossible.

I cursed his name for reminding me of better times.

The cleansing rain ceased for a few hours while I washed up and rested at home. At a quarter before six, Uncle Wally entered the library to find me curled up in the window seat with *Le Comte de Monte-Cristo*, desperate to escape my thoughts until necessity forced me to face them.

"There you are, my dear." He sat down next to my feet and released an exhale. "I don't quite know what to make of it, Mauve, but I received a note from Warrick, and he insists you come alone this evening. I can hardly find reason for him to expect a young woman would allow such an impropriety."

I tilted my head. "He has no hard evidence to prove that I *am* a young woman, with a protected reputation, or otherwise. It's simply another test. I am in no danger from him or any man. Any glance at my true appearance"—I gestured at my exposed face—"and they would have to be off their chump to lay a single hand on me."

My uncle gently patted my foot. "You are too hard on yourself. You have a unique beauty, it is true, but I take pride in the design and know the craftsmanship only enhances what is already there. It adds to your strength. It provides your vitality. That *must* resemble some sort of beauty."

I smiled. "Thank you, Uncle. That is true, and I shall never be able to repay your kindness for saving my life."

A shadow flitted across his brow. "Mauve."

His voice shifted. I examined his features with a renewed awareness. "Uncle Wally, what is the matter?"

"The time has come," he said, staring out the window. "You will perform my reading before you visit Warrick."

I frowned. "But you have never allowed it before. You said—"

"I know what I said. Reading family is always dangerous, simply because you can't erase what you see. However, secrets may soon be revealed whether or not I wish them so. And they need to come from me."

I blinked several times at him. "Secrets?"

He stoically stared back. Finally, he held out his bare hand. I swallowed the lump in my throat and searched his face. I trusted him, didn't I? Whatever he hid, it couldn't be as horrific as his expression indicated.

I reached out my lace-gloved hand and took his palm in mine.

The energy jolted through my veins, into my heart, and vibrated there with an unsettling force. And then my inner eye opened.

I stood in the past, before my childhood home, seeing my front porch through my uncle's eyes. I wavered. I felt intoxicated. I could taste the alcohol on my tongue.

"Éloïse!" I screamed, though through my uncle's voice. I staggered forward to the front door, the bottle of whiskey swinging in my hand and calling her name.

"Lo-Lo!" I shouted again, but I couldn't see very well. The moonlight, blocked by the cover of the porch, hid itself from my shameful cries.

The very moment I had entered my uncle's past, I understood. The history between my mother and him ran deep. Acting on her instinctive roaming ways, she teased both brothers endlessly, never fully satisfied with either. My uncle had come to convince her of his love.

I fumbled with the matchbook in my coat pocket. I simply needed to see more clearly. Perhaps I would write a note. Oh. No paper. Perhaps I could pick the lock on the door. I pulled out the matchbook. Although my present view could see the error in thinking, my uncle's aspect could not.

I lit the match with the same hand holding the almost empty bottle of whiskey. Even expecting it, the burst of light in my hand surprised me. I tumbled back at the explosion, instantly grateful the majority of alcohol was inside me. But from my position on my back, I watched the porch and wall light up with a hungry flame.

I scrambled backward like a crab but lost my strength at the steps and rolled down the majority, finally smacking my head on the stone walkway.

The blackness lasted an eternity. My uncle had knocked himself senseless while my house burned to the ground with my family, and myself, inside.

Finally, I felt roused by shaking. I didn't want to open my eyes, but some pressing remembrance told me I should.

I split my eyelids open and saw a young boy's face shouting at me. His ebony curls bounced with his gesturing and yelling, his grey eyes and rosy cheeks lit by an orange glow nearby. Intense pain in my leg yanked away my attention. I glanced down. Pieces of my whiskey bottle were imbedded through my pants, into my shin. It didn't hurt as much as it should have.

And then I saw her. My beloved Mauve. I saw her, laying in the grass, her face completely bashed in on one side. Adrenaline blew through my body and I leapt up, scooped up the boy, who screamed with pain and had a warm wetness across his middle, and grabbed onto Mauve, taking both directly to my restless horses and waiting carriage under the big oak tree.

I pulled my hand away from Uncle Wally's, my breathing ragged and shallow. I shot out of the window seat and stumbled back. "It was you?"

Tears streamed down his face, but he did not look away.

"My family! They're all dead because of you?" I screamed, wishing it wasn't true. He nodded his head and then covered his face with his hands. His shoulders shook, and all the anger came flooding through me. His pitiful sorrow, the apologies on his face, the sacrifices he had made over all the years . . . all resulting from the type of action a villain takes. *He* was the evil one. He killed my family! *He* should have been the one to receive my fortune. In all my fury, I took a step forward to deliver it, but something stopped me.

Those grey eyes. The desperation. The young boy who begged God to save me, even as he screamed in pain himself.

I had to know. I spun around and charged out of the room, down the stairs, grabbed the AirRidge key on the entry table, and ran out the door.

The cold night air whipped around my face as I stood on Inspector Warrick's doorstep. The wind chilled the path my tears had taken beneath my shroud, and I wiped them away again. I forced myself to bridle the emotions trying to take the reins, and knocked twice.

He answered his own door. "Madame Mauve, I am glad you are a woman of your word." He opened the door widely and gestured for me to pass. I held my chin up, allowing pride to rule my feelings. This man suspected my involvement in the death of many men. I could not fall prey to my emotions while under such scrutiny, regardless of my curiosity of his own past.

"Please, come this way." Warrick led me down the black-and-white tiled hallway and into a shadowy room. A fire in the hearth was on its way to obscurity, but it was comfortable, and I didn't mind the dark. It was a familiar companion.

"Would you like anything to drink? I make a terrible cup of tea. Or I have brandy?"

I shook my head. "No, thank you, Inspector. I prefer to just get on with it."

A smirk appeared on his devilishly handsome face. I suddenly had the odd realization that even if I smiled completely, it would only ever appear like a one-sided lift of the lips. The other side unimaginable.

"Already lost in thought?" he asked. "What do you think of?"

I glanced up. "Ah, nothing of consequence." He seemed to be stalling. "How can I help you, sir? I thank you again for helping me this afternoon, but I feel no obligation to you. Ask me your questions and let me be on my way."

He watched me carefully from his hutch as he poured himself a drink. "If you insist." The inspector finally crossed the room and sat in the wing-backed chair in front of me. "You see, I have a bit of a dilemma. Men are dying in this city, and even though the desolate and destitute ones do every day, no one cares about them. But many people care about the wealthy and superior ones. A despicable problem, if you ask me. However, in the last two years alone, we have had eleven deaths within the influential levels of society."

I decided I had better sit down on the sofa just behind me.

"People are beginning to talk," he continued. "Granted the cases have all been solved—suicides, accidents, or random murders—but they each have an interesting aspect to them. As a greenhorn a few years ago, I began investigating these closed cases, examining the types of lives these men led. While Good Samaritans on the outside, many had intricate webs of corruption spun beneath their layers of innocence."

I wished I had asked for a drink. A stiff one would have been great right about then.

"And then last night, I was keeping my eye on one Mr. Robert Bartlad, who had caused some nasty situations over the past few months, and to my surprise, something upset him while he was in the room with you."

Warrick stood up, walked over to the fireplace, and rested his drink on the mantle. He shoved his hands in his pockets and faced me. "My men outside knew to follow him if he left the gathering, so I was able to stay behind and see what happened next.

"When Charlie Vanderhook stepped out, I expected to see the same reaction. This was a man I knew to be in a troublesome position. He was under a great deal of pressure from some bank men, and my men reported he had been repeatedly approached about a Falco speculation scheme of one sort or another.

"While at the Cabots', I assumed he had already fallen into their trap. Thus you can imagine my surprise at seeing his smiling face as he left your presence, sure as I was of his guilt. But my lieutenant confirmed this morning that Charlie had again turned them down long before the party."

The inspector rubbed a hand through his thick curly hair and returned to his chair. "You must understand that I know what you do. It's quite simple, really." He leaned closer to me with his elbow resting on the armrest. "You see men for who they truly are, and it's quite terrifying if that exposes them to the truth of their vicious actions, but rather empowering if it opens their eyes to the possibilities of life."

"Inspector Warrick, you do go on at length. Is there a question in there somewhere?"

"Most definitely," he said. "But first, I wish for you to provide me with a reading."

"I'd rather not, sir."

"And why is that?"

My memories grew bright with my uncle's devastating mistake. Did I truly wish to know the truth . . . of anyone's past? The truth did not always accompany a solution. With the men under Falco's thumb, it was easy. I was not connected with them. It was different with my uncle. I breathed deeply, causing the whirring in my cheek to increase.

Warrick's brow furrowed. "What is that?"

"I think it is time I leave," I said, standing up. "You have yet to ask me anything of pertinence; instead you talk nonsense about my entertainment, for that is all it is. I—"

"Then why won't you do it for me?" Warrick stood up and gripped my arms.

"Be-because I don't know you, sir!"

"You knew Vanderhook? And Bartlad? What if I *want* you to know me?" He dropped his hands. "Do you think me unworthy of your talent? It is true; my blood cannot compete with the Lowells or the Saltonstalls, but I would not have thought you as snobbishly discriminating as that."

The insult was surely delivered with the intent to make me cave in to his commands, but my scrambled mind wouldn't formulate coherent thoughts. My chin quivered. Tears threatened. Why was I afraid to read him? I had never been so confused before. Everything had always been so easy—as black and white as Warrick's tile.

I took a few steps back. "You don't deserve what I offer, Inspector. I mean that in the most respectful way. You are not Robert Bartlad. Nor are you Charlie Vanderhook. I've never read a more complicated man in all my life."

He stepped forward. "You are reading me now?"

"No, it doesn't work that way. I reached that conclusion based on previous interactions with you."

He glanced down at my clenched fists. "Is the connection by choice?"

I knew his thoughts without difficulty. He contemplated touching me without my permission, to force a reading. "I'm leaving. This interview is over. I'm sorry I cannot help you with your investigation." I walked past him into the hallway toward the entryway. I put on my coat and gloves and opened the door. He stayed in the study and didn't try to stop me.

The visit hadn't gone anything like I had hoped. Or feared.

I slammed the door shut and stalked out to the AirRidge. Sliding inside, I started the powerful engine, revving it to fight the cold air. Warrick suddenly slipped into the passenger seat. I bit down on a yelp of surprise, and instead, offered a glare which he could not see.

He held his hands up in surrender. "I'm sorry. This has all gone completely wrong. I intended a very different experience tonight, but I think my nerves got to me."

I tamed my expression a bit. "It's not all your fault, trust me."

He searched my veiled face for a moment, and then said, "I want to show you something."

Grateful for the barrier between his sensual eyes and my vulnerable ones, I turned off the vehicle. "Fine."

He came around the front and offered his elbow as I exited. His hands were shoved into his overcoat pockets, and his expression offered the promise to keep them there. I shook my head at myself but took his elbow anyway.

He led me back into the study, sat me down in the wing-backed chair, and began to disrobe, first taking off his overcoat, then his dark vest.

"What are you doing?" I cried and stood up. My cheeks flared up.

"You are the primary suspect in my case, Mauve."

"That's Madame, to you, sir!"

He ignored me and continued to unbutton the top of his white cotton shirt. “While you may not have pulled a trigger or kicked a chair beneath a noose, you have driven men to their deaths. I cannot prove it, but I’ve learned enough to know the truth. And I need you to trust that I’m on your side.”

I choked on a squeal and turned my back on him as he pulled his shirt out of his trousers and over his head. My body thrummed with shock. “And this is supposed to cultivate trust? Put your clothing back on this instant!”

I heard him chuckle, though I heard shyness behind it.

“Turn around, girl. This is the only way I can open your eyes if you refuse to touch me.”

“Not on your life!”

“Oh, come, now. You’ve seen it all before, Mauve. Don’t you remember the morning we went swimming in our unmentionables?”

I gasped and spun back around. “You lie! I would never—” My words died in my throat.

Despite his breathtaking structure, that had not silenced my voice. From just under his left arm, across all his ribs and over to the other side of his waist, an enormous scar textured his abdomen strangely.

I stepped toward him, albeit cautiously. It was a great amount of skin to behold in one moment, but I bore it bravely. “What is this?”

“It was worth it, that’s what. Tell me you remember.”

I breathed hard and my heart beat a ragged rhythm against my chest. “I-I don’t remember everything.” And then instead of fighting the distrust and suspicion, I breathed in his aura. Answers came to me that I hadn't even sought yet. "It is you, isn't it, Abel?"

He smiled, but the sorrow behind it clutched my soul and squeezed.

He looked away. "I regret so much about that night. I wish I could have saved you from the collapse. The burning beam from your house fell onto both of us. Had my body not taken the brunt of it, it would have crushed you completely, but had I pulled you out faster, we could have walked away unharmed." He began to pace the length of the room. "And your little sister . . . if I had been thinking more clearly . . ."

I stepped in front of him and held up my hands, interrupting his walk, but reluctant to actually place my hands against his bare chest. "We were only children! You were only a year or so older than me! You must have been so terrified!"

"I was! I didn't even realize the danger at first! I just stared as your house burned and a strange man lay unconscious in your yard! Then something powerful called to me and I had to reach you."

"But why were you there in the first place? It was the middle of the night!"

"I came every night, Mauve. In the summers, and as long as I could tolerate the cold in the spring and fall. You rarely came out then. It didn't matter; I was still hopeful. But then your uncle—someone it took me eight years to identify and locate—took you away. I was determined to find both of you and exact justice for the wrongs of the past, but once I realized his important role in your survival, my anger against him dissipated into nothing. I wish I'd been a braver lad—to tell you how much I cared for you *before* I thought I had lost you forever. Your trust may have come more readily tonight."

The warmth in the room crept up exponentially. I took a deep breath. "Why do you tell me this now? Why must you torture me with the past?"

"Because I want you to remember!"

"How could I ever forget? Things were simple! Beautiful! Now look at me! I'll never know that life again! My curse has gone from bitter to unsavory, and I'm as delinquent as you suspect! Trust is not an option. I am a treacherous choice for an ally and you'd be wise to remember that." I turned away from him, angry at my own sore existence, and liable to collapse from exhaustion.

"I need you to let me help you," he said. "Falco has officers following my every move, and now yours. The Cabot party tipped them off, just like it did for me, and he knows I'm not interested in his business. He's out to get both of us, and I won't let him succeed. You need to trust the past, even if you don't trust me. It's enough to stand on—a strong foundation for our future, and despite its bleak outlook now, I mean to make it a beautiful one."

I heard him approach. The fire in the hearth had died down even more, though it still glowed with life. A glow which seemed to heat through my very core. "Your name was Bronson . . ."

"My mother remarried the year after that night." He stood close behind me and reached for my hand. For the first time in years, I didn't flinch away.

Abel gently wrapped his fingers around my wrist and turned me around. He lifted both hands to my veil, and I slowly grasped his wrists in warning. If he saw my face, his future would be made sure. My saving grace was another's deadly curse. But my willpower had diminished. My strength in protecting him from myself grew weak. I wanted him to know me. And that battled against my understanding of the consequence.

I shook my head as he began to lift the veil, and I closed my eyes to protect myself from seeing his disgust. Cooler air graced my left cheek and I knew my face was revealed.

"Mauve," he whispered. "I know you. You have only ever used your talents for good. You are no danger to me."

I took in a breath at the sound of his voice so calm and so close. His scent tasted sweet on my tongue.

He brushed his thumb across my non-mechanical cheek, and I opened my eyes. His own were warm with admiration. "You are still as exquisite as I remember."

Not realizing how tense I had been, I relaxed, no longer worrying about any future whatsoever. I reached for his hand without thinking. Our palms touched, and a vision ripped through me.

Falco sneering. His pistol aimed at Abel's face. The trigger pulled, and a snail-slow bullet spiraling toward him.

I yelped and jumped back. "No!"

"What! What is it?"

I shook my head, my eyes wide. I yanked my veil back down and shoved my way past Abel. "It's all my fault! I never should have let you!"

He called after me as I tore down the hallway and out to the AirRidge, but I was gone before he could stop me.

It was time to take fate into my own hands.

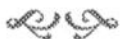

I drove slowly down the murky city streets of Boston toward the North End and the lowly indigent Italians, Irishmen, or Jews huddled under makeshift shelters, each in their own separate slums.

I had laid the foundation for the mess. The dominoes had fallen, many of them scattered haphazardly. I didn't know what I was doing. I never did. But instinct had never failed before, and I had to trust it. I simply didn't know how it would end. I couldn't see my own future. I stopped a few blocks away from my destination. The Green Parlor. A known location for Falco's dirty deeds.

With my pitch-colored clothing, I blended into the night and traveled unmolested. I'd never been to the Green Parlor before. No woman with any sort of reputation other than openly sullied should. I knew of Madame Tillant—everyone did—but I had never met her. Our paths did not cross. As owner and operator of the Green Parlor, she maintained a very busy lifestyle—one that wrapped itself tightly around the greatest kingpin Massachusetts had ever known.

I approached the heavy wooden door with trepidation. Once I entered, events would spiral uncontrollably. I stalled. To my right, leaning on the brick walls of the house, two beings went at each other roughly. It was difficult to decipher if the violence was born of passion or hatred. Despite my lack of street knowledge in that regard, I understood that it was very possibly a combination of both. I turned away.

To my left, a little dog with two mechanical back legs scrounged around in piles of refuse. Taking a deep breath, I began to open the door, but it gave way quickly as two smelly men crossed the threshold, pointlessly holding on to each other as they stumbled out into the street. I shook my head, removing the temptation to deliver their fortunes. They weren't beyond repair.

Stepping inside, I plastered myself against the wall to avoid contact and also the offensive smoke exhalations. The place would have been considered a fine crush at any high society party. The hostess must consider her number of guests a success for the evening.

I glanced up at the railing skirting the second floor. Several doors were closed behind the few women leaning on the banister, but I doubted they were empty. A shout caught my attention on the left side of the ground floor. A man stood up at a smoky table and threw his cards at another man's face. "Tha's what I said, ya lyin' sack of—"

He didn't have time to finish. The other man launched across the table at him, making cards and gambling chips and money fly in all directions. I scooted further along the wall, away from the ruckus.

Making my way to the stairs, I headed up, beginning to feel more than a few eyes upon me. I knew the dangers of such a place. But I didn't enter unarmed. I always had my protection with me, curse or not.

A more fully-clothed woman spotted me from the second floor where she had been overlooking the chaos with a pleased eye. She stood upright and approached.

"Bit out of your league aren't you, Miss . . . ?"

"Mauve. Madame Mauve. And I don't plan to stay long. You must be Madame Tillant." I curtseyed to show respect, hoping it would win me her trust.

"Mauve? Really?" She looked me over. "They've told me about you, you know. The men. Now I see why. What are you doing here, Madame Mauve?"

"I seek a man who owes a great debt."

"Don't we all . . . ?"

"Yes, but this man will actually pay it. And the result will serve the populace."

Madame Tillant's eyebrows knit together. "Who are you looking for?"

"Duilio Falco."

Her expression sobered. "You don't know what you're talking about. Go home, child, before you find yourself in over your head." She shooed me away with her finger.

I grabbed her wrist before she could turn away. She winced

at the touch, so I loosened my grip but met her eye. "I know what exists in his very marrow, Madame Tillant. I can feel it even now. I swear upon my father's grave, he will no longer take his payments from your flesh." She flinched. "Or from your soul."

"It doesn't matter," she said. "I'm dead anyway. If I give him up, he will kill me. If I do not, he takes my life every night. He hasn't paid a single coin to this establishment in over three years. His men beat my women. They run out the other immigrants until it only bleeds green, white, and red in here. *Tricolore.*"

She grasped my hands weakly. "But if I give him up and you fail—not that I doubt you; I have heard of your powers from men too incapacitated to remember their own names. If you fail, he will cut my heart out of my chest."

My own heart thumped a wild rhythm. I knew I had come for a reason, but I had thought it was my own selfish cause. From her words, more than choice had led me there.

"You have nothing to fear. It ends tonight."

Madame Tillant shook her head. Yet, she took in a deep breath and pointed to the last door at the end of the balustrade.

I took off my gloves as I approached. If I wanted full access to my gift, I would need to be exposed.

I didn't knock, knowing how much I may regret it. Turning the knob slowly, I eased my way in—thankfully, the room was silent, aside from the large, face-down, half-naked, snoring body on the bed. A relatively clothed woman stood at a dresser, brushing her long blonde hair. She caught sight of me in the mirror and stifled a scream.

Sometimes they think the veil is scarier than anything lying beneath.

I put a finger to my hidden lips and motioned for her to leave the room. She didn't hesitate. If someone had come to relieve her of her duties, she seemed more than grateful.

Falco continued to snore, a horrific grinding and popping sound. I wasn't sure what my plan had been walking into that room. Spontaneous decisions often ruled my life, but seeing him completely at ease, happy with his baneful existence, an idea came to mind.

What is more terrifying than reality? Our dreams.

I softly perched beside his bloated white and hairy body on the bed, and eyed his right hand, which was palm up resting beside his loosened trousers.

I breathed in, trying to clear my senses and troubled mind. There were many distractions and I needed to focus. Exhaling, I placed my palm against his, and took control of his peaceful respite.

After one shocking search through his past, I began to whisper. "As a child, you watched your mother's disapproval and died a little inside. Now you see her looking down on you from on high, and she visits you in all her righteous fury, but instead of a scolding or a blow to your cheek, she reaches inside your ribcage, into your foul heart, and removes it from your chest. You see its soot-covered onyx glory and all your despicable deeds, committed against the innocent and nefarious alike."

I felt his palm grow moist, his breathing speed up.

"You see into your mother's ghoulish eyes which no longer accept you. She screams into your face, 'Duilio Falco, you are no son of mine! You are not bone of my bones, flesh of my flesh! You shall be a lost soul after you leave this world, to ever drift alone, unacknowledged by any! You are utterly abandoned!' But then she lifts a finger. 'If you refuse to change,' she cries, 'you line your coffin with everlasting punishment!' She then turns her back on you forever!"

Falco stirred. His muscles jerked and twitched.

"You have tainted this community permanently, Duilio Falco—good men like Charlie Vanderhook, almost taken down because of your schemes. Men like Robert Bartlad completely ruined because of your organization. It ends now. Either you end it, or it ends you."

Falco's throat ripped out a snarl and he suddenly pushed himself upright. I jumped up, and flattened myself against the wall.

He remained on his knees on the bed, but dropped his face back down and began to sob.

I was weakened; the sentencing went beyond my normal scope of practice. Pushing my thoughts and words past his consciousness had taken its toll. My knees shook, so much so that I either had to sit down or risk betraying my presence. I didn't have to consider my options for long.

As I started to slide down the wall, I bumped a vase on a short table, and for a fractured second, I saw my future in that dropping glass. Had I time enough, I would have wept.

The ceramic vase crashed onto the hardwood floor and shattered. I shot across the room, aiming for the door, but Falco was faster than his weight indicated. He spun around, saw me running, caught me by my arm, and without a single question of interrogation, delivered a disastrous blow to the side of my face. The side that would leave no bruise, but one that couldn't afford that kind of damage.

I sucked in a breath, my head whirling. The clanking began. More than one thing was knocked loose.

He yanked me to him, grabbed my veil and ripped it from my head, hat and all. Pinned to my hair, it removed some of that as well, the rest in a mess around my face.

He bellowed ferocious words at me, but I couldn't understand a thing. His mother tongue was strong and fast. I just stared at him with wide eyes.

Had I forgotten my power? I still had it, didn't I? He could have battered me one more time, crushed the rest of my face, and yet I froze. His skin was a mere inches from mine and I didn't have the wherewithal to take full advantage right then and there.

He continued to bark at me, some little words I caught, but the gist was not lost to me. He raised his fist again. I knew it would be lightning fast, and I considered just taking it. But then a face flashed in my mind. First a boy, his rosy cheeks pushed upward with a huge smile as he lay beside me in the moonlight. Then a man, the same curled mess of hair, standing before me, seeing my imperfections and still wanting to know me, wanting to understand me.

I ducked just as Falco's beefy fist came toward me again. It breezed past my head, and I latched on to his less mobile left hand, palm to palm. Mentally frozen with fear, I could do nothing but squeeze my eyes shut and scream. Loud. Long. Bloodcurdling. Steam shot out of my face, along with loose gears and springs. By the time my lungs ran out of air, Falco's eyes had rolled to the back of his head, and he dropped into a heap of ugly on the floor.

I stood over him. Terrified. Empowered.

The door flew open. I expected to see Madame Tillant. Not the half-dozen coppers who barged in and shoved me against the opposite wall.

A great deal of shouting commenced, but I just stared at Falco as a forearm was shoved into my throat, my arms pinned behind me. I heard none of the commotion as they dragged me from the room as Falco began to wake. He spun his head around just as I was wrenched from his view.

They towed me out into the hall and down the stairs. At the entrance to the establishment, I saw Abel arguing with the chief of police. I couldn't hear their words above the chaos, but the chief had his hand on Abel's arm, restraining him. When they caught sight of me, they both stopped. Abel's eyes grew wide and he shouted my name, though I couldn't hear him. The chief wrapped both arms around him as he fought, and lifted him out of the way as the officers pulled me through the exit.

I should have known Falco wouldn't give up. At once, everything reached a fevered pitch. From the corner of the Green

Parlor, in front of the police cruiser cab, I watched Duilio Falco descend an escape ladder from the second story. I caught sight of Abel breaking free from the chief's grasp and running toward me.

Falco pulled the gun from his waistband. He lifted it toward me, but as he rounded the corner and caught sight of Abel approaching, he grinned and adjusted his aim.

With one swift movement that felt slower than the evolution of time, I stomped on the feet of both policemen confining me. They released their holds and I bolted toward Abel. I grabbed him and spun around so I was in front when I heard the crack of the discharged gun.

I felt a sledge hammer come down on my face and I dropped to the ground. Strangely enough, I heard another body drop at the same time as mine. I must have failed. Somehow the bullet had struck Abel as well.

~

Clink.

Click-click-click.

Tap. Tap.

My eyes felt full of sand. My head was braced as I lay on my back. I wasn't precisely comfortable, but I didn't desire to move.

Crank, crank, crank.

Abel!

I parted my eyelashes. Uncle Wally's face was closer than I ever would have wished.

"What are you doing?" I croaked. I had to speak with my teeth clenched, but I formed the words sufficiently. My head felt detached from my body, but in a pleasant sort of way.

He smiled. "Making you beautiful again."

"That's never going to happen." I tried to test my jaw, but he clicked his tongue.

"Don't try to move. You can't anyway. This strap is secure."

I reached up and touched the leather under my chin with uncoordinated fingers. "Where am I?"

"Jail."

"Oh."

"Right. They weren't quite sure what to do with you after you killed Mr. Falco."

"I what?"

"The .22 meant for Abel. It made an absolute mess of my creation here, but that bullet blew through the broken pieces of your cheek, hit the police cruiser cab behind you, and ricocheted straight back into Duilio Falco's eye socket."

He glanced toward my eyes for a moment. "Yes, I know! I wish I could have been there to see the look on the chief's face. A one-in-a-trillion chance to hit just the right piece of metal. It must have just missed you as it returned to him." He gave an unholy snort. "Fate at its best, yes? He dropped like a sack of potatoes."

So it hadn't been Abel to fall. I squinted my eyes, trying to picture how it had happened, but I regretted using facial muscles right away.

"Mm-hm," he said. "I'm sure your face hurts like the dickens now, but the doc gave you something to help with the pain. Otherwise, it'd be worse."

I grumbled in response. "Are you sure a bullet went through my face? How am I even still here?"

"Well, I use very good materials."

I smiled and winced.

He sniffed and changed the subject. "I understand you had an intriguing visit with Warrick."

"I've had a few interesting experiences over the past twenty-four hours."

"And what have you concluded?" He paused. "About me?"

I looked into his eyes. "Uncle Wally, none of us are perfect. If I thought you were a bad man, my intuition would have been going mad over the past eight years. We've all made mistakes. You've more than made up for yours."

He swallowed and continued working. A tear dropped onto my left cheek after a second. "Oh, sorry." He gently wiped it off and dabbed at his own eyes. "I really did try to repair the damage I caused—in every way I could. I did my best to support Warrick and his mother—anonymously, of course—but he was stubborn and suspicious."

Uncle Wally shook his head. "You know, he not only saved your life that night, but he permanently changed mine. Haven't touched the drink since. Still, I couldn't tell him about you until I knew he was ready to handle your situation. You're so special; he needed to put in the work. And did he ever. I'm sure he's been searching for you ever since I took you out of that hospital to fix you up myself."

He must have read the concerned and anxious look in my eyes. "Okay, okay, I'm almost done. He's fine and you can see him as soon as I finish." Uncle Wally paused to ratchet a piece back in place. "He asked me for your hand, Mauve."

My heart thudded violently against my ribs. "He did? What was your answer?"

"I think you already know."

I closed my eyes, refusing to let the excitement take over my wits. But the minutes began to drag. Could it be possible that I might be loved in spite of my appearance? In spite of my curse?

"Stop wiggling, girl," he said with a smile. "There. I'm done." He undid the strap beneath my chin and helped me sit up. The stone gray cell made me shiver, and my heart sank at the sight of the closed bars.

"What's going to happen to me?"

Uncle Wally patted my shoulder. "I'm sure the inspector will be able to answer those questions. Now, I believe you have a visitor."

I looked up and saw Abel leaning against the wall beside my barred door. He could not have been there long.

I hugged my uncle. "Thank you."

His breathing hitched for a moment. "No. Thank *you*, my dear." He packed up his toolbox and leftover machinery, stood up, and gave a little wave goodbye.

He shook Abel's hand at the door when the bars slid open. Their eyes met and each nodded. Much had passed between those two over the years. The beautiful things were what mattered. Acceptance, forgiveness, appreciation. I fought the burn of tears in my eyes.

Abel left the door open as he entered my cell with his hands in his pockets. His face showed so many emotions all at once. Worry, pride, desire. My heart refused to hold still.

"Well, my night was interesting," he started and leaned against the wall opposite me.

"Oh?"

"Indeed. I had my first real conversation with the woman of my dreams. She was strong and beautiful and intelligent."

"You're certain she was from your dreams, and not your nightmares?"

He nodded. "Very. But then she ran away from me."

"From you, or toward something else?"

"True, it was with the intent to save my life, but still! We could have worked together."

"Unless she was simply too desperate to change the future."

"That's likely. Criminals are whispering her name with terror as we speak." Abel pushed off from the wall and took a few steps closer, his hands still in his pockets."

"Such pleasant news."

He stifled a chuckle. "Right. But you'll never believe what she did to me to accomplish it."

"Do tell."

He stepped forward once more. "She caused my blood to run cold."

My eyes widened as I peered at his pale face. "Truly?"

"Yes. That—" He struggled with the words. "That savage swine-of-a-man tried to destroy the most beautiful creature I'd ever seen." Abel grasped my shoulders. "You put me half out of my wits, Mauve. We could have done nothing against the dastard for hurting you. He was well within his rights in that room. Swear you'll never do that to me again."

I shook my head. "How can you say that?"

His brow darkened. "I'm serious. You cannot put yourself in harm's way—"

"No, I mean . . . a beautiful creature? You're more out of your wits than you think."

Abel's shoulders relaxed and his expression softened. "I am the beholder, my dear. There's no arguing with these eyes." He grinned slowly, and I closed the distance between us by leaning my forehead against his chest.

"What will become of me, Abel?"

He wrapped his arms around me and pulled me close. "With no one to press charges, including the city, you are no longer a suspect and no longer detained by the Boston Police." He leaned back and lifted my chin. "Except you're still at risk for arrest."

I felt my heart knock against my chest. "What?"

"Unless you provide full payment for my stolen heart, I'll have to nab you myself."

I gasped and hit him on the chest. "Abel Warrick, you dog! I was scared to death."

He smiled naughtily. "Good. Now we're even." Without another word, he leaned forward and pressed his lips to mine.

Right then and there, that man provided the best reading of my life. I've little idea how he accomplished such a feat, but it's one I'd gladly relive all my days. For once, I was not the byproduct of someone else's choices.

I was just Mauve. And he was Abel.

And Abel loved Mauve.

Inspired by Emily Dickinson

Payoff for Air Pirate Pete

D. LEE JORTNER

Our well-designed and almost successful attempt to rob the train between Chicago and Rockford didn't end up as planned. My husband Clayton and I barely escaped arrest, and possibly death, when we jumped off the Zephyr about eight miles outside of Long Grove. Walking back towards Chicago, we vowed to forever avoid trains, at least in the Midwest. Too many WANTED posters plastered on train station walls might incite suspicion; our daguerreotypes surely graced a few of them. Shunning steam trains, although inconvenient, was preferable to spending months or years behind bars.

With a little ingenuity we found we didn't need to ride trains to stay in the burglary business. Using a little savings from a previous heist, we purchased a couple of decent steam-powered bicycles. Their speediness sufficed for a half dozen small jobs, but we always looked out for a faster, meaner mode of transportation. We intended to steal a steam-car, as soon as we found one available.

We didn't find a car; we found an abandoned airship. That's our story, anyhow. No one sat at the helm when we discovered a beautiful one tied up right behind a Chicago cattle yard. You can't tell me it wasn't abandoned!

Riveted under a billowing envelope hung an amazing enclosed gondola. It seemed huge to us—we, who, up until that day, could only pinch goods small enough to fit in the front baskets of two bicycles. And it appeared especially grand to me. Compared to the little ambulance dirigible I piloted extracting a wounded Clayton from Gettysburg, this airship was a flying mansion.

Our new airship could hold our bicycles, plus all the contraband we planned to pick up before we could retire in California and start a family. It came equipped with a galley, a captain's cabin, and a small bedroom with a real mattress. Luck had smiled on us. Lickety-split, we stuffed our bikes, and a small hope chest filled with tiny knitted booties and a little patchwork quilt in the freight compartment, untied the stays, stoked the boilers and charted west, intent on putting as many miles as possible between us and Chicago.

A soft wind carried us our first day out, so Clayton sat up in the co-pilot seat and we planned our next and, I insisted, final heist.

"I'm ready to settle down and start a family," says I.

"After we pull this off, I might be game."

I smiled, and took my left hand off the controls long enough to squeeze his for a second.

About a week later, I was of a different mind.

A middle-aged mercantilist on the Toledo-to-Chicago train last year told us about ZCMI, a Salt Lake City department store chock-full of jewelry, silver, and mechanical trinkets from all over the world. “In the back,” says he, “a large vault holds not only the store profits, but the amassed millions of that Utah Mormon Church.”

Two conspiring burglars like ourselves needed no more enticements. The fantastic stories of the riches brought over by those pioneers and the gold some had found and brought back from California had occupied our minds for years. We had no qualms about pocketing some. But to cross the Rockies the way the pioneers did, with oxen or handcarts, didn’t fit our style. Our airship made the heist possible and comfortable. We drafted a plan to fly over the mountains, steal the loot, and evaporate off to California.

It all sounded so easy, but like all our previous schemes, one little cog was stuck in the gears. We learned soon enough that our barn of a ship was great for transporting but not designed to fly at high altitudes. It sailed at a decent speed on flat or hilly areas. The Midwest Marvel, as we liked to call it, performed admirably in the slow climb to the west as far as the Wyoming Territory. However, as the prairie rose towards the mountains, the problems began. Try as I might, I couldn’t get it to achieve the loft I knew it needed to reach ten thousand feet.

By the time we hit the upper plains in Wyoming, I says to Clayton, "Maybe we can go another hundred miles, but no more."

He pulled his goggles down from their usual resting spot on the brim of his black bowler hat, and leaned on the window. "There's snow on them mountains. What's the date?"

"It's still June. These hills sure don't look like the Appalachians I flew through during the war. They must be mighty high, if there is still snow up there. We just don't have the lift."

Clayton threw his hat on the ground and swore like the mechanic and soldier he was. He kicked the gears, and when that didn't help, he huffed off to stoke the boiler.

I let him blow off his own steam for a while, before having another go at him.

Luckily, I had kept up with all the new airship designs, and Clayton whizzed at putting things together and making connections tight. His mech-arm replacement came fitted with the best wrench and screwdriver to be had.

"We can fix this," I says. "We just need a new part."

"What part?" he asks, his brown eyes hopeful.

"I read about the Kelster Aerolift Capacitor in a flyer. If we get one, we can increase lift by fifty percent and stabilize steering at altitudes above ten thousand feet."

"You sure?"

"It'll work." I sounded more confident than I felt.

It wasn't till supper that I explained this marvel wasn't yet available to folks like us. I hated to tell him that the price was set to start at $900.00 next spring.

"There's only test models, so far," says I.

"So what good does that do us?" Clayton slammed his spoon down and pushed his chair back from the table.

I knew we didn't have that kind of money, but we excelled at coming up with plans. "We'll come up with somethun'."

He looked at me with that look. "Got any ideas yet?" he says.

"The templates and test models sit in a factory in Green River, Wyoming, not far from the Rockies."

"Green River, you say? Chart the course."

To avoid detection we traveled at night, making quick time across the Midwest. But hiding an airship in the Big Sky country of Wyoming Territory took skill and luck. About twenty miles from Green River, we found the perfect spot in a canyon just northwest of the small town of Rock Springs. We dropped down, deflated our balloon, and made camp. From our hiding place, we rode our bikes into Rock Springs for supplies and kept our ears open for gossip about the surrounding communities.

Rock Springs, dusty and full of ranch hands, served as a stomping ground before the trains and airships would pick up cattle. At the general store, I overheard talk of Green River as a sophisticated mini city, with its rich people who had brought a little of the northeast airs with them. The folks in Rock Springs liked to dress up once in a while and take the train down the line to Green River, then eat out at the restaurant or gawk at the lavish homes which lined the brick-paved streets.

Rock Springs didn't even have a saloon. One traveler, dressed in a silk bustled frock and carrying a parasol, walked past me in front of the general store and whispered to her companion. "Why does the train even stop here in Podunk?" I bristled as I listened to the folks' snobby conversations. They thought they knew so much, but they knew nothing. Had they ever dropped down into the middle of a battle, ran out and pulled four injured soldiers out of the fray, and made it back to Delaware in time for dinner? Or did they risk their lives climbing and tapping into thirty foot telegraph poles behind enemy lines, like Clayton?

When they looked across their fans and down their nose at me in my goggles, leather boots, and holster, I returned their snooty glares with one of my own.

We learned plenty of tidbits of information loitering around the train station. Some of the best engineers from the east worked for the railroad, right there in Green River. The new western vice president had brought a team of designers out west to work on steam engines that could function high over the Rockies. Unfortunately, prototypes were so locked away and guarded that no one could snatch one out. We needed another way to get our hands on the piece.

After a long bike ride back to our ship, I brewed some tea, and we brainstormed.

"Maybe if we can get our hands on somethun just as valuable as the Kelster, we could make a trade," says Clayton.

I jumped up and kissed him, right in the middle of tea. "That's it! We'll take something ransom."

Since we couldn't sail our airship into Green River until the time was right, I volunteered to survey the area. This plan meant breaking my vow to avoid trains and ride the short distance to Green River incognito. Hiding my goggles in a satchel, and pinning my hair up under a fluffy, flowery bonnet, I pulled a blue calico frock over my leather corset and pantaloons. My goal was to figure out the best method of obtaining two of those Kelster Capacitors.

I arrived in Green River mid-day. For being way out here in the middle of nowhere, it sure had a lot of modern contraptions. Maybe all those engineers competed with each other in fancy transportation designs, for a lively assortment of steam– and sun-powered cars scared the horses as they drove down the brick-lined streets. When parked, the vehicles' shiny brass accessories reflected the high sun and sent sparkles of yellow light to dance on the two-story bank, jail, and few main-street mansions. Their beauty notwithstanding, I hated them. They foiled my first strategy of a bike-heist. Our bikes would never escape, and landing an airship in the middle of town would never work.

I didn't let this setback discourage me. I set to concocting a new plan: a plan with an infallible design.

Right in the center of town, on the north side of the square, sat the large brick Rothenberg family mansion. Mr. Joseph Rothenberg, the Vice-president of Wyoming Railway and Steam Company, lived in a square house topped with a white widow's walk on the roof. Yes, a widow's walk, making the house stand out like an elephant in a barnyard, there in the middle of a flat high prairie with nary a water body in sight. One gossipy nanny in a little park on the north side of town was more than willing to talk about the neighbors.

"Mrs. Rothenberg's family, the Billings of Boston, have been seamen for generations, and her family's house near the Atlantic boasted a white widow's walk. She loved the design. So there you have it," says she.

I just nodded and cooed at the little one wriggling her arms and legs in the perambulator. If I allowed myself, I could be totally distracted by this sweet pink bundle. Her lace bonnet and ruffled dress surrounded her chubby cheeks. But her adorable features only set my resolve to get this caper perfect. I wanted a baby of my own.

"What's this Mr. Rothenberg like?" I asked, slipping my fingers into the baby's tiny grasp.

"He's a stuffed shirt. He travels throughout the country on business."

I wondered if that meant we might be able to break in when he was out of town.

"I bet he has his own special train," I says.

"You should see it. So fancy! When Mrs. Rothenberg thinks he's coming home, I seen her stand on the roof, leaning against the white picket railing, and watching for him before we can even hear the whistle."

"Now, isn't that interesting?" says I. "Can she see far?"

"I 'spec' so. Last year a crew of workmen brought up a long spyglass of some sort. You can see it on the roof, if you walk around to the other side. My missus says that Mrs. Rothenberg can see when a train or airship is coming long before the sound of its whistle even reaches the town."

"That must be some spyglass!"

The bit about the spyglass concerned me, but this standout house had so much potential for us. When the nanny left to go home for lunch, I kept watch from my little park bench, stewing over possible heists. To hide my intentions, I fanned myself, nodding and smiling at the townsfolk as they walked by.

After school, a young boy, who I learned later was Pete Rothenberg, the family's only child, appeared in the widow's walk. He played with his toy cars, ships, and mechanical frogs. He tried to fly a kite, but ended up fishing leaves off the grass. He paraded up and down, wooden sword in hand, for almost an hour. A few times, he appeared to aim and drop something down into the street. Then he ducked behind the railing and peered between the slats as a gentlewoman would stop and touch her bonnet. I smirked behind my fan. This boy reminded me so much of how I imagined Clayton as a young'un. A middle-aged man in a tall stovepipe hat walked by arm in arm with a proper-looking lady. His wife says, "That Rothenberg kid is at it again."

He answers, "What an incorrigible rascal! If he weren't the boss' kid, I know what I would do with him."

I didn't question why he played alone on the roof. My stomach churned with excitement, but I did not let it show. Young Master Rothenberg was a unique opportunity, an opportunity we could exploit with ease. A plan started to form, and I scribbled a map on a scrap of paper.

On the long walk to our hideout that evening, I worked out the details. Back in our ship, over a dinner of biscuits topped with blackberry jelly that I had picked up in Rock Springs, I laid it out for my husband.

"We wait for a cloudy day, so they don't see us coming," says I. "Then I'll fly us over to Green River." We needed clouds—big puffy white clouds so we could disappear and confuse any townsfolk wanting to chase after the boy.

"So how's it gonna work?" Clayton asks.

"I'll fly right above the Rothenberg house, and you can drop the extension ladder and climb on down. Your mech arm will hold you secure, even if the balloon bumps a bit," I says.

"Finally, a practical use for this heavy thing," he says. He slowly lifted his arm, and rested it with a clunk on the table.

"It shouldn't be hard for you to snatch Pete off the roof, and I'll pull you both up into the ship. Then we skedaddle back here."

The day of the kidnapping started clear, and I feared we would have to put off our scheme. However, by noon, wondrous fluffy clouds blew in over the mountains and covered the vast Wyoming sky. We started the engines, ready for a 3:00 P.M. sweep in and out. I flew in high, coming down on the town from the north. We avoided the train-spotters checking down the line east or peering toward the mountains in the west. About a mile from our target, we dropped power and swept in low. I fought the easterly wind, and peering through my triple-powered goggles, I marked the Rothenberg house.

As I hoped, Pete frolicked alone on the roof wielding what looked like a toy sword or fishing pole. And just as I predicted, when he heard the whirr of our fans, he ran around the top of the house to get a better view of us through the spyglass. His eyes bugged as we came in fast. When the extension ladder lowered with Clayton, dressed in his long black coat, shining buckled boots, and goggle-bedecked bowler hat, latched to the side, Pete stared up, paralyzed in what might have been shock or maybe just awe. My husband's left mechanical arm clasped the lowest rung. With his right, he reached out and plucked Pete from the widow's walk and swung him upwards towards the ship's trapdoor.

Pete squealed, jabbed, and kicked, but he never let go of his little wooden sword. Fighting like a cornered bearcat, he slashed at my husband's arm and head, screeching like an angry mother prairie dog. But we had timed the abduction carefully, and the high-pitched train whistle sounded over the hollering, and Clayton's brass mechanisms held tight. I powered the balloons carefully, so we ascended as swiftly as we had descended. Pete looked down at the hard prairie 200 feet and more below, paused in his attack, and grabbed hold of the ladder above Clayton.

Using a special set of pulleys rigged into the cockpit, I set the crank to pull them up slowly while I stayed in the control room. I feared something was wrong. I clamped down auto-hold and rushed out and through the galley, arriving just in time to grab Pete as he pulled himself through the trapdoor. Catching him right then, before he could run back into the engine room to hide amongst the pistons and cranks, or escape to the living quarters and sneak under our bed, might have been my smartest move of the week. Too late, I learned I shoulda thrown the wiggly codger back right then and there.

Pete's sandy hair, his wry smile forming huge dimples on his cheeks, and his bright blue eyes beguiled me immediately. I'd been itching for a baby for a few years, but I hadn't actually spent much time with children. I laughed as the little urchin pointed his sword at my torso, took a couple of steps in my direction and pushed the pointy end against my leather corset. In a fake deep voice he says, "Lady, you better take me to the control room now!"

The last time I had been called "lady," a delirious soldier had mistaken me for Mrs. Lincoln. Ready to oblige, just to play along, I took one last look at the hole. The bruised, bloodied, hatless head of my husband popped up through the hatch. His voice boomed over the engine whirrs: "Put that sword down, right now!"

Pete's visage changed from a mischievous smile to a purple maniacal sneer. Oh, no, he didn't lay the play sword down. If anything he grabbed it tighter. Raising both hands above his head, he rushed Clayton yelling, "Pirate attack!"

I shook my head to gather my wits. I moved quickly and grabbed the little brat from behind. With my free hand, I forced his arms (sword and all) down and tight against his chest. I may be a woman with a natural soft heart for children, but nobody attacks my man. This adorable, belligerent scruffian was no exception.

I held tight.

Pete thrashed his arms and kicked my shins, but I didn't let go until my husband made it up through the hatch, locked it closed, secured the sword, and wrapped his mechanical arm tightly around the child's chest. Clayton rubbed his free hand on his head. I grabbed my nursing kit—no stiches, just a flesh wound, but treating him while he strong-armed the kid took a lot of skill and patience. Finally, I returned to the control room to steer our airship "home."

Sitting in my swivel chair, the lack of squabbles in the other room surprised me. After a couple of minutes, I heard high-pitched laughter, and a deep hee-haw. I climbed back to investigate. Clayton and Pete walked hand in hand, exploring the innards of the ship. They looked like two school boys who had just played hooky to go fishing.

I smiled as Pete asked Clayton question after question, pointing at every little gadget and gear. Even though Clayton says no to every request to turn a button, the boy was tenacious and asked to pull each chain and set every dial. My husband always enjoyed showing off the mechanical knowledge he had learned through hard work and experience. Pete gobbled it up.

Since we had no children of our own, the experience of having a youngster show uncommon interest in our flying machine enticed Clayton to forgive the bruises and curses too quickly. I feared being hoodwinked, but I didn't interrupt. Both boys smiled brightly, heady with excitement. Clayton looked at me, and I shook my head in disbelief. I returned to the cockpit and the captain's chair, and I hoped that this bonding might help Clayton see it was time for us to have our own family.

Even from my comfortable leather seat, I heard their intense conversation and started to find their excitement contagious. My mind drifted away from our simple plan: kidnap the boy, wait a couple of days for worry to overtake the town, contact the Rothenbergs, demand the Kelsters in exchange for the boy, and return the boy and collect the needed parts for our ship. But our simple plan didn't cover everything. We soon encountered a wrinkle or two.

Pete's boyish interest in our ship that afternoon endeared him to us, but it didn't prepare us for the coming hours or days. His unbounded energy and just plain disobedience wore on us. He ran back and forth inside the ship, touching and adjusting every lever and screw. Even after landing and securing the lines, he showed no interest in going outside into the cool evening. By the time the sun dropped behind the mountains, executing our plan and keeping up with a nine-year-old boy had drained us. Pirate Pete, as he insisted we call him, never seemed to wind down at all. We hated doing it, but we eventually resorted to hiding some sleeping powder in a brass cup of cocoa to get him to sleep.

The drugs worked for the evening, but unfortunately, they didn't have any lasting effects. The next morning, Pete woke us before sunup, ready to rumble. And rumble he did. Smart and cunning, he acted overly polite at times and downright rude and obnoxious at others. Whenever he wrangled away from our grasp, he explored the cockpit, undoing all the intricate adjustments that kept us in ready mode. We did let him look through the spyglass, but even that only kept his attention a short while. Finally, we shooed him outside by bribing him with a ride on my bicycle.

"Stay right near the ship, or Clayton will let you know how strong his mech-arm can squeeze," I warned.

He grinned at me for just a second before his gleaming eyes returned to the bicycle. "Yes, ma'am." And dropping his sword near the door, he sprinted out. That boy rode round and round the ship for at least two hours.

But riding alone didn't entertain Pete the whole day. He enlisted us to race with him. He threatened to run away if we didn't join in all his imaginative adventures. We may not be ready to meet St. Peter, but we do have our energy limits, and by early evening, I plum ran out of steam. After dinner, I could hardly keep upright. But Pete's vigor never waned. He had found a cave through my telescope and convinced us to climb the walls of the canyon and camp out.

I didn't want to resort to drugging him again, and I didn't want him adjusting the ship's gears while we slept, so we hiked. In spite of our fatigue, the climb up the canyon walls and sleeping in fresh air sounded like a first-rate plan to wear him out. Grabbing blankets, a casket of water and some six-month-old jerky, we trudged up a small goat path. I led, Pete followed and Clayton brought up the rear. We arrived at the cozy cave, checked for critters and laid out Pete's bed. The night was cool, the moon a sliver, and the kid worn out—a perfect campout.

Sitting at the end of the cave, our legs dangling, Clayton and I engaged in a hushed but heated discussion about the next course of action.

"I can't take this much longer," I says. I kept my voice soft but firm. "One day of waiting is enough."

Clayton sighed and looked back into the cave. "I'll get up early in the morning, and ride over to the wires and contact Mr. Rothenberg," says he.

"How are we going to get the parts?"

"There's a big willow tree right by the line."

"How would it work? We can't get caught."

"I got it all worked out. They can't lie in wait. They drop the thing, then skedaddle. We pluck the loot, drop off the kid, and hightail it over the mountains!"

I kissed Clayton softly before making our bed at the mouth of the cave. We didn't want to wake up and find a missing hostage.

When the sun first pierced the deep cave shadows, Clayton woke, scrambled down the path, grabbed a bike, and rode half way to the town of Rock Springs before the boy rolled over. For those twenty quiet minutes, I thanked my lucky stars that my husband got a clean getaway. But once Pete was up, the quiet dissipated. I faced the most rascally, sneaky, conniving, feisty, four-foot-tall, two-legged creature on Planet Earth.

I struggled to make my way back down the path with the boy and our supplies in tow. Pete, reminding me of my brother's hound dog, kicked every rock, veered off at every deer path, and stopped to pee behind every tree. And once back at the airship, he must have snuck out of my sight a dozen times, untied a half-dozen secure lines, and asked me three score questions. Finally, I agreed to play pirates, and he strapped me to the front of the gondola as a figurehead for a time.

By the time Clayton returned at suppertime, I hadn't even lit the stove to start cooking. Pete was out riding my bicycle. My husband found me barricading the door of our ship, nursing a sprained ankle, a broken fingernail, and a smashed goggle lens. My husband's face reddened, his eyes bulged, and he dropped the bike and grabbed me up in his one flesh arm.

"What's that kid done to you?" says he.

I didn't want to upset my husband, so I left out the part about being tied to the ship. "Oh, nothing I can't handle for a day or two more," I say. "We have been playing *Treasure Island*. I'm Long John Silver, and he's Jim Hawkins. First we swabbed the deck, then we climbed ropes, and then we did some sword fighting."

"You don't have a sword. What did you use?"

"The rolling pin from the galley worked okay, but it spun too much."

"So is that why your arms look black and blue?"

"This is the last time you leave me alone with the boy!" I glared at Clayton. His return nod let me know he understood.

Pete had snuck back into the galley. I spied him hiding behind the stove. He must have heard us talking. "Yes, and we need to ship out! Time to take off—it's time to find some treasure." He placed a childish treasure map in Clayton's hands. "Let's find the hideout of Billy the Kid. He has stolen so much gold from my dad's trains that he can't carry it with him."

Clayton stood up, placed his hands on his hips and glared at the boy. "We aren't taking you anywhere, you gangling gerbil."

Pete mocked him. Placing his own hands on his little hips he spoke in a singsong voice. "Don't be a willy, nilly, silly scared little filly! With our air machine, we can swoop in and grab the gold and leave."

"*Our* air machine? This machine is not yours at all! You can't just order us around!" I say. By this time, I was not only tired, but darn angry. *Why couldn't this kid just shut his trap?*

He didn't shut up. Instead, he turned to me and says, "Billy the Kid has robbed lots of my father's trains. I heard all about it. Papa told me where they hide out and everything! If we could get his gold back for him, he'll give us a big reward! I can help! I'm a great pirate; I practice sword fighting all the time."

He swung his little sword, getting awfully close to the astrolabe hanging in the middle of the little room. I gasped and reached out to grab him, but he ducked away. "Let's be real pirates! You can be Captain Smollett," he says, pointing to Clayton's scruffy whiskers. "Yo ho ho, and a bottle of rum!" He twirled around with his sword in the air. "Can we have something to drink? This is so much fun!"

"Of course not!" I say, my motherly instincts flaring. This kid ran hot and cold so fast, I couldn't keep up with him. Giving him spirits tempted me, though my conscience bit me in the heart. Two nights ago I had slipped the kid a sleeping draft; rum might not be a bad idea!

"We're the most terrible air pirates in all the western territories," says Pete.

I couldn't stay mad at him long. Catching his excitement, I walked to the cupboard and started to open the door before I stopped myself. Rum might have aided his sleep, but I only took out two glasses and one cocoa mug. Sneaking something into hot chocolate somehow sounded better than offering a shot glass to a nine-year-old.

I turned around, and asked, "Why would you want to recover your dad's railroad gold? What would you get out of it? Would he give you the money or let you play somewhere besides the roof?"

Pete just smiled.

Clayton and I exchanged meaningful glances, and he shrugged his shoulders. We agreed with our eyes, that of course we could rob Billy the Kid's treasure, but we certainly need not return the gold to the boy's dad.

We erred in not asking where a nine-year-old boy would have seen a map leading to the lair of the most famous criminal in the West. But his bright smile affected our judgment, and we believed him.

His little map was a start, and all our compasses, barometers, and gauges helped as we designed a flight plan to the

Green River Canyon where the boy assured us we would find the train-robber's cave full of gold. With plans to take off early in the morning, we didn't even remark at how easy Pete crawled into the makeshift corner bed and drifted off. I slept well that night and dreamt of filling our hold with crates of gold.

I awoke on the floor to a painful bump on the head and a sore backside. It took me a moment to realize why I lay on the floor. Our ship was airborne and rocking and jumping in the craziest manner! I stumbled out of the room, balancing myself as best I could until I reached the cockpit.

That weasel had stuffed his little head when Clayton had showed him the ship. I couldn't claim complete innocence, either. Before we played pirates, I'd given in to Pete's pleadings and offered him a grand tour of the cockpit. I had even let the conspirator sit in the captain's chair while I showed him how I readied the ship for flight.

Yes, while we slept, our little captive figured out how to get the ship in the air. Even though a brilliant student, Pete's navigation skills didn't cut it. He couldn't read the astrolabe or any of the other navigation instruments. I entered the cockpit, cursing the little brat who sat frozen in the chair. As I primed to whack him a good one, I glanced out the window. I did a double-take and found myself staring into the side of a towering granite mountain.

My jaw dropped. "What the ginormous gizmo?" I grabbed Pete's left ear and lifted him up out of my chair. With my free hand, I grabbed the wheel which strained under my pressure as I cranked it hard, and as far to the right as it would go. Pete let out a yelp, sounding like a beaver with a toothache, but I wouldn't let go of either the wheel or the ear. He needed to feel this pain. Unfortunately, I needed to yank the loft accelerator harder, and I needed to do it fast.

I dropped the boy, sat down quick, and grabbed the lever. The ship banked left, sending Pete flying into the window. He yelped again. A loud thump, a crash, and a curse assaulted my ears from behind. My husband's voice bellowed, "Jumping junipers! Where in buzzard's blazes are we?"

"Grab the boy," I yelled. "He 'bout slammed us into this Rocky Mountain!" With a quick glance, I eyed Pete on his hands and knees scrambling towards me. But Clayton must have seized his ankle because seconds later the boy lay sprawled, face down, limbs askew, sliding to the back of the room.

"You scandalous imp," Clayton says. "I should pulverize you right now!"

"I wanted to give us an early start," he cried in the high-pitched squeal of an obstinate urchin.

"You headed in the wrong direction!" I say. I pulled two aerostatic levers and turned the main wheel to the right. I managed to get the ship around while Clayton kept himself busy reprimanding the boy. "That's it! We are dropping you off in Green River on our way home," I says.

Clayton just looked at me, his expression impossible to read.

Jumping up and down, Pete broke in, "I am so sorry, I don't

want to go home. I want to stay with you pirates! I didn't mean to crash the ship. I didn't, really! I want to find the gold."

"*Sorry* doesn't hack it," I say. "You're on your way home."

Pete didn't take a second before he started apologizing. "I know, Mr. and Mrs. Pirate. I know I done wrong. But I have no fun at home. Mother makes me play on the roof every day to give her a bit of peace. Papa used to let me go to the train yard, but the foreman won't allow it anymore. My friends—their parents won't allow me to play at their houses. At least here I have some fun." Then he started to cry—and whether they were real or fake tears, I will never know.

Those have been the first honest words I had heard yet coming out of the mouth of that boy. Still, I wondered about the truth of anything he said. Everything made sense, sure. Our ease in nabbing him, his obnoxious behavior, and no signs of a search party! *What kind of kid was this? What kind of family did he have?*

My anger overshadowed my sympathy, though, so his pleas didn't touch me much. "Where's a gangplank when we need one?" I asked.

Clayton interrupted. He looked so torn. I thought he was ready to give up on Pete, but his head bouncing back and forth from me to the kid bothered me. When the man started thinking, I got worried.

"Effie," says he, "we should just stick with our plan. I already sent the ransom demand."

I folded my arms across my chest and glared. "The course is set," I say. "Green River."

"Not yet!" Clayton says. Then turning the boy around—but still holding him tight by the shoulders—he looked directly in Pete's face. "Pete, if we allow you to stay a bit longer, will you quit these shenanigans? Will you control yourself?"

"Oh, I'll be the best! I'll wash the dishes and shine the clock-works," he pleaded.

Not the promise I wanted. I didn't trust him. But when he put on his cute begging face, it took all I had to resist. "No you won't," I says. "You won't touch anything on this ship ever again."

"He can play outside and ride the bikes," says Clayton, "but I'm not ready to give up on our big score yet. His father is super rich, so I know we'll make out fine. After we get the device from Mr. Rothenberg this afternoon, then we set him loose."

"How much would anyone be willing to trade for this one?" I asked, pointing my finger directly at Pete's nose. "I still vote for pushing him out the trapdoor as we pass his house, but it looks like I am outnumbered." I let out a slow breath, and flew on quietly for a few minutes. Then I turned towards Clayton and the boy and says, "We won't be going off chasing Billy the Kid, either!"

"Okay, no Billy the Kid," Clayton answered. "But Effie, just wait until tonight. You'll see."

"Last chance for him *and* for you!"

"Don't worry. By tomorrow night, we'll be in Utah scoping out ZCMI."

I spotted the secret entrance to our canyon and descended carefully. After landing, Pete helped tether the ship. That afternoon, Clayton rode off towards the town.

"I'll be back in a few hours with the parts," he says. He waved to me, looking confident as he took off on his bike down the path. A slightly humbled Pete stuck to tweaking and riding my bicycle. He made a few adjustments, and I admit he did make that bike smoother and faster. But then the questions started again. How many boys had we kidnapped? What was our next plan? Who had we stolen the airship from? How many trains had we robbed? When did I meet Clayton?

After each question, he lapped around the ship, blasting the klaxon, scaring the wildlife, and grating on my nerves. I made up fantastic answers, hoping he would give up on asking. We kidnapped twelve boys. We planned to fly across the Pacific Ocean and attack China. We snitched the ship from the Royal Canadian Mounties. We didn't rob trains, only millionaires. Of course, I told him I met Clayton at finishing school where Clayton waited tables. Even when I claimed that I was secretly a princess from Arabia, he said he believed me. My stories were quite mixed up, but he didn't care. He just circled the ship again and asked another question.

By the time my husband returned to camp in the early evening, I had collapsed, exhausted. Clayton, though, with his downcast eyes, furrowed brow, sunburned face, and still hatless head, looked worse than even I felt. This scheme had taken its toll on both of us. Only the kid seemed unaffected.

Ordering Pete to gather some kindling for a campfire—which I hoped would be the last—I joined my husband in the galley. I looked at him expectantly.

"I don't see a Kelster in your basket. Did you get a response?"

"Yes," he says. He didn't look up; his hands were busy opening and refolding a small piece of paper.

"And? Will he give us even one? I am willing to compromise. I think I can still make an altivolant ship with just one Kelster Capacitor and a few extra alterations. But the kid needs to go, even if we get less than what we hoped for."

Clayton sat at the table and dropped his head into his hands. "Oh, we will get less than we bargained for, that is for sure. Here, read the note they left," he says, shoving the paper across the table. The last three days babysitting Pirate Pete should have prepared me for the words I held in my hands. Printed in neat letters, the response shocked me nonetheless.

Kidnappers:

Received your demands. I must be blunt; you are asking too much. Instead, we have a proposal for you to consider, one that we feel is much fairer considering the situation. You bring Pete home and pay us three hundred dollars, and we will take him back, no questions asked. But don't bring him to the train yard, as the foreman has sworn an oath that he will shoot him next time he comes near, and his shot isn't that great. Bring him by the house at night so as not to alert the populace of his return.

Sincerely,

Joseph Rothenberg

I dropped the paper to the table and tasted sour bile working its way up my throat. "We put up with this kid for days, and now we can't get rid of him without paying his parents? What in tarnation is that?" Clayton stared at the table. "I don't even think he wants to leave! And when he doesn't want to do something . . . We might be stuck." The idea terrified me. "We don't have three hundred dollars!"

Clayton placed his hands firmly on the table, stood up, and turned to the door. Leaning out, with his arms above him braced on the doorframe, he watched Pete speeding down the east trail. I joined him. The boy maneuvered my bicycle so fast and quick. Neither of us had that much skill.

"I have an idea," Clayton says, "one that may solve the problem." He proceeded down the ladder. "Pete!" he called out. "Come show me what you've done to that bicycle."

"Sure, Captain Clayton. I can take the corners much faster now. Did ya see me ride down from the cave?"

"I sure did, Pete. You are quite the mechanical engineer!"

"Will you race me?"

"Oh, I could never beat you with my bike! Yours has so much added power." Pete beamed at him.

"I have a proposal for you," says Clayton, putting his hand on my bike's handle. I couldn't believe what I was hearing. *What was he doing?*

"A proposal? Like a business proposal? You want me to help you attack China?"

Clayton laughed, a little confused, and glanced at me. I

shrugged my left shoulder and winked, so he continued. "No, just tell me how much you like this here bicycle."

"I love this bicycle! You're not going to give it to me, are you?"

"That depends," says he.

I was about to interrupt. That was *my* bicycle he was about to give away! I loved that bike. But I bit down hard on my bottom lip and let him continue uninterrupted. I didn't see as I had much of a choice.

"Here is my proposal. We let you keep the bicycle, if you will let us take you home. It seems we owe your Dad some money. No matter what, we need to drop off the bicycle on your roof tonight. We can drop you off, too. So the choice is yours: come with us and we'll drop you off with the bike or we leave you here by yourself—we won't be coming back, and we won't be leaving the bike."

I had to hold tight to the door to keep myself from barging out and stopping him. Clayton had no right to give away my bike—the one thing I had bought legal, though I'm not saying how I got the money to do so. I sat down right in the doorway and let him negotiate away. The kid couldn't hang around and endanger our airship, or my sanity, any longer.

Pete pleaded with Clayton to take him with us to China, and Clayton explained honestly that I had been joking—our ship simply didn't have the power to make it that far. That left Pete without much of a choice either.

"Okay, take me home," he says. His drooping face and low voice conveyed his disappointment.

Our sticky predicament left few options. My script was a bit better than Clayton's, so I wrote out a note to Mr. Rothenberg explaining our financial position. I asked him to accept the bicycle in lieu of the three hundred dollars. Of course the bike was worth far more than four hundred with the newest modifications, but we also didn't have much of a choice. I tied the note to the bicycle handle and made Pete promise to show it to his father.

In June, the sun sets late, so we didn't lift off until long after our dinner—roasted squirrel Pete had run over with my bike. The boys brought some rigging down from the top deck and tied one end of the line to the bulkhead and the other end to the bicycle with a set of halyard hitches. I double-checked the knots myself.

We flew in silence: a quiet of battling emotions and worries. We watched the stars in the clear night sky.

No clouds obscured our arrival, and as we neared Green River, I slowed down to adjust my goggles. I easily located the large cubed house on the edge of the square. All the windows shone with gaslight. The Rothenbergs expected us.

When Pete ran into the flight cabin to give me a goodbye hug, a tear formed in my left eye. He wasn't my child, but for a few days, it almost felt like I was a mother. I blinked away the tear. He returned to mount the bike. Clayton asked if the belt was tight enough. 'It better be,' I thought. I heard a clang as Clayton knocked on the dishpan protecting Pete's head. Pete was ready for the flight of his life.

"Time to go," says Clayton. "Don't forget to give your pa the note."

"Give me a shove!" Pete cried.

"Hold tight," says Clayton.

I positioned the ship directly over Pete's house and dropped as low as I could without knocking out one of the chimneys. Clayton cranked the wheel by the trapdoor and lowered our human anchor down to the roof. I held our ship steady. From my window, I couldn't see directly below and be certain he made a safe landing. But Clayton gave me the thumbs-up, and I let the ship rise as he turned the winch to pull up the line. We needed to skedaddle way out of town before the neighbors or the foreman caught sight of us and had time to load their shotguns. A few seconds later, a loud Clayton-sounding whoop echoed through the hull. He was loud enough to wake a hibernating possum. I turned back to see my husband waving his missing and now returned goggle-bedecked hat above his head and dancing around in a high-stepping jig.

Smiling, I turned the ship 180 degrees and set the calibers on the chronometer south for Green River Canyon. Maybe Pete did know something about Billy the Kid's hidden stash.

It was worth a look.

Styled after "The Ransom of Red Chief" by O. Henry

Rise of the House of Usher

J.R. POTTER

13 October 1837

Dearest Brother,

Roderick, the house is alive once more! Father is up morning and night, ever feverish in the pursuit of "his glory" as he now calls his work. I do not know what he is building, only that it sounds like a full orchestra of hammers and pipes. The floors creak, the bell jar slides across the mantelpiece and shatters. Waking or in dreams, I find myself running through this lost mansion picking up the decay of its quaking walls, while the sound of his voice booms through the endless corridors and chambers: a grim laughter, rising behind locked doors.

I have seen Father twice in the past two weeks—*twice, Roderick!*—and always trailed by the Creature. His faithful servant hasn't aged a day, believe me, while Father—*may the Lord forgive me for saying this*—looks as if he's already "festering in his shroud." But the Creature remains frozen in youth's eternal stream, the same milky-white complexion, the same bulging, glacial blue eyes, almost tranquil-looking, if not for the things he has seen. . . .

He refuses to speak even a word to me in English when I press him about what Father is building in the damp grotto beneath the east library where we used to play as children (do you remember?). Perhaps his mind insists on returning to his Germanic roots, as if speaking the words might grant him a momentary relapse into that former life before Usher, before Father.

Perhaps it's his only way to survive these days that are nights.

Tell me: can you return to a place that Time has gutted completely, leaving only the barren shell, a skeleton no more resembling the original article than one human ribcage placed side by side with another of equal age and size?

Answer this for me, dear Roderick, before leaping to your pen.

Ever yours, your faithful sister,

Maddy

P.S. I thought you would approve of the Shakespeare reference. Tell me, how do the women in Paris take to a lawyer who can quote Elizabethan verse?

18 October 1837

Dearest Brother,

I awoke last night (was it night? The sky told me so, but there was an urgency in my heart that suggested morning) and found the Creature standing in the courtyard just beneath my window, a few paces from the sluggish pond that is the reflective witness to our house's misery.

Do you remember how we used to speak of the Creature's "secret ears," how we believed he could even hear our own thoughts beating around in our heads? Well, I tell you his ears were well tuned last night: before I could let the curtain fall from my hand, he spied me in my bower, his pale face jerking up to meet mine, as if attached to a marionette's string.

He had a bundle in his arms—which he didn't dare drop on my account. I caught something peeking out of the sack—a hand, or at least what was left of one.

The skin cased only a portion of its God-given form, while at least three of its fingers were wholly metal, each one jittering in a manic *frisson* that told me the thing—*for how could one still call it human?*—was not so easily put down.

I do not know where he buried it, but in the east library several hours later, sipping the chartreuse you brought me last Christmas, I think I heard the thing clawing outside the bay window like a five-legged spider searching for its nest back in the infernal grotto below.

Even now, three-quarters of the chartreuse emptied, my desk swims beneath me in this abyss of a room which candlelight has all but forsaken. Nothing burns in here, Roderick: the air is as damp as the deepest crypt, perhaps made damper by my tears. I think this little desk is my life raft, bearing me across the frigid Atlantic towards you. And then comes the cracking—always *cracking, cracking*—up through the ice and wood, the thing that once was someone's hand, coming for the girl who once dreamed that life rafts always get recovered.

Write soon. Even a few words would settle the tremor in my heart!

M

23 October 1837

Because I can only take your silence as complicity in Father's dealings with the devil, I will continue to prattle on my life story like one of your overeager witnesses, or better yet—like the school girl who would follow you around by the tail until you collared her behind the schoolhouse wall.

But I must be my own teacher and counsel in this matter since you have departed Usher, skipping eagerly in your own bookish way towards the skirts of *les belles dames de Paris*.

Yesterday, I resolved to venture beyond Usher's curse—*beyond him*, I mean, and the Creature.

For a few brief hours, I confess, I managed to break free of the fog that entraps Usher day or night, the same fog that made me mistake you for an ogre once (do you still have the scar? I've often wondered. Even now, here in this gloom, just thinking of it makes me smile). I made it all the way to the river, and I must say it was the most pleasant afternoon I've spent in years.

Do you remember how beautiful our land is? Surely, in all your travels abroad you have seen more majestic vistas that would make the grounds of Usher pale in comparison (if the pale fog would allow it). For the first time my lungs filled with sweet, temperate air, not the usual damp asphyxiation that chokes all breath; the mask of everything that is Usher fell away, and I regarded the streams, the rivers babbling on to Babylon, the selfsame that must have inspired Mr. Coleridge to his pen.

And then everything changed.

Despite your silence, I feel compelled to describe what happened next as a testimonial to the great crime that is at this very moment being committed in your own land, in your own home, Roderick.

I know how you frown upon my daily imbibing (I will not say "drink," for the word assumes that a thirst is slaked, whereas mine, as long as I dwell aboveground in Usher, shall never be quenched from its many secret fires). And before you draw up the brows of judgment, let me state, for the record, I had not had even a sip that afternoon. It all fell in line with my escape from everything that is Usher; I wanted to cleanse my soul.

But what would happen there in my seemingly impregnable cloister would darken my heart, filling it with a terror that no man-made concoction or spirit shall ever remedy. The day had begun its turning. I must have drifted off into one of my reveries again, but one so peaceful it made my sudden awakening all the more brutal.

Through the thatched hands of the trees, the light came now in golden slivers illuminating only fragments of my secret bower. There were three figures, three I could detect, just beyond a strand of oaks skirted by tall grass. My instinct was my pen knife—the one you gave me the day before you left, making that ridiculous little joke that "the pen is now truly as mighty as the sword." I reached into my garter, but it was nowhere to be found. I must have left it on my desk.

There was no pathway back through the woods that was not barred by my assailants. The only sure escape was to dive into the river which was now as cold as the grave, and would surely become mine were I to hazard that route. Three men I spied—men, that was my instinct, Roderick—but my instinct was wrong. They were not men at all, at least not any more.

As I shivered, flattening my belly against the damp earth like a snake to hide my position, through the fingers of tall grass I watched one approach. He had not bothered to wear a coat or even a shirt, but was naked as Adam save that the rib borrowed by Jehovah from his breast remained clearly missing. In the cavity of his chest were the lineaments of a true watchmaker's hand. Even at twenty paces I could hear the *click, click, click* of the infinitesimal gears, his mechanical heart beating for his dear watchmaker, our father, and perhaps now for his watchmaker's daughter—*though what desire could animate such fleshless beating?*

I felt my body start to wither down into the dirt, sinking farther and farther as the creature approached. Before I fainted into the nothingness that is the icy grip of fear, I saw his—*its*—face. Since I am writing this letter, you have surely deduced that I survived that afternoon, and I will confirm that—*Yes*, the shell of your Maddy survived that encounter, but not the soul gripped by fear within her. I am no more since I've looked upon that visage; I am that visage entirely now myself.

I must describe it in detail as one last effort to beseech you to return and help me destroy what Father has achieved—the mechanics of disaster.

A beehive of leather encasing the outline of a face down to the exposed mouth . . . the naked skull peeking out from the chin beneath the womb of leather . . . chattering, gray chips of teeth and jaws held together by copper wiring. There are no eyes, Roderick! The creature *feels!* Yes, it *feels* the world through some sensory detection that is mysterious to me but not to him, its watchmaker god. There is no tissue, no skin, no remnant of humanity left in these animated corpses. *He has cooked their humanity down to the bone. . . .*

As the thing crouched over me, its mechanical heart clicking in well-timed frenzy a foot above my own, I could smell the shell of what it once was. Was this a grandparent? A noble ancestor? The frenzy of its mechanical being rose like an ocean in my ear, and I fell beneath its jittering void, my nothingness being hammered out until everything in the world, and everything you knew to be your sister, turned black.

23 October—*later*

The face of a bird upside down in a tree: a small thrush. The ground close to my face. Then darkness. Something hammering in my ear. A memory? Your voice shouting, "I am Arthur Pendragon! I am the slayer of the Great Worm!" Then the light again and the bird gone from the branch. The hammering in my ears falling away to the steady heaving of two breaths—mine and the Creature's.

I cannot see him from my position slung over his back, but I feel his cold hands grip my waist. And without looking I can sense his massive form, see his deep tracks retreating behind us through the mud. As for the others, I see nothing of them in the woods. The mist swirls back round us and we are in Usher again.

Minutes—moments?—later we slip through the tall stone arch, into the shrouded doorway, up the long staircase. I have not the strength to break free, to run back down the stairs to the cracked door hissing with dark air coming from the watchmaker's studio. All I can think of is the pen knife stabbing through his heart—not the Creature's, but Father's—and putting a stop to this madness. But the thought leaves me like a dream.

I fall back, my head hitting his back and smelling the dampness of his jacket slickened by my tears. Darkness falls over me. I awaken later in a pitch black room. As my eyes adjust, I spy the watchmaker by the window. His hair is a bloom of lightning white, the only light in the room save for the twinkling of his two eyes that now turn at the change in my breathing.

There is a reflection on the nightstand next to me: a glass, not one I remember leaving there. Though the hammering is still echoing in my ears, it doesn't take me long to realize that he has drugged me, his own daughter!

This is what we've come to, Roderick! Where are you, Roderick? Where is Arthur Pendragon to slay the worm that has burrowed into our keep, who has devoured all our treasure and our kin, who has found only a girl left alive, a flimsy shield against the oncoming storm? He inches closer to my bedside smelling of the dead fat of a corpse. I close my eyes to rend the thought of his busy hands from my sight.

"Did you truly think, my dear, that you could stop my ascending glory? Did you think I would let you escape my rising gift to the world?"

One finger: on my throat. Testing my pulse? No—the first lace of a strangling glove. My mind is on fire, but my lips are frozen messengers of sense.

"I . . . I . . ."

Laughter: the same as Beelzebub's. The finger releasing. His face turning back to the window. The moon pulling back the layers of a man who once was a man, now no different from his work: *the devil is in the details. The devil is in the glorious work. The glory of Man is not God's. The glory of the grave hath no sense. . . .*

"Kill me? I know you want to, even before everything I am about to show you. But you cannot kill me! You cannot kill any of us!"

He turns—slowly, slowly, a thrushing sound like a raven's wings spreading wide, like an archangel unfurling his dark egress.

"I shall live on through my work. And you, little Madeline, you shall see the House of Usher rise again!"

The hand: at my throat again, the breath getting choked out

like a coffin lid lowering. And his eyes! *His burning, brilliant eyes!*

"The dragon is hungry! And the dragon shall lift its wings over us all!"

It is the impossible thing that we imagine, Roderick, but it is the improbable thing that is all the more surprising when it comes to pass.

The tip of the pen knife slices up through the back of his neck. He staggers, screaming, falling backwards into the arms of a figure as tall as the room itself. He gargles out his last breath, blood spraying like a shower all over the room. His wingless body lowers to the foot of the bed and in his place a figure—pale and monstrous and filled with glacial tears—the Creature, the first creation of his hand, his twisted insides not mechanical, but riven by hatred and misguided guilt . . . but riven no longer.

Me on his shoulders fleeing. And then the sound: *a wild scratching up from the depths below.*

The House of Usher will rise again.

10 March 1838

At the refuge of Our Lady of Deliverance, months after the horrible night.

Dearest Roderick,

It was good of you to come see me today. Sister Margaret said that you reminded her of our dear president, Van Buren, with your new muttonchops. I told her they would never let you in the office if they knew of the trail of broken hearts and bodies from questionable duels you've left across several continents.

The comment made her giggle like a girl—a chaste one, of course. I sat for several hours after your visit on the porch where they put the consumption victims to alleviate their suffering. I think I share a common bond with them: the dark air of Usher has crippled me mortally. And now, tomorrow, I am to return again to the place I fled and I alone escaped.

I am not sure if I will survive or escape again. I feel a dark gravity calling me, Brother, as one magnet feels another and must fly to it. The peace and serenity of this place is a blessing, and yet the curse of Usher is stronger, and I am bound to it, as are we all, bound by our blood, and how can you escape your own blood? Perhaps it is well that I am to return, as there is no instrument possessed by a doctor that may locate the source of my agony, for it is buried deep in the mind, in the memory of what I have seen.

So, to that end—perhaps to *my* end if I can still be your dramatic Maddy—I will return to you, but first I will put down for the record the rest of that October night, may it serve you to fight the demons that still haunt Usher, though the monsters from your report have either fled or died, if death is still a possibility for them.

I found the letters, dear Roderick, the ones he never sent to you. The Creature knocked over the table in our flight and out of the secret hatch they fell like doves. You have found them by now, no doubt, and I only ask that you include this letter as the last chapter. May it be my last testament to the House of Usher.

Though the effects of the laudanum were starting to wear off, I swore I saw the tail of something slither past the banister outside my door. Perhaps, in my mind, I still heard your voice saying you were Arthur Pendragon and that the great worm was yours for the slaying. When we return, I will look in every room for evidence of that dragon. I am certain it sleeps, balled tightly in one of the dark wings of the house. It is invisible most of the time, but as the patron mascot of Usher it cannot forever go unseen. I am certain you will see it one day, dear Brother, and when you do, I am certain I will be gone from this world.

Forgive these digressions, the habit of a mind not wishing to remember the pain it has endured and survived. We made our way from the bedroom where his body still lay warm, his mouth still open in its final scream of agony. The staircase swung like a circus platform beneath us as we descended—I again on his back, the Creature heaving and cursing low in German. We got to the foyer when one of Father's infernal creations broke up from its hole in the ground, rising up from one of the pores in the brain of the mastermind of Usher.

This one had something installed in its mouth: not just chips of teeth, there were little metal mallets like the tongues on a piano. It made a discordant noise as it came for us. It was then that I realized its creator had endowed it with speech: the mallets struck patterns of sounds, the sounds conforming to words.

"*Give us . . . give us . . .,*" was all it could utter, perhaps all it needed to.

The Creature's hand ripped open the door, but we were mistaken. There were two others in the courtyard. "*Give us! Give us!*" they chanted in operatic chorus like one of Herr Wagner's new cycles. The Creature set me down, slamming the door shut first, then twisting the handle and locks with his bare hands until the door became stuck.

The sickening swoon was starting to wash over me, the plummeting back into the hammering nothingness. I clung to the metal knocker, which strangers always mistake for a horseshoe, the apotheosis of luck, but truly is the opposite: the first U in the name of Usher, signifying now the Unclean, the Undead, the Unredeemable.

The thing beyond the door beat with unrestrained fury, a few inches behind my ear. I watched through glazed eyes as the Creature battled the first monster, lunging to the side with surprising quickness as the bone and metal arm swung forward like a pendulum aimed at his head.

For all his taciturn mystery, the Creature may be the fastest man I've ever met. Reaching behind the neck of the first monster, keenly aware of its anatomy, he grabbed a long cord that appeared to be the central seam in the monster's leather-wrapped chest. The cord ripped free, one of the monster's shoulders coming apart instantly. As it staggered backward, the Creature kicked his heel into its back and it went sailing into the tarn, where, upon impact, the open seam in its back separated even further.

By now the beating behind my ear had become a sharp cracking: the *door was coming apart*. The Creature's "secret ears" detected the change, and brandishing a small pistol from his coat, he unloaded several rounds as the second monster descended upon him.

BLAM! CRACK! BLAM! CRACK! The sound of gunshots and the splintering door alternated for several seconds. I clambered down from the steps, holding onto the metal railing for dear life. He caught me in his arms, and in one swift motion bore me up onto his shoulders, then turned back to fire at the monster that would not be put down by such mortal instruments.

It reeled towards us, its leather face rent backwards from the last blast of the pistol. The beehive-like wrap of its head had split open, and in the subsequent crater, an amalgam of twisted gears and bone burst forth. We had only a few seconds before the door would split open behind us or the monster in front of us would reach us. We needed another way into the woods.

There was only one other way that I could think of, the only way you, had you been in my place, would have chosen: the underground mausoleum where the bodies had been taken to build Father's "glory."

I could see the place in my mind as if standing there twenty years ago as a child, the day we wandered in chasing that squirrel: the stairs leading down, the freezing air, the silence of the breathless crypt. And then—at the far end—a pinhole of gray light, a partially collapsed wall, the evidence of Nature's omnipotence above the curse of Usher.

The squirrel found it before we did, escaping back into the woods. I trusted, like a girl trusts her father or mother before she truly knows their hearts, that the hole still remained, that the light would still guide us, that Nature still rises above Man's mischief to return him to his rightful place beneath—never above—the stars.

I yelled to the Creature to drop me. He swung out, catching the oncoming monster and driving him back with the butt of his pistol. As he wrestled with him on the ground, in his back pocket I could see the glint of the pen knife stained red in the moonlight.

Rushing towards him—perhaps a little too eagerly, the effects of the laudanum still strong—I fell forward, smacking into the monster's hand that slashed out, cutting open a wound above my eye which immediately began to pour blood. Screaming in agony, I stumbled backwards into the stone wall of the tarn where the other creature grabbed my hand just as the door to the house blew open.

The touch was frozen. With my other hand I winched open the frenzy of jittering fingers, freeing myself as the Creature went down on top of his adversary. I had no time to waste. I reached him a second later, and ripped the pen knife from his pocket. He spun the flailing monster around and, seeing me, told me without speaking—his eyes seemed to summon my hand—to undo the beast. With a slash I ripped open the sewing joining the shoulders and back, and like the first one struggling in the pond, I undid my father's creation.

The epileptic shaking came immediately as the gears inside him began to jitter out of control. The Creature let go of him and, staring at me, ascertained—I am confident now through some sort of telepathy—my intentions to find the hole in the wall of the mausoleum, the tunnel which lead secretly out into a corner of the woods that would prove difficult to reach by regular footing without going another half mile around, as a dark finger of lake jutted up in the middle of the forest, whereas the path through the crypt lead directly up onto the opposing bank.

And so, he gripping his pistol and I my flimsy knife, we took off across the courtyard, headed for the stairs, down into the profaned resting place of our ancestors. We reached the spiked fence surrounding the crypt a few seconds later. With a swift kick to the rusted bars, the door blew back, and the Creature turned to take my hand. He neither smiled nor frowned: his face was a milk-white resolve of what he had to do. I didn't understand until I reached the bottom of the steps that he was sacrificing himself.

To this day, I don't understand why he made the decision. I hated him all my life, and surely he hated me—the flesh and blood of his master, the creator of his anguish. As you know, he owed Father a debt of loyalty that prevented him from ever breaking his tenure of service. Perhaps now, severing his bond with his master by knifepoint, his loyalty, in its strange way, had passed on to me.

I heard the door slam shut behind me, a body slinking down against it to bar the way. Then the sound of gunfire and shouts in German. As I trembled alone in the dark of the crypt, I could hear his cries as they descended upon him like a sea of daggers, scraping and slicing away at his blockading flesh. What would you have done, dear Brother? Would you have laid down in the crypt and waited for the end? As I slunk to my knees, I thought about the silence of such an end—no more hammering, no more scraping, the sea passing over me like a wave and me sinking down with it into nothingness. But in that nothingness there was a second void and there was your face. I knew then, dearest Brother, I could not go to the grave without you. For beyond that empty silence there was still a voice—your voice. And that voice was telling me to get up.

In my eyes: blinding tears laced with blood. In my nostrils: the stench of death. Then something . . . alive brushing past my arm. The two open doors yawning like toothless, black mouths before me—the profaned cellars of our father's desire. And behind my head: the breaking of a door into madness.

Where was the light? Where was it, Roderick? I could hear the silence around me turning to the hum of gears, timeless watches in the monsters' chests continuing their rotations though their watchmaker god was no more. The hammering rising in my ears again. And then—at the far corner, where hope shields its face from the critical eyes of disbelief, an opening—a gray spout of light with the bricks crumbled beneath it.

I ran for the hole while across the floor a scraping hum signaled their attack. I reached up through the window of my freedom gripping only wet dirt. The remaining bricks scraped my arms as I pulled with everything that was still alive within me. There was something at my ankle as I climbed up and out.

But it was too late. Staring down into the trap below, I could see it: its head without a leather mask, its long dark hair still attached, its face still half of Mother's.

"*Give us . . . give us . . .,*" it whispered reaching again for my ankle. It was the nightmare of the past he couldn't let sleep. The nightmare started to ascend. I forgot everything that was ever good about her. I thought only of him and kicked it back into the crypt.

The boat. Two rotting oars. The oars pulling through the water as black as the tarn. Seven shadows on the bank hesitating—one with long hair, half of a white face hovering through the mist seeing me, but me not seeing it.

April? May ~~1837~~ 1838

What are days, years? All life and death is a circle. And the circle leads back to Usher.

There is a dragon in this house, Roderick. I am that dragon. Every scale of my armor—can you see it? Can you see reflected in every scale the face of Usher?

I am a mosaic of all its evils. I am every face twisted and remolded by its unclean hands. I am the Creature, I am Father, I am you even—what you will become if you remain in this house. Just like you cannot stop the dragon from uncoiling in the corner, you cannot stop the legacy of this house from rising again.

From my bower, I see a man standing at your doorstep, Roderick, the one you have wanted to join you for so long. He has no sense of the dragon slumbering in the depths of this house. He comes as a confidant, a trusted friend to whom you can open your heart. But what will he say when, looking into the heart, he beholds only darkness and the mechanics of disaster? Will he spy the handiwork of the true architect of this place, not the work of great God in Heaven?

You do not believe it—you cannot see it, not yet—that we are etched with the same furious hammer strokes as what once climbed out of our profaned playground. We are the patchwork of his desires, and even now, bloodless in his shroud, he is reaching up through the dirt and mud and placing a finger on our throats.

Send this so-called friend away now from your doorstep; he comes with too little and too late for either one of us.

I'm looking down at him from my bower now. He is persistent. I'm wondering who is more the foolish servant—your man opening the door or the one standing just beyond it. My chartreuse dragon eyes scan over his weak, unarmored body, piercing down to his warm, beating center which is the target of all Usher. He brings it now to you like a gift with no notion that it is like a deer tail to a hunter. His innocence shall herald his end.

But I am the dragon, Roderick. My arms reach all the way to touch the black, extinguished stars. My wings shall wrap around you like a thundercloud. My scalding breath will singe back the years and years of withering mold that has grown round our bodies, our souls. From the slumbering evil of this place we will rise, we will rise, we will rise, WE WILL RISE WE WILL RISE WE WILL RISE WE WILL RISE WE WILL RISE WE WILL RISE WE WILL RISE WE WILL RISE WE WILL RISE WE WILL RISE WE WILL RISE WE WILL RISE WE WILL RISE WE WILL RISE . . .

Styled after "The Fall of the House of Usher" by Edgar Allan Poe

The Silver Scams

M. K. WISEMAN

Jan Kamphuisen sat bolt upright in his bunk, ear cocked to the side, listening intently to that which had woken him. The soft creak of canvas, the whine and whirr of the massive gears, the gentle straining of the cords and battens that held the contraption together—all serving to drive the man to distraction in their own small way.

The windmills. The damnable windmills.

Creaking, cracking, clattering away. Jan sighed noisily, as if in an attempt to drown out their cacophony. He turned over in his cot.

The poor fellow—if indeed one could pity a criminal, a murderer, such as Jan—the poor fellow was exhausted, having bailed himself out of an early and watery demise the day before. It wasn't his first trip to the *Waterhuis*, the prison's water dungeon, named for the frantic and constant bailing its occupant was forced into. All told, Jan had dug a hole in water for fourteen thousand, two hundred eighty minutes. He knew. He'd counted each time he'd been sent there. Indeed, the *Rasphuis* had its own method of justice and, while Jan could see the demented reasoning behind the torture, the cruel cleverness of the neat little system, he was angry. And it was never a good thing when Jan got angry.

More often than not, people got hurt when Jan got angry, because when he did, he usually forgot to think. Take that old fool Raff Brinker, for example. There wasn't a day went by that he didn't regret bashing that nice man's head in. Especially as Jan had only done it to cover the escape of him and his companions, an effort that had allowed Pier and Laurens to flee, and earned Jan a waterlogged five year imprisonment in the *Rasphuis*.

Restless, Jan turned again, mentally shaking his fist at the monstrosity of lumber and sail peacefully marking time above him, the dumb object unaware of the slumber it disturbed and the passing hours it tallied up against the prisoners who toiled below.

Jan hadn't been the brains of his operation, that was Pier's calling—make no mistake about that—but he was no unlearned idiot either. Jan held a passing familiarity with the story of that Don Quixote gentleman and could now see why the crazed Spaniard had taken up such a vendetta against the windmills. *Ha!* Jan could only imagine the look on that Spaniard's face if he ever espied the great country of Holland.

But with all his frustration at the noisome windmills, he did have great respect for their power and clever engineering. It was his business, after all. Well, the brawn end of it was.

Jan turned over on his other side, contemplating the coming day. Not that there was much to contemplate. The day would either be spent rasping wood or bailing water. *Rehabilitation. Bah!*

Five years. *One thousand, eight hundred fifty-four days.*

Jan felt the telltale racing begin anew and tried to calm his mind, taking deep breaths. Deep breaths that, unfortunately, ended up timing themselves along with the creak and sway of the windmills above. *Calm yourself or you'll be bailing again today,* Jan repeated the mantra in his head, trying to drown out the numbers that threatened to run away with him.

Aggravated assault and murder. That was the charge against Jan. And it was true. For Jan was easily aggravated.

A big man with an oft vacant expression, one might easily dismiss Jan Kamphuisen as a simpleton. But that would be completely dismissing the tortured turbulence that ran under the surface of a placid face that could so easily turn purple with rage.

Like one of those fascinating adding machines one might find at the World's Fair, poor Jan was beset by numbers. His brain ran rampant with calculations, with odd observations. On more than one occasion, it had impeded his better judgment . . . finally landing him in the *Rasphuis* with blood on his conscience. And since that point, Jan's shortened fuse has cost him seventeen days bailing.

Working for his friend, Pier, had provided an outlet for this maddening mental energy, had kept Jan largely out of trouble until that fated night five years back, when Jan got pinched and Pier, it would seem, fled for safer parts.

Not for the first time, Jan wondered what his cohort had done with his half decade abroad. *Likely cozied up to that spineless son of a doctor to cover up our having framed him for murder, made himself a pretty pile, then retired having forgot all about his old partner, Jan.* Bitterness and the dwelling upon of revenge were common pastimes within the *Rasphuis*, and Jan considered himself an adept.

A rattling in the hallway roused the prisoner from his bunk. Anything from the Outside generally served to distract idle minds—or as close to idle as Jan's ever ran. But this was different. Even from his tiny porthole, Jan could see that no less than three guards—*22.5 stone*, his mind quickly calculated—were making straight for his cell.

"Prisoner stand back from the door," the foremost of the guards called out, his voice detached from his duty. The lock rattled, then yielded. Jan stood to the side, trying to look as unthreatening as a big man with a short temper possibly could. Resentful of his captivity or not, he did not wish to repeat yesterday's exercise in survival.

Pier! Jan's prison-short hair stood on end.

It was not possible.

The third guard, the one who so resembled his former partner in crime, winked. It *was* possible. And said possibility was confirmed in less than four seconds when the other two guards gave a sigh and appeared to fall asleep on the floor of Jan's dark cell.

"You've lost weight. I had figured on the fatter one's uniform for a man of your size. Well, no matter. The other fellow's trousers will simply be a touch short on you," Pier Hoogsvliet spoke in low, crisp tones, just as he always had.

Jan gaped . . . just as *he* always had.

Pier had planned the jailbreak perfectly, and with nary a shot fired from his curious looking pistol, the two men gained freedom within several tense minutes—*three hundred eighty-two seconds*. It was only when they were down the canal a fair piece and holed up in Pier's safe house that Jan dared question his former boss.

"Is he dead?" Jan's first question spoke to his most pressing fear.

"Which one?" Pier laughed. "Wessel? Raff? That doctor's sainted son, Laurens?"

"Any of them," Jan added a laugh of his own. Quickly assessing his companion, he could tell that the five intervening years had been kind to his old cohort. In addition to the technologically advanced equipment Pier carried on him—Pier alluded to something called an "aether pistol" as being instrumental in the escape, answering Jan's unspoken question—expensive clothing had lain in wait for the jailbird. Jan wondered at the slight accent his friend now bore. It was all very posh.

"Wessel succumbed to illness; one *not* perpetrated by us. Raff's head injury just about did him in. Lives up the way in a place they call the Idiot's Cottage with his wife and two kids. So he's not doing any talking, and if he does grow lucid, we've possibilities for leverage on the man. And Laurens? I went into business with him, actually."

Just as Jan had predicted. *Sly old crook.* He looked to his partner—nay, his rescuer—and wondered just what it was he wanted.

What Pier wanted at present was a hot meal, apparently. The self-styled aristocrat stood at the stove, shirt sleeves rolled back to the elbows and sweat on his brow. That he hadn't asked Jan for help—or even just to cook the whole meal—was a surprise.

Jan spared a glance around, valiantly resisting the urge to tally the stones. The place looked cozy. Respectable. Not the sort of place one would look for a crook who'd previously fled the country and his recently jail-broken cohort. Jan didn't ask whose place it was. He knew better than to ask such a stupid question. Clearly Pier's new operation was long in setting up—Jan's untimely release from prison just another step in a complicated dance.

Jan was just glad to be invited to the ball. Pier had a new look to him—no doubt out of necessity. After all, he was wanted for far more than petty larceny, whether all witnesses had been dispatched or not, and just over five years had passed. No, the changed look went beyond a new cut and style, a thick mustache that curled and drooped daintily over thin hard lips . . . Pier's very walk was altered, his speech—never boorish—was now manicured and polished. Even in clean stylish clothes, Jan felt dirty in the man's presence.

Pier was a con man, a criminal gifted in the art of selling water to a mermaid, wind to a miller, and lies to politicians. And the plan he laid out to Jan over a rich and restorative dinner was pure genius.

Taking a sip of well-seasoned port, Pier at long last fixed a gimlet eye to his newly freed companion. "Who'd you talk to in the *Rasphuis*?"

"Sorry, what?" Jan spoke around his mouthful of potatoes and gravy, unsure he'd understood the question.

"Who knows about us? What we've done? Who our connections are?"

His stomach rapidly filling with a feast fit for kings, Jan found his temper greatly subdued. "I'm not a blab, Pier. You know that." He continued to tuck in, waiting for Pier to get to his point.

Pier nodded, satisfied. "No, you're right, Jan. You're not a man to squeal. You're more of the strong, silent type. A man with dependable broad shoulders. I bet you that a man like yourself could lift the capital and the surrounding five miles clear out of the reach of its waterways. You've been bulking up during your . . . rehabilitation."

Jan smiled and took a deep draught of his wine to clear his throat. "Now that's just too kind, Pier."

"I tell it like I see it, Jan. You know me."

"Honest a man as ever broke bread." Jan lifted his glass and guffawed. "So what's the plan then, Pier? What're you needin' me for?"

Pier kept his answering smile inside. Jan was truly a treasure: big, strong, imposing, and just barely smart enough to go with a plan but not outwit his partner.

"You and me and those big strong shoulders of yours . . .

we're going to lift Holland." Pier sat back and waited for the words to sink in.

The telltale dull look of confusion crossed Jan's face, the man looking as if he was waiting for either an explanation or a punch line. "Lift? Holland?"

"And eliminate the need for the dikes, the pumps, the worry, and the sleepless nights that come with each and every storm. Yes, Jan, we are going to raise the countryside above sea level."

"But how?"

Pier basked in Jan's befuddlement. He was going to enjoy this one.

"In my five years abroad, I learned a great many things from the modern cities of Europe, America, The Orient, even the far reaches of Antarctica."

"Antarctica . . ." Jan breathed the word, bedazzled.

"Stop interrupting. Yes. And I have seen miracles of engineering, learned from the best." Pier postured grandly in his chair for his rapt one-man audience. "With the extensive low-lying waterways crisscrossing the countryside and cityscapes, we have the perfect outlet for my pneumatic naval mines.

"You see, Jan, it is a well-known fact that the country is seven meters, at most, below sea level at any given place. Submersible pylons, placed at strategic positions below water and terrain, would act as a grid to lift everything out of harm's way."

Pier rose from his chair, striding off to the far end of the room where he dramatically shifted aside a velvet cloth revealing an object that Jan did not recognize. It looked like a copper version of a whiskey barrel.

"I give you my remotely deployable pylon. Controlled by waves of electromagnetism, these contraptions open like a lady's parasol, blossom like indelicate flowers, pushing the earth up, up, up . . . until, voilá! We can shovel the dikes into the gaps left by the lifts, the windmills can be dismantled, and we can all sleep better at night."

"Amazing." Jan's eyes had grown round as moons. "But will it work?" Already he was running the numbers in his head.

Pier sniffed disdainfully at Jan's skepticism. "Heard of New Orleans? Laurens and I perfected the technology there."

"Laurens . . ." Jan growled, eyes darkening.

"Yes, I was lucky enough to get out with my plans—the traitor thought he was going to commercialize the process, whereas I thought it best—noble even—to bless our homeland with this incredible technology."

Jan shook his head, past regrets again rearing their ugly head and dulling the shine on Pier's plans. "Too bad what happened to Raff. Brave man like him who'd worked as he did on the dikes . . . Coulda used a mind like his."

"Cut the remorse, Jan. He was a meddler. A sharp snoop like him would have questioned the whole thing."

"I can have regrets if I want to, Pier. I've been rehabilitated, after all." Jan shrugged off his partner's sharpness, the old dynamic returning to the two men with the ease of a well-worn glove. "What I don't get is how you'll convince anybody that we can do what nobody's done before. I . . . I think they *like* their system of windmills and water, ditches and dikes."

"They love it because it's the only thing keeping everything from floating away. No more, no less," Pier corrected. "Now, if something were to happen, something to remind them of how fragile their system is . . ."

"They'd come a-runnin' back our way with hope in their eyes and money in their fists."

"Exactly," Pier concluded. He let the enormity of his plan sink in before approaching Jan with his first task. "Tonight we'll assess what we're up against. And I'll need you—you with your head for figures—to find their breaking point. We need a devastating flood. Nothing critical, mind you, but enough to wake these people up to the fact that the whole damn country could well be underwater without our help."

Lightning arced across the roiling skies, briefly illuminating the faces of two figures bent on dark purpose. Wincing, the second of the two-man-cavalcade braced himself for the thunder sure to follow.

Jan hated storms. The odds were never good. Recalling the number of sleepless autumn nights he had suffered through, his brain awash with gallons of fears, stopped him in his tracks. He cast bleak eyes over the heaving waters of the nearby channel, sure that they were in for the storm of the century.

"Isn't this terrible?" Pier's wind-whipped words flew at Jan.

"Yes. Terrible." Jan shuddered, his mind trying to gauge the contents of the engorged clouds that pressed from above.

Pier laughed, looking like diviner and madman as he raised his hands to the sky, begging the rains to come and provide the very emergency they'd wished for but hours before. But the storm seemed more sound than spate, the noisy prelude heralding little more than a few fitful showers.

Ineffectively holding his arms over his head in an ill-conceived attempt to stay dry, Jan whined, "Come on, Pier. We're not gonna get anything done tonight. And I'm gettin' wet."

This last didn't help his case. Pier's own disappointment made his tongue especially sharp. "Big man like you afraid of a little rain? Then you should have brought an umbrella."

Scowling, Jan pointed out that the weather wasn't right for an umbrella.

Pier, on the other hand, was impervious to the rain-dampened squall, compliments of an intriguing little device he'd pocketed before going out into the thunderous evening. An invisible bubble of clean, dry air surrounded the man and Jan was jealous.

"You coulda had two . . ." Jan muttered.

"Hush."

At Pier's request for silence, the two men stood atop the dike, Jan wondering at his companion and Pier gazing westward along the channel.

"There." Pier pointed, reaching out impulsively to grab Jan's arm and thinking better of it when he realized how saturated Jan had become.

A pitiful cry arose from below, borne on the still-fitful wind. There was a boy down near the water's edge. Small and dressed in farmer's clothes, he couldn't be more than six, maybe seven, years of age.

"Go to him, Jan."

The resentful bullheadedness that had been growing within Jan now reached its apex. "Why me? You spotted him."

Pier gave Jan an arch look that seemed to say, 'In these immaculate clothes?'

"Fine." Jan grumbled the entire way down the mud-slick slope, finally reaching the terrified young lad.

The boy refused to leave his spot on the bank.

Come on, you fool boy. Jan beckoned from several paces off, unaware that his large stature and rain-drenched appearance had rendered him a fright.

"I can't."

"Why not?" Jan was exasperated. He risked a look up to the top of the levee. Pier was nowhere to be seen.

The boy's response pulled Jan's attention back to the situation at hand. "If I leave, the dike will fail and we will all drown."

Jan now saw where the boy had—rather ineffectively—pressed his thumb into the steep embankment. Water streamed down the boy's outstretched arm, dripping off his elbow and causing the child to shake with cold.

Jan thought quickly—as quickly as he was wont to do.

"We'll fix it. My friend 'n me. You'll only catch cold." Jan opened his arms, beckoning.

With a reticent sniffle, the boy removed his muddy hand and approached his rescuer. Just as Jan suspected, the dike held.

"Ahoy there." Pier's head peeked over the edge of the precipice. "You there, boy, is your family nearby?"

"Yes. The farm is just up the way." The boy pointed.

"As I thought," Pier nodded sagely. "I think your father is coming this way, lad."

Reaching the crest of the sodden dike, Jan noticed that Pier had stopped using his rain shield. He, in fact, looked downright disheveled, but Jan had little time to ponder it when the boy broke free from his arms to run across the field.

"Father!"

Pier had spoken the truth, the boy's father had come looking for his son. Father and son embraced, the boy letting loose a torrent of words. "He saved me, Father. I was looking for the stray cow and then the storm came and then there was all this water coming out of this hole in the wall and so I was afraid that the dike would fail so I stayed and—"

Following in the boy's wake, Pier cracked a weak smile. "I found your son, good sir."

"Thank you. Thank you. How can I ever repay you?" the boy's father cried out.

Jan approached, sodden and shy.

Pier rushed to keep talking. "Yes. I found your son and signaled you while my friend here kept the dam from busting wide open. Your son is a hero, sir, a real live hero. If it wasn't for him we'd have all been floating away right about now. Seems *we* are in *your* debt."

Jan opened his mouth to correct his partner, shutting it when Pier shot him the darkest of looks.

In the end, it worked out better than Pier could have dreamed.

All of Amsterdam hailed the farmer's boy as a real living embodiment of the Hero of Haarlem, the little Dutch boy who'd saved them all from a watery demise centuries before. By the following afternoon, everyone within a ten-mile stretch had an account of the drama that had taken place during the nighttime storm, as well as a description of the two strangers who'd saved the boy who'd saved them all.

Told over and over, the story was being bandied about with pride. A leak of such magnitude stopped by a finger? A mere child's finger? In town to gather the supplies needed for their own carefully orchestrated disaster they'd planned for the following week, Jan rushed back to Pier in a panic.

Pier, by contrast, was delighted at the news. Heartache, sacrifice, imperilment of a child . . . and all without the risk of themselves getting caught in the act of sabotage. He counseled his overactive stooge to wait and see. Get their equipment readied, by all means, but wait and see.

Patience was rewarded. Curious citizens came to gawk at the famous leak, instead seeing the gleaming copper panel that Pier had quickly placed over it, effectively and dramatically stemming the flow.

Doctor Thomas Silvertongue—for Pier, of course, couldn't go by his known name amongst countrymen who might yet recognize him—was quick to embellish the story and claim credit. Truly, disaster had been avoided, compliments of his unique and proprietary engineering techniques. The limelight turned from the soggy seven-year-old to the dashing engineer.

As the newly-minted hero of the saga, Doctor Silvertongue wasted no time in proposing a system of his own—one that would replace that of the terribly outmoded and dangerous dike and canal system, one that would not put the safety of the nation in the hands of its innocent children.

Heartstrings wrung by this new sentiment, the old bearded gentlemen who ran the country put their venerable heads together and unanimously elected to hear Silvertongue out . . . and pay him generously for his efforts.

And now to look busy, Pier smiled to himself as he pocketed the first of his advances.

Jan was less overjoyed. Feeling he had far more invested than a mere finger in an earthen dam, he could already feel the weight of responsibility crashing down on him like so many gallons of water. More than once he'd exposed his concerns to Pier. The numbers just didn't work.

As usual, Pier scoffed at his friend's ignorance, telling him to run them again, verbally berating him, threatening poor Jan into believing himself in the wrong.

And perhaps he was. Pier called the hefty brass cauldron that sat splendidly on display in Pier's warehouse a submersible. Curious. Gazing upon it, Jan could not help but dream of their plan coming to fruition. And yet, in his mind, they needed a hundred such vessels, nay, a thousand, submerged and dug into the earth beneath the countryside in order to raise everything properly, else they'd merely be fixing one small problem to create fifty others. But saying as much only got him into trouble.

And so Jan continued to work his numbers as was his wont.

"I do not like it!" The forceful pronouncement cut through the chatter of one hundred restless men. The *Staten-Generaal* was meeting once again to discuss the progress of Doctor Silvertongue's massive undertaking. While the sentiment was doubtlessly shared by no less than half the representation, the outcry served to produce an audible grumble.

The plan had to work. The country was in peril, they could sink at any moment. Silvertongue and his exotic, newfangled ideas were their only hope.

Technological mastermind or not, where Pier excelled was reading the human heart. He'd maneuvered and manipulated such that they could no longer conceive of any other solution to their newly-urgent plight. Especially as, "We've put so much money into it!"

Ah. There. At last the *true* reason for their discontent, and for their blind faith in Silvertongue's plan: the nagging feeling that it was too late to turn back now.

It was just that, now that the proposed plan was well underway, the doctor kept needing more and more. Materials were expensive. His consultant, a quiet man whom they'd rarely seen, came dear. Never mind his usual fees for such large-scale work. Why, he'd reportedly found and raised two of the eight major islands of the Kingdom of Hawaii for *twice* what he was charging the Dutch.

"If we could just see his progress, talk to his man, than maybe we could rest easily and justify such an expense."

Pandemonium erupted in the venerable hall, a hundred angry men wagging fingers and grey beards at the suggestion. Who could they send on such an errand? What man was to be entrusted with such an important task of judgment? Surely Holland's leading engineers had no knowledge of such things, else they'd have raised the country instead of working out an intricate system of bailing, watering, and channeling all those years ago. Silvertongue seemed to be the only expert around.

There was a vague rumor that Doctor Silvertongue had a partner abroad, a supplier for the massive metal parts that arrived weekly via steamship. However, nobody knew who he was, and for the most part did not care. After all, their savior was here, and had a name and a face.

When faced with trying times, there is but one thing about politicians that is utterly predictable. Politicians will be political when given the chance. Tours of Doctor Silvertongue's factory were arranged, divided into a dozen factions—both to accommodate the modest size required to produce an informative tour and so that each political faction within the *Staten-Generaal* could keep an eye on their opposition.

Doctor Silvertongue was more than receptive to the idea of informative tours. He, in fact, welcomed the opportunity, going so far as to open his warehouse to all comers . . . for a modest fee, of course. After all, he needed to do something to control curious crowds, prevent severe loss of production time to gawkers, hawkers, and protesters.

And protesters there were.

While the ineffective men of the *Staten-Generaal* seemed content to "ooh" and "ahh" over Silvertongue's massive submersible, returning to their government seat to bicker over other mundane things, such as who had dared question the efficacy of this marvelous plan, the dike workers were not as content to merely take Silvertongue at his word.

Jan was shortly afforded the opportunity to flex some of his more obvious muscles, cracking the skulls of several hotheaded men who'd rather Holland stay as it was. A country below the level of the sea, marvel of the modern world. How could anyone dare take away its sparkling channels and silence its windmills?

Eighty-six thousand, five hundred twenty-two. Five million, six hundred thousand five. Seventy-six . . . Lost in his numbers,

Jan nearly missed the telltale flicker of light as he exited Pier's warehouse and made for home, having worked long past sundown. The light flashed again and caught the eye of the former felon.

Jan ducked down behind a low fence, instinct taking over where intellect failed.

Within moments, seventeen men made landfall, dragging their boats up onto the bank of the channel that had brought them near. Lanterns carefully shuttered, they conversed in low tones, finally fanning out around the dark perimeter of the hulking warehouse.

Risking a glance down the channel to where home lay, where Pier had long since gone at day's end, Jan considered running for help. But that meant losing track of the ne'er-do-wells that hovered around the doors of Pier's prized facility.

Flexing muscles and calculating fast, Jan made a snap decision and took off at a run.

A frantic pounding upon the door woke Pier out of a shallow sleep. Grabbing his aether pistol, and checking that the safe was well and truly concealed, he confronted a white-faced Jan on his stoop. The none-too-gentle giant had blood on his hands.

"Damn it, man!" Pier leveled the gun at his partner.

"What? Wait! Pier, it's me, Jan."

"You think I don't know that?" The gun stayed level. "I can't have none of your trouble, now. You get into some sort of fight, you get yourself out of it."

"It's your fight, too." Jan moved to the side, gesturing feebly to the bright glow a good quarter mile—*five thousand, two hundred seventy odd feet, Dutch miles being four times the English standard*—distant along the channel.

"No!" Pier lurched to the doorway. "No, not the submersible. I am undone . . ." He swayed on his feet unsteadily. "You. Stay hidden. I'm calling the guard."

"Guard? What guard?" Jan puzzled, his brain fuzzy. Suddenly, following Pier's order sounded mighty tempting.

"Mine." Pier was cryptic as he slammed the door shut in his cohort's face.

"He has requested a guard, now?"

"No. He has requested materials to construct a guard . . ."

The exchange in the *Staten-Generaal* was less enthusiastic than in previous sessions.

"After people have been hurt?"

"Ruffians, m'lord. Bent on destroying what the man has built. That's government property."

"His crony is the ruffian, more like. If you'd have seen some of those men after that fellow got to them . . ."

"Men who were intent on burglary, vandalism, and worse."

The murmur rose to a fevered pitch, became a dull roar. Objections and counterarguments to providing this Silvertongue with his own mechanical militia jostled for dominance. The suggestion was made that they were throwing good money after bad.

"Order! Order, I say!" Somewhere amongst the throng, a gavel was heard pounding. Chastised, one hundred angry old men fell silent.

The speaker continued, "You saw what he did for that child? He deserves our respect and trust. Give the man what he needs to protect his—*our*—investment. I spoke with Silvertongue himself and he believes that this armored guard of his can be recycled into the project. His assistant has provided him with new numbers, and it would seem that he would have required far more of those underwater metal chambers than previously thought—the one that we saw in his facility being but a model for demonstration."

"Demonstration? Bah!" a disgruntled voice cried out in response. "I've seen naught but posturing, promising, and a load of metal junk on display. More suitable as museum pieces than functioning machines capable of raising farmlands and buildings."

"Well, I daresay it is time for a demonstration then, yes?" Silvertongue himself spoke from the doorway. Pier strode sinuously amongst the greater men, smiling his way to the center of the room, strange metal canister in tow.

It could best be compared to a fish barrel, although that would likely have irked its creator. Coming in at about half the height of an average-sized man, and twice as big around, the metal barrel moved on unseen wheels, creaking and cranking its way across the polished *Staten* floor. Covering its surface, a dazzling array of knobs, levers, and shiny buttons all begged fiddling and pushing.

"Behold!" Silvertongue cried out—quite unnecessarily, mind you, for all eyes were fixed upon the gleaming wonder. "You have seen, no doubt, the marvelous interior of a windmill, its wind-driven engine pulling and pushing water this way and that. Some of you have, perhaps as boys, noted the intricate workings of a clock as it tick-tick-ticked along. Mayhap you've had a glance at the miracle of deployable pylon engineering from tours of my facility. But I promise, not one of you has seen the like of this before." He bent and adjusted a control on the metal-barrel's side.

And it exploded.

Well, not quite exploded—though many a politician was sent scurrying for cover under the assumed threat. Rather, the barrel opened up, revealing pistons and shocks whirling furiously inside the staves. Steam hissed and poured out from half-a-dozen places, while the entire contraption rocked and rotated in place.

Now, shouting to be heard above the din of his invention, Silvertongue explained, "These automated sentries are impervious to most firepower and can be set to automatically deploy upon sensing vibrations in the ground or sounds of a certain frequency. Equipped with two fully rotational Derringers and self-destruct mechanisms, they're the smartest guards on the planet and, I daresay, *would* protect *your* investment as I finish my work on the submersible that will, in the end, raise all of Holland *permanently* above sea level."

He turned another lever and the machine quieted, settling back into its unassuming barrel shape once more. "When the weaponry is removed, they can double as supports for my underground hydraulics system that will keep your country elevated beyond the need for dikes and windmills. Any questions?"

Silvertongue was granted the extra funding he'd requested. And his warehouse was left alone at last.

Knee-deep in steam-powered copper barrels and up to his elbows in grease, Jan once more debated the wisdom of expressing his worry over Pier's grand plan. *Twenty-seven hundred . . . Fifty-seven . . . Eighty trillion, five hundred sixty-five* . . . Things had gotten out of hand. Perhaps he was becoming paranoid, the numbers wearing at his mind but . . . Armored copper barrel sentinels? It seemed a little extreme.

For all that they'd antagonized him and attempted to thwart their grand scheme, the engineers with whom Jan had conversed had seemed decent fellows. Decent and *knowledgeable* fellows, who truly did have the country's best interests at heart. Jan felt . . . lonely . . . now that they, and all other comers, had been chased away by Pier's new security measures. He had nobody, nothing but his numbers, to console him in his fears that something about Pier's plan simply did not add up.

They were one week away from putting Pier's plan into action. One week away despite Jan's insistence that they hadn't near enough power to lift the entire landscape. They were talking ponderously heavy earth and water, not feathers and soap bubbles, after all!

The concept was astoundingly simple. Pier's cauldron—correction, submersible—would dive into the channel nearest the factory carrying a payload of sentinel barrels, deploying them at regular intervals. And herein lay the potential for trouble. Jan suspected, but could not confirm, that the *Staten-Generaal* had advanced payment for sufficient sentinel-barrels but they had simply not been built.

But Pier said that Jan was wrong. And so Jan assumed it to be true, having heard as much his entire life.

Jan is such an excellent fall man, Pier chuckled to himself as he did another check on his submersible, having only just loaded in the heavy safe containing payment for his project. He stopped to watch his poor simpleton of an assistant shuffling the heavy copper barrels about on the channel's edge.

He was right, Jan was. The plan would never work with the resources that they had in hand, nor would it ever have no matter how much they'd poured into the project. But time was running out. He'd stalled as long as he could. Pier had his king's ransom, had his escape plan ready. Now all he had to do was grab his luggage from the storeroom, eke out a little more of the government's silver if he could, and away Pier would fly! Fly to freedom and a gentleman's retirement, surrounded by all the luxury his great mind could conjure.

Pier fingered the rectangular object in his pocket. Heavy with the radio mechanisms that made it function, the switch was in itself as high-tech as the machines that it controlled. One press of the button and each of two dozen sentinels would snap to attention, covering his escape nicely. Poor Jan would never know what happened until the sentinels deployed, firing indiscriminately. The authorities would snag the only one of the duo left within the *Staten's* jurisdiction.

Pier ducked into the submersible once more, debating where to stow his luggage and wondering how long he would be able to tolerate the cramped quarters. His initial designs had included a much more plush and gentlemanly interior, corners that had to be cut in order to maintain the cover that his copper conveyance was a tool of the trade rather than a means of escape.

Sounds of a disturbance somewhere up the bank echoed down the hill into the channel. Pier sighed, "Now what?" This morning he'd noted the glassy look in his partner's eyes. He knew that look, had been waiting for it, even. The numbers were again getting to Jan and he barely held in check his famous temper. But Pier had counted on a few more hours—days if he could get them—to siphon off a little more money from those fools in the government.

Holstering his pistol, Pier went to confront and then deny involvement in whatever was happening up the hill at his factory.

"Yes. Box that up, too." A well-appointed gentleman stood brashly in the center of Doctor Silvertongue's warehouse, giving orders to a host of soldiers clad in the uniform of the *Landmacht*, the Dutch Army.

"By what authority—" Pier stormed into the factory, stopping short and choking back the short and angry accusation. He stared at the newcomer with a face gone white, hand straying to the pistol concealed beneath his coat. "It's you! Laur—"

"Thomas. Thomas Higgs." The man stopped Pier's hasty words, flashing his former partner a wicked knowing smile. "And I believe you, sir, have something of mine."

Pier narrowed his eyes. Two could play at this game. Had Laurens come to claim his cut of the scam? Or was the man here on some sort of a benevolent mission, recompense for his own previous involvement with Pier and Jan? Clearly Laurens, too, did not desire that his fellow countrymen recognize him just yet.

"I was just explaining to these gentlemen that most of what you see here is my property, rather than yours, Mr. Silvertongue." Laurens raised his eyebrows, hand straying to his own weapon of choice.

One of the soldiers inserted himself between the two gentlemen, eyeing Silvertongue with a look of apology. "See here, now. We've orders to inspect this claim. I'm sorry, Doctor Silvertongue, but we're going to have to confiscate this lot until it gets sorted out. Mr. Higgs here apparently has some pretty damning evidence of intellectual thievery on a grand scale."

Pier found himself staring down the barrels of a dozen military issue rifles.

Where the hell is Jan? he wondered. He scanned the warehouse and saw nothing but scrap metal, half-finished copper sentinels, and the hardened, suspicious eyes of his accusers.

Pier raised his arms in a gesture of surrender, a gentleman to the last. He had a better chance of making it to his submersible if he played along than if he challenged the trained men and was shot for his efforts. He was also curious as to what "damning evidence" Laurens had managed to dig up on him.

"So, what were your plans, Silvertongue?" Laurens allowed Pier's alias to roll across his tongue. "Looks here as though you're playing at war." He ran his fingers gingerly over a half-finished sentinel barrel. "Decent work. Shoddy craftsmanship. Who's playing engineer this time?"

"Now, now. Have a little respect for the doctor," one of the soldiers cut between the two gentlemen, diverting their smoldering looks. "He's promised to raise Holland. Bring her up over sea level like the rest of Europe."

It was Laurens' turn to look shocked.

Pier allowed himself an ingratiating smile. "You see? I haven't anything but noble thoughts in mind." He turned to the soldiers. "The rest is amassed on the bank of the channel. My partner and I were going to perform our feat of engineering—our miracle, if you will—tonight. Most of what you'll find in here are test-runs and experiments. Come, let me show you."

He turned on his heel and strode out. He sincerely hoped that he had guessed correctly about his opponent, namely Laurens' curious-looking weapon was not a firearm and that, even if it were, the man was too honorable to shoot someone in the back.

Pier was correct on one count, namely that Laurens' holstered weapon was not, in the traditional sense, a firearm.

However, it did hurl lightning, a fact which Pier soon discovered the hard way as he made, not for his assembled sentinels, but for the safety of the submersible.

The air crackled with energy as Laurens aimed and fired, using the prod in his hand as one would a sword but with much better range. Pier gasped and arched his back as the first of the shockwaves hit him, falling to the ground with a shudder. Slow to pick up on what had just transpired and admittedly afraid to interfere, the soldiers had only managed to raise their own guns, dividing their efforts to cover both gentlemen, when Pier's questing fingers reached the small control box that had fallen from his pocket as he'd gone down.

"Get down! Everyone!" Laurens' shouts of warning came but a moment too late, as he recognized his adversary's intent. Most of the soldiers went down in the first volley, as Pier's deadly sentinels sprang into action, spraying bullets in sweeping arcs. The rest were pinned to the ground under the steady and lethal hail of shots.

Laurens himself remained unharmed, but unable to use his weapon effectively nor gain the necessary ground to stop his quarry. He crawled a hasty retreat, back around the warehouse to where he'd secured his own escape vehicle.

Disgusted as he was by the dirt his ill-used suit was accumulating whilst he lay in the grass outside, Pier waited for his head to stop swimming. Even if it was only for the space of a few moments, getting up before the electricity had dissipated would be a bad idea. Concentrating instead on the lovely music his sentinels were creating in the warehouse behind him, he enjoyed the repetitive ping of the bullets, wondering how long it'd taken one to find his friend Laurens.

Laurens. Pier's eyes narrowed as he performed a double-check on his pulse. Shakily finding his feet, he stumbled off down the embankment.

What in the world is that glorious weapon that Laurens brought with him? Pier wanted one. But not bad enough to go back. No, a quick look around had confirmed that Jan was nowhere in sight. And with the guard pinned down in the factory, it was time for Pier to flee.

Slamming shut the door behind him and locking the seal, Pier slid into the pilot's seat of his waiting submersible.

"That didn't go so bad," he muttered blackly to himself. It had all gone so horribly wrong! How had Laurens figured out what Pier was up to? How had he known him to be in Holland?

Fist angrily jamming different controls into position, Pier struggled to calm his nerves. Thinking of the massive payday that lay in the cargo hold of his ship helped a great deal. Taking a steady breath and checking the vessel's cruising depth, Pier leaned back heavily into his captain's chair and allowed a slow smile to creep across his face.

"Pier? Beggin' your pardon, but I think we're goin' a bit too fast to drop our first payload."

Jan! The captain of the cramped submersible whirled around in surprise. "How the–? What the–?" He sputtered ineffectively, as his partner took up residence in the only other seat in the diminutive craft.

"I heard a commotion up on shore as I came in for the final check and figured I'd better stay put and get the submersible ready for launch. Found some big ol' box in the hold that had to be removed before we could load in the copper barrels. Heavy sucker. You'd 'a thought it was filled with gold bullion." Jan chuckled and shook his head, every inch the dolt that he was. Seeing Pier's face turn a tight-lipped red, the ex-con grew solicitous. "Everything alright, Pier?"

"Yeah. Yeah, fine. Everything's fine." Pier tried not to fume, concentrating instead on navigating the narrow channel. He'd explain it all later . . . minus certain details, of course. "Plan's changed a bit, though." He paused, considering his next move. "Jan? How much do you know about Venice?"

Styled after *The Silver Skates* by Mary Mapes Dodge

Nautilus Redux

SCOTT E. TARBET

In compliance with the request of a friend of mine, who has been nagging me on Facebook for months, I called on my good-natured, garrulous old aunty, Simone Wheeler, in her little assisted living apartment. Simone is a spritely one hundred and five years old, pushing—as she likes to say—a hundred and six. I was there to ask her about a bundle of hand-written pages she has had in her possession for years. She says they are notes of an interview conducted by a certain famous nineteenth-century writer, whose love child she has always claimed to be.

I make no claim for the authenticity of the papers, the interview, or Simone's claim that her mother had a May/September dalliance with the Great Man. But I couldn't in good conscience let the result of my visit pass from history without becoming known. Therefore, as the man himself would have said, I hereunto append the result.

You're trying to get me drunk, aren't you? Come on, Sam! Admit it! Don't kid a kidder! You think you're the first so-called journalist who tried to pump ol' Ned for information? You know I'm fond of my drink, so you think it will make me stupid? Nice try. I suppose I can't blame you for taking a shot.

Let me tell you, my friend: there are two kinds of reporters who try that. The first are the ones who want to make Professor Aronnax out to be a liar or a madman. They think because I was there for that fantastic voyage of twenty thousand leagues beneath the seas, and the professor talks about me in the book, they can get me to say the whole thing was made up. Just one problem with that: it wasn't. Every word he wrote was true. Every experience he wrote down actually happened. And then some.

The second kind are the ones who think Captain Nemo might still be alive, that he's still out there somewhere. They pump me for information to help them find him. Wouldn't that be a sensation? "Killer Captain Still Haunts the Seven Seas!" Wouldn't they just sell lots and lots of newspapers? Make a name for themselves? Sure! Trouble is, I don't know a thing more about what happened to Captain Nemo than when we were cast adrift from the *Nautilus*.

Exactly like the professor wrote in his book a couple of years ago. Will he ever choose to write another one? Search me! If he knows more—which I don't think he does—you'd have to ask him.

Sam, you seem a nice enough young feller. And you went to all the trouble to scour every waterfront dive in San Francisco to find me. What's more, I've read a few of your pieces in the *San Francisco Alto California*, and even though they're funny, and stretchers, they seem pretty respectful. I read that book of yours, *Innocents Abroad.* Matter of fact, I read it aboard the *Nautilus* when there was nothing better to do. Which happened a lot. It was exciting for Professor Aronnax, seeing all those animals and corals and fishes and whatnot, but most of the time I spent in the salon or in my cabin. With my feet up, reading books. Without 'em, I'd have been dead bored. I need to be doing things. I need to be moving. Being cooped up underwater in an iron tube was not my idea of fun.

Reading your stories over and over—that saved me, more or less. I'll tell you what: you gave me all those good tales in *Innocents Abroad* and in the newspaper, so I'll give you another. I hope you write more. Lots more. Maybe one with me. Maybe you'll make me as well-known as that famous jumping frog from over in Calaveras County.

There's a part of the story of that journey aboard the *Nautilus* that the professor left out. On purpose. Why? Because there was a loved one of somebody involved who was still alive, who deserved protection from the public. But I hear tell she just passed on, so I don't suppose telling the tale can hurt anyone now.

You've read how the professor, his funny little manservant Conseil, and I all came to be aboard the *Nautilus*, so I won't go into that, except to say that it surely was not Captain Nemo's choice. When it first happened I figured it was nip and tuck whether he would throw us all overboard or set us adrift or maroon us on some godforsaken island. But he was a true gentleman. In most respects.

You've also read about the sinking of the Nantucket whaling ship *Pequod* some years back. And that's a story that is near to my heart, me being a whaler myself. Well, sir, you just get us another drink—might as well get a whole bottle—and I'll tell you a tale that happened aboard the *Nautilus*, but concerns the *Pequod* too.

It happened in the middle of our winding, back-and-forth, up-and-down voyage around the world.

Way out in the middle of the South Pacific there's a part called the Coral Sea. And out in the middle of the Coral Sea there's a string of islands called the Solomons, more than a thousand of the little buggers. Look at a map, and you'll see, way off by themselves, a little cluster of the Solomons called the Duff Islands. Look way off at the end of the Duffs, and if your map is big enough, you'll see one called Elingi. European maps call it Obelisk Island. I don't know why anyone ever named it that, or drew it all angular on a map. I'd lay you odds, though, that it was some European map maker that drew it, and named it, and never set foot out of his office.

The reality of the place is very different. It's not all angles and cliffs. It's a regular Pacific Island, just like in a picture postcard: white sand beaches, waving palm trees, coconuts lying around on the ground, thick jungle once you get much past the beach.

But tiny. Too small for a village to live on. Nobody goes there, except once in a while maybe a native out fishing who gets blown off course.

One morning at breakfast, Professor Aronnax announced that Captain Nemo had invited us on a hunting expedition. Seems the *Nautilus'* galley was in need of restocking. We ate a lot of fish, as you can guess, and Cookie had a real fondness for coral trout and red bass. He was a wizard with those fish. Prepared them every which way, until most times you forgot you were eating fish for breakfast, lunch, and dinner. Hardly missed beef and salt pork at all. Usually. Why, sitting here with you now, I wish I had a plate of his trout filets.

So we went hunting that morning, the captain, the professor, Conseil, and me. We put on Nemo's fantastic suits he invented for underwater light and breathing. They worked just great, those suits, allowing us to trudge a long way, carrying those pneumatic spear guns he invented. That man was a regular genius engineer.

We left the *Nautilus* on the sea floor, barely a hundred feet below the surface. We walked along, gradually up hill, chasing fish this way and that. Mostly, though, we dawdled, while the professor and Conseil gawked and marveled with each other, pointing out this coral, that fish, and this animal. They couldn't talk through those bulky helmets, but it didn't stop them. They were giddy as a couple of old maiden aunts over a bunch of colorful critters. So we wandered further, and were out longer, than we first expected to. And that led to one of the great adventures of my life.

We had strayed close to Obelisk Island, right up to the rocks along the shore. We had climbed and meandered through that underwater coral forest until the water was pretty shallow, the troughs of the waves no more than an arm's length above our heads.

The sun shone almost straight down through the crystal clear water, and lit up all the colors of the rainbow in that coral forest. It was really something to see. The professor, in his book, did a much better job of describing it all than I can, being just a sailor.

We were walking along, parallel to the shore, when a flash of movement caught my eye. I don't mind telling you I have a sharp eye. Right proud of it. Many a time on watch on one whaling vessel or another, it has been me that has picked out the far-off spouts of single whales, which others couldn't even pick out when I pointed to them. But I was always right.

I saw something move on the bottom, a dozen feet away, just the barest twitch of movement.

I stared, and gradually made out the biggest lobster I have ever seen anywhere, easily sixty inches from the tips of its little claws (the Atlantic ones have bigger) to the tip of its huge tail. And it's that huge tail that's the good eating.

Even though it was so big, you almost couldn't see it. It was grayish-white, with light gray stripes running across it, just like the sea bottom there. Perfect camouflage. I wouldn't have noticed it if it hadn't twitched.

I tapped the Captain's shoulder and pointed it out. He thought about the situation for one quick second before he arranged our little party for the attack. Bagging this lobster would be a big coup, and a real delicacy for the ship's table for days to come. It would take our best teamwork.

At his direction, Conseil and I crept around the sides of the beast, while the Captain and the professor stood in front of it, waving their arms and holding its attention. I got within a fathom of it, and Conseil a step closer, before it broke its habit of perfect stillness when it feels threatened. It finally reacted to Conseil and spun toward him.

Its back was to the vertical rock of the shoreline, and it started to edge slowly back across the sand, toward the deep horizontal crack where it hid out. Conseil saw this, and must have figured it was about to get away, because suddenly, without warning, he dove for it.

He threw himself flat on his face on the sand and managed to get a grip on the animal, his gloves clamped around the claws. Conseil and the lobster froze for a second, staring each other in the eye. Then its six strong spidery legs went to scrabbling for purchase, trying to back into its crevice, pulling Conseil with it.

I dove on my friend's legs, but lordy, was that lobster strong! It was dragging us both backward.

Suddenly there was a flash from above. A heavy antique harpoon speared down through the water and buried itself in the sand directly between the heads of Conseil and the lobster.

I'd seen many such a harpoon as a lad, when I first went to sea. It was the old kind, the kind the Nantucket whalers used. Six feet long, two-thirds of its length made of stout American oak, as big around as a strong man's wrist. The rest of the length was iron, thick as my thumb, and barbed at its tip with the razor-sharp, gleaming white tooth of a sperm whale.

There was a stout hemp rope bound along the harpoon's length and knotted to an iron ring in its hilt. That rope was stout enough that when a strong man—and it took a strong man, I'll tell you—hurled it deep into the flesh of a whale, and the whale would run, the rope would easily tow a whole whaleboat full of rowers and their heavy gear. The whale would sometimes run for miles, pulling the whalers along the surface. That became known around the world as the Nantucket sleigh ride.

Now one of those old harpoons had come within a whisker of skewering Conseil and nailing him to the sandy bottom.

Quickly the rope tightened, and the harpoon began to be pulled up from above. It dawned on me that whoever had cast that harpoon knew he had missed, and was likely to strike again.

I forgot all about the lobster and grabbed hold of the harpoon. Captain Nemo did the same, and with all our force and weight, we gave it a mighty heave.

We were rewarded with a splash directly above us. Our attacker was pulled from his footing on the rocks, and plunged headlong into the breakers above us.

All four of us jumped forward and grabbed his legs. The element of surprise had now gone over completely to our side: all of a sudden he was in the water, fighting for his life against what he had to figure was some unknown creature of the deep. But his struggles got him nowhere, since we had him outnumbered four to one, and we had our lead boots holding us to the bottom.

Ever since, I've thought how easily we could have just drowned him. But all of us—even the Captain, who you could call ruthless for attacking all those ships of war—automatically held our prisoner up so he could breathe. After all, he didn't know he was attacking people. He was just after his dinner.

So we just held him there, with his head above water, waiting for him to gather his wits and calm down.

Imagine my surprise when I noticed that the leg that Captain Nemo and I had hold of was hard to the touch and gleaming white. It was polished whalebone. And it was bound to the stump of the man's leg with very ship-shape leather straps, obviously crafted by a ship's carpenter.

He finally figured it out, strange as it was: whatever had him wasn't some monster. It was intelligent, human, and it wasn't trying to hurt him. He stopped struggling.

With one hand Captain Nemo signaled to us, and together we all moved toward the shore. We pushed our prisoner up onto a rock, and one by one the rest of us climbed out of the water.

We must have been a strange sight in our underwater suits, the great brass helmets with their thick isinglass lenses, and our pneumatic spear guns. You can imagine how our prisoner stared and stared.

And we stared right back at him. He was not, as I thought before, some native fisherman. He was burned nut brown by the tropical sun, and his skin was old and wrinkled, as wrinkled as a sperm whale, but his eyes were gray and alert. What sparse hair remained on the sides of his head was as white as the driven snow, and hung dripping over his shoulders.

His beard reached at least to his waist, gnarled and twisted as roots of trees blown over, bleached white by time, sea, and sun. An ancient, puckered scar ran from his hair, down the side of his face and neck, and slanted across his chest. No, this man was no South Seas native. He was as Caucasian as the four of us.

He sat there on the edge of the rock, glaring a nation at us as we stood above him in our bulky suits. Captain Nemo seemed to realize that we must seem like sea monsters to the man—or something from another world altogether. He reached up and unlatched his helmet, and it released with a great whoosh of air. The professor, Conseil, and I were not as used to the equipment, and it took us longer, but we finally got our helmets off.

We stared at our captive, and he stared right back at us. The professor, always a man of words, was the first to speak.

"*Parlez-vous Francais*?" he asked our captive hopefully. He received only a glare back.

"*Sprechen zie Deutsche*?" asked Nemo. No answer.

My turn, I thought. "Do you speak English?" I tried.

"Aye," answered the old man.

"Good!" I answered. "I am Ned Land, of Quebec."

"I am Professor Pierre Aronnax, of Paris," said the professor. "And this is my manservant, Conseil." Conseil gave a tiny bow.

"And I," said the Captain, "am Nemo, Captain of the *Nautilus*."

"Ahab," grunted our prisoner. "Master of the *Pequod*."

❧

The solo journey of the great albino sperm whale bull, which had begun far away in the gelid abyss of the Southern Ocean and would terminate in the balmy, shallow waters of the tropical Pacific, was nearing its end. The deep-diving, cold water squid that were his preferred prey, and on which he had grown to such great size, could wait. Now his females called him to rejoin them in the mating grounds around the Duff Islands.

More than sixty times he had made the annual trek from the south since his own father's return had driven him from his mother's side. It had been late in his fifteenth year.

For the next twenty of those years he had made the annual northward pilgrimage alone, wandering between the pods of females and their young, seeking the opportunity to mate. Again and again he was driven away by the larger, more experienced bulls.

But he was eating more than a thousand pounds of squid each day, and grew quickly and unusually large. More importantly, he battled tenaciously and with growing skill, both with his giant prey and the other young bulls.

Eventually his bulk and skill grew dominant, and after a battle that lasted two entire days and nights, he prevailed: he rammed, bit, and battered a mature bull, still in his prime, into submission. The older bull fled, and the White Whale assumed his place. He was now the protector and breeding male of the pod.

Fifteen journeys later he had finally achieved his full growth, and had fathered two dozen strong, healthy calves. Half had his unusual albino coloring. Had that been the end of his story, nature would have considered him an outstanding success. But fate and cruel humanity had much more in store for him.

He was a massive eighty-seven feet long and eighty tons when he met the whaling fleet for the first time. Hurrying north, he paid no attention to the wooden hulled English whaling ship, the *Samuel Enderby,* that turned to parallel his course. The clattering of the oars of the whaleboats and the shouts of their crews were unusual, but he didn't yet have reason to be wary. He continued on his way.

The first sting of a harpoon, totally unexpected, provoked an automatic response: unlike the cows the whalers usually slaughtered and stripped of their flesh, the white bull did not retreat to others for protection. The cows would surround the most vulnerable, their ring of powerful tails pointed out at the orcas or schooling sharks, their teamwork discouraging their tormentors. Unlike them, the White Whale turned. And he fought.

But his opponent was not one of the colossal squid of the black depths—no powerful, barb-ringed suckers, no enveloping tentacles or vicious, slashing beak. Nor was it another sperm bull challenging for his harem, nor was it orcas, which could sometimes harry a young whale calf away from its pod. No mindless shark. He had faced and bested each of these many times, until it had been many long years since anything but another full-grown sperm whale bull had been a serious threat. This was something new.

His unwitting speed and great size had saved him—the pursuing boat had been hard-pressed to catch up. When it finally did, at the end of the rowers' endurance, they found that this bull was so unexpectedly huge that the sweet spot, the kill spot beneath the high, bulging head and behind the pectoral fin, lay far under water, out of harpoon's reach.

The hapless harpooner standing in the prow of the boat only managed to embed his weapon in the hump of the bull's back. It was painful but not lethal, and served only to enrage him. His massive, muscled tail, which had driven him through the thousands of miles of his migrations year after year, lashed around and swept the wooden boat from the surface in one mighty blow. The whaleboat, built light for the speed of pursuit, was instantly pounded to matchwood. The White Whale's powerful, narrow lower jaw, with its rows of crushing, grasping teeth, by itself longer than the whaleboat, snapped from side to side as he twisted and rolled, exactly as it did when he battled colossal squid thousands of feet below the surface. But here was no squid flesh to seize and swallow whole, only the splintered planks of the boat. And, incidentally and unnoticed, the arm of its skipper, Captain Boomer. This one-armed captain would live to spread the fame of the White Whale abroad through the fleet.

But that day, there was no further attack. The bull continued on his way.

Over the next several seasons, through repeated encounters with the whaling fleet, the leviathan's reputation grew steadily, until his notoriety among the whalers gained him a title: Moby Dick. Like other legendary bulls, he was both feared and coveted. The captain who flensed him stood not only to assure the profit of his voyage, but to guarantee himself preeminence among the whalers of the world.

A new mating season, a new campaign, a new ambush, this one more organized, this commander better versed in the ways of the greatest prize—the massive bulls that yielded the largest bounty of precious spermaceti, oil, sea-ivory, and ambergris.

The wooden hull of the newcomer was weathered and blackened by the sun of the tropics around the world, the ice storms of the Southern Ocean, the smudgy, oily fires of the rendering, and the passage of the years. She was hung about with the grisly trophies of many campaigns: intricate scrimshaw—the cunningly carved bones of her conquests—decorated every conceivable space. Her bulwarks were studded with long, sharp sperm whale teeth, making her deck appear one continuous gaping jaw. Her antique tiller was cunningly fashioned from a sperm whale's jawbone. Even the sheaves of the ropes were carved of sea-ivory. On her stern, in plain Quaker script, her name: *Pequod.*

But Moby Dick was oblivious to the old black ship whose captain seemed to have an uncanny knowledge of the whale's course, and hove to directly in his northward path. Nor did he pay any heed to the three longboats that splashed into the water and sped off before the *Pequod's* sails were fully furled. The swift longboats set a course to intercept. And kill.

⁂

"The ancient mariner is clearly quite mad, Master," opined Conseil.

"Be that as it may, my friend," the professor answered, "he does seem to believe sincerely that he is that notorious Ahab, whose obsessive pursuit of the white leviathan Moby Dick nearly circumscribed the globe."

I wish you could meet Professor Aronnax, Sam. He's a pip. He really does talk like that. Maybe someday you will.

But Conseil wasn't having it. "Impossible," he insisted. "His shipmate Ishmael records that Ahab got tangled in his harpoon line and the White Whale pulled him to his death."

For someone who supposedly got pulled out of a whaleboat and drowned twenty years before, the old man was doing a splendid job of picking his way ahead of us up the steep path that lead from the beach to his camp. The old man was clearly used to leaning on the harpoon as a walking stick, but I was carrying that. There was no way I was going to risk him taking another poke at somebody.

So he muttered and complained, a mournful, low, singsong sort of tirade. Listening to him made me think the same as Conseil: the old man, whoever he was, was crazy as a ship's rat. And it made me wonder how crazy I would get if I somehow wound up marooned for decades. And how long it would take. But from all the stories in all the whalers' forecastles I had ever been in, the distance from Ahab to crazy had never been a long one in the first place.

The professor and Conseil followed behind us, carrying the old man's previous catch: a fine sea trout. Captain Nemo, true to his oath against setting foot on dry land, had immediately put his helmet back on and returned to the *Nautilus*. He promised that the ship's launch would return to a nearby beach before nightfall to carry the four of us—the professor, Conseil, the old man, and me—to the ship.

"I've read the book too," I told Conseil. "Ishmael didn't actually see Ahab die. All he really knew was that the Captain was pulled overboard. He certainly wouldn't be the first sailor to be washed up on a tiny Pacific island."

"But it has been twenty years since the *Pequod* was holed and sunk by the charge of the White Whale," said Conseil stubbornly. "The story has spread around the world, from whaler to whaler, and now to the rest of us. Books have been written. Certainly the tale has grown in the telling."

"Without a doubt, my friend!" the professor answered. "But from that same account we know many details of the men, the ship, and the voyage. They should be more than ample to test the old man's veracity, if not his sanity."

We kept climbing. Finally, we topped the spine of the narrow island and emerged from the trees into a tiny clearing with a small, weathered, palm-thatched hut. In a pit ringed with coral, the remains of a fire still smoldered. At the edge of the trees near the fire pit lay a considerable mound of shells, coconut husks, and clean-picked fish bones. Someone had obviously been living here a long time.

The old man picked his way to a large cedar log that lay alongside the fire and settled with a groan. It was painful to watch his gnarled old fingers unfasten the straps that held his whalebone leg. He sat rubbing the stump.

When he spoke, it was to Conseil. "In my cabin," he said, "lies a shell with the pressed oil of the coconut. Fetch it for me. And step lively, young Pip!"

Conseil stared at him, then looked to the professor, who smiled at him apologetically and nodded. Conseil left grumbling under his breath at suddenly being cabin boy to a crazy sea captain, and soon came back with a coconut shell, which he gave to the old man. I thought he would massage his stump, but instead he did the ship-shape thing, and carefully massaged the fragrant oil into the leather straps that bound his leg. He took care of his gear before he took his ease. A careful sailor indeed.

"Sir," said the professor, in that stuffy way of his, "I perceive that you are accustomed to leaning upon your harpoon as a staff. I apologize for depriving you of its use during our climb. It is my fond hope that we may soon come to trust one another. I hope that depriving a master harpooner such as yourself of his weapon will soon become unnecessary."

But the old man paid him no heed, talking instead to the leather straps that he so carefully doused with oil. He muttered under his breath, "T'will hold, old gentleman. Long heat and wet, have they spoiled thee? Thou seemest to hold. Or truer perhaps, life holds thee; not thou it."

Only when he had properly tended his gear did he massage his stump. “Bear the oil hence, Pip!” he barked at Conseil.

“Pip?” muttered Conseil. “Who are you calling Pip? Away, you crazy old loon!”

The old man glared at Conseil. “The greater idiot ever scolds the lesser,” he answered. His hearing was obviously just fine.

He hauled himself up and grabbed a slender length of bamboo that lay nearby. Using it as a crutch, he hobbled to the gigantic trunk of the towering cedar tree that spread over his “cabin.” He unknotted a slender homemade rope, and lowered a bosun’s chair from the branches. This line ran compound through doubled sheaves of bone, polished smooth by the long rubbing of years. As we watched with our mouths hanging open, he heaved himself aloft into the branches. I pulled the bosun’s chair back down, and quickly hauled the Professor aloft, then myself.

When I reached the top, I found myself on a large horizontal branch, wide as a sidewalk, thicker than any yard on any sailing ship that ever floated. It was easy to walk far out along its length, and that’s where I found the professor and the old man gazing out over the ocean, the old man seated on an improvised watchman’s stool.

The branch, which was the height of a man-of-war’s mainmast above the ridge, shot from the highest point of the tiny island. It had clear views away to sea on the east and west, and along the spine of the ridge to the north and south. From the old man’s lofty perch he could see anything that moved, at least five leagues in every direction. The surface of the sea sparkled crystal blue below us, shot through with the rainbow hues of the coral reef beneath. But nothing moved on the surface.

As I came to stand beside the professor, the old man addressed him, not breaking his surveillance of the sea to look at us. "Where away thy vessel, Frenchman?" he asked. "No sail dots the horizon. No mast or spar strains the sky." Slowly he turned to survey the circle of the horizon, over the vast distance afforded by our great height.

"The *Nautilus*, sir, goes not upon the waves, but beneath them. Yonder she lies, resting upon the ocean's bottom, a league distant." The professor pointed to the west, where the long dark shape of the great submarine could be seen clearly. The old man stood, and peered at the sight like a hawk for a long time before he spoke.

"Hear me, Frenchman! Full two score years, from a boy harpooner of eighteen, waged I war upon the horrors of the deep, until the White Monster snatched me away and cast me up on this desolate shore. Another score of years from this lofty perch watch I day and night. By God's grace, my eyes remain undimmed, my ears unmuffled by the passing of time. Seventy-eight years abide I in this veil of tears, cursed to remain until the Fates decree my release. I see the whales great and small frolic above and beneath the waves. Betimes methinks I spy my nemesis, the White Whale. Oft-times I think myself mad, for I see him frolic among the other cetaceans, in incarnations large and small, betimes almost near enough to the shore for a harpoon thrust. I have seen the great Maelstrom. I have endured ice typhoons that would strip a man's flesh from his bones, and raging seas piled up like the o'er-cresting Alps. I have witnessed unspeakable wonders. But never in all those years, not even in the most fanciful foremast yarn, have I heard tell of a ship that goes beneath the waves."

As it would happen, even as the old man left off speaking, the *Nautilus*, her captain returned to her, blew her ballast tanks. Great jets of water from her powerful pumps rose high into the air, and the ship, all fifteen hundred tons of her, shot suddenly to the surface in a roiling mass of air and water. Her enormous propeller beat the waves and her rudder turned her toward the sandy shores of the tiny isle.

"By heaven, there's a sight! There's a sound!" the old man exclaimed. "Blind and dumb might well be envied now! Hark ye what coffin rests there between the worlds! Beneath the waves and above them! What conveyance from mortality into immortality! What dark harbinger of death and destruction!"

Like noiseless nautilus shells, the light prows of the *Pequod*'s longboats sliced through the sea. One of the boats, her sails more efficiently set and managed, quickly outran the other two. Her men pulled hard at their oars, driven by the shouts of their tall, gaunt commander, who stood at the tiller, both feet planted wide, as steady as if he stood on dry ground. Ahab, already "The Old Man" to his crew, was recently turned fifty-two. Though he could not know it, he and the whale with which his fate was intertwined were born on the same day, half a world apart. Now their paths were destined to cross for the first, but far from the final time.

"Pull, lads!" Ahab cried. "Pull ye for the prize!" Each knew that flensing, rendering, and stripping one big bull like this would fill as many oil barrels as three of the cows they usually slaughtered. They knew that the spermaceti, ambergris, and ivory from this behemoth would fill out the *Pequod*'s cargo and allow them to turn for home. They had already been away from Nantucket more than two years, and were anxious to be on their way, their fortunes secured.

No one had more incentive than Ahab. Just after his fiftieth birthday, he had finally married. After all his long life at sea, after a hundred ports of call, he finally had a reason to hurry home: his girl-wife, of half his years. And a son he had never seen. He urged on his oarsmen with all the fervor of a heart awakened late in life.

From more than a mile away the whalers could see the white line of foam that rippled in front of the great beast's head, bearing straight down on them. Seabirds of several varieties followed above him like a wavering halo, feeding on the small fish that rushed and leaped out of his path.

Ahab maneuvered the nimble boat in a wide semicircle to bring the speeding whale up the boat's starboard side, where the Persian harpooner in the bow would have a good stroke to deliver a fatal blow as the bull shot past. "Stand steady there, ye Farsee!" Ahab cried. "Ready your lance!"

A scant half mile astern of the small boat, the whale disappeared momentarily beneath the waves, leaving the surface unruffled. A nervous murmur swept through the rowing whalers. "Pull, lads! Pull for your fortune!" Ahab cried. "Match his speed! He surfaces again very near!"

"The gods grant he breach not beneath us," muttered a nervous seaman. Every eye strained aft, as the wheeling cloud of sea birds drew within a cable's length.

Hard astern, the surface of the sea pushed upward before the monster's bulk. Preceding even the great brow, the tall but shattered pole of a recent whaling lance broke the surface, rising like a battle standard. Finally the whale's wrinkled forehead rose into view. Its natural striations were overlaid with scars of the battles of decades. A thousand confrontations with giant squid, orcas, and the whalers of a dozen nations had left their grisly brands. Taller than three men, the immense bulbous forehead loomed out of the water, pushing its own foaming wave. The whale rushed unheeding straight at the longboat. So precise had been Ahab's anticipation of the whale's course that he was forced to swerve aside to avoid being overrun. With a curse, he threw the tiller hard over.

On came the undeviating leviathan. A gentle joyousness, a mighty mildness of repose in swiftness marked the unwavering beat of his mighty tail. Tumbled by the breaking wave pushed up by the monster's head, the longboat was flung peremptorily aside. It swung wildly, heeled over, and capsized, entangling the rigging with several harpoon lines that trailed unheeded behind the rushing bull. The longboat's mast and spars were twisted and crushed in the tangle as a man would crush a fistful of dry twigs. Men, oars, and splinters of the boat spun high into the air, mingling with the spray of the whale's spout and the whirl of seabirds. One by one the men fell unharmed back into the whale's foaming wake. One man only, Ahab himself, fell wounded. A whistling scythe-like section of the tiller had neatly severed one leg just above the knee.

The White Whale continued on his uncaring, unconscious way. Ahead lay the Duff Islands. And his females and young.

I could hardly contain my excitement as our usual trio—Aronnax, Conseil, and I—waited in the salon for the old man to emerge from the cabin that Nemo had assigned him.

The *Nautilus*' cook had taken pains to prepare filets of the fine sea trout that the old man had speared, along with an array of the other fruits of the sea that we usually ate. As we waited, I voiced a thousand questions that were on all of our minds.

"How old do you think he is, really? It's very hard to tell. How did he survive all these years? Could he really be the same Ahab of the story of Moby Dick? I thought that was just a sailor's yarn."

"I hope we shall soon know," the professor answered. "He is of the ancient age and possessed of the reported characteristics of the legendary captain of the *Pequod*, and he certainly has the manner of speech of the Nantucket Quakers. I think we shall soon have the opportunity to put him to the test."

At that moment the door to the salon opened. The man who entered was very changed. In fact, I found I recognized him only by the halting, swinging gate and the whalebone leg. The halo of white hair and the tangled beard were gone. His tattered rags were gone. Some kind soul among the *Nautilus*' officers had outfitted him with the polished boots, creased breeches, and double-breasted, navy blue coat of an officer. It hung on his tall frame like a scarecrow, but gave him back his overwhelming dignity. He wore that uniform as if he had worn it all his life.

You've probably heard and read a lot about Ahab's eyes. What eyes they were! They were piercing, like an eagle staring down at a rabbit from the sky. They were eyes that had squinted into the sun of all seven seas, eyes that had seen hardship, gory death, and long solitude. Eyes that were haunted and driven by an inner fire that only death could quench.

You'll pardon me, Sam, if I wax a little poetic. By this time, the old man had clearly conquered my imagination. If he were indeed Ahab, what stories he could tell! I longed to put a thousand questions to him directly.

He sat without a word and stared down the table, glaring at the food, prepared in rich French sauces of butter and wines from around the world, scowling like the strict Quaker he was. At last he chose a small filet from the very sea trout he himself had speared, took a glass of water, and ate slowly and in silence.

I ate in something of a hurry—not unusual for me—but my brain felt like it was churning in my head. Finally, I could hold my tongue no longer. "Sir," I said, breaking the silence, "is it true what they say, that you are that same Ahab who hunted the great white sperm whale, Moby Dick?"

The old man looked at me out of the corner of his eye.

"Thou sayest," he said flatly.

"But that cannot be!" I exclaimed. "Ahab's shipmate, Ishmael, saw him pulled from his longboat to his death."

"Beshrew the man! Only a rogue or a fool reports as truth what he only supposes to be true!" the old man growled. "He could not see my death, for the Specter has not yet come for me. The gods forbid it, for the devil beast yet lives that took my leg and robbed me of my ship. With malice aforethought, he cast me away on that desert isle.

"I have seen him with my very eyes, amid the shoal of spermaceti that haunt the shores where I dwelt marooned. From the depths of hell he returns, regular as the circuit of the earth around the sun, to afflict and torment me."

This gave me pause for thought. "The legend of the White Whale is a tale told in every forecastle I have ever manned. But I have never laid eyes on him, or met an honest man who claimed to have seen him with his own eyes. And I have harpooned the whales of every sea."

The old man finally turned his attention completely to me, and stared at me intently. "Upon your word, you have hunted the great sperm whale bulls?"

"That I have," I answered. "And the old-timers tell of eighty-foot bulls, including the famous Moby Dick. But such stories are not to be believed. The largest I ever saw with my own eyes barely exceeded sixty feet, and he was a true monster."

"Fah!" the old man snorted. "In my day, sixty feet was at best a respectable catch."

"Indeed," the professor put in, "in these latter days of steam-powered steel ships and steam-propelled harpoons, the catch the world around is progressively less. The bulls are smaller every year."

"Moby Dick is not of this world," the old man insisted quietly. "He is an unnatural monster. A creature from hell. When I pursued him halfway around the world, when I battled him to the death of my ship and crew, he was every inch of ninety feet. And eighty-five tons if he was an ounce. Even at rest, the white dome of his head rose above the waves to the height of three men. When he threw himself aloft out of the sea to survey the scene, his fall cast such a wave as to rock *Pequod* until her yardarms nearly dipped. When later he ran at her and struck her in her starboard bow, her death was foregone. She was doomed for the bottom the moment he set his malignant eye upon her."

As he spoke, Captain Nemo entered the room behind him and stood listening.

"Sir," the professor said, "the whole world is familiar with Ishmael's account of the sinking of the *Pequod*. You will forgive me if I have questions that will confirm for us your identity—"

"Forgive you? I will not!" he spat. He rose to his full height and glared at the professor like some Old Testament prophet come to life. "What care I for your questions? What care I for your confirmation? By all the powers of heaven, I am neither a madman nor a liar. I know who I am! My word abideth."

"My deepest apologies!" said the professor, as soothing as he could manage. "It is my native scientific curiosity, not the desire to offend, which prompts me."

"Science!" the old man huffed. "Your science can neither prove nor disprove me. You have my word. It is enough."

"But the details of the men, the ship, the voyage—"

"And if I tell you some detail that disagrees with the penny dreadful scribblings of this fool Ishmael? A man I barely noticed, twenty years since? What then? Will you have disproved me?"

A hush fell over the salon, broken only when Nemo, who had not made his presence known until now, cleared his throat. "Perhaps, sir, you will permit me, as captain of this vessel, to inquire if there exist loved ones who would rejoice at the news of your rescue—those who have long considered you sunk in the depths of the sea?"

This stopped the old man in his tracks. He sighed, and half turned in his seat to face Nemo. "Captain," he said, "therein lies a sad tale. For I left a young girl-wife at home, whom I widowed the day I married her past fifty, and sailed for Cape Horn the very next day. And there is a son born to me after my departure. Never did I set eyes on the lad. I know not if mother or babe yet live."

That made all of us silent and thoughtful a moment.

And now, Sam, now you know why Professor Aronnax did not include this part of the story in his book, *Twenty Thousand*

Leagues Under the Sea: that same girl-wife old Ahab spoke of. It is she who only recently passed away. She was the reason that Aronnax forbore: he felt he had to protect her.

"New wonders have arisen during your isolation," the professor said, breaking the silence. "Steam and electricity are transforming the world. It is a marvelous new age. When Captain Nemo consents to put you ashore, your family can know of your rescue within hours via telegraph. You may be certain of reunion in Massachusetts within a few weeks. Why, Mr. Phileas Fogg has recently gone around the world in eighty days."

The old man eyed him with distrust. "Eighty days? What sorcery is this?"

"No sorcery, sir. Science. Steam engines drive iron ships over the seas and locomotives over the land at unbelievable speeds. Ships of the air—dirigibles and balloons—traverse the tallest mountains with ease." We were all silent another moment while he pondered.

"Gentlemen, with my own eyes I saw the vessel in which we dine rise from beneath the waves," he answered finally, his manner slow and deliberate. "I must indeed allow that there are new wonders beneath the sun."

The old bull was late. The passing of the long decades since his last encounter with Ahab and the obliteration of the *Pequod* was taking its toll. This year's journey back to the pod had taken a week longer than in years past. When he arrived over the folded trenches and underwater plains of the Coral Sea, the contest for his females was already well underway. Three young bulls in the prime of their lives, each more than forty tons, battled for supremacy. They butted each other, pushed, rolled, and snapped, raking each other with their powerful jaws, each intent on intimidating and outlasting the other two. The sea boiled and frothed around them. The females and young huddled at a safe distance.

The White Whale, already ten years older than the most long-lived of his breed, and forty years older than the three hearty contenders, knew instinctively that he would lose a long battle. The young bulls would combine to wound, exhaust, and drive him away. Instead he relied on sheer mass, speed, and the guile of his long life to tip the balance in his favor. He dove deep, down, down into the inky darkness. From the depths a quarter mile below, he sped upward.

As you might expect, it was my keen eye that first spotted the spouts and the frothing sea around the three young bulls. After all, I had been searching the sea for years for the signs of the various great whales. They were some two thousand yards to windward off the *Nautilus'* bow. We cruised on the surface of the Coral Sea, which was calm as glass that day, except for the rolling and spouting of the three big bulls. The three of us—the professor, Conseil, and I—were taking our daily bit of exercise on the deck. Nemo's mate stood hard by, shooting the sun as he did every day.

"Professor!" I said, pointing to the spouts. "By my eyes, those are the spouts of sperm whales! See how they slant to the side! Only the spermaceti does that."

"I doubt you not, my whaling friend!" the professor said. "Conseil! This is a scene that perhaps Captain Ahab would relish to witness again after so many years ashore." But Conseil, who was as watchful of his master's wishes as I was of distant whales, had foreseen that suggestion, and was already scrambling down the ladder to fetch the old man to the deck.

The mate barked an order into a speaking tube, and the *Nautilus* altered course to approach and get a better view of the three whale bulls.

Alerted by his mate, Captain Nemo appeared first, followed some minutes later by Ahab. "Where away?" the old man demanded.

Without taking his eyes from the battling trio, Nemo handed Ahab his own brass spy glass. "Five points off the starboard bow."

The old man handled the glass like a veteran sea officer—another confirmation to me of his identity—but after a moment he handed it back to Nemo, disappointed. "Spermaceti indeed. And bulls. Full grown. But young. Not the monster. Not Moby Dick."

He turned to me. "Spiest thou the shoal, harpooner? The cows and calves? Half a league beyond the bulls. A dozen spouts and more. There lies the prize."

So preoccupied were the young bulls with their battle that they were blind and deaf to the doom from below. Ninety tons of ancient juggernaut White Whale, twenty tons of it concentrated in the battering ram that was his forehead, slammed like a runaway locomotive into the vulnerable underside of the largest of the young targets.

The shock wave of the impact echoed backward through the old bull's towering forehead and spermaceti, and was reflected and magnified forward by the natural amphitheatre of his supremely adapted skull. The young bull was carried out of the water, a hundred feet into the air. The impact was instantly lethal. In a moment, skull, brain, ribs, lungs, and heart were obliterated, life extinguished.

The White Whale shot vertically out of the water, a towering white T crossed by the corpse of his rival. He twisted and bit as he fell. The long serrated blade of his jaw closed over the second bull's spine behind the head. The crushing weight of the ancient bull's falling bulk folded the young bull nearly in half, snapping his spine. Death was slow but inevitable. The third challenger fled.

The old bull lay quiet in the water a moment, recovering from his charge, his echo-locating clicks taking fresh stock of the world around him. The broken, dying remains of his rivals. The females and young, huddled up a mile away. The canyons, ridges, and coral plains of the sea floor. The distant islands. And in the other direction, slicing silent and smooth through the surface waters, a strange new rival: the *Nautilus*.

~

To those of us watching from the deck of the submarine it was as if a volcano had erupted without warning. One moment we watched with delight something none of us had seen before—not even me: three great bulls twisting and turning together in the water, butting their great foreheads together, raking and biting with their long narrow jaws. The next moment the largest and strongest of them was thrown high out of the water, almost in the same moment another was broken nearly in half. One moment it was all curiosity and wonder, the professor and Conseil bantering whale anatomy back and forth; the next instant Moby Dick arose from the deep, impossibly huge and white and towering high out of the water. He scattered the three strong young bulls like leaves before a nor'easter, and ended two of their lives in an instant.

"Ah! Ah! By all that is holy!" old Ahab cried. "Is there no rest upon this earth? Not three hours afloat and the monster has found me afresh!"

I had not taken my eye off the great beast. In all my years of whaling I had never seen an animal so beyond all understanding. So monstrous huge! So overwhelming! He seemed like some scourge straight out of the Bible, some unnatural beast from the depths of hell. Suddenly I could well understand everything Captain Ahab had been saying about him.

I became aware that the beast had wheeled his towering white forehead in our direction. Slowly he rotated his great body from one side to the other, turning toward the *Nautilus* first one eye, then the other. Slowly he accelerated. His deadly intentions were clear.

"Captain Nemo!" I cried. "The White Whale fixes his eye on us!"

Nemo barked into the speaking tube, and the ship's powerful engines hurled her forward like a racehorse leaps from the gate. Caught off guard, the professor was nearly thrown from his feet, but I caught him, hoisted him upright, and shoved him and Conseil toward the hatch. Nemo pushed Ahab ahead of him. We hurried down the companionway, the others hard behind us. The heavy iron hatch clanged shut and immediately the boat tilted beneath our feet as Nemo tried to turn away from the charging whale.

But as quickly as the *Nautilus* accelerated, Moby Dick was faster. The boat was turning hard to port, diving steeply, when the collision came. I was thrown from my feet, and fell sliding down the sloping passageway, in a tangled heap with my companions.

Luck frowned on Ahab again. The old man was thrown hard against an iron hatchway, opening a great gash across his head and face. As he fell, he threw his hands forward to break his fall. I heard a horrible crunch as the old bones of his left arm and shoulder gave way. His face was twisted with pain as I hoisted him to his feet yet again. But, he clamped his jaw, and didn't make a peep.

Suddenly the tilt of the deck shifted the other direction. The *Nautilus* was climbing back toward the surface. And turning hard. A seaman ran toward us down the passageway, headed astern to the engine room, and I grabbed his arm as he passed. "What has happened, shipmate? Tell us!"

"The whale overran our stern!" the man yelled. "The rudder is jammed, bent hard over. We're going in a circle. The captain is surfacing the boat." As he spoke the tremor of the engines died away.

Conseil and I helped the old man to the salon and made him comfortable. The boat leveled out on the surface and the hatch clanged open. We heard running feet. I, too, hurried to the deck, the professor close behind. The *Nautilus* lay hove to on the surface, with serious damage to her stern. Several men already hung from ropes over the jammed rudder, with cutting torches and heavy sledge hammers, working like demons to cut it loose.

Nemo stood with his glass, observing the White Whale, who paused some two hundred yards off, blowing regularly. Blood stained the water around him. Several large sharks had already arrived on the scene, circling, waiting for their opportunity.

After several tense minutes the whale stirred, circled away, then rounded to face us. Nemo shouted orders and the men at the stern scrambled up the ropes and down the hatch. On his command, far below, someone turned the boat's wheel. The rudder creaked, groaned, rotated beyond center a few degrees, and stopped. The *Nautilus* could travel straight ahead but could vary her course only a few degrees.

The screw began to turn slowly, and the boat crept forward.

"Captain!" I called, "the bulls fight on the move. They don't sit still and wait to be hit. Even though the *Nautilus* is bigger, maybe if we go fast enough, the bull will think that he has frightened away the last opponent. He may turn back to his pod and leave us alone." Nemo nodded and gave orders. The boat accelerated.

The gashes on the White Whale were deep. He had been wounded by the submarine's prop and rudder, but not nearly bad enough to kill him. He was enraged, and—despite my hopes—he was not going to be distracted so easily. He had not reached his great age by shrinking from a fight, or leaving the outcome in any doubt. Even though the *Nautilus* was three times his length and twice his weight, he seemed determined to put an end to any threat once and for all. He faced us, accelerating to full speed, pushing up a wall of foam before him as he came.

Professor Aronnax stared horrified, frozen as if he were mesmerized. "Captain, will you dive?" he asked.

"No," Nemo answered grimly. "I cannot steer, and dare not give the brute the chance to get above us again. The hull is thick and stout, but who can tell what damage he might do us? He is mighty, and the depths are his home. He might even carry us down with him, or may prevent us from rising." He sighed, but did not slow the boat. "You must be prepared for impact, Professor. I shall attempt to evade him, but I fear he means to strike us head on. Helm!" he called. "Hard over!" We looked aft. The rudder was still fouled. Although the helmsman tried mightily, the rudder merely creaked and groaned, and our course did not change much, if at all. We cut through the waves at the *Nautilus*'s maximum speed, her prow throwing back a foaming wave.

Suddenly behind me I heard the rhythmic clank of footsteps, and looked up to see the gaunt, ancient figure of Ahab striding toward the bow, leaning heavily upon his harpoon. His left arm hung useless. His face was a mask of bloody rage. "Captain!" I cried. "You should be safely below!" His pace quickened. His whalebone leg clanged on the iron deck.

He was old, he was badly injured, one leg was missing, and he had been marooned ashore for years, but he climbed like a monkey out onto the *Nautilus'* dancing bowsprit. He stood there like some avenging sea god on that great serrated iron battering ram.

"Towards thee I roll, devil beast! To the last I grapple with thee! From hell's heart I stab at thee; for hate's sake I spit my last breath at thee!" he screamed.

"Come back, sir!" I cried, desperate. "You'll be killed!"

"Nay! By all that is holy, I am the law, and I am the judge! I am the oppressed, and there is the oppressor! Through him I have lost all that I loved, cherished, and venerated—country, wife, child, father, and mother. I saw all perish! All that I hate is there! Say no more!"

The beast hurtled at us like a great steam-powered locomotive, his monstrous tail beating the sea to froth. Captain Nemo swerved the bow away as best he could, but the White Whale matched his every move. He had no choice. "Heave to!" he cried. "All back full!"

The whale's snow-white dome filled our view, hurtling at us like some towering blank wall. The dark figure of the ancient mariner was silhouetted against it like a child's shadow puppet.

"Have at thee, thou fiend of the eternal pit!" he screamed. At the moment of impact he raised his harpoon high, leapt from the bowsprit, and buried the lance in the whale's wrinkled forehead. An instant later the needle-pointed prow of the *Nautilus* pierced the old man from behind, nailing him sprawled across the forehead of the White Whale.

The great whale and the great iron creation of modern science ran together so hard, with the old captain sandwiched between them, that they were both hurled out of the water. The whole length of the ship's iron prow passed through the captain, and was buried deep into the whale, halfway down his length.

Sam, all this may make you wonder if my brain is baked, but I saw it with my own eyes. I'm telling it to you as I know it happened—nothing more, nothing less.

The crash threw me forward into the whale's leathery, barnacled hide, only to be hurled backward by a gushing flood of spermaceti and blood. Locked together, the submarine, the whale, and the old captain fell back into the water with a mighty splash that nearly washed us all overboard.

The propeller spun hard, blurring in reverse. It bit the water as it fell. Steel and iron strained and screamed. The prow pulled free with a lurch and the *Nautilus* backed away. Bound together in death, Ahab and Moby Dick sank into the black depths.

Well, Sam, this bottle is dry as a bone, and there isn't a whole lot left to tell. After our encounter with Moby Dick, the rest of our voyage—our famous twenty thousand leagues under the seas—passed as the professor wrote in his book. Like he said, the three of us—the professor, Conseil, and I—parted ways with the *Nautilus* a few months later.

I will tell you I believe Nemo and his crew are dead, their ship torn apart in the Maelstrom of Norway. But as Ahab told us, only a rogue or a fool reports as truth what he does not know to be fact. I am no rogue, and I certainly had no desire to be the second fool to wrongly report a great captain dead. With my own eyes I saw Ahab perish and sink, pierced and crushed almost beyond recognition. I did not see Nemo die—not with my own eyes. So even though I can hardly imagine how even the mighty *Nautilus*, tough as she was, could have survived the Maelstrom, I won't say he is dead. I will only say what I know to be fact.

I traveled with Professor Aronnax for a while after our survival and escape, in order to tie up one loose end.

Several months later we made our way to the United States, to Massachusetts and the whaling island of Nantucket. We had what we all believed was a painful but necessary errand of mercy.

Ahab's widow was a charming woman of later middle years. Her son was a strapping young man with a wife and child of his own. Both had lived on Nantucket all their lives, so neither was a stranger to the hazards of whaling, and both had accepted Ishmael's word that Ahab was killed when the *Pequod* went down. Both had long ago resigned themselves to the loss of their husband and father.

The young man, who never knew Ahab, had made a life for himself, far from his father's fame. He was anxious to spare his aging mother, his wife, and his child the pain that would come with the public revelation of the old man's long years as a castaway, and the dramatic account of his rescue and death. Old Ahab's obsessive pursuit of the whale would be held up to be gawked at by a whole new generation. I was one hundred percent in agreement with the young man on that.

Even though it wasn't public, the news tore the widow's wounds open all over again. She was tortured by the thought of her husband's torment, long isolation, and violent end. For weeks she took to her bed, close to death. Her faithful son and daughter-in-law were constantly at her side, and eventually she recovered. But she remained in mourning until the end of her days.

But now she has passed on, and is beyond sorrow. The son . . . I trust you'll keep his name and whereabouts out of it, if you ever decide to put all this down on paper.

I don't know if anyone will ever believe a word of any of this, Sam. But you're the tale swapper. You decide.

Styled after *Moby Dick* by Herman Melville and
Twenty Thousand Leagues Under the Sea by Jules Vern

Mr. Thornton

SCOTT WILLIAM TAYLOR

John Thornton stood on the banks of White River and surveyed the scene before him. 'Damn fools,' he thought to himself as he watched that horrid woman and her two companions head away from his camp. He was glad to be rid of them, and spit as a physical expression of that disgust. The spittle froze moments after it hit the ground.

The young man, aged beyond his years by the cruel experiences of life, watched as the trio increased the distance between him and them. The wretched people represented everything he hated about the human species. He had hoped prospecting in one of the remotest locations on earth would separate himself from such people.

However, his experience taught him that human stupidity could never fully be eliminated as long as others were allowed to live and breed and populate the planet. No, moving to a world of indescribable beauty, a world where life and death co-existed in a macabre dance of skill and luck, couldn't save John from the likes of the human dregs he had the misfortune to meet.

"Damn fools," he said as he watched the disaster unfold. After the screaming ended, the silence of nature engulfed him.

"Son, time to go. Best get home before dusk."

Something in the air sparked a memory in John's mind, to the point where he turned to see if his father stood beside him. As the water stilled, visions of the man's childhood returned to him to a time when he and his father rested on the banks of the Ohio River on a warm summer Sabbath day, the only day John Thornton, Sr., abstained from working. The son turned and followed the strong blacksmith to their home on the river's banks. Tomorrow meant another day of hard work, when the young boy loved to run errands and do whatever he could to please his hero.

The cold and remoteness of Alaska dissolved, replaced by the warmth and humidity of the Ohio River Valley.

"Dad!" John saw the memory of himself turn and race after his father. "Wait for me!" John Thornton's life as a boy differed greatly from that of the bitter cripple standing on a cold riverfront in the Yukon Territory. In fact, anyone lucky enough to know him then thought a more pleasant child could not be found.

"We need to be heading home," his dad said with a wink. "I've got a lot of work to do this week, and I'm going to need a well-rested helper in my shop to get it all done."

The five-year-old looked at his dad with the admiration only a child has for his father and tried to return the wink but only succeeded in closing both eyes, something that made the boy's father laugh. As the pair left the riverbank, John Sr. thought of the life that lay ahead for his son.

Born the year the horrific American Civil War ended, John Jr., growing up in Cincinnati, lived in a world reeling from the inhumanities of man. The blacksmith and other Civil War survivors vowed the next generation would not grow up in a world of hate and evil. Theirs would be a new beginning, and the offspring from this new beginning would be as pure as a newborn child.

The parents of this chosen generation looked upon their children as a saving force for good. They would succeed where their forefathers had failed. They would not allow their sins to sully mankind's last great hope. This next generation would represent the hopes of thousands of parents and grandparents. He prayed his son would act well his part.

They held hands as they returned home under a brilliant orange sky.

Years passed, boys grew to men and experience passed from one generation to the next. The small blacksmith shop grew in size and importance until a new *Thornton & Son* sign hung above the door.

"Excuse me, sir," the well-dressed stranger, who appeared to be in his middle years, said after walking into the shop. "Do I have the pleasure of addressing John Thornton?"

"You do," John Jr. said. "But you probably want my pa, John Thornton, Sr., the twenty-one-year-old said as he set down his hammer and tongs. "He's in the back."

"No," the man said. "It is you, John Thornton, Jr., with whom I wish to speak. I am Charles LeBrock, and I represent the Whitney and Company Shipbuilders. We're looking for a boiler designer, and I'm here to offer you a job."

As John Jr. grew, life as a blacksmith's son proved as great an upbringing as any adventurous boy could wish for. From his earliest recollection he thought of nothing else but the fabrication of metal, bending that collection of elements to the will of man until truly miraculous products existed. In awe and reverence he watched his father take the liquid material, form it, manipulate it, urge it to become those things most coveted and needed by the paying customers. Every waking minute John thought of learning the trade and, one day, taking over his father's business. Thornton had become Thornton & Son, and when he had children, the tradition would continue.

School, church, baseball, nothing could pry the young man's interest away from the forge and bellows. As a teenager, John spent more time in the shop than his dad. John the elder watched with prideful eyes as his son began taking on projects he had not the time to complete, then he allowed the boy to assume more responsibility and bigger jobs. Each time John touched the forge, he impressed. It was clear to all who noticed that the younger Thornton worked metal like a master conductor commanded an orchestra. He had a gift. John controlled steam as if it were his right arm.

The young man's rise in fame coincided with the explosion of steam power as man's greatest achievement in the manipulation of nature. The world was changing at a speed unparalleled in human history. Technology in steam power resulted in machines to replace beasts of burden. Mechanized horses and oxen prototypes found their way from factories into barns and shops across the country. John worked every day to learn all he could about the age of steam. All who knew the industry understood John Jr.'s day would come.

"Beg pardon, sir, but I think you'll want to be speaking to my father," John Jr. said to their visitor. "I've never taken on a project so grand."

"Be that as it may," came a voice from inside the shop, "I do believe John Jr. is the man you want." John looked to see his father walking toward them.

"Father, this is Mr. Charles LeBrock from the . . . what business was it again?"

"The Whitney and Company Shipbuilders of Chicago."

"A pleasure to meet you, sir," John Sr. said. The two men shook hands and began speaking of business. The younger blacksmith started to imagine the proposed commission, a job giving him the chance to learn the skills that would allow him to open his own blacksmith shop one day.

"No, my son is mistaken—he's the one you want," the father said, giving the son another knowing wink.

With a new job and position, John worked feverishly for the next two years on his invention, a steam-driven engine unique in its design and unsurpassed in its efficiency. The Thorntons worked in secret, hopeful their new engine would eclipse anything currently being used in ships or trains or mechanical animals. Finally, the day came to unveil John's contribution to mankind.

"Son, I couldn't be more proud," John Sr. said as he escorted his wife aboard *The Missouri Pride*. The young inventor beamed as he watched his parents, as well as 1,525 other passengers and crew, climb onto the decks of the beautiful vessel. Under his feet John felt the raw power of the engine waiting to be released. He knew in mere moments the whole world would see something they had never seen before.

However, John Jr. didn't know that the night before, the captain of *The Missouri Pride*, a man named Chester A. Jones, entered a brothel on the outskirts of Cincinnati and began drinking. The drinking evolved to boasting and soon the drunken man was placing bets with anyone within the sound of his obnoxious voice that his ship, the newest craft in the company's fleet of ships, could best anything currently on the water. More than a few souls took up the challenge thrown down by Captain Jones. Gambling purses and inflated egos fueled the reckless behavior and the man captaining *The Missouri Pride* vowed to crush the competition.

Steamboat racing remained a common practice, even though laws were created to curtail such contests that many times resulted in the destruction of one or both ships and far too many deaths.

The ship's maiden voyage from Cincinnati to Louisville began at 8:30 a.m. on the morning of August 7, 1888. John's father stood proudly on the bow of the beautiful ship, knowing his son's talent and ingenuity allowed it to make record time as it chugged up the Ohio.

Had not Captain Jones' claim of his boat's superiority been offered the night before, the captain of another vessel, *The Stockton*, would not have been waiting to accept the challenge two miles upstream.

The passengers aboard *The Missouri Pride* knew nothing of the bet when they saw the other ship as it begin to mirror their progress toward Louisville. Passengers stood outside and felt the rushing humid and pollen-filled air as it brushed past the elegantly dressed women's hair and smartly attired gentlemen, causing more than one patron to use a hand to steady either bonnet or bowler. They laughed and waved to spectators on the riverbanks as they flew by. Those watching were also impressed by the ship's speed. Several on mechanical horses tried to keep up with the steaming vessel. The horses could not match *The Missouri Pride's* impressive power.

One man ignored the carnival-like atmosphere surrounding him, however. John Jr. knew something had changed the moment *The Stockton* came alongside. He felt an adjustment in the boilers and he knew internal pressures were being forced upon the virgin engines to which they were not supposed to be exposed. Not yet, anyway. Vibrations in the ship told John that if the captain continued to push, the metal boilers would fail, and fail spectacularly.

He raced to the boiler room. "In the name of all that's holy, man!" h roared at the workmen. "What in the hell are you doing?

You're pushing it too hard!" His pleas were ignored as the obedient seamen continued feeding the fires with more and more fuel. These men knew of the captain's bet and, like dogs scrounging for table scraps fallen from above, they understood that they too could profit from the race.

The blacksmith climbed the stairs to the bridge, passing excited travelers—including his parents—who were enjoying *The Missouri Pride's* incredible speed, something no one had experienced before. The captain was right; his new ship was fast. The speed surprised even him as *The Stockton* began to lag and then fall behind.

"Captain Jones!" John yelled. "For the love of God, please stop! The boilers cannot take this punishment, not now! It's too early!" The young man's imploration was met with an indifferent stare from the man who only smiled and turned his attention back to the river.

As John inhaled to begin a new appeal, the floor beneath his feet disappeared as the ship's boilers exploded. Because he stood in the doorway, the shockwave blasted John from the room and into the river below. When he finally surfaced, the scene before him was one of indescribable hell, as if Satan himself rode the river and had dispensed his own brand of twisted justice upon mortal men.

The ship was gone; its burning frame was quickly disappearing in the water. A huge cloud of black smoke curled skyward, and the air was filled with screams from the wounded and dying in the river. His heart almost stopped as he thought of his parents.

In desperation, John searched the river for any sign of his loved ones. The carnage of dismembered and burned bodies barely registered. He had to find them. Passengers and crew from *The Stockton* rushed to offer aid by jumping into the river whenever they saw someone alive. As his eyes continued to scan the river, John felt strong arms encircle his chest and draw him from where *The Missouri Pride* once sailed. He pleaded with his rescuers to allow him back to the water but to no avail.

"It's no use, son," he was told, the words an attempt at comfort. "You won't be finding anyone alive out there."

John continued fighting as they lifted his exhausted body to the deck of *The Stockton*, but once he surveyed the damage from his elevated view, he knew the men spoke the truth. Of the 1,527 people listed as passengers, only thirty-five survived, all of which, like John, were blown from the ship as they stood on deck. John's parents had perished.

The months following the tragedy proved difficult for John. An investigation found the ship's captain solely responsible for the explosion. Still, John's reputation suffered. His love of blacksmithing faded to the point where he questioned whether or not he would return to the trade. Each time he worked the ore, nightmares and the sight of mutilated bodies, the smell of burning flesh, wood, and metal returned. He tried pushing it out of his mind. He failed.

One day, while John tried yet another time to return to the forge, a visitor came to his shop. The aged man walked with a cane, but there existed a fire in his eyes.

"Be ye John T'ornton?" he asked, his thick Irish accent filling the humble shop.

"I am."

"Me name is Geoffrey Connelly. I've come to speak to ye about *The Missouri Pride.*"

John stopped his work and stared at the stranger. A smoldering rage began to burn inside him. Those who knew the devastated young man refrained from bringing up that particular topic.

"That's not a good idea."

Geoffrey stood his ground.

"I understand the vexation ye must—"

"I don't think you do," John said, cutting short the man's empathetic words.

"I apologize. I have no right to presume. Such a terrible accident on the river."

"It wasn't an accident."

"Of course it weren't. I mean not to gull ye, lad. I have studied what happened. I've read the report, and I know t'were the captain's own daft head that caused the problem. If he'd acted different, the disaster wouldna' happened."

John paused, set down his hammer and approached Geoffrey. "What is it you want?"

"Let's take a tour, somewhere without so many memories."

The two men spent the next three hours discussing the

future of steam power in the world. Geoffrey Connelly lived in Canada, an industrialist originally from Ireland who created his nation's second largest railroad, then sold it and moved to North America in hopes of growing his fortune.

In the new world his luck changed. With more failures than successes and the knowledge that his deteriorating health was seriously impacting his ability to invent the intricate designs that existed only in his mind, Geoffrey knew he needed talented men to mentor and train. When he heard of *The Missouri Pride's* impressive speed that tragic day on the river, he began his search for the blacksmith responsible for its boiler design.

"I'd like for ye to come and work wit' me as me employee," Geoffrey said as the conversation between the two continued. "I believe one look at me factory in Calgary and any misgivings ye may have will disappear."

"Calgary? Where's Calgary?"

"Canada, in the western regions, a wee journey of a week or so by train, west then north."

"Any great rivers in Calgary?"

"It be a prairie settlement with no steamboats there, but there's water, to be sure."

John considered the man's offer. He loved the Ohio Valley, but his forge and the ghosts that haunted his memories made living in the area bittersweet.

"Mr. Connelly, before I answer, do you have a project in mind, something specific you want to create?"

"Ye come straight to the point, lad, and I like that. I'm going to be the first to successfully construct mechanized dogs."

Mechanized dogs . . . the thought of which caused even experienced designers nightmares. Some had tried, but all had failed. Building a machine to replicate the function of an animal was one of the most involved and difficult endeavors ever undertaken. Horses, oxen, even elephants in Asia proved a natural choice for replication, for these were large animals. Even rudimentary blacksmiths could create the metalwork required for such contraptions, and repairs to the beasts were relatively simple.

But a dog? Even if someone could successfully build a functioning replica of a dog, what purpose would it serve? Dogs were used for hunting or companionship, neither of which benefited from an artificial version.

"You want to create a dog? Reaching for that brass ring?"

"Aye."

"Sir, you've got guts, but . . ."

Geoffrey held up a hand.

"The western territories in Canada resemble yer western states in many ways. It be wild, untamed, raw. In the west, a horse be as important to a man as his gun. When ye travel into the northern territories, ye can say the same of a dog. The animal can lit'rally mean the difference between life and death."

Geoffrey emptied the glass of beer that had gone largely ignored as they spoke. He then stared at John, the man's steel blue eyes burrowing into John's soul.

"I want to build an apparatus that will allow men to travel into the deepest regions of the north. Large animals, they're too heavy. They sink in the deep snows, but a dog, wit' steam coursing t'rough its veins, will glide o'er the snow and ice of the frozen Yukon and into Alaska. Wit' your help, it'll happen."

Geoffrey continued talking, but John heard none of it. The realization that Alaska would be his new home brought the feeling of contentment he had longed for, prayed for.

Fifty years earlier, news of gold finds in California reached John Sr. when he was a child. The young man tried convincing his father—John Jr.'s grandfather—to move to California, but to no avail. He often spoke to John of the disappointment he felt being unable to join the other adventurers in search for gold. When news hit that gold had been discovered in Alaska a year earlier, John Sr. was dead. The younger blacksmith remembered fondly the times his father spoke to him of his unfulfilled wish. Now, thanks to Geoffrey Connelly, John had a chance to see his father's dream achieved.

"Work for you, eh?" The blacksmith had only worked for one man in his life.

"To start, but a full partnership once we build and sell our fahrst order."

"When can we leave?" John asked.

"Immediately."

The Canadian plains presented a new canvas on which John could repaint his life. As the pair journeyed first to Denver, then north to Calgary, they discussed the latest developments in steam-driven automation. As the train continued onward, John understood better the genius of his traveling companion and now partner.

"Why Canada?" John asked. "Why not Pennsylvania or Michigan? They have everything you need."

"Lad," Geoffrey said, "those places be good, aye, but Canada has somethin' neither can boast—a proximity to the Yukon. Also, the area be rich in iron ore and there be water a-plenty. 'Tis ideal for our operation. Wait until ye see me laboratory," Geoffrey said, a phrase he used often as they traveled. "I can't wait to return and build the designs that have lived in me dreams these many years."

The dreams of mechanical beasts began to live inside John as well. He envisioned the smallest of gears intersecting with larger gears until an entire metal animal took shape. His fingers tingled with anticipation. His skin yearned for the heat of the forge, the smell of elements transforming with fire and sweat.

Geoffrey spoke often of his factory. "I call it *Il Laboritorio*. I'm sure you're going to love it."

The truth turned out to be somewhat different.

The train stopped in Calgary and the West's newest entrepreneurs were met at the station by Geoffrey's personal assistant who transported them via mechanical horse and buggy to *Il Laboritorio*. The building wasn't quite what John envisioned. The converted dairy barn needed attention in a most desperate way.

"So, this is it?" John said, revealing his disappointment in his words.

"Close your eyes, lad," Geoffrey said as he came and stood next to the younger man. "I know the site be unworthy of our dreams, but just imagine—imagine the world's finest laboratory right where we stand." John tamped down his temper and followed his partner's instructions.

"We approach the pinnacle of greatness! No one stands even close to where we are, even *with* our humble accommodations. No, lad. This building is only temporary. It *will* improve, and once the world discovers the potential of our combined genius, nothin' in heaven or earth can stop us."

Geoffrey watched as a smile formed on John's lips. With closed eyes, the young man began to slowly nod his head.

Within twelve months the pair had built their first fully operational mechanical animal. With little fanfare, the final panel on the dog's outer shell was set in place and John lit the boiler that provided power to the beast. John named it Buck in honor of his father, John Buxton Thornton, Sr.

"After all these months," Geoffrey said as the two waited for the gears to engage. "We finally have our fahrst product."

"Not yet. We still don't know if last month's modifications will prove successful."

They watched as Buck rose slowly from its prone position on the assembly table.

"What about now?" Geoffrey said.

"A little more time . . ." Both men listened to the animal's heart and heard the inescapable sound of water converting to steam.

"Careful, now," Geoffrey warned as John reached for the steering mechanism located just behind the machine's metal ears. Each mechanized animal, be it horse, oxen, or now dog was controlled with reins. Leather strips ran from the operator to a central control box usually located between the head and the back of the contraption. Many overanxious metal workers failed to complete their inventions because they lacked the patience required to adequately build a proper control box. Though not equipped with reins, John worked the controls with a slightly nervous hand.

The dog responded and leaped from the table. It stood proud on the floor of the laboratory waiting for its next command.

"Eureka!" Geoffrey cried. "We have our dog!"

"I do believe you are right!" The men celebrated well into the night. In the morning they woke with the hangover of success throbbing in their brains.

John spent the next week refining Buck. He fashioned a small sled and harness and hitched it to the contraption. As he labored, he pictured a team of such dogs all working together to pull men and provisions across the frozen mountains and valleys of Alaska. Buck was beautiful. Its sleek metallic face gleamed in the warm Canadian sun. Every time he saw that face, John wished his father could be there to see it. He would most certainly be proud of his son, but thoughts of his father also brought pain, a pain he felt might never leave his heart.

As he worked on the animal, John felt a growing attachment. Buck became more than just a machine; it became a symbol, a symbol of renewed hope that the young blacksmith would overcome the sadness of his life and see those unfulfilled dreams come true. The fact that this symbol came in the form of a dog meant even more. Dogs had always been part of the Thornton household. Memories of hunting and summer walks returned to the now-grown man as he worked with Buck.

The two learned to work as a team, operator and device. They returned each day, John exhausted with new information on how to improve the designs even more, and Buck walking with a subtle intermittent hiss in the place of a tired pant. Each day brought new revelations, new discoveries, and a bond that John would have imagined impossible only weeks before.

Months passed and the work progressed. The team of Connelly and Thornton worked at a fevered pace to build as many dogs as possible before the summer. On one spring day, the plan came to an end.

"John," Geoffrey said after returning from town with supplies, "I apologize, but I've been called away."

"No, Geoffrey. You can't leave! These dogs are nowhere near being done. I need your help now more than ever."

"I'm sorry. It can't be helped. I'm duty bound to an investor from San Francisco. I received a telegram from him just today.

I'm to be on tomorrow's train to Boise and then to California. I must go, lad."

"Then git!" John turned away. No one in the local area possessed the expertise needed to offer help sufficient for John to continue in the man's absence. "You know I can't finish this team until you return."

"Aye, I'm afraid that's true. I do feel terrible about leaving, but I have no choice."

"You always have a choice," John said as he looked his partner in the eye. The older man met his gaze, then looked away.

"I shall return in three weeks' time. Goodbye, John."

The words proved to be the last either man ever spoke to one another.

John began the daunting task of building his team of dogs alone. He knew Geoffrey's absence almost certainly guaranteed they would miss the chance to sell their beasts to prospectors in the summer. The plan had been to sell enough of their animals in the coming months to gain capital. That would allow the business to improve their factory so that more units could be built and sold the coming year. Everything hinged on getting these machines ready. They needed to show the world the superiority of a mechanical dog over a living animal. Geoffrey's actions threatened more than just a delayed product.

Three weeks passed, then four, then two more with no sign of Geoffrey. Each day John arose, hoping for some news that their endeavor would somehow be saved. When he traveled into town he checked with the telegraph office for any word. When none came, he worried his business partner had fallen victim to foul play. He had no choice but to continue his work.

The greatest difficulty in manufacturing a team of dogs dealt with the steering mechanism. A dog represented an entirely new problem in controlling an automated animal. Horses and oxen either worked in pairs or alone. The control boxes on a team of horses, for example, only had to mirror each other with slight deviations for steering. A team of dogs pulling a sled could number in the teens. The control box complexity would need to grow exponentially with the addition of each dog. John worked day and night until he felt confident his new invention could handle the job. This all but guaranteed a working team of mechanical dogs would fetch top dollar to anyone heading north in search of gold. He couldn't wait to show Geoffrey upon his return.

John never got the chance. After several weeks of waiting, he woke one morning to the sounds of men and wagons. As he dressed, he saw scores of men break into the factory and begin removing dogs—both built and under construction—and loading them into their wagons.

"What the *hell* are you doing?" John screamed as he raced partially dressed from his living quarters.

A member of the Northwest Mounted Police confronted John before he could reach the building. "Sir, you are to return inside your house until we have finished our business."

"No! I will not! You! You put down that dog *right now!*" John shouted at a man carrying Buck from the building.

"Mr. Thornton! We have legal authority to remove all machines and records of the business from these premises. We are only carrying out orders delivered to us from the Court of Alberta District. We intend on completing the charge given to us, and no one will impede us from our duties."

John stood, his body enveloped by rage. He looked into the eyes of the officer and saw the unyielding determination of a man upholding the law. After several moments, John spoke.

"Sir," John said, fighting the urge to break into a sprint and level any and every man loading up the wagons with his animals. "I don't understand why you are here."

The policeman produced a document. "This may help, Mr. Thornton." He handed John the papers.

The shock of seeing a small army rob him of his livelihood paled in comparison to the physical effect the words printed on the paper had on the young man. As he read in silence, his usually strong legs buckled as the truth of what happened became known. Geoffrey Connelly had sold ownership of the company and all its assets to financiers in San Francisco.

The transaction was legally binding. John was only an employee and had no right to any portion of the business. The new owners demanded immediate transfer of the company, and Mr. Connelly obliged. The document stated that all previous employees were to be fired upon completion of the transaction and was signed by the new owners, a Mr. Charles Phelps and Mr.

Hal Phelps of Carson City, Nevada. John stopped reading and allowed the papers to flutter to the ground.

"I'm sorry to be the one to tell you," the officer said. John heard the sincerity in his voice. The broken man could only watch as more of his dream disappeared into the back of the wagons.

"No, no. You're only doing your job." John bent and retrieved the order. He began reading, searching the papers for something.

"Uh . . . There's nothing in the order concerning your personal belongings."

John stared at the officer.

"I made sure of it before we set out. However, I cannot allow you to take anything from the factory."

"I understand."

"Anything in that building now belongs to the Phelpses."

John chuckled a bitter laugh.

"Good luck, Mr. Thornton. From the looks of it, I'd say you've accomplished something amazing here. A talented man like yourself should have no trouble finding work someplace else."

John could only nod as he watched the men complete their task. He saw the dogs being loaded one by one into the carts, Buck being the last to go, the beautiful, expressionless metal face staring. He wished the dog would somehow find its own will and bound from the wagon to join him at his side, but he knew this was impossible. The dog obeyed its new master now, and the thought almost broke his heart.

The Mountie shook John's hand then left to assist the others. John walked slowly back to his quarters and shut the door behind him.

After a week of drinking and not much else, John realized if he wished to remain alive he needed to leave Calgary. Thankfully, when the officers took Buck away none of them bothered to search John's quarters for any items that could be considered company property. John left the factory with his tools and a small boiler, one of their prototypes that powered the dogs, buried among his belongings. He almost left it behind, for the thought of it brought him immense pain. In the end, he stowed it, along with a handful of coal and his tools, and set out.

John walked into town, sold almost everything he had to a local blacksmith, bought a non-mechanical horse, and rode west.

After losing his business, the thought of Alaska turned his stomach, yet somehow John knew that's where he would ultimately end up. Since everything he held dear had been taken from him, he still had one chance to make something of his life—if not for himself, at least he could fulfill his father's dream. If there was gold in Alaska, maybe he was due for some good luck, having already experienced a lifetime of the bad.

As John pushed west, he had trouble finding work. The people, though friendly, were weary of drifters. They'd seen men like him pass through their small towns before and what little work there was went to the locals. Paying a stranger for something they themselves could do didn't make sense, and besides, many of the men passing through were only answering the siren song's promise of untold riches hidden in Alaska's vast territory.

When he could find them, John worked odd jobs as he made his way west and then north after reaching the British Columbia Territory at Dawson Creek. When he could not find work, he survived by begging or eating food left for animals. He stayed only a short time wherever he stopped, never getting close to anyone nor allowing anyone to get close to him. He never told a soul about his past, of the steamboats or mechanical dogs. After building fences for one rancher, or doing farrier work for another, the silent man asked for directions to the next settlement, then saddled up and left town. Soon any memory of him ever being there disappeared as well.

There are at least three things a man expecting to survive on his own should know before setting out on a trek to Alaska. He should bring with him adequate supplies, or a way to get those supplies. In other words, he should have a gun. A man must know his limitations; know the terrain and what dangers lay in store. And most importantly, a man should know to never embark on a trek to Alaska in October.

For John, he at least had a gun. Unfortunately, a gun can't guarantee survival when up against a blizzard. As he traveled, John knew enough by the signs of the animals that a storm was brewing. After living in Calgary for a year, he had experienced temperatures reaching 30° below zero. Geoff's laboratory lacked many things, but it did keep two men alive under terrible conditions. Now, as the storm bore down on the solitary rider he realized his violation of two of the three survival rules, and his ignorance could prove his demise.

When the storm hit, John had at least a two-day ride until he reached Whitehorse, the next settlement, but as the snow began to pile up and the wind screamed across the valley, he wondered if he'd ever see another human being again. He sought shelter, anything to give cover for himself and his horse. He made his way over to a grove of pines hoping for relief.

Things looked bad as the pair searched. Finally, they found a small pocket of protection between a tall pine and a large rock that shielded them from the wind. John managed to get the horse tied off, then he sat on the frozen ground. As he searched for additional clothing to stem the damage of the biting cold, he found the forgotten boiler and the few nuggets of coal. As if his life depended on it, he worked feverishly to light the boiler. At last the fuel caught and he tried gleaning heat from the small object. Against all odds, he fell asleep as the storm raged around him.

John woke covered by snow. Miraculously, the clouds that tormented the man had vanished and a bright autumn sun burst over the snow-covered valley. The man's spirits rose when he spotted the sun, but one look around brought his world crashing down upon him.

His horse was gone.

"Damn," he said. He survived the storm, but it may have all been for naught. He planned on arriving at the next settlement in two days. Now he would need the better part of a week to get there on foot. As he prepared to leave, he stowed his boiler and thanked God he had it with him.

John's trek to Whitehorse proved as difficult as he feared. As he trudged through the snow, he worried the damage being done to his feet was irreparable, but he knew if he didn't press on, death would be his only reward. When he stumbled into town, two men found him and took him into their home. They provided him with food, drink and warmth. However, they could not reverse the damage inflicted on his frozen feet. It took several weeks for him to recover to the point where he felt he could sit up. He had lost several pounds on his already thin frame, but he was alive.

The man said not a word when he finally saw the extent of the damage to his feet. Of all the hardships and trials in his life, nothing compared to this. For the first time in his life, John lacked the physical ability to do simple things, walking being the most basic. He cursed his luck and wondered how he could have ever complain about anything before this latest setback.

During the winter months, many prospectors remained in Whitehorse as a refuge from the weather. As John convalesced, he came to rely heavily on his two saviors, Pete Sutter, an older man from Kansas and Hans Larsson, a Swede who dreamed of vast wealth in North America. Both had lived in the Yukon for several years in search of that elusive metal.

"We got gold fever," Pete said.

"Yeah, we gots the fever bad." Hans's strong Swedish accent hung in the air as he spoke.

"You find much?" John asked.

"Depends on how much you call *much*." They laughed at the joke. The men got John to walk, first by carrying him under each arm as he took his first timid and helpless steps, then by constructing crutches, which greatly improved his mobility. In the weeks and months of his recovery, the three became fast friends.

"No!" John said to Pete and Hans over beers. "I'm telling you, mechanical dogs *are* the future in the Yukon!"

"You're drinking funny water," Pete said, slightly slurring his words. Ever since leaving Calgary, John had never told another person of what he and Geoffrey built.

"It's too complex," Hans said. "Horses? Sure, they're big, not difficult at all. But a dog?" He waved his hands in the air to communicate the impossibility of the idea.

"Wait right here!" The two men watched as their friend rose and left the bar.

"Where do you think he's going?" Hans asked.

"Hell if I know. Maybe he's got one of them dogs in his saddlebag." Alcohol enhanced the joke's impact. They continued snickering until John returned to the bar. When they saw that John had brought back his saddlebag with him, they exploded into laughter.

"You want proof?" John withdrew the heart of the mechanical dog. "I got it right here." He slammed the boiler, slightly larger than a man's fist, down on the oak table. The laughing stopped immediately.

"Where did you get that?" Pete whistled.

"I built it."

"You didn't?"

"Damned be I if I'm a liar," Hans said as he picked up the boiler and turned it over in his hands. "It's beautiful, my friend. I've never seen anything like it. Does it truly work?"

"Like a dream," John said, smiling as he returned to his seat. The men stopped drinking as John told them of his adventures. He cried as he relayed the history of *The Missouri Pride*. The mood in the room changed as John spoke of his time spent in Calgary and the incredible experience he had designing and building his dogs. He told them of Buck and the man for whom the animal was named. It felt good for John to finally tell someone else of his life before Whitehorse. After answering as many questions as the impaired men could ask, the three parted. John hobbled to his room, flopped upon the bed, and slept the best sleep he had in years.

As spring slowly reached the upper Yukon, the prospectors prepared for the season. John had spent weeks hearing stories from his friends, and he dreamed of the day he could join them prospecting. The three readied their provisions, including John who had spent much of the winter fashioning metal prosthetics for his legs. The braces extended from his knees to below his feet where they took the place of the removed portion of each foot. The invention allowed John to walk unaided by crutches. With his new mobility, John felt whole enough to accompany his friends.

The trio traveled by traditional dogsled up the banks of the Yukon River, passing Kluane Lake. It wasn't until they reached White River that they realized their early departure was adversely affecting John's feet.

"I'm sorry," John said, dejected. "I'm going to have to stay and rest." All three knew he was right. He would need to remain behind while the other men ventured farther north to scout locations for their next attempt at a profitable claim.

They spent several days setting up a camp for their friend, but the men were anxious to leave. Frozen rivers provided the quickest access to some of the most remote locations, and each day they waited meant a previously accessible path might turn into an impassable body of water.

John sat on the banks of the frozen river and listened to the sound of the dogs fade as he watched his friends disappear into the vast expanse of God's creation. It was then he felt truly alone.

After several days, John wondered if or when his friends would return. He hoped they had not deserted him like so many had previously done in his life.

The thought was not unfounded. Men had killed friends over a disputed claim when gold was found. Hans and Pete had dedicated much more of their lives to this endeavor. If they found gold, a two-way split meant much more profit than a three-way divide. John might never hear from them again, and in his condition, being stranded on the banks of this half frozen river, his chances of survival looked bleak.

John spent some of each day searching the horizon for any sign of human life, and he hoped he and his friends would again be reunited. It was on one particular morning that John did notice movement along the riverbank. However, in his wildest dreams he could never have imagined the events that were about to take place.

It wasn't movement that first caught John's eye, but a flash of light reflected off something. The cloudless sky allowed a brilliant sun to wash the valley in light. Somewhere miles away something caught that light and sent a gleam of illumination back at him.

John continued looking in the direction of the anomaly. Minutes after the first spark, he saw another, then another. Soon the small area became alive in burst of lights, as if the river were no longer frozen but shimmering in the morning sun, but only in that small area.

"What could that be?" John said to no one. "It almost looks like . . ."

A gasp caught in his throat. The scene before him reminded him of a time when he watched a pair of stagecoach mechanical horses going through their paces on the plains near Denver. Whatever it was approaching, he knew it was mechanical. When it came within 100 yards John knew exactly what it was and had seen something he thought he would never see again as long as he lived.

"Hello!" A voice cut through the chilled morning air as a team of mechanical sled dogs drew near. John stood, unable to answer, unable to even move.

"Hello, there!" The man yelled again as if John had not heard him.

"Damn you, man!" The team stopped at John's camp and a well-dressed older gentleman stepped from the sled. Obviously a man of means, his gear and equipment were of the highest quality. "Are you deaf?" he asked.

John mostly ignored the man for he could only stare at the team of dogs. He recognized them immediately because he designed and built them.

But it was the lead dog that drew most of John's attention. Buck. John began to limp toward the dog, ignoring the man who continued yelling at him. As he hobbled to the team, a flood of emotion poured over him.

"Hal! Leave that idiot alone," said another man getting out of the sled. "He obviously doesn't understand you—maybe he's just an uneducated Russian." Only then did John notice the sled brought a party of three people, two men and a woman.

"Sir!" said Hal. "Stay away from *my* animals."

"Excuse me?" John whispered.

"Oh, so you're not deaf and you can understand," Hal said. John turned back to the dogs.

"Stay back! Those are extremely complicated machines. You'll damage them if you get any closer."

"Oh, Hal," the woman said. "Would you just forget about those infernal dogs for once. Can't you see it is Charles and I that need to rest?" Hindered by weight, the woman struggled to climb from the sled. Her clothes were expensive, but in need of attention.

John could only stare at these people as if their words made no sense. He turned back to the dogs and what he saw made him sick.

The machines he spent so much of his soul building looked as if they were about to literally fall apart right in front of him. His eyes scanned the condition of each dog and he saw neglect. He saw mistreatment. He saw a total lack of respect for the inventions he had worked so hard to build. In his wildest dreams he could not imagine anyone inflicting the type of abuse they had been subject to.

Still, the other dogs looked in better shape when compared to the lead dog, Buck. His once beautiful face was dented and scarred. The oversized pads on its paws were disintegrating. Soon the animal would only have metal spikes that would sink into the snow, rendering the dog useless for transportation. He saw gaps in the metalwork where gears were exposed to the elements, something he and Geoffrey spent weeks trying to prevent. With the animal's inner workings open to outside influences, corrosion and destruction were all but guaranteed.

"I'm not going to tell you again, sir," Hal said. "You leave those dogs alone, or by hell, you'll be sorry. Now, my sister and her husband are in need of your assistance and I demand you help us."

John turned from the team and limped back to his chair by a fire. Without looking at anyone he picked up a stick of birch wood and resumed whittling on what would eventually become an axe handle.

Hal, realizing his demands and profanity had no effect on the man, decided to change his strategy.

"Sir, I apologize for my behavior," he said with an exasperated exhalation. He slowly sat on a log to rest. "We have met with misfortune on our way to Dawson. My sister has fared much worse than a woman of her stature should have to bear."

John continued to whittle.

"I also failed to introduce ourselves. I'm Hal Phelps, and this is my brother Charles and his wife Mercedes. We came by way of Carson City, Nevada, then San Francisco and Seattle."

As Hal continued expounding on the many problems they experienced in their search for gold, a memory burrowed from the back of John's mind until it hit his consciousness with such force, his heart began to race. These were the men who had purchased Geoffrey Connelly's business, the men who sent officers to take his dogs, the same dogs that obediently stood only feet away from him. It took every ounce of energy in his body to not stand and confront the pompous men, especially after seeing how they treated his creations. Hal continued speaking but John didn't hear him. He thought only of the dogs.

As anger welled up within him, he realized his invention had worked. He had proven that mechanical sled dogs—if treated correctly—could not only survive the untamed northwest, but excel in sending men to areas as yet unexplored. The realization of his ultimate success cut through his depression and gave him a sense of accomplishment he never knew he could feel.

Eventually John spoke. Hal and Charles asked several questions to which he gave simple answers. When pressed, John was brutally honest, but deep down he knew much of his advice would be ignored. Besides, the sight of the three made him sick to his stomach.

"Time to go," Hal yelled using more volume than was needed. "We need to get on the trail if we're going to make Dawson by tomorrow night."

"You're not going to make it to Dawson by then," John said with complete confidence.

"How would you know—you're nothing but a cripple!" Hal quipped. John ignored his insult and continued whittling.

"Charles," Mercedes whined from the sled. "Maybe we should listen to him."

"Maybe you should be *quiet!"* the man screamed at his wife.

"I mean, he knows the area and we don't."

"No," Hal said. "They told us up above that the bottom was dropping out of the trail and that the best thing for us to do was to lay over. Others told us we couldn't make White River, and here we are." Arrogance seeped from each word the man said.

Even though he hated these people, John couldn't allow them to leave without giving his opinion. They were idiots, but even the biggest fool deserves some compassion.

"And they told you true," John said. "My friends—experienced in such matters—said the bottom could likely drop out any time. Only fools, with the blind luck of fools, could have made it as you did. I tell you straight, from what my friends say, I wouldn't risk my carcass on that ice for all the gold in Alaska."

"That's why we're headed to Dawson and you're stuck here. And where are these so called *friends* now?" Hal smirked at John then walked to the sled.

"Sir, if you take your team on that ice, there's nothing I can do to help you."

"Help? You can barely walk. How on earth could you ever help us? Charles! See to the dogs. I want them ready for a full-day run!"

John watched as Hal's brother accessed the boiler on each of the dogs, inserted several lumps of coal, and topped off the water. The man who created the magnificent animals sat patiently as he watched the greenhorn add too much fuel, further damaging the amazing creatures. Several times he felt he should say something to them as they made mistake after mistake, but no. The dogs were no longer his. He held no claim to them. The stoic man who endured so much pain in his life shed a single tear as he tried to ignore the madness happening around him.

"What's wrong with the lead dog?" Hal asked in disgust.

"I don't know," Charles said as he tried adjusting the gauges on the boiler.

"I'm tired of that dog always breaking down." Hal walked to the front of the team. After a moment of inactivity Hal picked up a club and brought it down hard on Buck's head.

"Damnable thing!" he roared. "Next time we get to some thin ice, I'm going to cut that worthless dog loose and laugh as it sinks to the bottom of the river."

John could take no more.

In an instant, the impaired man rose and rushed at the team. Both Charles and Hal saw the rage in his eyes and backed away. In doing so, Hal tripped over his flailing feet and Mercedes screamed. John stopped before Buck.

"That's *my* dog," Hal said, his voice cracking in his failed show of bravery. John said nothing. Hal produced a long knife and thrust it forward, to which John simply knocked it from his hand with the axe handle he still held fast. John picked up the knife and cut the reins connecting Buck to the rest of the team. Without saying a word John cradled Buck in his arms and with great difficulty carried the damaged animal back to the fire.

To John, the rest of the world disappeared as he knelt and investigated the extent of the Phelpses' disrespect. At first sight he wondered how the animal was functioning in any capacity, the damage was so extensive. So absorbed was he in Buck's condition that he didn't hear the thread of profanity directed at him from Hal and Charles or the threats of retaliation they hurled at him from the banks of White River.

"This is your last chance! Don't take the river!" John yelled to the team as they set off for Dawson.

"You can go straight to hell!" Hal roared and pushed the team out on the frozen ice.

As the Phelpses left, John did turn to see if they would follow his advice and take the longer route around the weakened ice, or if they would direct the team toward the path they vowed to take, a path which meant certain disaster. As expected, they chose the latter.

'Damn fools,' John thought and spit. He knew the team and the three people were doomed. He continued watching as the sled dogs began to cross the unstable ice and saw the hole open up. In an instant, it engulfed dogs, sled, and people. The trio of screams echoed off the frozen ice then stopped as the woman, her husband, and her brother-in-law sunk into the freezing water.

The master turned his attention to his dog. "You poor devil," he said, and Buck nudged his hand.

Styled after *The Call of the Wild* by Jack London

West End

NEVE TALBOT

Theodore Laurence loved Josephine March. That was the cold, hard truth. He had loved her since that first time he laid eyes on her. Sitting at his desk, he had stared out over the hedge, and there she had sat in her attic window next door. Her laughing eyes had reached out and claimed him. His mates all called him Laurie, but she began calling him 'Teddie' when he was but sixteen, as if she owned him, and he knew then and there she did.

Thoughts of that day five years gone filled his mind as he closed the door and left his grandfather's house behind him. Before him, a new life, a new adventure, and the Cassiopeia: a massive triple-envelope airship unlike anything else in the skies, then tethered not a hundred yards off on the March family's farmland, out of reach of milling crowds and prying eyes. The legendary inventor, Edward Rochester, had developed its revolutionary alloys and unique design; the crystal arrays that captured the light of the sun and transformed it into power; and the engines that translated that power into speed with maximum efficiency.

Laurie would depart that very hour. He had graduated with the highest honors from the new Massachusetts Institute of Technology, and in the process gained the notice of the genius Rochester who made himself Laurie's mentor. Laurie would continue his education at Rochester's foundries in Great Britain. It should have been a day full of joy. He should have been giddy with anticipation.

Should have been.

Laurie followed the automaton that propelled a trolley overladen with steamer trunks and bandboxes across the garden lawn. Such menials were hardly new, but the machine before him resembled nothing ever before put into service. Sleek and graceful, strong and durable, with technology unmatched elsewhere, the Mandroids could accomplish nearly any physical task capable of man—all but intentionally harm or inflict death. That they would never do.

The warmongers had their rail guns and cannon, their armored trains and incendiary devices, their fifteen-foot-tall mechanized monsters with Gatling guns for appendages, euphemistically dubbed 'Peacekeepers,' that mindlessly trammeled friend and foe alike. After the devastation of the American Civil War, in the face of British, French, and Dutch empiric brutality and conquest, Rochester swore the world needed no help from him to slaughter wholesale. He would never invent a weapon nor allow his technology to be used as such. He maintained an uneasy peace with the British Empire by allowing his foundries to remain in its territories; they smelted the alloys and fabricated the shells, but nothing more.

Instead of selling killing machines, he sought the help of Laurie's grandfather, Mr. Laurence, and Jo's father, Reverend March, in giving away the Mandroids to the war-ravaged refugees of the New American Alliance, the tattered remains of the United States, still destitute and starving two years after the end of the war. The two friends had become integral to the operation and true partners in the venture. Profit would come after the devastated nation got back on its feet, but the Mandroids would first change the world. They would plow fields and harvest crops, build roads and clear away rubble, and provide much-needed manpower for the decimated population.

Laurie pressed one of several glowing crystals set in a small brass box that he held, and the machine immediately halted at the gap in the hedge between his grandfather's estate and Orchard House, the March family property. Since his first day in Concord, Laurie had known he belonged there. How many hours over the past five years had he spent snug in the attic with Jo and her sisters, acting out Jo's ridiculous plays? Meg and Beth were like his own sisters. Little Amy was his pet. But Jo—Jo was part of him. She ever would be.

Not even her denial of him the previous morning would change it, and therein lay the rub.

Laurie huffed at himself and his pining, and reactivated the Mandroid. A simple sequence of commands directed it through the hedge, across the Marches' kitchen garden, and into the cow pasture to the Cassiopeia. Another flick of a switch, and the machine effortlessly moved its burden up the cargo ramp and into the hold. As he stood at the bottom, staring up into the cavernous expanse, it felt empty without Jo's luggage beside his own, despite it being filled with rack upon rack of factory-new Mandroids awaiting dispersal.

Laurie would never begrudge Beth the support of her sisters, but she made a terribly convenient screen for Jo. They all had come to take their leave: Jo, Beth, Amy; even Meg had dragged her new husband, John Brooke, away from his morning coffee to be there. Mrs. March—Marmee to the girls—stood with her husband, the good reverend, as he consulted with Rochester.

Laurie deeply felt the family's notice, but Jo's dodge sent him a clear message to keep at arm's length. But then, he didn't need her words to understand her. Her thoughts came across perfectly clear.

Well, he would do her one better: never mind arm's length. He refused to see her at all.

He could be too busy to notice. His old school chum, Freddie Vaughn, made that easy enough. Laurie had to brief him on preflight procedures. Freddie only got the nod for the venture to England because Mr. Vaughn, a major investor in the Mandroid project, demanded it, but Freddie was thick as a brick. Rochester carefully chose his battles with the father, and Laurie must suffer the son.

Rochester's experiments with mechanical prostheses and neuro-electric implants fired Laurie's imagination, and he considered medical school as another option across the pond. Whatever he did, he would follow in the footsteps of the brilliant young inventor. Like Rochester, he would do some good in the world. With Jo by his side, he knew he could not fail.

Except, Jo had no interest in England or Scotland or taking the Grand Tour—at least, not with him. She had always dreamed of going, but when he asked her to accompany him, she turned him down flat. As she put it, she didn't love him—not enough, not that way, and she had no interest in playing wifey with a ruffled pinafore and a calico cat, sitting alone by the fire for who knew how many years while he engrossed himself in his studies yet again.

All through university, whenever he returned home, Laurie could not disgorge what he had learned fast enough for Jo. If she could not go herself, his attendance was the next best thing, or so she said. He felt he went to university for her as much as himself.

But that wasn't good enough any longer—he wasn't good enough—and not even the promise of Europe could tempt her to accept him. It had never before occurred to him that she would deem his offering unworthy of her, and the stark realization blindsided him. Of a sudden, they were strangers, and Laurie's expansive, glorious horizons felt dark, gloomy, and hopeless.

Laurie tried to focus on Freddie, but his thoughts would turn to the sisters haunting the periphery of the field. Even so, he had his pride, however wounded; he would not go begging—not again. England and the Empire beckoned, and he would show her nothing but defiance, while he inwardly prayed she would somehow change her mind.

"Will you not part well with me, Teddie?" Laurie wheeled at the sound of Beth's gentle voice. She looked too pale. Jo, so strong and hale beside her, accentuated Beth's air of frailty as she clung to her sister's arm. "Do you mean to go without saying goodbye?"

"You should not have come out, Little Bit," he chided. "The morning damp will do you no good."

The trace of an impish grin flitted over Beth's face. "If Mohammed will not go to the mountain—"

"I would have come to you had you given me half a chance."

Beth wagged her head and clicked her tongue in mock severity. Laurie felt the heat rush to his cheeks. To cover his prevarication, he took Beth's free arm and threaded it through his own, despite Jo's continued support of her. "Come with me, Miss Insolence, or I'll bodily remove you to the house."

Beth acquiesced far more easily than her brave front should have allowed, and within a few steps, she leaned heavily upon him, although she stubbornly maintained hold of her sister. The uneven terrain of the cow pasture caused her to stumble, and put her in constant danger of falling to the ground. "Shall I carry you, darling?"

Beth denied him but leaned her head on his shoulder. He slipped his arm around her waist to keep her on her feet, and knew Jo resisted the urge to do the same. "You should not have come out," he chided. He shot a look of indictment at Jo for allowing it.

"Mr. Laurence," Beth answered, "I am not so vain as to believe that your love for me is stronger than your . . .

disappointment—than your awkward situation with my sister. You would not have come to the house, and I could not allow matters to remain thus between you. I will not have it. So I came to meet you halfway." She gave a little shrug. "She could attend me or stew in the attic—a simple choice, really, for I know she loves me quite nearly as much as—"

"Beth, you go too far," Jo snapped, the first word Laurie had heard her say all morning.

"—as much as she will miss you when you're gone."

Laurie eyed Jo askance, although he avoided revealing the weakness. "You mistake her, Beth. She's glad to see me go so I will no longer hang about to bother her."

"I am right here," Jo protested.

"There you are wrong," Beth persisted. "She already misses you."

Laurie jerked his chin in denial and let the matter drop. Jo still glared at the ground as she plodded along beside them. For all of Beth's good intentions, the ploy accomplished nothing.

Beth tripped once more, and Laurie scooped her up in his arms. "Don't bother to protest," he growled softly.

Beth buried her face in his neck. "Don't let Marmee see."

Laurie hurried to Orchard House in great, ground-chewing strides and Jo scampered along beside him. Of all the injustices in the world, Beth's bout with scarlet fever and subsequent weakened heart angered him the most. There had to be something someone could do. The medical profession could perform miracles. Why had they not yet invented a mechanical heart?

Jo bustled about in the kitchen putting the kettle on as Laurie gently laid Beth on her sofa beside the fire. He quickly had her tucked snugly in a counterpane, propped in pillows, and breathing more easily. Next step, a roaring fire.

Laurie realized the house had gone silent but for his own muttering at a bank of stubborn coals. He looked up—straight into Jo's tender eyes, the silence rich and redolent between them. If he could bottle that look that professed all her voice could not, he could endure his time away—the time she needed to reconcile her mind to her heart.

The fire popped and a clinker bounced out onto the hearthrug. Jo dropped to the floor to fetch it, but he scooped it up and threw it onto the grate before she burned herself.

She reached out to warm her hands. "I think the fire is hot enough." She smiled gently to soften her words.

"Perhaps," he answered, "but we want it to last."

"We do," Jo murmured.

"Just the kindling catching the flame isn't enough."

"No . . ."

"A good fire takes time. It must get hold of the logs."

Jo nodded, her words scarcely breathed. "It will. I am certain . . ."

"I can wait," Laurie whispered.

Each word had drawn them closer, until the space between them charged electric, like one of Mr. Tesla's famous coils. Her swimming eyes bespoke her wishes and Laurie leaned to close the distance, but she ducked her head and rested her forehead against his, as much surrender as she allowed herself.

Far too soon, she moved to rise, but he took her hands to retain her. “Marry me.”

“I just can’t,” she whimpered.

“No. Of course not.” His words fell harshly—more harshly than he intended. He tried to force it back, but the surging anger and frustration propelled him to his feet. “We belong together. You know it, Jo, as well as do I, but your blasted pride won’t allow you to admit it. Well, I wish you the best of luck with it, but it has brought me naught but heartache.”

He turned to storm away and met the sight of Beth on her sofa, feigning sleep. His sadness washed over his anger, dampening the flame. He bent to kiss her head. “I’m sorry, Bethy,” he breathed, but his words caught in his throat. Beth opened her eyes and threw her arms about his neck and he dropped to his knees to hold her. “You’d best be here when I return, or I’ll fight the archangels themselves to fetch you back again.”

The Cassiopeia’s steam whistle blew, demanding his return to the ship. Beth released him without a word, offering only a sad smile. “Goodbye, you scamp,” he murmured softly. He kissed her once more, then strode away, leaving Jo and his hopes behind him.

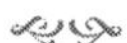

Four years. How had four years come and gone in that instant—less than a blink of an eye? The first year felt as if it flew by as he and Freddie Vaughn studied metallurgy with Rochester's partner, Rottstieger. That is, Laurie studied. Freddie primarily took up with lordlings and courtesans, and only caused trouble when he did show at the foundry.

Laurie marked the time by posts from home, letters Jo sent him that allowed him to hope. Long, chatty, light-filled letters that between every line seemed to count the days until he would return to make her his own.

But then, as that year drew to a close, the University of Edinburgh came calling. They had seen his designs. They liked his ideas. The advances in metallurgy and electricity made them more than fanciful dreams. Surely, he wished to expand his studies into medicine and press his theories as far as they would go.

Such opportunities did not simply fall from the sky. Laurie never imagined they would come seeking him out. Surely Jo would understand. Surely. Surely she would now join him.

Surely not.

Instead of Jo, only a cold denial met Laurie and his roses at Liverpool, in the form of her passage refunded by the booking agent. Her formal answer to his cable came after weeks of waiting. The letter left no doubt of her intent and dispelled the last of his self-deception.

Laurie occupied his mind with his studies, but his heart felt a lead weight within his chest. For three years, he plodded through the damp and dreary cold of Scotland, enveloped in the darkness. The long winter nights felt eternities. The short span of long summer days were only torment.

Freddie Vaughn remained in England as he polished his libertine credentials, paid lip service to the company, and advanced from lazy and spoiled to corrupt and malignant. His friendship with Laurie grew caustic, and soured more whenever business took Laurie to London and they met in society.

The letters from home stopped coming. Even Laurie's grandfather had become terse and uncommunicative. The news that did come, which should have given Laurie comfort—given him joy—bored a canker in his soul. Meg had given John twins. Twins. That should have been him. That should have been him and Jo.

But all that was over and done, just like medical school. He had to move forward. He had no other choice. And, when push came to shove, he could move on to places far worse than Jamaica. The crystal blue seas, clear skies, and verdant hills leeched the tension from him and scrubbed the taint of martial, mechanized, greasy, smoke-choked London from his soul. Powered by Rochester's sootless solar arrays, free of slavery and oppression, clean and sunny Kingston seemed an Eden by comparison.

An army of orderlies swarmed the Cassiopeia once it touched ground, and Laurie stood at the bottom of the gangplank handing out credentials as each ex-soldier amputee filed past. He admired Rochester for purchasing their freedom; enslavement of debtors more evidence of the Empire's oppression. As the agents for the absentee buyer, Laurie hoped they had filled the commission well, for he hadn't the least inkling of Rochester's plans for them. He supposed he would find out soon enough. Surely, the man would meet the flight.

"Quite the entourage, Doctor. Fifty-three new patients . . . ambitious."

Laurie turned to the deep voice that assaulted him from behind. Not overly tall but broad of shoulder and ramrod straight, Edward Rochester made Laurie think of a bulldog: not the most comely breed but compact and strong, elegant in its own manner. Coupled with his dark, saturnine features and high, intelligent brow, he appeared severe and aloof despite his mere thirty years. His changeable moods and erratic actions made him difficult to know, but he was a good man, benevolent, passionate, fiercely protective of his friends and his inventions, stalwart in his beliefs, a formidable foe to cross. At that moment, he wore a smirk of self-satisfaction.

Laurie hesitated. "Of a truth . . . we brought fifty-six."

"Do tell."

Laurie nudged his chin the direction of the three men detained at the top of the gangway: one small, wiry miscreant whose eye-patch enhanced his sinister air, and two sidekicks.

"We were halfway to the Azores when we discovered them. After all the burglaries at the foundry and the fire at the warehouse, we felt you would wish to see them. It's the closest we've come to any answers."

"We know Vaughn has been lobbying for the Empire for four years," Rochester growled. "We know that blighter will stop at nothing to achieve his own ends, and none else but that worthless son of his had the necessary access to get as far as they did. I trusted Freddie and he betrays us all. He makes himself the Empire's stooge. We know the answers, Dr. Laurence. What I need is proof!"

"As I said, these blokes may be worth interrogating."

"No papers. Stowaways."

"Indeed, sir. And certainly spies. We found several restricted areas breached."

Rochester's looks darkened. "And the schematics I sent Julian to collect?"

"Safe and sound, but we redoubled security and strengthened protocols."

A storm brewed on Rochester's visage. "Get them off my ship," he snarled at the guard. "Throw them in the gaol—what in Hades is *that*?"

Laurie need not follow Rochester's gaze to the cargo ramp. He had anticipated that moment for days. "A Mandroid, sir."

Rochester strode to the automaton. "Mandroid," he barked as he closed the distance. "What is your designation?"

The thing turned its head, then the rest of its body to face its Maker. "Mr. Rochester?" it answered in a tinny, mechanical voice.

"Your designation, now."

"Mandroid 69-0257NA-D, under contract to Mercedes March, Plumfield, Concord, Massachusetts."

Rochester spun on Laurie. "March's blasted aunt took my Mandroid—my *Delta* to London for the Empire to get their hands on?"

Laurie fished into his pocket and surrendered the machine's large control crystal hanging from a long silver chain. "Yes, sir. She took the Mandroid with her when she and Amy embarked on the Grand Tour. We discovered it the evening of our departure. The old lady knew well enough to keep it out of sight when I visited Amy, but apparently, showing off to society outweighed any sense—"

"What need has the Empire of thugs and felons to commit industrial espionage when vain old dowagers deliver my secrets to them hand over fist?"

"When we confiscated hers, she complained that the Vaughns yet had their Delta in London—"

Rochester's upraised hand brought Laurie's briefing to an abrupt halt. His steely eyes locked Laurie's own as he produced a newspaper tucked beneath his arm, then carefully unfolded it. A blazing headline and a Daguerreotype of a mighty conflagration filled the space above the fold, dated a week since. "EXPLOSIONS ROCK SKY-HARBOR, SABOTAGE FEARED!"

"Tell me, Dr. Laurence," he demanded, his voice menacing. "Where exactly is the Vaughns' Delta model?"

"We speculate that it has been decommissioned, sir."

"Tell me I am imagining it. Tell me this catastrophe"—he jabbed his finger at the paper—"was not the product of a Mandroid self-destruct."

Laurie stood firm. "We have every reason to believe it was, sir. We activated the universal recall function as soon as we confiscated the March Delta, but the countdown expired before the

Vaughns' machine reported to the Cassiopeia. . . . Then, BLAM! We scarcely got away. Another moment's delay and we would have been caught in the sky-harbor lock-down."

Rochester scowled first at the newspaper, then at the Mandroid, then at the paper again. Laurie watched as his visage softened and his eyes began to twinkle. "Blazes! I wish I had been there to see it. Was it as terrific as I imagine?"

"More, sir. It seemed they stored it at a munitions dump."

Rochester barked a laugh. "Serves them right, the fools!" he snorted. "What will it take for the Empire to get the message? My Mandroids will never fight their wars for them." He looked up from the paper. "What of the warning signals for the self-destruct? They had not disabled them, surely."

"We heard them, sir, and we were a half mile out. Anyone closer would run away just to escape the sound."

Rochester nodded in satisfaction. "Blasted Brits." Laurie wondered exactly when he had ceased to consider himself a citizen of his homeland. Rochester spun on his heel and strode away. "Come!"

Laurie fell in beside him just as Rochester stopped abruptly to look him in the eye. "Tell me: are you content?"

Laurie hesitated as his mentor set out once again for the low bungalows which skirted the landing field. "I'm afraid I don't take your meaning."

Rochester eyed him askance. "It has been four years since we made these plans. Men grow, change. You have been abroad, seen a bit of the world. Is this still what you want?"

"I would have wasted a great deal of time and money were it not."

"Indeed," Rochester smirked. "So, how do you like the Royal London? What of Edinburgh?"

"Frankly, they lack vision, sir. They would never attempt what you did when Julian Meeks broke his back and lost his leg. They would have written him off, but you put him back on his feet. You restored his future."

"The man is my friend. Should I live to be a hundred, I'll owe him a debt that cannot be repaid."

"But that's just it, sir. It's about quality of life. I do not mean to solely follow either metallurgy or medicine. The two together should be taken more seriously. Those Edinburgh chaps believe if they strap steel and brass and gears and leather onto a man, with no regard for what he suffers, he should be grateful. But that is not enough, sir. It is inhumane, inefficient, and barbarous."

Rochester grinned. "And you believe you could do better. You would marry the disciplines."

"Aye, sir. I am here because of what you did for Julian. You did better with him than they ever could, and you never went to medical school. Perhaps that makes you more qualified than any of them—you are not limited by preconceptions."

"You are correct, Mr. Laurence, I am no physician. I am most fortunate that we didn't kill Julian in our efforts to help him. The doctors I brought here didn't know enough, and I was arrogant and reckless, but we muddled it out. But that was six years gone.

"We have learned a great deal since then. I have brought like-minded physicians, metallurgists, electrochemical engineers, all to my estate at West End to study the matter. But you, my friend, are the only one who has studied both metals and medicine. You are uniquely qualified. Julian's patch job begins to wear down, but with your help, we will be ready—well and truly ready—when he needs us again."

"It seems too good to be true."

Rochester grinned. "Wait until you see West End."

They had reached the largest bungalow and made their way through open, airy rooms, and past segregated offices. Rochester paused with his hand on the latch of a louvered door. "I've pressing matters to attend. Wait for me here, and when I return, we'll discuss your new discipline of physiological metallurgic engineering." He turned the handle and pushed open the door, then strode down the passage without another word.

Laurie stepped into what seemed an antechamber of some sort, with a broad bank of windows opening the prospect directly before him, chairs against the wall to his right, facing a desk on the left, which sat before several cabinets beside a second door. His back to Laurie, a young man absorbed himself with filing stacks of manila folders and accounting ledgers in the drawers.

"Pardon me," Laurie hesitated. "Mr. Rochester told me to wait."

"We're all in an uproar because of this new doctor just arriving," the boy answered without turning from his work. "Make yourself at home."

The voice fell with comfortable familiarity on Laurie's ears, and he cursed himself and his weakness. Despite the intervening years, now and again some random sight or sound reminded him of Jo, and the old wound would ache.

However, the thought forced him to look beyond the cropped riding pants and tall boots the boy wore, to the curves that filled them out so nicely, and the loose blouse that revealed not the slight form of a sprouting youth but the shapely form of a young woman well grown. She wore her hair in a short, loose mop of curls, and a leather jacket and goggled helmet hung from a hat rack in the corner.

"We are all in a muddle, but feel free to help yourself." She waved a file over her shoulder toward the general direction of a sideboard. "There's no telling when Mr. Rochester will return."

Laurie attempted to say something, but he could only think of Jo and how she would have reveled in the freedom of such attire. Jo, who was three thousand miles away and hadn't thought of him from one year to the next.

Rather than indulge in a useless bout of self-pity, Laurie turned to the windows. The airfield resembled a kicked anthill as all the workers scurried about and unladed the Cassiopeia's cargo.

"I suppose you're quite used to this sight." He nodded at the bustle of enterprise. "For you, that is business as usual."

"Of a truth—"

Laurie turned at the sound of stacks of paper hitting the floor. The lady, his own Josephine March, stood and stared at him, dumbstruck. He blinked at her, willing the vision away. He had been from home for far too long. His eyes surely conjured that which he most desired. "Of a truth?" he choked.

"You?"

"Whom did you expect?"

Jo blinked at him, and Laurie watched as she flushed as pink as she had been pale but a moment before, but a visible act of will pushed back her astonishment, replaced by a familiar consternation. She set her jaw, her shoulders stiffened, and her voice took on a decided edge.

"Of a truth, Mister Laurence," she pecked out, as if her tongue had become the hammers of the typewriting machine on the desk before her, "I never gave it a second thought, except to curse the man who brought this down upon our heads."

Her eyes shot daggers as sharp as her tone, then she dropped to the floor to collect the records. "This is not business as usual. Fifty unexpected soldiers in need of immediate medical attention have strained our facilities to breaking."

"What are you doing here?" Laurie managed. He hurried around the desk to assist her. "Jo, what are you doing here?"

"Mr. Laurence—" she replied coldly, "or is it Doctor Laurence now? I've lost track of the time."

"Which you would not have done had you come to me."

"Which I need not have done had you returned when you promised."

Laurie bit down on his angry reply. "It is Doctor Laurence," he said instead. "It has been for some time. Surely Amy told you."

"But of course," Jo laughed bitterly. "Amy. How could I possibly forget Amy? How is my dearest sister?" She scooped up the remaining papers to prevent his reaching them, then threw the shambles onto the desktop. She began slamming the packets, one atop the next, in cadence with her words.

"Beautiful Amy, charming Amy, Amy the pet of Aunt March. Amy, who stole my Grand Tour because she is beautiful and elegant and worthy. Amy would never shame our family. You finally finish medical school and what do you do? Rush straight to London—to Amy, the perfect match for you and all of high society!"

"I finally finished medical school and moved on to my exams at The Royal London. Amy just happened to be there. I was there scarcely three months—"

"And spent every spare moment with her, escorting her into society. Making a great show of sporting her about town."

"I have no idea where you get such preposterous notions."

"Where else would I get them? From Amy, who writes once a week specifically to tell me how much time you spend together, how charming you are, how brilliant in society, and how intimate you have grown. Surely by the end of your residency there, you will be ready to settle down."

Laurie forced his jaw shut. Her accusations left him stymied. "I spent twenty hours a day at hospital, Jo. When exactly was I supposed to be this gadabout?"

"I haven't the faintest idea. Why don't you ask Amy?"

"What the devil do I care about Amy?"

His exasperated tone brought her up short. She blinked at him. He pushed back his hair with both fists and stepped away. He folded his arms across his chest, his legs braced for impact, and stared out at the Cassiopeia. "And my residency is here," he muttered. "At least get your facts straight."

Stillness settled over the room, he knew not how long—probably only moments. It felt an eternity. "If you do not care for her, you should not toy with her thus," Jo said at last. An angst-riddled mixture of empathy and compassion weighed heavily in her soft tone. "You will break her heart."

"Perhaps Amy interpreted things the way she wanted to see them," he told the windows. "Perhaps she would have done no matter my actions." He turned to her. "Or, perhaps what she wrote and what you read were two different things. But by my life, Jo, I never courted your sister. She only made me want . . ."

Laurie bit down on his accursed tongue. He refused to make a fool of himself yet again. After her three-year silence, he owed her nothing. She lost the right to be jealous of anyone after his disappointment at Liverpool. "What are you doing here?"

"Surely Amy kept you well enough informed," Jo retorted.

"Apparently she felt no need. Perhaps she assumed we communicated. Perhaps you never told her of your directive to stay away."

"My directive? You mean to put the blame on me?"

"Forgive me, but it sounded very much a directive to me. When a man asks a woman to be his wife—"

"Your wife? You booked my passage and sent me a cable that said 'come.' "

"—when he asks and gets nothing but an empty cabin and silence in reply—"

"What are you on about?"

"Do you know what it's like to search a luxury liner for a bride who never boarded it—who never so much as declined the invitation?"

"I wrote, Laurie. As soon as your cable came, I wrote."

Laurie wagged his head in denial. "Whatever you did, I waited for two months for word, and 'I value your friendship more than I can say, make sure to keep in touch,' at the end of it left no doubt of my banishment."

"Then you're a fool."

"Indeed I am, for once upon a time I believed your words and your intent were one and the same."

"Once upon a time, we required no words to understand one another."

"And just see how well I profited from that bit of felicity."

"What would you have me say?"

"Was 'yes' too much to ask?"

"Was your presence?"

He proffered no reply, and she turned again to mutilating Rochester's reports.

"Jo," Laurie insisted. "Jo!" He took her shoulders to turn her to him, but her look was all fire and ice. Her eyes scalded to the touch, and he dropped his hands. "Jo," he said more gently.

“Why didn’t you tell me you were here? I would have come as soon as I had word.”

“And make me responsible for you giving up your studies? I think not. You got on with your life. I got on with mine.”

“There are places far more suitable for a young lady to exert her independence—places close to home, where her family can protect her, or come to her rescue when she gets herself into scrapes.”

Jo’s eyes grew narrow and flinty, her voice low and still. “Do I appear to need rescuing, Dr. Laurence?”

Laurie blinked at her. She appeared strong and self-confident, a vision from heaven, bloomed into full, breathtaking womanhood, the glow of the tropical sun golden on her skin and setting fire to her thick brown hair. He drank in the sight of her, and she again flushed and turned to her filing.

“Perhaps I should have said, where fools can reach you when they stand in need of rescuing—fools rather prone to getting into scrapes.”

“I have no time for fools,” she spat, and slammed another drawer.

Laurie placed his hand over hers as she reached for another file. “Miss March,” he said gently, “pray, what draws you here, of all places?” He eyed the door that he felt certain led to an inner office. “What would induce you to accept such an unprotected situation?”

She clutched several thick ledgers to her breast. “We brought Beth,” she finally conceded, “to see what could be done. They can do things here no one else can.”

Laurie blinked, startled, but before he could produce aught to say, she had pushed past him and assaulted the unexplored door. She shoved it open so forcefully, it bounced off the wall, but she caught it as she stood on the threshold and glared into the adjoining room. "You have done some low-down, despicable things, Edward Fairfax Rochester," she accused, "but this is positively the worst. I will not be managed thus."

A burst of deep laughter answered her indictment; her look professed she expected as much. She slammed the ledgers in her arms onto the floor. They scattered at her feet. "You think this is so funny, you clean it up. I am not your secretary."

She spun on her heel and marched from the room, sparing a volley of javelin looks for Laurie as she grabbed her coat and helmet. He yet stood, dumbfounded, when she appeared out the window a moment later. Parked just outside the window, a motorized velocipede—the most elegant two-wheeler Laurie had ever seen—sprang into life as she climbed aboard, opened the throttle, and sped away in a hail of dust and gravel.

"How do you like my handiwork?" Rochester grinned from where he stood in the doorway. "I've just about got that filly trained to the bit."

He chortled, deep and throaty, but paused as he turned back to his office. He gestured with his cigar to the scattered documents in both rooms. "Clear away your mess, Laurence. We've got work to do."

Despite the renewed turmoil of his sensibilities, when Laurie lost himself in his work, he found peace. Nowhere else on earth were scientists allowed to explore their theories and test their ideas with so much encouragement and support. West End went beyond the wildest imaginings of the world at large. Sometimes they left it centuries behind.

All things considered, he enjoyed his time there, soaked in as much knowledge as he could, and began to gain enough confidence to put his own ideas to the test. Life was good at the surgery. Most of the time.

Laurie perched on the edge of a pretty little divan in an airy sitting room. Tropical plants bloomed in the corners and on stands. Birds twittered in a cage by the open French windows that led onto a private veranda. The perfumed breeze wafted in, bringing with it the smells and sounds of the surf on the cliffs below. It would have been perfect, had it not been a room in the sanatorium. An exclusive suite in a private wing, granted, but it felt a cage nonetheless.

Laurie's patient reclined on the chaise beside him. He felt her pulse. "I wish you weren't so pale."

Beth laughed. "Yesterday, you told me I got too much sun."

"Yesterday, you did," Laurie smiled. "But your body needs more than fruits and berries, Bethy. You need to eat more red meat."

She eyed him, all teasing and insolence. "There is not a lot of beef in the Caribbean, Doctor, and I can't bring myself to eat goat."

"There will always be enough beef for you, my girl, if I have to fly to Texas and fetch it myself."

"You fret too much."

"I'm your doctor. It's my job to fret."

Beth's gaze wandered through the open doors. She remained silent for some time, and when she spoke, Laurie strained to hear her. "Do you suppose heaven is much like this?"

"What kind of talk is that?"

"I hate to leave you unhappy."

"Then don't leave me. Marry me instead. We shall run away."

"Indeed. To where?"

"Where should you like to go?"

"I hear the Caribbean is lovely. Or perhaps the West Indies."

"St. Kit? Barbados? Do say you will."

"When?"

"Now, of course. This moment."

"Oh, dear me. I'm afraid I have another engagement—with my doctor."

"Reschedule."

"I fear I cannot. He is very busy, you see, in much demand. Should I cancel, I may have to wait weeks or months before he can see me again. It will not do."

"Lucky blighter."

The laughter in Beth's eyes subsided; in its place, that fathomless compassion that seemed to define her. "I can recommend someone else, however," she said gently, "whom I know you love far better than me."

"Bethy—"

"She loves you. I know she does."

Laurie looked away. In the months he had been there, they had thus far managed to avoid the subject. He knew Beth bided her time, but her failing health spurred her sense of urgency. He wished he could oblige her, but some things—too many things—were beyond his control. "That ship sailed a long time ago. It's best we both admit it. She has other . . . interests."

Beth reached out her hand and allowed it to slide down his shirtsleeve. "I know her heart."

"I know her actions." Laurie pulled out his otoscope. The maneuver had served more than once to change the subject.

Beth was having nothing of it. Instead, she pushed his hand away from her face and held it to prevent his escape. "What actions? What do you mean?"

Laurie shrugged. "She is so natural. She can't imagine anyone being interested in her, but there are half a dozen blokes round about who would court her if . . ."

"If what?"

"If she only opened her eyes and saw them. They form a queue."

Beth's brow furrowed. "Such as whom?"

"Beth—"

"If you want me to leave off, convince me."

"Such as Friedrich Bhaer, for one."

"Friedrich Bhaer?"

"That German bloke, the friend of Rottstieger's—the schoolmaster."

"Him?" Beth burst out laughing. "Teddie, the man is twice her age."

"Fifteen years, at most."

"Twenty."

"Even so, with Jo teaching at the school, they are constantly together. He captivates her. She soaks in everything he says. She likes brainy men."

"Teddie, you have advanced degrees from two of the world's best universities, and you could just as easily have earned another from Herr Rottstieger. You shall have to find another excuse because that will not do."

"She doesn't think of me that way, Beth. As smart"—he shrugged—"challenging, with something to offer her mind. And he is in love with her."

"And she is in love with him, you say?"

Laurie wagged his head. "Every time I think I understand her, I do or say something stupid, she gets angry, and . . . I just know what I see in her admirers."

"Admirers? Someone beside Bhaer? You had better try again because Professor Bhaer does nothing for your argument."

Laurie pushed back his hair with both fists, then dropped his head between his shoulders, his elbows on his knees. "Rochester, then. Edward Rich-as-a-sultan Rochester. It's only a matter of time before he speaks, and when he does, she will accept him. I feel certain of it. Everyone does."

"And who is everyone?" Laurie looked up at the distinct sound of a smirk in Beth's voice. Her eyes twinkled, and laughter flitted across her face like a will o' the wisp.

"Just about every doctor or scientist at the surgery believes it so; every lad at the school. You cannot watch them together and not see what she does for him."

"She takes him down a peg or two."

"Just so."

"She makes him toe the line, just like all her boys."

"You have seen it as well. He adores her. He pretends to be contrary just to raise her ire."

Beth's smile faded. "And that looks like love to you?"

Laurie again shrugged and looked away. "And how could I say what love looks like? I thought I knew, but . . . He seeks out her company. He goes to the school when he has no business there. If he's in Kingston or Spanish Town or Montego, he always gets back by Sunday. He makes a point of being here on her visiting days with you. She calls him 'Edward' as if they already were man and wife. He acts . . . proprietary toward her."

Laurie lay his hand over Beth's when she rested it on his arm. "Silly man," she smiled gently. "Edward Rochester will never ask Jo to be his wife."

"How can you be so certain?"

"The crystal around his neck, do you know it? The one he fiddles with in moments of abstraction? It was a gift, a sort of talisman, from his one true love. He sets great store by it. The lady married another, then died in childbirth, but he never ceased loving her. He cannot give his heart away because it is all bound up in that crystal."

"If he has no intention of ever asking Jo to be his wife, why is he raising her expectations?"

"Jo has no expectations, Teddie."

"Well, you can be blamed well sure the rest of the island does."

Laurie drew up short at the sight of the constriction of ill-concealed pain on Beth's face. He gently assisted her to sit erect that she may breathe more easily. A small tablet from the vial in his pocket quickly gave her relief. At last, she leaned her head against his shoulder. "I'm so tired."

"Nurse Ratchet says you spent too much time on the ward yesterday."

"I was needed."

Laurie refused to argue the point with her. The only way he would win was to empty the post-surgical ward of patients. Her sunny, smiling face was the best medicine any of those men could receive. He just wished it did not come at such a cost.

He pulled his stethoscope from around his neck and settled it into his ears. She had grown accustomed to his listening to her heart. She scarcely noticed his delicate maneuver between her opened buttons. She knew the routine, breathed deeply, allowed him to prod, but still rested against him.

His brow furrowed, as it ever did, at the angry red scar that sliced her sternum in two. "You should have told me, darling," he fretted for the one-hundredth time. "You should have told me and I would have come."

"And you would have stopped them and I would have died anyway. Somebody had to be the first."

"I should have been here."

"You would have stayed and ruined your chances at medical school. Then where would your career be? Whatever Jo has claimed, I begged her not to tell you. We made Amy promise not to mention it. You needed to stay in school."

"You're my sister. What if you had died?"

"But I didn't, and you're here now. That's what matters."

He sighed. "You know the pig valve they sewed into your heart is failing."

"I know."

"I don't know what to do."

She looked up at the catch in his voice. "My lad." She rested her hand against his cheek. "There is nothing to do. It's just time."

"I'm supposed to fix this."

She smiled and shook her head. "God gave me three years and more than I had any right to expect. I've come to love this beautiful place and its people. I've been useful. I've been happier here than I ever imagined I would be. Every extra day is a blessing. I am not greedy."

"I am. The past six months here with you feel like no time at all." Beth again leaned against him, and he wrapped his arms around her. "I make a terrible doctor."

"You are a wonderful doctor," she said into his shoulder, "but you don't make a very good god."

He laughed despite himself, as she made so many do. He didn't know a man she had attended who didn't dote on her.

"You should go," she nudged.

"You send me away?"

"I do. You have duties to attend."

"You are a harsh taskmaster."

"That's me."

Laurie gently eased Beth back into the pillows on her sofa. "Rest," he murmured. "Sleep."

"No football?" she whispered.

"Not today, Miss Priss. Perhaps next time." He leaned and kissed her, but she already slept.

Laurie eased closed the door to Beth's suite, then turned on his heel, intent on his long list of duties. He stopped short at the sight of a tall, broad Jamaican in the passage.

When away from the island, Julian Meeks carefully concealed his mechanical modifications, but at home, he dressed for comfort, the prostheses readily apparent. An accident with a cane harvester took his left arm, but a terrible hurricane broke his back and right leg, paralyzing him and necessitating an amputation. But Julian was Rochester's closest friend, and the inventor refused to rest until he devised the means to restore the man to health.

Laurie knew Rochester trusted no one as he did Julian. He had become his right-hand man in running his Jamaican businesses, but he did so chiefly from Kingston. To see the man at West End boded ill.

Despite his apprehension, Laurie rankled to see Rochester and Jo appear at the opposite end of the hallway. Surely they came to visit Beth, but for Laurie, their joint arrival provided further evidence of their mutual attachment. But all other concerns fell by the wayside as the two men conversed. It seemed Laurie watched a storm roil on the horizon and quickly close the distance. He felt a guilty flush when Rochester spied him observing their consultation, but a look from the man beckoned him to the group.

"We have a situation," Rochester announced as Laurie approached. "Eye Patch and his cronies have escaped from the gaol."

"They've been there six months," Laurie protested. "Why would they bother? Their sentence is up in a fortnight." He looked from one man to the other and the silent communication between them. "They're harmless. Aren't they?"

Rochester glared eastward, toward Kingston. "Perhaps last week . . . Now—"

"There has been a break-in at Hangar One," Julian interrupted. "The office there has been ransacked."

Laurie cursed. "Blast. Did they get anything?"

"There's nothing there to get," Rochester answered, "unless they find some value in flight plans and launch schedules."

"What could they hope to gain by it? Where do they think they can run?"

"We also have unexpected visitors," Julian explained. "Freddie Vaughn."

Laurie felt a pit sink in his stomach as the last piece of the puzzle dropped into place. Rochester confirmed his suppositions. "He comes with an entourage—in an Empire warship."

"Not a warship," Julian denied. "It's an advanced model, and I have never seen the like, but there are no guns, no cannon—"

"That you can see," Rochester countered.

Julian nodded his concession. "That I can see."

"And the governor will fold at the first sign of trouble if I'm not there."

Laurie shuddered. Freddie had at last tipped his hand. "I assume you leave for Kingston immediately."

"We leave for Kingston," Rochester corrected. "You're my new ambassador."

"Me? What could I possibly do?"

Rochester clapped him on the shoulder and Laurie winced with the force of it. "Didn't you know? He brings his new bride, Miss Amy March that was. You're all but brothers-in-law."

Bedecked in white tie and suffering for it in the sultry summer evening, Laurie stood in the large drawing room of the King's House in Kingston, one of the few structures on the island to survive the devastating hurricane that nearly killed Julian and took thousands of less fortunate lives. Amy—the charming Mrs. Vaughn, as she quickly became known—moved amongst the Governor General's hastily organized reception, the perfect socialite, her London polish buffed to a high sheen. The mime came as easily to her as quiet grace settled on her sister.

While convivial and charming in the elegant gown Amy had pressed her to wear, Jo did not campaign to win the favor and admiration of everyone in the room, as did Amy. Amy did not come across as false, exactly, but in London, she had seemed as natural as the sun. That evening at Kingston, she glared like one of Rochester's electric iodine lamps.

"I don't mind you looking, old chum. Just so long as you don't touch."

Laurie refused to turn at the sound of Freddie's voice. The man had been attempting to corner him all evening, and Laurie had thus far managed to avoid it.

"She is a tasty dish," Freddie continued. "I got what I paid for there."

"How fortunate for you her aunt died."

"It did make up Amy's mind for her, and high time, too. I don't know that I could have waited much longer." Freddie chortled. "I nearly took the matter in hand once or twice, if you take my meaning. Then the old bird would have forced her to marry me."

Jo's glance of concern from across the room brought Laurie's attention to his own clenched fists and scowling brow. He forced himself to appear more cordial. "That's what I like about you, Freddie," he muttered. "You're an incurable romantic."

"I followed her to Monaco, didn't I? And to Paris in the spring? The little witch just toyed with me. All that talk of love and soul mates was only so much twaddle. Well, she came round to her senses soon enough once we put that battle-ax in the ground."

"One can't help but wonder why you bothered, knowing her so reluctant."

Freddie laughed outright. "She was the best thing on the market: beautiful, charming, a handsome dowry, and then the old lady's fortune . . . Cold fish where it counts, though, but that is neither here nor there. I certainly can afford a stand-in."

Laurie glared at the man, incensed. "Do you have a point, or did you just come over here to prove to me—just in case any doubt remained—what an unmitigated heel you are?"

"Don't pretend you haven't sampled the wares of that piece of work," Freddie accused, jerking his head towards Jo. "You may think you have people fooled, but I've seen the way you look at each other."

Laurie turned to walk away, but Freddie caught him by the arm. He wheeled on the man. "What do you want?"

"I have to talk to you. I've been trying for two days."

"If this is your idea of conversation, I want nothing of it."

"Just hear me out, and I'll leave Amy here when I go. You know she wants to stay with Beth."

Laurie again looked to Jo and caught the pained look she wore when watching Amy. With a parting glance to the society manikin Amy had become after only four weeks of marriage, he stepped out onto the veranda.

With the noise of the reception muted behind closed doors, Laurie challenged his adversary. “What do you want?”

Freddie paced away and back again. Laurie’s disquiet grew the longer the man took to screw up his courage. “I need your help,” he finally blurted. “I need the complete plans for the Mandroids.”

Laurie barked a laugh. “Oh, is that all? Give me five minutes and I’ll run fetch them.” He moved to walk away, but Freddie blocked his path.

“I’m perfectly serious, Laurie. I need those plans, and you’re going to get them for me.”

“Indeed. And why would I do that?”

“Because you’re not one of them. You’re not like Rochester. The man is a butcher.”

“What are you on about?”

“I’m talking about the Mandroids. Do you know how long the Brits have tried to sort out those blighted crystals? They can’t make heads or tails of them. And then he invents the Deltas and tosses out the control unit completely. Voice commands? Invisible energy waves? Stuff and nonsense! They need to analyze his designs. The best engineers they have can’t even get the head module open, let alone examine it.”

“And you know the reason why. Rochester won’t weaponize the Mandroids—”

“That’s not the real reason. You strut around with your nose in the air because you’re so smart, but you accept everything Rochester tells you as if he were some sort of god. Well, I’ve finally figured it out. I know how he can just talk to those Deltas and they do whatever he says."

"Indeed. Do tell."

"He uses brains."

Laurie gaped at the man, speechless, the idiocy so baffled him.

Freddie made use of the silence. "When we learned about Rochester's interest in the amputees—"

"The amputees?"

"Soldiers, sailors returned from their posts without arms or legs."

"I know what amputees are, Freddie. What are you talking about?"

"Rochester! Six months gone, he bought a whole shipload of amputees from the poorhouses. The government allowed it. They wanted to see what he would do. He brought them here and they disappeared. I tell you, he uses their brains. He puts them in the Mandroids. That's why they seem like they're human—they really are—at least, they have the minds of humans."

Laurie found unfathomable how one man could be so deluded. "Let me see if I understand this," he said at last. "You're telling me Rochester buys up slaves, cuts open their heads, removes their brains, and installs them in the Mandroids to make them function as they do?"

"Yes! The amputees are perfect, don't you see? They're already soldiers. They don't need training like others would, and no one cares about debtor slaves. Rochester can do whatever he likes and no one misses them."

Laurie stopped a waiter who just then passed with a tray overladen with hors d'oeuvres. "Jenkins, stop a moment?"

The man's blank service face bloomed into friendly recognition. He proffered his tray to the two men. "You bet, Doc. What else can I get for you?"

Laurie took the platter from the man and set it aside. "Do you mind showing my associate your arm?"

The man shed his jacket without a second thought. "Not a bit, sir," he answered, rolling up his sleeve and removing a glove from his hand. Freddie gasped in surprise. Laurie smiled with pleasure. Jenkins was one of the first to receive Laurie's new designs, and the prosthesis was a thing of beauty.

The waiter grinned at Freddie's gaping response. "Dr. Laurence, he's a magician."

Laurie pressed his point. "If you wouldn't mind, would you loosen your collar? I should like to prove to my friend that you aren't a Mandroid."

"A Mandroid?" Jenkins laughed. "Everyone knows we ain't got no Mandroids on Jamaica. Too many real men needs the work."

"Humor me."

The waiter obliged, but completely doffed his shirt and rolled up his pant cuffs before Freddie was satisfied in the man's humanity. "Jenkins," Laurie said at last, "we've replaced your right arm and both legs—"

"And you give me a glass eye." He turned to Freddie. "I'll be the first to try Doc's new mechanical eye, when he figures out the fiddly bits."

"But are you in possession of your brain?" Laurie queried.

The waiter grinned. "Now, some says I ain't, but that weren't your fault, now was it, Doc? Maybe if I had more of 'em, I'd still have my arm and legs. 'Twere the best thing Rochester ever did, says I, buyin' us all up like that and givin' us new arms and legs and such."

"Thank you, Jenkins. That will be all." Laurie turned to Freddie who looked decidedly green. "Are we finished here?"

Freddie wagged his head, still dazed. "I was certain . . ." He blinked and shook his head as if to free it of the preposterous notion, but it only amplified his panic. "No brains only makes it worse, Laurie. You have to help me. If you ever were my friend, you have to help me. I need those plans."

Laurie snorted in disgust. "You were my friend once, mate, but that ended the first time you broke into Rottstieger's office and ransacked it. Did you think we didn't know who it was? You will never get your hands on those schematics. Even if I could get them, I would never give them to you."

"You have to. One way or another, they're going to get them. It will be easier on everyone if you just give them to me now."

"Who is 'they'?"

"The Empire! The military! Do you think they stay away from here just to be nice? Jamaica belongs to the Empire, but they know Rochester has the whole place armed to the teeth. They can't even get close without being blown out of the sky. They know about his submersibles and his bombers. They know he armed the Americans."

"You have gone stark raving mad."

"And that explosion was my imagination, I suppose? Any chance I had of convincing them they were wrong ended that night. One Mandroid—one 'disabled' Mandroid—leveled half of Southwark. They couldn't even find the husk of the casing when they finally got the fire out."

"Rochester never hid the self-destruct from anyone, Freddie, especially not you. If you hadn't tried to take it apart, it would have returned to the airship and nullified the command. You should have never taken it to London to begin."

"Don't you get it?" Freddie charged. "You don't just say 'I can't' to the Empire. You don't shrug them off and walk away. I came all the way here just to get those plans, and I can't go back without them."

"Then don't go back." Laurie stepped away. "Return to Boston, Freddie. You're out of your depth."

"They'll kill me!"

Laurie stopped and turned to his one-time friend, the pit in his stomach filling with lead. "And how many people will die if they turn Mandroids into killing machines? How many innocent people, all in the name of wealth and might? Whatever you did to put yourself in their power, I am sorry for you, but I will not give such a weapon to those madmen."

In the wee hours of the morning, as the whole West End contingent dragged themselves across the veranda of Rochester's sprawling hilltop bungalow, sudden brilliant lights filled the Kingston airfield below. The Empire dirigible dwarfed even the massive Cassiopeia, and its running lights blocked out the stars in the sky when they threw the switch, making visible the thick black smoke belching from the airship's multiple stacks.

"Good riddance to bad rubbish," Rochester spat.

"They're not leaving tonight, are they?" Jo fairly whimpered.

Laurie took her arm and threaded it through his own. "I'm sure they aren't," he soothed.

"The men who designed that ship are fools," Rochester cursed. "It will end in tragedy, mark my words."

"Why?" Laurie wondered. The ship was a thing of beauty. It gleamed in the night sky, all silver and sparkling, its long, thin gondola extending nearly three-quarters the length of the envelope.

"It's an inferno awaiting a spark."

Laurie stared at the dirigible, attempting to take Rochester's meaning. "They use hydrogen for lift, but that doesn't burn without oxygen, and the envelopes are sealed. It should be safe enough."

"It's not the hydrogen but what's around it," Rochester countered. "The canvas is coated with powdered aluminum and iron oxide. The engineers were boasting to me about it, how light and durable it was. But that's Thermite. Thermite coupled with hydrogen? If I had anything to say about it, I'd never allow anyone I loved aboard that ship."

Jo clenched Laurie's arm and buried her face into his sleeve. Rochester startled, as if he saw her there for the first time. He shrugged. "But then, they haven't had any trouble yet, have they? It requires an immense deal of heat to get it started . . . but once it's lit . . ." He abruptly turned on his heel and strode down the veranda.

"Amy's not on it," Laurie attempted to reassure her, although he had no faith in his words. "Freddie promised he would leave her. I'm sure she's sound asleep in her bed in the King's House."

As he walked Jo up the stairs and to her own rooms in the streaming moonlight, neither spoke, each so focused on the airship that the moment completely escaped them. Later, when he sat alone on the sill of his own window, the shutters thrown open as he watched the full moon on its descent to the horizon, he realized how natural his arm felt around Jo. They just fit.

The roar of the dirigible's engines reached up to the bungalow from the airfield, and Laurie watched as it floated effortlessly into the sky. The propellers engaged, the airship swung hard about, then glided out over the harbor. Laurie watched until it disappeared over the western hills. "What do they expect to find in Spanish Town?" he wondered to himself.

The light from Jo's room suddenly spilled out through the shutters, just as he flipped his own switch, and he knew she had likewise stood in the darkness, watching, waiting, until the dirigible vanished. He wondered if she wished he had said more, or if she thought of him at all. Her mind surely overflowed with concern for Amy.

He dragged off his tie, loosened his collar, tripped the light switch, and flopped onto his mattress. Sleep washed over him before he could kick off his shoes.

Laurie opened his eyes, still in a fog, uncertain of exactly what had roused him. An urgent scratching intruded into the silence.

"Laurie?" He could scarcely hear the whisper, but he heard—or perhaps felt—the strain in her voice. "Teddie, are you awake?"

"Jo? What is it?" Laurie stumbled from the bed to the door in the darkness. With his turn of the knob, Jo rushed into the room, more agitated than he had ever seen her.

"You have to help me, Teddie," she insisted. "He has Amy. He's going to hurt Amy. You have to help me now."

"Who has Amy?"

"Freddie! He has taken her. We have to get her away from him."

"She's his wife now, Jo. There's little we can do—"

"And she ceased being a person because she's his wife? He can do whatsoever he likes to her because they are wed? He can force her to—" She broke off abruptly and turned away.

Laurie followed her as she paced frenetically. "Freddie is a wretch, I know. I tried to tell Amy, but . . . but I shouldn't have left her in London, I own. She will have a difficult time of it, but he's all talk, surely."

"And her bruises are all talk, I suppose?" Jo demanded. "She tried to hide them, but she couldn't—not from me. I made her tell me, Teddie, and it wasn't very difficult. Were she not his wife, he could be hanged for what he does to her. He should be hanged, and by heaven if you don't help me—"

She abruptly spun on her heel and made for the door, but Laurie was faster and managed to bar her way. "Stop, Jo. Just stop and take a breath."

"Get out of my way, Theodore Laurence, or I will never speak to you again."

"No, Jo. I will not. There's nothing you can do that won't make it worse—not tonight. Tomorrow—"

"Tomorrow? Tomorrow will be too late! He expects me at dawn. I need it now!"

Jo again attempted to get past him, but Laurie clasped her shoulders and held her fast, despite her attempts to shake him loose. "Expects you where, Jo? What is going on? For once in your life, will you just talk to me?"

Something in his face or his words broke through her panic and fear. She blinked at him, taken aback. "Did I not say?"

"No, darling. You did not. Now, tell me what has happened, and let me help you."

Jo held out a crumpled sheet of stationary. "I found this on my floor. I don't know who left it," she explained. "They slipped it beneath the door."

She paused just long enough for him to read Freddie's demand that she get the schematics, tell no one, meet him at the rendezvous by dawn, and deliver them alone. "What are we to do? How are we to save her? How can he expect us to get to West End so quickly?"

Laurie glanced at the missive, then back to her distraught face. He knew her anger could not hold against her fear much longer. They had to move forward. "He expects you to rush off in a panic, without thinking things through. He doesn't know you."

"How does he expect me to get the plans? Why would I have any sway with Edward?"

"Perhaps he heard the scuttlebutt. Or maybe seeing you together—"

Jo stopped her pacing to stare at him in the dusky light. "Seeing us together? When? Doing what?"

Laurie shrugged. "At the garden party, at the reception, arriving in town with him from West End. Any time he saw Rochester, you were at his side."

"It was the only way I could see Amy! That wretch refused—what do you mean 'scuttlebutt'?"

Laurie stepped to the lamp and feigned examining the letter in better light. "It doesn't matter."

Jo followed him, then pushed herself into his view when he refused to turn to her. "What are you talking about?"

"What good does it do to discuss this? You'll kill the messenger and we still won't be any closer to helping Amy."

"What scuttlebutt? What do people say?"

"Jo—"

"What do they say?"

"People wonder when you and Rochester will wed."

Jo searched his looks, and he found himself unable to escape her careful scrutiny. "Is that what you think?"

"I just want your happiness, and if it's with him . . ."

“I should be his rightful property, just like everything else around here, regardless of what I want.”

“How am I supposed to know what you want? You stopped talking to me years gone. I only tell you what I see.”

Jo blinked at him, nonplussed. They stood there, silent, feeling themselves at some sort of crossroads and uncertain which way to turn, or even where the paths led.

“What about Rochester?” she said at last.

“Rochester be damned.”

“He will never give the Empire the Mandroids. What do we do?”

Laurie reached for the leather jacket that hung on a peg by the door. “Exactly what Freddie says.”

Laurie crouched beneath the hibiscus bushes at the base of the lighthouse at West End. He thanked his stars for Rochester’s speed skiffs that skipped along the coastline like a stone on a pond, even carrying Jo’s velocipede.

Above him, the Brits had tethered the airship to the tall stone tower, but it strained against its moorings, unhappy with its turbulent berth. The chuff of the idling dirigible engines competed for predominance with the surf on the jagged rocks at the base of the forty-foot cliffs and the gusts of wind rushing up from the sea.

Freddie paced along the ledge of stone, his hand clamped down on Amy’s own as she rested it upon his arm. At first, Laurie wondered that he had backed himself to the sea with no open escape route. Then, the man turned and stumbled over a long line that hung from the airship, the slack lying upon the ground. It attached to the body harness Freddie wore, and Laurie saw only too clearly how he intended to extricate himself from the situation. The only way out was up.

Just as Freddie began to appear impatient, the crunch of gravel announced the arrival of Jo's velocipede. The man visibly tensed as her otherwise silent two-wheeler drew to a stop, and the figure wearing riding breeches and a helmet climbed off.

Freddie looked up at the dirigible and jerked his chin. From his hiding place, Laurie cursed beneath his breath as Eye Patch opened the cargo hatch and trained a scoped rifle on the newcomer. "You shouldn't have come, Laurie," Freddie called out to the rider. "I told her to tell no—" His words choked off in his throat as Jo pushed back her goggles, peeled off her helmet, and shook out her hair.

"I brought what you want. Now let Amy go."

"How did you get them?" Freddie demanded.

"How humiliating," she taunted. "After four years of trying and only four years of failure to show for it, you have to beg a woman to save your sorry hide."

"Show me the plans, b—" Freddie cursed.

"Jo, don't!" Amy cried out. Freddie flung a look at his wife, and she cringed as if he had struck her. Only Eye Patch in the dirigible above kept Laurie from leveling the man then and there.

Jo slid off the satchel strap. "Release my sister."

"Is that it?" Freddie demanded.

Jo held up the molded leather bag. "It is. I know where he keeps the codes to his safe room."

"Safe room?"

"Do you want these or not?"

"Roll it here."

"Release my sister."

"Not until I know you brought what I need."

"You won't make heads or tails of them anyway, mate," Laurie muttered under his breath. "But, it's not as if you'll have the chance to try."

Jo carefully removed the cylindrical tube from the satchel. Laurie bit his lip and held his breath. He said a silent prayer . . . as he had done since he walked out his bungalow door. Everything had thus far gone according to plan, but one slip on Jo's part and it all would go up in smoke.

Jo unscrewed the lid of the tube with great care. "Listen to me," she explained as she worked. "There is a trick. You must do it exactly as I say."

"I don't need some woman to explain my business to me."

"You mustn't trip the firing mechanism," she insisted. "If you don't open the right end, the self-destruct—"

"Just show me the blasted plans!"

Jo set down the tube and unfurled the blueprints. She held them up for Freddie's inspection. With each nod, she revealed another page, until all ten had been displayed.

"I can't believe you actually got them," Freddie muttered

as Jo gingerly returned the sheets of schematics to their container.

"It's a man's world," Jo answered. She held Amy's eye. "A girl does what she must to survive."

"Now, roll them here."

"We had a deal. You're not taking my sister anywhere."

"My wife, you mean to say." Freddie grabbed Amy by the hair and turned her cheek toward him. "Tell that shrew to give me the plans if she ever wants to see you again."

"Amy, walk over to me now, and I'll roll—"

In a flash, Freddie whipped out a dagger and pressed it into Amy's throat. She whimpered and clutched at his arm that pinned her to him. "Bring the satchel to me! Now!"

Jo hurried to obey. As she thrust the tube at Freddie, the dirigible's tether to the lighthouse dropped to the ground. The airship gunned its engines and began to turn away from the tower, taking up Freddie's slack, and Laurie at last saw how wrong he had been. Freddie never meant to release his wife but had secured her to the same line as himself.

Jo lunged for Amy, but Freddie leapt back and pulled them both off the ledge. "Amy!" Jo screamed as her sister plummeted from sight.

Laurie rushed from his hiding, took a running leap, and flung himself off the edge of the cliff. As he flew through the air, he collided with Freddie who was again on an upward trajectory with the airship. The flying machine jolted with the sudden added weight. Laurie clenched his legs about his adversary's and held on for dear life. The dirigible struggled to turn hard about against the buffeting winds, but the sea dropped away from them as it quickly gained altitude.

Freddie dangled by his harness, fumbling to secure the satchel. Amy swung wildly several feet below. Her body hung limp and lifeless and, as she hit the cliff-side, Laurie understood it wasn't the first time.

Laurie clambered higher along Freddie's torso as the man struggled to free himself. Laurie grabbed the satchel secured around his neck. "Get him off!" Freddie shouted up at the dirigible. "Blast you, get him off!"

Laurie landed a solid right hook to Freddie's jaw, but the line again jolted, and his grip slipped. He slid down a few feet but managed to hold on. The grind of a winch told him time was running out.

Freddie rammed his elbow into Laurie's temple and dislodged him. Laurie grabbed hold of the line at Freddie's harness, but a solid boot to the ribs knocked Laurie loose. With only one wrist tangled in the line, he plummeted toward the sea. Amy's unconscious body interrupted his descent, and he grabbed hold. Dangling with naught but one elbow hooked between the line and her harness, he rifled his pockets with the opposite hand until he at last found his Swiss knife.

Laurie could hear Freddie shouting orders at his henchmen as the winch continued to raise them and he closed on the hatch. The sea below looked hard and unforgiving, for all its crystal blue serenity, but Eye Patch grinned down at Laurie through the sights of the rifle.

Laurie had no choice. With the press of a button, the blade snapped out of its housing. Two swipes on the line, and the pair plummeted toward the unforgiving surface of the sea.

The encroaching black void vanished as quickly as it had come, and with its retreat came an onrush of pain. Laurie opened his eyes into an azure world. At the nadir of his plunge, his mind cleared enough to send him clawing for air and the surface once again. The light shimmered above him, much farther than it appeared. When he finally broke the surface, he gasped for air, feeling as if his lungs would explode.

Still disoriented, he turned about in the water, attempting to gain his bearings. At last, he found the shoreline, just in time to see someone fly off the forty- foot cliff and slice into the water in a perfect swan dive. "Jo!" he exclaimed. "What in blazes—?" He raced toward the shore but had only gone a few meters before he could truly think clearly.

"Amy!"

Laurie rotated frantically as he scanned the unbroken surface of the water. He again plunged below, searching desperately. At last he saw her sinking toward the bottom.

Laurie thanked God for the crystal clear waters of Jamaica. He found Amy quickly enough but had nearly expended his air before he could reach her. As it was, he managed to grab a hank of hair, then frantically kicked for the light.

He broke the surface with a gasp and hauled her into the air with him. "Amy! Amy!" he cried, slapping her cheeks. "Come on, Amy. Wake up." Dread filled his heart when she failed to respond, but he could do nothing for her while scarcely treading water. Her heavy skirts dragged them both down, and the screaming pain in his bruised ribs slowed him, but Laurie had only one choice: sink or swim.

"A boat would be useful," he grunted as he hooked his arm around her and set off toward shore. The sound of racing skiffs answered him, and he breathed a sigh of relief as Rochester and a whole flotilla of dinghies rounded the point. "Late, as always."

"Come on, Amy," Laurie pleaded as he pressed down upon the girl's chest with one heel of his palm atop the other. "Don't do this to me. You can't do this to me."

He tipped her head back and plugged her nose, then sealed her mouth with his lips. For the tenth time, he filled her lungs with air from his own, then returned again to pumping her heart.

"Laurie—"

"Shut up, Rochester," Laurie cursed. "Two, three . . ."

"She's gone, mate."

"—four—I said, shut up!—five." He again bent and breathed for her, when of a sudden, she convulsed, vomited, and then gasped for air. He sat her up and held her as she emptied her stomach of seawater, and coughed and hacked her way to breathing again. Utterly exhausted, she crumpled against him, and he clutched her to his heart.

"Great Scot," Rochester cursed. Laurie followed the direction of his nod. On the horizon, out over the open sea, the Empire airship gleamed a brilliant silver in the morning sun, but flashes of red and a curious white smoke ran along the fuselage of the gondola.

"Jo was supposed to tell him about the trip wire," Rochester swore.

"She tried. He refused to listen. . . . But, I thought you wanted the contents destroyed when he opened the tube."

"I didn't mean for the fool to set alight that death trap!"

"I don't understand."

"The chemical reaction started to fade the ink the moment the sheets hit the air. Without the reagent, they would have been blank by the time he managed to open the tube again. We needed more time."

"You had no choice but to use that tube. If anyone is to blame, it's Freddie." Laurie watched the growing flame with trepidation. "They will put out the fire, surely."

Rochester jerked his chin. "When I do a thing, I do it right." He glued his eyes on the airship as the smoke grew thick and black, and the fire licked from the gondola up to the envelope. Laurie thought he may vomit himself, so quickly did the white-hot flames melt away the fuselage.

He never saw the order given—Rochester certainly never issued a verbal command—but the four other skiffs hovering about them raced off toward the horizon and the catastrophe. Without warning, the whole ship dropped like a stone from the sky. A massive explosion shot water and steam a half-mile into the air. Three more blasts followed the first in quick succession, then the flames and the smoke vanished beneath the surface of the sea.

The rescue skiffs stuttered to a halt. Any hope of survivors disintegrated when the ship's boilers hit the cold water. Only the fish could retrieve what little of the passengers remained.

Amy whimpered and buried her face in the crook of Laurie's neck. Laurie pulled her closer, then leaned his cheek against her hair. "Hush, precious."

"How long is the proper mourning period for a merry widow?"

Laurie looked up at the acid remark. Julian's skiff had silently drawn alongside, Jo looking a scalded cat, barefoot, and wrapped in a blanket. He had no idea how long they had been there. "Before what?"

"Before you can marry her, of course."

"How many times do I have to tell you, you've got it all wrong."

Jo shrugged. "I don't know. That kiss seemed pretty definitive to me."

Laurie fought to keep his ire from boiling to the surface. "And that swan dive—are you obliged to marry her because you jumped off that cliff?"

"I didn't dive after Amy, you idiot! I—"

Laurie willed her to finish the statement, but she looked away, and he knew himself quite properly dismissed. “I need to get Amy to the infirmary,” he told Rochester. “Drowning is the devil on one’s health.”

Despite the heat, Beth lay wrapped in a cocoon of counterpanes, and yet her hands were still as cold as ice. The French windows to the veranda stood open wide, allowing in the fresh breeze and opening the broad vista of another stunning sunset in the making. It was Beth’s favorite time of day, and Laurie always ensured she had the best seat in the house.

She smiled to lend Laurie comfort as he took her pulse, but was too weak to speak. He fluffed and adjusted her pillows that she might breathe more easily, but she at last raised a hand to stop him. A simple gesture, and he sat beside her and again took her hand.

“I have a confession,” she whispered.

“Hush,” he answered. “Save your strength.”

“For what? Are we boating later?”

“Right after lunch.”

She smiled but held his hand more firmly. “I need you to listen to me.”

As she spoke, Jo paused at the open door, hesitant to cross the threshold. Laurie moved to rise and surrender his place, but Beth clung to him. She gestured to Jo, who entered and sat opposite Laurie. Beth reached out and Jo took her hand.

"I have a confession," Beth said again to Laurie, "and you must be still until I've had done."

"Bethy—" Jo objected.

Beth closed her eyes, as if calling upon some inner strength to control an impatient tongue. "We had a deal," she insisted. Tears welled in Jo's eyes and she looked away but said no more.

Beth again looked to Laurie. "Four years gone, I was very, very ill—"

Laurie swallowed hard. "You don't need to do this, Bethy."

"Please, Teddie. Let me." He too looked away. It was far too difficult to gaze upon her face as she struggled to bare her soul, but he found it equally disconcerting to watch Jo's turmoil unconcealed. "Four years gone," Beth pressed on, "I was very, very ill. While we were at the seaside, my sister received an urgent wire.

"I saw it in her face. Relief, love, excitement, anticipation, joy, it was all there, but only for a moment. Then, she hid it away and pretended to be angry. I was dying, you see, and she would never leave me, not even to rush to the side of the man she loved.

"Then, Mr. Rochester sent for us and we came here. The doctors helped me and I improved for a time. Then, I was dying again and the doctors told me they wanted to build me a new heart, or at least patch up the one I had. The operation was a success, but by the time I was on my feet again, another year had gone by. All that time, my Jo refused to leave me. She knew she had broken your heart. She never blamed you, but she gave up hope. Then, when Amy started writing from London—"

"There has never been anything between me and Amy, Bethy. Never."

Jo twitched, as if she would speak, but she refrained.

Beth smiled weakly. "Amy has always worshiped you, silly man, but she never had the sense to admit what was real and what were wishes."

Beth closed her eyes a moment and drew in a few deep breaths. "Jo knows you saved Amy's life, that you helped her heart pump and her lungs breathe when she couldn't do it herself, but it must have been very difficult to watch."

Laurie glanced across to Jo who feigned deafness to the conversation. "There is nothing romantic about having vomit spewed into your own mouth, Bethy."

"The head knows what it sees, but the heart knows what it wants. When that desire is so compelling, the heart silences the head." She paused a moment as she searched Laurie's face. He wondered if his own sensibilities were written as plainly upon it as Beth's were upon her own. "Thank you," she breathed. "Thank you for saving my sister—from Freddie, from the sea. Thank you."

Laurie offered her a sad smile. "Anything for you, m'lady."

"Jo gave you up for me, Teddie," Beth forced herself to say. Tears seeped from her eyes unheeded. "She has always put me before anything else. She shouldn't have had to choose between me and you, but she wouldn't have been Jo otherwise. It's my fault, Teddie. If it weren't for me—"

"Hush," Laurie commanded. "If you start blaming yourself, I will leave the room. I will not sit here and listen to that drivel."

Beth eyed him in protest.

"Drivel," Laurie insisted. "Say it, Bethy, or I walk out this instant. That idea is pure drivel."

Beth sniffled and scrubbed at her tears. "Drivel," she said feebly.

"Drivel," Jo agreed.

Beth closed her eyes to rest. Her breaths came shallow and quick. Her mother and father appeared in the doorway, following along in Amy's officious train. Laurie again attempted to rise, but Beth retained him. "Stay," she breathed. "But a moment."

He settled, and she opened her eyes. "You promised me a last request."

Laurie attempted to smile. "I gave you that last month, and the month before that, and the month before that. You're spoiled rotten with last requests."

"This is my last one, I promise."

"Tell me."

"Promise to answer me true, without obfuscation." She opened her eyes to hold his gaze. "Promise me."

"We have no secrets, you and I."

"Promise me."

"I promise."

"Do you love my sister? Do you love Jo?"

Laurie shook his head. "You know that answer."

"Tell me."

Jo jumped to her feet and stepped to the open doors, her back to them all. She wrapped her arms about herself. "Do not press him, Bethy," she begged. "I cannot bear to hear him say the words."

Laurie thought to oblige her, but Beth's silent insistence left him no recourse.

"More than I can say," he croaked. "More than I ever dreamed possible, for I never imagined Jo would become the breathtaking lady before me."

"Would you marry her?"

"Jo doesn't want me, Bethy. I've never been what she wanted. I've never been . . . enough."

"Don't tell me what she wants. Would you marry her?"

Laurie again lifted his gaze to Jo who had turned and inched closer. She stood with her hand clamped over her mouth while her tears streamed and her shoulders silently wracked. But her eyes pleaded for the words to provide her relief. In that moment, he knew beyond doubt what those words should be.

Laurie rose and stepped to her, produced a handkerchief and dabbed at her wet cheeks. "In a heartbeat," he murmured. "Now and forever and five years gone."

Beth managed another feeble smile. "Jo, would you—"

"Yes," Jo interjected. She barely breathed it. Her lip quivered and her trembling hands grasped his own as they cradled her face. "Oh, Teddie, yes."

Laurie drew in a great draft of air, awash with a maelstrom of sensibilities. He could do naught but release her despite his strongest impulses, but she intertwined his fingers with her own as they turned to their gentle mediator.

"Promise me, Teddie," Beth instructed. "Promise me you will always love her."

"I promise, Bethy."

Beth again forced her eyes open. "Promise me, Jo. Promise me you will allow yourselves this happiness."

"I promise, darling."

Beth looked to the reverend, her father, who presided from the door. "Is it enough?"

The man smiled. "Enough for me, Jamaica, and I'm sure the Good Lord." He looked to Laurie and Jo who had given him their undivided attention. "I now pronounce you husband and wife. You, son, may finally kiss the bride."

Laurie looked to Jo who looked just as startled as he felt. But he had no idea if she was pleased or dismayed. "May I?" he finally asked. "Is it enough for you?"

Jo offered him a shy smile. "It is. You may."

Laurie meant to merely seal their pact with a gentle, petal-soft kiss, but before he knew it, he held her in his arms, her feet suspended from the floor. He clung to her as she buried her face in the crook of his neck and wept, and, truth be told, he shed more than a few tears of joy and hope and relief and regret himself.

"I love you, Mr. Laurence," she whispered. He set her down to look into her eyes. He again took her face in his hands, his thumbs tracing its graceful lines. "I love you, Mrs. Laurence," he answered, then bent and made good on his original intent, and more.

At last, he drew away from her but held her firmly about the waist. As one, they turned to Beth, and their joy became bittersweet. Marmee and Father had assumed their respective places. Despite her look of sublime serenity, Beth lay motionless. Marmee tenderly folded her hands across her chest. Reverend March gently closed her eyes.

Amy fairly huddled in a corner, weeping uncontrollably. Jo rushed to her and gathered her up in her embrace. Laurie knew as a physician he should declare time of death, but all that would wait. As he stepped to close the open doors, two shadowy figures retreated from the veranda. They turned one last time before they disappeared around the corner of the bungalow.

Rochester met Laurie's eye and saluted. Laurie knew Rochester attempted his devil-may-care insolence, but no one escaped Beth's influence. Not even Rochester. His self-congratulation melted into acknowledgement, his taunt into shades of grief. Julian merely nodded, and between the two friends, that spoke heart to heart.

Before he drew closed the doors, Laurie paused to gaze at the purples and golds and magentas and blues that blazed across the evening sky, reflected upon the Caribbean sea, as the sun melted into the horizon. "Yes, Bethy," he told the night. "Heaven must be very like West End."

Styled after *Little Women* by Louisa May Alcott

About the Authors

From the editor: *Mechanized Masterpieces* is by far the most popular anthology at The X, as well as a top-rated title. Because the concept of Steampunking classic literature so captures the imaginations of readers and writers alike, we decided to conduct a special invitation-only competition, open exclusively to team members of Xchyler Publishing. Competition was fierce and judging excruciating, as evidenced by the length of this book. However, we know all lovers of Steampunk will be pleased with the results

And now, introducing those X-peeps who made the cut, including three authors from the original work:

J. AUREL GUAY

J. Aurel Guay writes fantasy and science fiction with an emphasis on strong plots and meaningful themes. Having played at writing fiction since grade school, he revived his passion in reaction to his day work in biomedical science. "The Death of Dr. Marcus Wells," published in *Shades and Shadows: A Paranormal Anthology* is his first published work. His current work in progress *Jagerund* is a novel expanding on the previous short story.

http://jaurelguay.wordpress.com

www.facebook.com/JAurelGuay

www.twitter.com/losthawken

www.amazon.com/J.-Aurel-Guay/e/B00FXTW89E

www.goodreads.com/author/show/7336990.J_Aurel_Gua

MEGAN OLIPHANT

An editor at The X, **Megan Oliphant** has studied creative writing since college, taking classes from the founder of LTUE, Marion K. "Doc" Smith at Brigham Young University, and attended Orson Scott Card's Literary Boot Camp in June of 2014. Her primary interests are in fantasy, ranging from dark urban to high epic, but she's a sucker for a good mystery that she can't guess the ending to before she gets there. She divides her time between reading, writing, and "familying" with her husband and five children in North Carolina.

JAY BARNSON

Software engineer, video game developer, and father, **Jay Barnson** is a transplant to the state of Utah from the east coast. He grew up on a diet of science fiction and fantasy ranging from

Howard, Heinlein, and Tolkien to Lucas and Spielberg. His wife and daughters had to drag him to his first steampunk convention. And now they can't drag him away from the genre. Jay's first short story with The X, "Dots, Dashes and Deceit," appeared in *Terra Mechanica: A Steampunk Anthology* (2014).

www.rampantgames.com/

www.rampantgames.com/blog/

www.facebook.com/russell.barnson

www.twitter.com/RampantCoyote

plus.google.com/100149974806519304027

www.linkedin.com/pub/jay-barnson/0/a2b/ab3

www.goodreads.com/author/show/8194589.Jay_Barnson

M. IRISH GARDNER

A daydreamer at heart, **M. Irish Gardner** has dabbled in imaginary worlds from Day One and developed an incurable addiction when she finally began recording her ideas. Her bachelor's degree in recreation management does nothing for her writing, but she sure knows how to play. She lives in Arizona with her husband, two daughters and all the other characters in her head. Gardner's first published work, "Reformation," appeared in *A Dash of Madness: A Thriller Anthology*.

www.facebook.com/MIrishGardner

www.goodreads.com/author/show/8102226.McKenna_Gardner

D. LEE JORTNER

Playing with imaginary friends and writing and directing plays in the neighbor's garage filled **D. Lee Jortner**'s childhood. Today she lets her imagination flow onto her keyboard as she writes mystery, fantasy and steampunk stories and novels. "Payoff for Air-Pirate Pete" is her first short story for Xchyler Publishing. She also enjoys her marketing role with the company and teaching English composition at Ivy Tech Community College in Valparaiso, Indiana. When not writing or working, Jortner is usually busy with her husband, children or grandchildren.

www.facebook.com/pages/D-Lee-Jortner/246452102210796

www.amazon.com/D.-Lee-Jortner/e/B00PUMDVL8

www.goodreads.com/author/show/10645104.D_Lee_Jortner

http://livingwritingteaching.blogspot.com

www.pinterest.com/dleejortner

www.twitter.com/dljortner

J.R. POTTER

J.R. Potter gravitated towards the paranormal world from an early age. Watching the first episode of The X-Files was a transformative experience, and an education in great storytelling and mythmaking.

Since "growing up," James has devoted his time to finding his voice through writing, publishing short fiction in *The Portland Review*, and winning two international short story competitions for science fiction and horror. When he's not writing, he tours with his incredible wife Amy as "The Crooked Angels," an Americana duo specializing in rocking your socks off.

Potter is currently collaborating with artist Klaus "Plaid Klaus" Shmidheiser in the graphic novel series *Glimmer Society*. His first short story with Xchyler, "Dr. Pax's Great Unsinkable Bird," appeared in *Terra Mechanica*. A full-length novel, *Pneumatica: Harbinger of the Skies*, is slated for 2015 release.

www.glimmersociety.com

www.facebook.com/jamie.potter.146

plus.google.com/u/0/104738328865653094370

www.goodreads.com/author/show/8194590.J_R_Potter

M. K. WISEMAN

A Wisconsin gal with a Southwest soul, **M. K. Wiseman** can generally be found wandering happily amongst the pages of the largest book she can get her hands on. She came upon writing rather accidentally, finding that, sometimes, there are stories that simply must be told. "The Silver Scams" is her third short story published at Xchyler. Other titles include "Clockwork Ballet" in *Mechanized Masterpieces: A Steampunk Anthology* (2013), and "Downward Mobility" in *Legends and Lore: an Anthology of Mythic Proportions* (2014). A fantasy novel is scheduled for release in 2015.

A techie with a penchant for typewriters, she is a magnet for misadventure, though her own story has yet to unfold. Harboring such dreams as someday possessing a library complete with hidden bookcase doors, piloting a hot air balloon, and running away in a sailboat, she currently subsists contentedly between worlds, plotting and dreaming.

http://mkfauble.wix.com/home

www.twitter.com/FaublesFables

www.facebook.com/FaublesFables

www.goodreads.com/MKWiseman

SCOTT E. TARBET

Scott E. Tarbet writes in several genres, sings opera, married in full Elizabethan regalia, loves Steampunk waltzes, and slow-smokes thousands of pounds of Texas-style barbeque. An avid skier, hiker, golfer, and tandem kayaker, he makes his home in the mountains of Utah.

Tarbet's short stories with The X include "Tombstone" in *Shades and Shadows: a Paranormal Anthology* (2013), "Ganesh" in *Terra Mechanica*, "Year of No Foals" in *The Toll of Another Bell: A Fantasy Anthology* (2015), and "Nautilus Redux" in *Mechanized Masterpieces 2*.

His full-length novel, *A Midsummer Night's Steampunk* (2013), receives excellent reviews. Tarbet's next endeavor, *Dragon Moon*, a speculative fiction thriller, will be published by The X in 2015.

http://scotttarbet.timp.net

www.facebook.com/ScottETarbet

www.twitter.com/setarbet

plus.google.com/u/0/103022248044977989570

www.linkedin.com/pub/scott-tarbet/b/568/543

www.pinterest.com/scotttarbet

SCOTT WILLIAM TAYLOR

Scott William Taylor grew up in Utah living on the side of a mountain and lives on that same mountain today with his family and a dog that loves cheese. Scott is married with four children. Scott is a contributor to *Flash 500* e-book, and creator of *A Page or Two Podcast*. He also wrote the award-winning short film, Wrinkles.

Scott's first work with The X, "Little Boiler Girl," appeared in the first *Mechanized Masterpieces* anthology. His short story, "Split Ends," which appeared in *Shades and Shadows*, and "Mr. Thornton" tie him at second for number of contests won at The X.

www.scottwilliamtaylor.com

www.facebook.com/ScottWilliamTaylorAuthor

www.twitter.com/HyggeMan

www.amazon.com/Scott-William-Taylor/e/B00CN0M7YC

goodreads.com/author/show/7073542.Scott_William_Taylor

www.linkedin.com/profile/view?id=7796172

plus.google.com/u/0/117260351777137513756

NEVE TALBOT

As a child, **Neve Talbot**, developed the habit of lulling herself to sleep by dreaming up continuations of her favorite books too soon ended. She first cracked open a spiral binder in high school, and has spent the past decade dutifully penning her prerequisite one million words of bad writing before getting to the good stuff.

Now author, editor, story coach, and journalist, Neve currently lives with her husband under the pseudonym of Penny Freeman, in a quasi-reality filled with fantasy, sci-fi, historical fiction, Regency romance, the classics, and history books, suspended between the piney woods and sprawling metropolis of southeast Texas.

"West End" is Neve's third outing with The X, the others being "Crossroads" in *Shades and Shadows*, and "Tropic of Cancer" in *Mechanized Masterpieces*, of which "West End" is a sequel.

http://about.me/pennyfreeman

About Xchyler Publishing

At The X, we pride ourselves in the discovery and promotion of talented authors. Our anthology project produces three books a year in our specific areas of focus: fantasy, Steampunk, and paranormal. Held winter, spring/summer, and autumn, our short-story competitions result in published anthologies.

Additional themes include: *The Strange Island of…* (Steampunk spring/summer 2015), *Losers Weepers* (paranormal, fall 2015), and *Worldwide Folklore and the Post-modern Man* (fantasy, winter 2016).

Visit www.xchylerpublishing.com/AnthologySubmissions for more information.

LOOK FOR THESE RELEASES FROM XCHYLER PUBLISHING IN 2015:

The Toll of Another Bell: *A Fantasy Anthology,* January 2015*Vanguard Legacy: Fated* by Joanne Kershaw, Book 3 of the Vanguard Legacy trilogy, March 2015

Blondes, Books & Bourbon by R. M. Ridley, a White Dragon Black anthology, April 2015

Kingdom City: Revolt, an urban dystopian fantasy by Ben Ireland, Book 2 of the Kingdom City franchise, spring 2015

Lock 12 a young adult urban fantasy by Johannah Spero, summer 2015

Hohenstein, a historical romance set in pre-war Germany by Didi Lawson, summer 2015.

To learn more, visit www.xchylerpublishing.com.

Sneak Peek:

A STEAMPUNK ANTHOLOGY

MECHANIZED MASTERPIECES

Tropic of Cancer

NEVE TALBOT

My father went to his grave without a word of praise for me falling from his lips. He never truly knew me. Even so, he knew human nature, and therein lay his genius and my downfall.

My father knew the profundity of the fable "Sun and Wind."

Sun and Wind argued over who wielded more power. They determined to settle the argument with a competition. They spied a traveler walking down the road, wrapped in a cloak. The contest: wrest the man's protection from him.

Wind accepted Sun's invitation for the first go. It blew and loosened the man's wrap. Then, Wind blew harder, forcing the man to struggle to keep his mantle. However, the stronger Wind blew, the fiercer the traveler held to his cloak. At long last, Wind prevailed by blowing his victim from his feet.

Despite Wind's self-satisfaction, Sun took its turn with confidence. It shone upon the wayfarer. The air warmed. The man loosened his grip upon the cloak as he walked. Then, he removed it and slung it over his shoulder.

Thus, my father wrested my dreams from me.

A passionate youth, a lover of all things mechanical, I fancied myself a changer of the world—an inventor—and so earned my father's patrician contempt. I nursed great ambitions but assumed no generosity on his part. I knew the entire Rochester fortune portioned to my elder brother, Rowland.

I desired only two things from my father: the freedom to make my own way in the world without interference from my family, and his ward and niece, Yvette Fairfax, as my bride. My father bequeathed me neither.

My attempts to keep the latter concealed from him failed. My father's actions professed him perfectly sensible of the attachment between Yvette and me. However, he never mentioned it.

Instead, the man sent me into the sun.

As my father's agent, I traveled from London to Spanish Town, Jamaica, in the prototype airship of my own design. My father assured me linking my fortunes with Jonas Mason, a wealthy cane planter, would set me for life. My friend and partner, Professor Heinrich Rottstieger, accompanied me. Afforded little choice, we resolved to make my father's dictates serve our own ends.

All manner of airships abounded at that time, but with Herr Professor's metallurgic discoveries, and my own invention, a sunlight-dynamo power source, our design would revolutionize air travel. In Jamaica, I would conduct further investigations into the energy-retentive powers of crystals.

My sweet Yvette provided the impetus for every scheme. My hopes in her propelled me forward. And, lest my recollections of her fade, the engraved crystal that hung about my neck continuously brushed my skin and thrust her to the forefront of my thoughts.

Not yet one and twenty, I had never before traveled beyond the shores of Great Britain. The trappings of "progress" and "civilization" defined my world: coal, steam, copper, and steel. Creation seemed made up of these things.

However, in every port of call—Lisbon, the Azores, Bermuda—the greater the distance from my homeland, the more alien and strange the world became to my limited experience . . . the stronger Nature clung to that which is rightfully her own: clear skies, blue sea, unpolluted shores. The breath of life.

We had nothing but ease on our journey: fair winds and a furrowing sea, so to speak. In clear skies over deep waters, with the silver of our triple envelopes gleaming in the sun, our image shone back at us. Our configuration, long and sleek—the fins and rudders, the stern propellers and engine houses—created what appeared a strange creature of the deep running beneath us.

We cleared the emerald-green mountains northeast of Kingston on the morning of the fifteenth day. The absence of man-shaped mechanoids patrolling the streets grabbed my attention. Where were those brutal implements of totalitarianism? Those clockwork weapons with head, arms and legs, but no conscience or compassion?

I realized nothing of mechanization had invaded that island—no airships, no dreadnaughts, no rail guns or steam engines. No sub-aquatics patrolling the deep in an illusion of absolute control. No steam-sweepers or horseless carriages chugging and puffing, filling the air with their noise and soot. The light shone pure and clear, the sky as azure as the sea.

Heinrich circled low over Spanish Town. Children raced the *Andromeda* to her landing site. At the broad expanse of lawn before the Mason mansion, they hesitated. When the airship belched our engineers from the hold, and they rappelled down the lines to anchor us to terra firma, the children cheered. The adults who trailed after them seemed only slightly less eager.

Not the least trace of soot smeared the pure faces before me. Likewise, the weary existence and unending toil of the downtrodden in London seemed absent in Jamaica. In this sea of humanity, their black skin a grace of Nature, rather than the curse of industrialization, I could yet see hope.

Did I see poverty? In abundance. The need for reform? Without doubt. But unlike Mother England, I saw happiness in the faces of the poor. I saw dignity; belief in themselves. I felt myself the serpent in the Garden of Eden with my hold full of cargo and my brain full of technological marvels. I wondered what mischief I had wrought in this island paradise simply by bursting onto the consciousness of those people.

Thus, the inescapable paradox of my life lay bared before

me: mechanization had long since become my great passion, but I detested its natural consequences. Young, sincere, and green as new spring, I swore Jamaica would not suffer the fate of England.

As I copiloted the airship in its final descent, a pair of women on the veranda of Mason's home caught my eye. They stood on the balcony; an old crone leaned heavily upon a cane. Her weathered, ebony skin stood in sharp contrast to her hair of brilliant white. Her bright eyes shone sharp and quick. An aura of calm surrounded her.

She stood beside a young lady at the balustrade, a statuesque beauty whose complexion glowed like aged ivory. A gossamer robe provided token coverage of her nubile form. Her jet black hair hung in loose curtains down her back, and along with the folds of her dressing gown, ruffled in the morning breeze.

She appeared intent on the windscreen behind which I sat, which bubbled out from the cockpit of the airship. Eventually, the heckling of the old woman gained her attention. She then glanced at herself, tugged at her wrap, and turned into the house.

As we landed, Yvette's crystal burned with an icy sting against my chest. I failed to understand the significance at that time, but with the chill, I relived the occasion when Yvette presented the gift, as I often did in future days.

We lingered, just we two, in the Andromeda *cockpit. Yvette sat in the captain's chair, fiddling with the knobs arrayed*

on the consoles before her. I knelt beside her, drinking in her lovely, grief-stricken face.

"I dread your departure, Edward," she murmured softly. "I fear you will plunge into darkness and never escape. I cannot . . . It must not be so."

*"I told Father one year, Yvette. I go to make my fortune—*our *future. All of this is a means to an end—a bridge to my heart's one desire. Tell me you—"*

Her fingers on my lips silenced my tongue. Her looks forbade my speech. She held my gaze, her eyes swimming in tears.

She took my hand and held it. She turned the ring upon my finger. She had woven it of her own silken tresses. It shone like pure gold. "Promise me you will never remove this ring. No matter what else happens. Give me your sacred honor."

I searched her features, unsettled by the desperation which laced her tone. "Never. I promise."

"And yet, it is not enough," she murmured. A look of firm resolve added complexity to the sadness and loss upon her face. Then, warm stone and cold metal settled into my hand. I raised into the air Yvette's prize crystal hanging from a silver chain. The sunlight refracted through the stone and projected upon the bulkhead an image of the Andromeda *herself, ablaze in rainbow colors.*

"I had it done. A crystal from your workshop could serve, but this stone . . . you need it for protection."

More than a mere line etching, a master craftsman had carved a relief of our airship onto the stone in minute detail.

Deep in the recesses of my mind whispered the certainty that Yvette had employed forces I would never understand to accomplish what, I dared not speculate.

Yvette loosened my collar, clasped the chain about my neck, then tucked the crystal beneath my shirt. Her hand rested upon my bare chest as she whispered her instructions. "It must rest here, next to your heart, touching your skin."

I riveted my eyes on her, willing her to meet my gaze. She busied herself in setting my attire to rights, yet would not look into my face. Her lips whispered some silent invocation I could not hear. Then, she gave her final instructions. "Use this to remember me. A token of my . . . friendship. To keep you afloat. To light your way home."

I took up her hand and held it to my cheek. "I shall never remove it."

Tears again welled in her eyes. "See that you don't."

"Edward! What the devil are you about?" Herr Rottstieger's intrusion brought me to my feet, and one glance at the lady's ducked head caused him to hesitate.

He harrumphed to clear his throat. "Well, then, mein junge. *We must weigh anchor tout suite."*

Yvette rose and stepped to the hatch. I moved to follow her. "Just as soon as I see Miss Fairfax home."

Yvette wheeled on me. "No, Edward. No. I have Rowland."

"Yvette—"

"Please, Edward," she breathed. "Let us part here as we are, the best of friends."

My whole being revolted at the notion of such a cold parting. I would take her in my arms and bespeak my heart. I would profess my undying devotion, secure her to me. But I knew she meant to avoid such a scene. I could not discomfit her.

"The best of friends," I repeated, forcing a smile. She extended to me her hand, but I leaned and kissed her cheek.

"Remember your promise," she whispered, and then was gone.

At Spanish Town, Rochester coin opened the doors of the colony's finest families. Naturally taciturn and unsocial, I found answering the demands of society a most onerous duty, but I got on by degrees. I dare say, I became good at it . . . at least, I gained confidence. I became, so it was said, the most popular young blade on the island.

Every now and again, Miss Bertha Mason—for such was the beauty on the balcony—would flit across the social stage, but remained otherwise elusive. I scarcely knew her.

Even so, she wormed her way into my consciousness. She battled with Yvette for my dreams. In them, the breeze which caressed the nymph's soft skin with silken tresses, which flirted with her robe and offered teasing, tantalizing glimpses of a round of breast, a length of thigh, also wafted jasmine around me. It encircled and enfolded me until I awoke in a sweat, the scent still palpable in the air.

But then, the crystal would again cool my skin, and the fever which fought to control me receded at its touch. The clouds lifted, my mind cleared, and dreams of Yvette, fresh and clean and pure, would fill my mind. It felt a brisk early morning after a suffocating, sticky, and stultifying tropical night.

My father's plans progressed apace. Within three months, I shared ownership with him and fully managed West End, a cane plantation at Negil, on the westernmost extent of the island. Within six, I had completed the initial phase of our planned rum distillery. Within nine, I had established myself as a member of the West Indies elite. Investors lined up to underwrite our airship manufactory. The sunlight dynamo in both distillery and sugar mill proved an unqualified success.

I wrote to my father and begged Yvette's hand.

At the end of a year, I had done with waiting. My father's silence on the subject and Yvette's failure to write caused me no small amount of concern. I would attend Herr Professor on a three-month publicity tour of the East Coast of the United States, and from there, we would go to London. I would return with my bride.

Twenty hours and counting. I itched to be gone, but last-minute business at the governor's mansion detained me. There, an acid etching illustrating a newspaper article on the notice board caught my attention.

I burst into the offices high in Hangar One and slapped the yellowed clipping onto the desk in front of Herr Rottstieger.

"Look at it! Just look at it! Tacked up with the notices in the lobby like some tawdry bit of gossip!"

Lately, All Souls Church, Langham Place, London: Mister Rowland Fairfax Rochester, son of Rupert R. and the late Camilla Fairfax Rochester of Thornfield Hall, —shire, wed to heiress and society beacon, Miss Yvette Fairfax, daughter of the late Colonel and Mrs. Harrison Fairfax, last of Hyderabad, India. Couple to honeymoon on the Grande Tour before returning to their home on Wimpole Street.

My friend eyed me warily, without a single glance at the paper. I stepped back, undone by the truths I read so plainly on his face.

"You knew." The words stuck in my throat. Herr Professor winced. His eyes fled mine. "By the devil! You knew and you hid it from me!"

He flinched as my palm hit the desk, a tiny jerk of the head as he stared at the floor. I pushed my hands through my hair with both fists to press back the whorl of disjointed thoughts that assaulted me. Tears rushed my eyes. A leaden weight sat on my chest. I could draw no air.

I stepped away from the violence bursting to free itself. My back to the man, I leaned against the windowsill, my outstretched arms pushing hard against it, as if somehow I could hold back the cataclysm. I stared blankly through the glass, wrestling with a gale of sensibilities, resolves, reckless, insane schemes to make her mine, struggling to cease my trembling and stifle a wail of despair-laden rage. A knock at the door at last shattered the silence. Herr Professor rebuffed it. Footsteps scurried down the wooden stairs.

"I didn't hide it, *junge*." He spoke softly, feeling his way. "You never read the papers."

"You just neglected to tell me, is that it?" I turned to him. He no longer sat, but propped himself against a file cabinet situated against the wall. "How long ago was 'lately.' There is no date here."

"Six months."

I felt kicked in the chest by a mule. Herr Professor surely read my outrage. "I have not known for six months, Edward—only three months, perhaps. It has been six since the day."

Realization of the truth settled over me like an arctic blast. "My father told you . . . That blasted bounder wrote and told you when, exactly." Rottstieger again winced. "And all this time—all this time you have pretended to be my friend—pretended to encourage me, *to share my joy*! You played me for a fool!"

"No, Edward. When you wrote and asked Yvette to be your wife, I knew nothing of the matter. The letter from your father came after you told me what you had done."

"And so for three months, every time you delayed our departure—all of it was a lie to put me off!"

"I delayed because Rochester told me he would write—*they* would write. They would tell you themselves in their own time. In their own way. I kept waiting for that letter, Edward—for

Rowland to do the honorable thing. I had resolved to tell you . . ."

"When? When, exactly, were you planning to extend me that courtesy?"

"Before we got to England."

"But after we left Boston," I spat. "It would not do to spoil your precious tour."

Herr Professor closed his eyes in capitulation. "No. It would not." His pulse throbbed at his throat and he swallowed hard. "I never wanted this to happen, Edward. I never expected it to end like this."

I peered at him. "What are you not telling me?" He heaved a sigh and I felt the last piece of the puzzle drop into place. "You have been in on it all along," I whispered. "You took his part."

"No, Edward. I never took his part. Anything I did, I did for you."

"For *you*, you mean to say!"

"No, *junge*. For you."

"How much? How much did he pay you to get me away from Yvette so Rowland could marry her? How much to properly merge the Fairfax and Rochester fortunes?" He hesitated, tongue-tied, and I slammed my fist on desk. "How much, Heinrich?!"

"The matching funds. If I could get you to Jamaica, he would match whatever other investors gave you—gave the corporation."

"*The matching funds*? His *club dues* are more than his precious matching funds! You should have asked me, Heinrich. I could have got you better."

"You have no idea what it meant to have Rupert Rochester

invest in us. He is respected, known for his perspicacity. His endorsement gave us *gravitas*. That he would not invest in his own son's inventions—it damaged our cause more than you can imagine. But what harm could a trip to Jamaica do, eh? How much good would come of it . . . at least, so it seemed to me."

I snorted, then flopped to a chair and dropped my head into my hands. A storm raged within. I gripped my hair fiercely, clinging to something—anything—to keep from going under.

My friend sat beside me and placed his hand upon my shoulder. "*Mein sohn*," he ventured after a long moment, "no one could see you together and not know she loved you. That day—the day we left—when you were together in the cockpit, with the door locked and Rowland so frantic to get inside . . . I thought you had secured her promise. By my life, I thought you were secretly engaged."

The pall of his words settled over me and I looked up. I could not deny the overwhelming sadness in his eyes, a mere glimmer of the grief my new clarity gave me. "No, Professor . . . No. She would not hear me. She sent me away."

My anger vented, the resentment seeped from me. In the fog of my self-deception, I believed with all my heart she would wait, but the cold, stark truth revealed my folly, and I could not begrudge Herr Rottstieger his own.

I leaned back in my chair and pushed the hair from my face. I heaved a sigh. "What now?"

"What do you want to do?"

"Besides hurl myself from the highest cliff?"

"*Junge . . .*"

"What is there for me now, professor? Everything—*everything* I have done has been for her, for our future together. What good are my dreams without her to share them?"

"Edward, without you, I would be nothing but another iron monger, an engineer forging the inventions of other men without enough mettle to build my own. But with you—I became bigger than myself. Like all the men you employ, who now earn a fair wage and can send their children to school instead of into the fields, I flourish because of your dreams. If not for yourself, *junge*, soldier on for these people. They dare to dream because you live yours."

I could not say how deeply his words sunk into my heart then, but they have since become my mantra—more or less. Then, as now, I felt the caveat: I lived the dream I managed to scrape together from the rubble of my castles in the air. But that had to be enough. I had to prove to them all—to my father, the blasted blighter, to Rowland, to Yvette herself—that they had not inflicted the mortal wound to my soul that then bled bitter tears—and bleeds still.

I rose to my feet and moved to collect the scrap of paper, but my hand hesitated over the desk, distracted as I was by an envelope edged in black sitting on the blotter. I glanced at Herr Professor. "Heinrich? Have you lost someone?"

His brow furrowed with concern. "Nein, *junge*. That came for you this morning."

He must have moved a chair behind me, as I did not hit the

floor when my knees buckled. The letter rattled in my hand. The black border hissed, rearing and ready to strike. I forced myself to rip open the envelope and read my brother's smooth hand.

I snorted. "The old buzzard popped off." A bitter, ironic laugh surged through me. "He gives me precisely one hour to curse him to the devil, and then denies me the pleasure of hating him for the rest of his days."

"The man was the picture of health!"

"Apparently, a rogue mechanoid didn't like the cut of Old Man Rochester's jib. He stepped from his carriage and . . . Do you recall, Professor, my outrage over their use as peacekeepers? He derided me for a stupid boy who could not understand such things. What do I know, eh?" I snorted my disgust.

"And Yvette? She is well?"

The name leeched a bit of acid from my soul and my manner softened. "Yvette is in indifferent health. They have taken a house in Athens for a time until . . . until she is safely delivered. Rowland will not leave her, thus requests that I see the solicitors myself."

Herr Rottstieger peered at me. "And you, Edward? You have just lost your father."

I flapped the papers at my friend. "And gained full ownership of the plantation and all of my father's interest in the corporation."

"There. Do you see? He always intended—"

"No, Herr Professor. I will not temper my feelings. *Rowland* had a momentary flash of guilt, not my father. My brother has relinquished the rights, and now fancies he has purchased absolution for his greed and treachery."

Silence descended over the office. I again stepped to the window and gazed at the horizon, where the sky melded with the sea. I felt Herr Professor's eyes upon me . . . the only thing I felt. It seemed as if the loss of Yvette and the loss of my father canceled one another. The tidal wave of grief left nothing in its wake—not even the flotsam and jetsam of the cataclysm. I felt . . . blank.

"So? Now, what will you do?"

I turned and headed for the door. "Today, West End. Tomorrow, the Cubans; then, on to conquer the Yanks. Then, to England to do the dirty work while my precious brother enjoys his spoils."

Styled after Jane Eyre by Charlotte Brontë

Continued in

Mechanized Masterpieces

A Steampunk Anthology

[2013]

Xchyler
PUBLISHING

Made in the USA
Charleston, SC
21 August 2016